MacGregor's Lantern

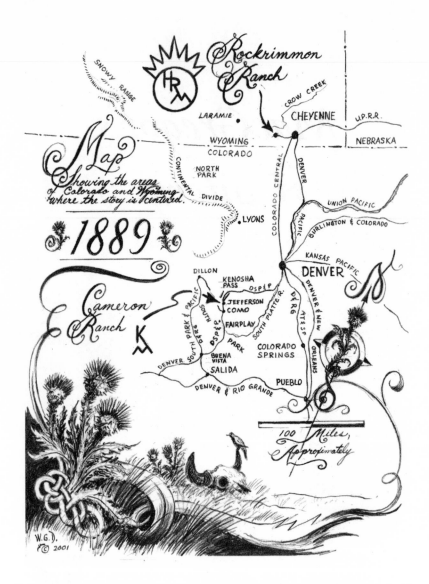

Rockrimmon Ranch

HRM

Map

Showing the areas of Colorado and Wyoming where the story is centered.

1889

Cameron Ranch
K

SNOWY RANGE

LARAMIE

CHEYENNE

CROW CREEK

U.P.R.R.

WYOMING
COLORADO

NEBRASKA

NORTH PARK

CONTINENTAL DIVIDE

LYONS

DILLON

KENOSHA PASS

JEFFERSON
COMO

FAIRPLAY

SOUTH PARK

BUENA VISTA

SALIDA

DENVER SOUTH PARK & PACIFIC

DSP&P

DSP&P

D.SP.&P.

SOUTH PLATTE

COLORADO CENTRAL

DENVER PACIFIC

UNION PACIFIC

BURLINGTON & COLORADO

KANSAS PACIFIC

DENVER

DENVER & NEW ORLEANS

D.&R.G.

A.T.&S.F.

COLORADO SPRINGS

PUEBLO

DENVER & RIO GRANDE

100 Miles, Approximately

W.G.D.
© 2001

MacGregor's Lantern

Corinne Joy Brown

Five Star • Waterville, Maine

This novel is a work of fiction. Names, characters, places, and incidents are either the product of the author's imagination, or, if real, used fictitiously.

Five Star First Edition Women's Fiction Series.

Published in 2001 in conjunction with Jane Dystel Literary Management, Inc.

Cover art by William G. Duncan.

Set in 11 pt. Plantin by Al Chase.

Printed in the United States on permanent paper.

Library of Congress Cataloging-in-Publication Data

Brown, Corinne, 1948–
    MacGregor's lantern / Corinne Brown.
        p.   cm. — (Five Star first edition women's fiction series)
    ISBN 0-7862-3227-7 (hc : alk. paper)
    1. Women ranchers — Fiction.   2. Married women — Fiction.   3. Colorado — Fiction.   4. Wyoming — Fiction.   I. Title.   II. Series.
    PS3602.R69 M34 2001
    813'.6—dc21   2001023417

To my husband Avi,
without whom
this book could
have never been written

Acknowledgements

The writing of this novel drew upon the experience and opinion of many people who gave of their time and expertise to develop the story. Not necessarily in the order of importance, deep appreciation goes to: the late Mrs. Tweet Kimball for her personal contributions to the Colorado cattle breeding industry and for founding the Cherokee Ranch and Castle Foundation in Sedalia, Colorado; to Penny Coffman and her knowledge of Colorado's early law; to Dr. Les Lockspeiser, cardiologist; to Charles and Wendy Groesbeek, Bea Bartles and the Columbine Ranch, plus Isabelle and Richard Firestone and Ginah Moses of the North American Scottish Highland Association, and Ms. Jane Nelson of Scotland, all for their insight into the raising of Scotch Highland cattle. To Karen Dennison and Laurie Wagner Buyer for their knowledge about South Park; Carol and Earl Cox for their understanding and love for life in the West; to Margie Earlywine for her knowledge of early ranch life in and around Cheyenne, and to Jean Casson for her links to the Colorado Scottish community. To Les Langford, ballistics expert; Michael Lancaster and Susan Thornton, bagpipers; Ron MacGregor for his knowledge about the MacGregor Clan, Mark Henderson, rancher, for sharing his life as a cattleman; Loretta Thompson for her knowledge of Celtic music; John Beech of Edinburgh for his knowledge of Scottish anthropology; and Willam G. Duncan, artist, illustrator, westerner and friend.

Preface to MacGregor's Lantern

What follows is a story inspired by real events anchored in the history of the American west. The characters are fictional, although based on certain individuals who actually occupied the landscape described. Political figures are portrayed as found and remain unchanged in name or position.

Many English and Scottish immigrants explored and settled the West in the 18th and 19th century, having come first as explorers, fur traders, and eventually, cattlemen. Their efforts invigorated the cattle industry with solid growth, leadership, and livestock, still reflected in many ways today.

Twenty miles south of Denver, a 6000-square foot reproduction of a Scottish castle built in 1923 sits atop a hill on a 3500-acre cattle ranch. Now a conservation easement, open to the public, the castle and the woman rancher who lived there for 54 years were of infinite inspiration for this story.

In spite of common preconceptions about the "Old West," please be aware that by the late 1800's, electricity, the telephone and other modern conveniences had already touched major population centers, ushering in an era that would respond rapidly to technological change. That, as well as dramatic shifts in politics, transportation, economics, and growth continued to shape dramatically the evolution of the west of myth and reality. Nonetheless, a greater debt is owed to the gifts of every immigrant culture that found its way to the region and left its inheritance.

To this I dedicate this story.

The Author

*The emancipation of women may have begun,
not with the vote, nor in the cities where women marched
and carried signs and protested, but rather
when they mounted a good cow horse and realized
how different and fine the view . . . from the back of a horse,
the world looked wider.*

*Joyce Gibson Roach
Historian*

Part One

Maggie turned in the saddle, searching the valley behind for the last traces of town. As she did, her split skirt bunched, exposing her chafed legs to the mule's coarse and bristly hide. She had hoped to see just one more curl of smoke or other reminder of a settlement, but instead, saw nothing but a curtain of pines which hid the silent trail.

How could one grieve for rooftops or a fence, she wondered. *Dogs barking?* The last climb into the hills placed them all behind her, fragments of another life. Maggie focused her eyes on the woods ahead and flinching as her heels pressed down, urged the old mule forward, trying to close the uncertain gap between herself and McKennon's long-legged pacer.

"Move!" she groaned. The hooves of the mule shuffled, then slowed. From up ahead her husband shouted back at her, "D'ye think ye can keep goin' till nightfall?"

"For God's sake, yes!" replied Maggie, regretting the thought of even another hour astride the stubborn beast. Although she hated the mule, she couldn't help but notice that it plodded skillfully over the stony trail and that McKennon's spirited blueblood stumbled often, its long neck arched and its haunches black with sweat. In spite of herself, she had come to trust the mule's efficiency and common grace. "I'm doing just fine; you needn't worry about me." She feigned a proud smile, then added, "We're keeping up as well as we can."

Maggie ducked low, clenching her teeth, and as the dense

woods closed in, she pressed the animal's sides with her calves. All around, dark trunks blotted out the sky, shredding patches of light. McKennon disappeared into the pines until only his mount's long tail could be seen here and there, swaying through the brush. Above them, noisy silver jays began to swoop and dart among the boughs, while a hungry hawk riding a night wind with wings extended hovered overhead. Seeking prey, it descended before them, gliding through the trees.

Frightened by the shadowy intruder, the champing mare suddenly reared and wheeled. Shattering branches overhead, she dislodged Kerr McKennon, tossing him to the ground in a clatter of timber and stone that tumbled like an avalanche down the difficult trail. Maggie screamed. The trembling mare stopped short, coming to a halt dangerously close to the stunned rider who now lay motionless by her hooves. Maggie's mule, ears pricked straight and head thrown high, stopped in its tracks, jolting its own rider while surveying the chaos before them.

McKennon scrambled to his feet as forcefully as he'd been thrown. "Ye damn daughter o' a witch, ye are!" he exploded in a rough brogue, dusting himself off while he grabbed the terrified mare by the bit. Heavy foam lathered his hand as he pulled her back onto the serpentine path of the trail. Swinging back into the saddle, he nudged her forward once more, then followed with a firm kick in the flank. "Tryin' tae kill me, are ye? Na' yet, ye won't!"

The skittish horse balked as he urged her against the shoulder of the mountain and shortened his hold on the reins. Without hesitation, the Scotsman used his whip to remind her just who was in charge, cursing as the leather snapped against her hide. Finally she came around and he remembered Maggie.

"Hey now! Are ye wi' me, lass?" he shouted, peering into the twilight gloom.

Maggie nodded and waved a leather-gloved hand. "I'm still here, just a scare! How about you? All in one piece? Nothing broken?"

"Aye, I'm fine, fine . . ." He straightened his hat, pulling it back down tightly upon his brow. "Verra' well then . . . come along." He reeled in the packhorse that had shied far out of the way, saying, "Stay close, lass. An' dinna' be fallin' behind."

Far to the east the first star brightened. Maggie breathed a deep and wistful sigh, straightened her tangled skirts, and sat as tall as she could. The mule, ears pricked forward, ambled slowly, searching for a sound to follow.

Maggie McKennon rode with caution, keeping her eyes on the mare. Each mile brought her closer to the dream of South Park, while a jumble of childhood memories, already a universe away, continued to fade. Thinking back, she realized her entire world had changed in less than a season, new horizons shifting in the wake of the one word—*yes*—her acceptance of the proposal from the Scotsman, Sir Kerr McKennon, which betrothed her to a stranger whom she was certain had come to save her from herself.

At the time, Maggie felt no doubt about her hasty affirmation. Chance had lured her, stifling reason. Quite confident that such a proposal would never come again, she relied on fate, which she trusted blindly, and hoped for luck, which she trusted not at all. At the time, either seemed reason enough to leave a society that shunned unmarried women and escape to the West to find a new life.

Maggie never told a soul she'd have gone just about anywhere to become the person she wanted to be, one who could defy convention and make up her own mind about the way women ought to live. Nearly every organization she belonged to had confronted the question of women's rights to choose, to work, and to be compensated fairly. Even her simple sewing circle bred heated discussions as others like herself dared to think of becoming equal under the law. Maggie resisted taking a more active role at the risk of her father's wrath, but couldn't ignore the voices of dissent rising from both privileged and working women everywhere.

Wishing Kerr would slow their pace, Maggie hoped she hadn't made a mistake. There'd been no time to reconsider, the arrangements had happened so fast. And although the awkward frame of the packsaddle now reminded her that the present seemed painful and hard, she sensed that returning home would be even harder still.

Margaret Lyndon Dowling had heard that the frontier was an adventure not to be missed. The thought of going West consumed her. Her parents, however, assumed she would continue to teach at the Ladies' Grammar School while living at home and eventually rise to the position of headmistress. The scenario appeared acceptable, if not ideal. Either teach or marry, her mother had concluded, although her chances to accomplish the latter had gradually grown more and more slim.

"Prettiest of the three, if you ask me," Magnes Dowling often bragged. "And too smart for her own good! That's the problem." His explanation gave little solace to Anna Dowling, his pluckish and doting wife, who bemoaned her daughter's spinsterhood as though the family had acquired the pox. Blaming her daughter's distant manner and bold intelligence for discouraging possible suitors, she could not hide her contempt for the young woman's obvious indifference to the matter.

"Really, Margaret, you must try harder," Anna prompted. "A girl your age needs to be visible. Accept the invitations that come, few as they are. Your refusals raise questions about your well-being, not to mention our own. An education is a fine thing and you were wise to pursue one but not at such a cost. You should be thinking about a husband and a family."

Anna almost never let a day pass without reminding her

daughter of the burden she'd become. "You could at least try to find a steady beau," she added one evening as the family sat together in the library. "Someone who might provide you escort, companionship. You know how often I'm required to entertain and couples are so much easier to place." This problem Maggie failed to find significant, as nearly all the men to whom she'd been introduced left her uninspired. She therefore ignored the complaint, forcing her mother to proceed to other fronts.

"How does it look, after all, when your father and I step out for an evening and leave you staying at home? No, that will never do. It's my duty to remind others that you are still available. I'll continue to insist that you're included whenever we're invited until such time as it is no longer necessary."

Maggie considered moving out, if only she could, to take her own residence on Hamilton Square. She knew such an idea was uncommon, if not unheard of in their circles, for proper women simply did not live alone. Predictably, her father would have none of it, not for a moment, since such a move appeared a clear admission of ineligibility in the eyes of any decent person.

"What?" he said, the only time she dared bring the matter to his attention. "Move out? What for? Live like some pariah or outcast? Ridiculous. Your place is here, in the Dowling house. We've plenty of room for a woman grown. Consider the matter closed."

Magnes knew well the demands of Philadelphia society and had abided willingly by its long-established rules. Yet all around him, old money competed with the new and the city's social strata cracked and groaned in response to forces rising from beneath its gilded crust. Industrial titans, first-generation immigrants, and self-made men systematically broke through the barrier that had been thought to protect all those fortunate enough to have inherited wealth, as opposed to the rest, who had not.

As he explained circumspectly to Maggie on her twenty-eighth birthday, "One must never settle for less. A woman marries up or across, or not at all. If one is fortunate enough to be born on the top, it is imperative to remain there. Position," he lectured to all his daughters, "is like virtue. Essential, though fraught with limitations."

Based on such sage thinking, he had decided that Margaret would stay at home until the proper time, or the right suitor arrived, and that was simply that.

The primary school served Maggie well. Each morning she taught reading and writing to giggly young girls, but to pass the afternoons, sought the tales of the West that held her interest fast. She scoured the papers daily, thrilling over every incident and venture and musing over the exploits of famous characters on both sides of the law. Illustrated dime novels lay hidden under her bed to be read in private, late at night, when she could recite passages aloud. The very sound of the strange Indian names, settlements, and boom towns worked a kind of magic on her soul.

Even among her closest friends, there wasn't one she dared to tell about her dream of riding with the likes of Buffalo Bill or the scandalous Calamity Jane. In her world, most women rode in carriages if they rode at all. Or they stayed safely at home, pursuing domestic arts and the classics. She alone read the diaries of explorers and pioneers, wanting to see for herself what others had written about, adventurers who'd gone West, daring to take the chance.

When the esteemed clients from Edinburgh returned for the second time to court her father, Magnes L. Dowling IV, a fourth-generation Philadelphia banker and financier, they succeeded in charming him entirely. Hugh Redmond MacGregor, originally from the rich farm area of central Scotland near Stirling, and MacGregor's elder partner, Sir Kerr McKennon, a Highlander with a talent for raising meat-producing breeds, had presented themselves at the bank in a mannerly fashion that invited both instant confidence and respect. Like many other British adventurers, the Scots had been engaged in the rapidly growing cattle business in the western territories and appeared entirely credible in their success. As the director of the First Bank of Philadelphia, Dowling received them warmly and found their financial portfolio both acceptable and intriguing.

"Damned if those Europeans didn't seize opportunity when they saw it," Dowling grumbled to his wife as he reviewed the day's affairs. "My colleagues in London and Edinburgh have been behind the cattle rush for years while we've preoccupied ourselves with the railroad and the Indian. These Britons have brought their beef stock and manpower to consume the open plains, funding the use of the public lands with investor groups of solid wealth. Now just where were the rest of us?" he demanded, unwilling to admit that he had been reluctant to join the fray. No longer, he resolved. He sensed that the time had come.

Dowling had to give the English credit for their success, the result, no doubt, of coming from a sea-bound empire with limited resources. Indeed, he believed the great West still lay open to those who would master it, and for those who succeeded, the profits promised to be staggering.

After rounds of meetings, the partners parted company, and MacGregor apologetically left to return to pressing matters at his ranch. The senior executor of the plan, Kerr McKennon, accompanied Dowling to his home to discuss at leisure what had been presented earlier in the day, as well as the possibility of an additional personal loan. Magnes often entertained major clients at home, preferring the privacy of his own library and the close company of family to whom the bank would eventually belong.

"My sincerest compliments on yer daughters," the Scotsman offered as the Dowling girls were presented one by one. "Where I come from, such women would make any man proud." In the blur of conversation that followed, Margaret overheard him inquire as to their individual eligibility and merit. She pretended to ignore his questions but listened more sharply to their comments than before.

Watching her father confer with his client, it was easy to admire the fine-looking Scot as he proceeded to present his lifelong dreams. Margaret thought the widower seemed somewhat old to be starting over, yet ambitious enough to be tempted by fortune. Whatever the assumptions might have been, Kerr McKennon made sure everyone understood that he'd been an established authority in Scotland, not only on agriculture, but on ranching, familiar with precisely everything a man needed to know about cattle and how they made men rich.

Anna Dowling, elegant in bustled bronze brocade, presided at the foot of the table, beaming as she rang a tiny silver bell. "Ladies and gentlemen, dinner is being served," she announced, and sought her place beneath the gleaming candelabra, smiling broadly at her husband as he took his own place at the head. With a good deal of effective folding and rustling, she adjusted her tasseled skirts and mantle to preside over the meal.

Emily, her youngest, barely ripe at nineteen and still cherubic with blond ringlets and innocent blue eyes, sat with her husband, Charles Leeds, who sat at her mother's immediate left. A junior officer in the bank, the ambitious Charles had become the pride of the family, both a confidant and advisor in all of Magnes Dowling's plans. High hopes had preceded the year-old marriage, as the young man's family had deep ties to shipping in the northeast and beyond.

Anna's middle daughter, Wren, five years older than Emily, joined her husband, Arlen, who sat at her mother's right. She brooded, pursing her thin lips into a petulant frown while waiting impatiently for the meal to begin. Arlen chatted at her side, cross-examining their dinner guest with youthful bravado. A self-styled entrepreneur, Arlen boasted shamelessly, having started a small company importing wine and spirits that now flourished with auspicious success. With gypsy eyes and dark curly locks, he played the dandy and got away with it, fawning over women at every opportunity.

Maggie noticed that her mother extolled his shrewd sense for business and made much of his clientele, name-dropping with obvious delight. One could see clearly that she favored him, handsome and amusing as he was.

The guest of honor sat at Magnes Dowling's right hand, well positioned to speak easily to his host and still observe clearly Magnes's only remaining single daughter, Margaret, who occupied the chair next to Wren. Finally, at Magnes's left hand sat Benjamin Farrell, the inscrutable family attorney who had become personal counsel to Magnes since the bank had solicited its European investments in the spring of '82. He had a disagreeable habit of always offering his opinions, whether invited or not.

"My dear ladies," he interrupted, "such elegance! Don't we all look our loveliest this evening? Magnes, my friend, I must say, how *do* you ever bear it?" Farrell bowed and feigned bedazzlement, covering his eyes in jest with a handkerchief. The sharp points of his white collar pressed up against flabby jowls and an insistent paunch pushed hard against a silk vest, visibly faded and stained. He winked hard at Maggie, reminding her as he often did, that although he might be a confirmed bachelor, he was neither blind nor shy.

The attorney's insatiable appetite made him a frequent guest at the Dowling table. Margaret had grown to loathe both his manners and his breath and avoided him as much as possible. Under contract with the bank for more than twenty years, he had nonetheless become an important friend of the family, and she knew that his opinion and blessing would be required in whatever ventures lay ahead.

Crocheted lace lay over fine linen, setting off the first bouquet of the season: fragrant lilacs, jonquils, and lilies, their creamy petals opened wide like satin stars. Elegant place settings bore layers of blue-and-gold trimmed Lenox, complemented by goblets of the finest Irish crystal. McKennon's invitation to present his plans informally, yet in confidence, to the Dowling family, apparently called for Anna's most festive table.

Hoping to catch Maggie's undivided attention, the hopeful Scot looked her way at every chance and by the time the main course was served, had made it clear that he had far more than business on his mind. Maggie's observant father, sensing a match, catered paternally to his new colleague and his eldest daughter as well, attempting to engage her in the evening's conversation in every possible way. No matter that the potential son-in-law nearly equaled him in age, he felt sure that should the negotiations prove successful, a betrothal to an older man would help to tie an even sturdier knot.

"To Scotland!" Dowling proposed a toast.

"Aye, an' tae a fine host," returned McKennon, raising his glass. He then solicited the rest of the family's support. They all knew what was important—there was money to be made.

Each one at the sparkling table put down their glasses and listened, trying to envision the future as Kerr McKennon shared his scheme. With his prudent planning and First Bank's money, he and the great Scottish cattle barons would replace the buffalo and the Longhorn with imported pure-bred stock, turning the West into a bonanza of infinite reward.

"Now, now, that's sure tae be enou' talk o' this," McKennon announced. "We'll be borin' th' ladies soon." Smiling at Maggie and thoughtfully stroking his beard, he added, "*Och*, nae more o' business. I hope we hav'na been too rude. Pray tell, what might th' ladies ha'e tae say?"

The aristocratic, silver-haired Scot looked dapper in a crisp linen shirt and charcoal tweed, his burnished skin aglow against a dark green ascot of finest silk foulard. His blue eyes sparkled, their depths as dark as the sea. Glancing at all three sisters and back at their father, he hesitated, as if seeking permission to continue. Then, turning toward Maggie, who sat listening enraptured, he picked up a butter knife, examining it slowly as he spoke.

"I say, Miss Marg'ret, ha'e ye e'er seen th' kind o' flowers that grow abo'e timberline?" He paused. "Or bands o' Indians, campin' in th' wild?" His Scottish accent had a rough burr in it, yet a musical and pleasant lilt that Maggie liked, familiar words accented heavily on the second syllable. "*Och*, now, that's a sight tae see . . ."

Kerr moved his chair closer to the table and leaned forward, studying her appreciatively. The candlelight created bright auburn streaks in her hair, pulled back into a twist, and glints of fire sparkled off the gold brooch fastened at her throat. Once she found his eyes focused upon her, she found herself speechless, so taken aback was she by his direct approach.

"Why, Mr. McKennon," she replied, regaining her voice, "what questions! Indians! I've been no farther from home than New York. Though I have a mind to see such things, Pennsylvania is the only frontier I know. But I *have* read of the adventures of Buffalo Bill and the tales of Geronimo too, as well as the works of James Fenimore Cooper. Does that count?"

Magnes laughed approvingly and cut in with a note of caution. "My dear sir, you are talking to the one daughter who's always got her nose in a book or is engaged at a civic meeting. Can't seem to get her mind off cowboys and Indians, however, or even worse, what she calls women's progress and politics. A regular libertarian. You'd better beware!" He looked at Maggie with a mixture of exasperation and tenderness.

"Intolerable," Farrell chimed in, patting his lips as if to wipe away the very word. "If I've said it once, I've said it before, too much reading will fill a female's head with nonsense. Our Margaret's far too bright for such fantasies, aren't you, dear?" He squinted at her with accusing eyes as he stabbed his dinner anew. "Those Beadle stories I know you subscribe to are pure myth and hogwash. I would never touch them myself. Surely, you could do better." Maggie glared and sisters Emily and Wren tittered like birds, staring her way without blinking.

"James Fenimore Cooper, nae less . . . ?" McKennon replied, rolling his r's deliberately. "Ye wouldna' be teasin' me, now?"

Lowering her eyes, she continued respectfully. "Certainly not. I don't tease. I read what's available. But just what, might I ask, sir, is timberline? Is that the word you used?"

"Hah! So ye' hav'na learned everra'thin' in that big city school o' yers! Yer father tells me ye're th' brightest o' the bunch an' ye still don't ken how th' trees grow! What shall we do abou' that?" A smile escaped his lips.

Maggie flushed scarlet, wondering what kind of answer he expected and took a sip of wine. Kerr, staring intently, hunched down in his heavy jacket, looking her straight in the face, platinum brows shading his merry eyes.

"Well, young lady, I willna' tell ye. Perhaps ye'll just ha'e tae see fer yerself. Let it be said I invite ye tae it. Come an' join me if ye will. I'd like ye tae be my guest."

McKennon did not elaborate. Instead, he continued to look at her, as though appraising real estate or fine horses, his expression growing more serious and sincere.

"Look here," he continued, his voice softening. "Life's na' easy fer a woman out in th' wilderness—nor fer anyone. But th' Colorado territory is more bonnie than I can e'er describe. There's more land there than in all o' Scotlan', more than all th' miles o' water in th' North Sea. An' th' sky! Why, 'tis so vast it confounds th' mind just tae stand beneath it."

Here Kerr paused, searching for the right words. Lines in his long jaw deepened and his voice lowered as he went on. "But a man gets lonely. Wants fer a special somethin'—company I s'pose ye'd say." Clasping both hands, he laid them out before him like an offering, interlocking his fingers in a tense hold. "Days on a cattle ranch seem full, Miss Marg'ret, full enou' tae overflow. But th' nights wane empty, that's th' truth. I think ye'd like it out there, that I do. Such great country needs fine women like yerself . . ." Kerr focused on the centerpiece to gather strength, then looked back at Margaret directly.

Arlen and Charles simultaneously cleared their throats as Maggie's mother suppressed an exasperated sigh. Then, silence. Kerr looked as though he'd surprised even himself with his impassioned speech, as though he'd said far more than he planned to say, then or ever. Painfully conscious of the incriminating hush, he turned to the small butler's tray by the sideboard.

"D'ye mind if I ha'e a wee dram o' th' malt here?" he said, reaching for a carafe. Not waiting for an answer, he poured a drink and downed it in one audible gulp, avoiding the immediate stares and whispers that flew across the broad damask. He refilled his glass before replacing the carafe.

Magnes Dowling came to the rescue. Rising from the head of the table, he said, "Well now, gentlemen—would anyone care to have a smoke?" McKennon stood up immediately as if glad to retreat to the safety of ritual. Arlen, Charles, and Farrell all rose too and headed for the library where a box of fine Dunhills passed between them. Dowling took the first puff, then doubled over with an explosive cough, his weak lungs protesting the imported cut. He leaned against the closest chair gasping for air while Farrell patted him on the back, motioning to Arlen to bring water. The young man rushed to assist him, as he had often done before.

Stunned by what had just transpired, Maggie sat mute and motionless at the table. While waiting for the last course, she replayed the conversation in her mind and tried to decipher its meaning. Although the year was 1889, unmarried women did not accompany single men on trips. *No, this was something else, altogether.* This was a proposal of marriage if she had read him correctly, a proposal made in front of the entire family. Her head began to ache and she cradled her temples between her fingers as she pondered just how to proceed.

His audacity embarrassed her. *How dare he approach such a subject in public?* Yet, she knew that when he'd spoken, she'd felt a hidden door unlock, her life bursting forth before her. Then again, she wasn't sure if it might not have been a door closing as well. *Who was he? And what was this invitation really all about?*

Maggie didn't notice when her mother rang the bell and announced that coffee and dessert would be served. The men re-assembled in the dining room, McKennon taking his seat again across from Maggie. Quivering cherry trifle layered with cream appeared in individual serving bowls. Emily and Wren smiled, raising their eyebrows at Maggie, still the object of attention, only to catch Kerr's eyes fastened on their sister once again. Wren extended a high-buttoned boot under the table and nudged Emily's ankles.

"Unbelievable," she whispered through closed lips, "how could he possibly be so forward, right here, in front of everyone?"

"Maggie has a suitor!" hushed Emily. "Who'd have expected it?"

The butler presented fresh mint and custard sauce while Maggie stirred sugar into her tea, its fragrant depths clouded by a flurry of finely cut Lapsong leaves. She studied them intently, hoping for an answer to magically appear.

"Look here, McKennon, about this cattle empire," Magnes began abruptly. "The way the prospectus reads, it appears that ten thousand acres of settled land controls a grazing area of nearly a million acres for freehold use. I'd say that's a fair amount by any estimate." He bridged the awkward situation, changing the subject with businesslike aplomb. "That's over fifteen hundred square miles, my good man. And according to your projections, we expect at least two hundred thousand acres of those to be fenced by barbed wire, enclosing fifty thousand head of cattle on the hoof."

McKennon nodded with a smile.

"As I understand it," Magnes continued, "at least three new rail outlets between Leadville and Colorado Springs will cross at convenient junctures to speed the stock to market when the time comes. Now, are you trying to say you can actually manage such a parcel?"

"Ye may rest assured, Mr. Dowlin'," McKennon responded. "My Glasgow an' Aberdeen promoters ha'e us cap'talized at nearly four hundred thousand pounds, more than enou' tae start. I've got water, a full staff, an' horses. Wi' yer help, we'll expand th' Colorado project in stages an' event'ally, fence it all if we ha'e ta', keepin' our investment intact. That way, we needna' worry about a bit o' liftin', or cattle-thievin', now an' then. We'll brand an' divide, as we should, sellin' off th' surplus when necessary." Here he paused to study the effect of his words. "O' course, I daresay we'll ne'er equal what th' English ranches ha'e done in Texas. Some twelve million head at last count. 'Twas written only t'other day that at this moment there are single herds that outnumber all th' cattle in th' North country, in all o' Angus per'aps, or Perthshire. That's a fact!

"My own partner, Hugh Redmond MacGregor, is but a few years ahead o' me in this venture in th' Wyoming territory. He's known well in Edinburgh fer his success. I beg ye tae inquire about his fine establishment na' six miles out o' Cheyenne, th' well-known Western Land an' Cattle Company, otherwise known as Rockrimmon Ranch. He was runnin' Herefords by th' thousands last time I looked, an' he's returned tae his investors seventy-seven percent o' th' original share capital in only five seasons."

Heads nodded approvingly and Maggie looked up to see McKennon beaming at her father. The Scotsman caught her eye and winked. "I myself am testin' a smaller but much hardier breed, more suited tae th' mountainous terrain. Short in th' leg, deep in th' brisket, an' bold as a banshee, but so tender an' delicious. Th' Highland or Kyloe we call it, 'tis a breed almost as old as th' clans themselves. A fine specimen o' cattle both tae raise an' tae eat. The English table canna' get its fill o' 'em, act'ally. Brings a proud guinea at th' market everra'time, an' still th' Queen's favorite. Are ye familiar wi' th' type?"

"No, sir, can't say that I am. Can't say so at all. You must tell me more, but why don't we continue this discussion in private? Over a brandy?" Magnes gestured toward the library. "I see we have much to cover."

"Indeed. Ye're quite right." McKennon finished his glass of whiskey and pushed his chair away from the table. "But may I invite Miss Marg'ret here fer a walk first, while th' evenin's still young?"

"Absolutely," Dowling replied on her behalf.

"Marg'ret?"

Maggie rose as Kerr offered her his arm and they strolled through the paneled library, Magnes following a few steps behind. They paused before a portrait of Maggie's great-grandfather who himself had immigrated from the British isles nearly a century before.

"*Och*, Miss Dowlin', fortune is on my side. I dinna' count on such luck," Kerr began. "Ye're na' only a lady, but one wi' a sense o' adventure, I can tell. An' a *guid* family '*tae* boot. How did I ever land in such a fine kettle . . . ?"

Folding his arms thoughtfully, he studied the portrait. "There's nae use wastin' th' point. 'Tis a *guid* match, I can see that. Indeed, it seems we were meant tae meet."

"Perhaps we were, who knows?" Maggie answered. "But I'm not sure I know what you mean by a match, sir. If you are suggesting that I join you, sir, then I presume you mean as your wife?"

Kerr nodded. She'd understood him after all.

"I'm flattered, I suppose. But you may as well know that the West is something of a passion of mine, a place I've always wanted to know. If you are sincere, I believe I'd be willing to make my dream and my destiny the same." Maggie's words spilled out between shallow, hurried breaths. "That is, I'm open to your offer and willing to take whatever comes. The West doesn't frighten me in the least, not any of it. I want to explore it all."

Kerr stood quietly before her, taking in every word as freshly turned earth absorbs the first spring rain. "Go on," he urged.

"If you truly intend to show me the West, I don't need you to ask me again. I am willing if you are." Maggie felt her hands perspire, her heart racing, now faster than before. "Let me also say this, Mr. McKennon. That if I go, I shall never look back. I'd like to see your South Park in Colorado and the great Wyoming Territory as well. I've heard that there a woman has the right to vote, just like a man—to actually serve on a jury, to be heard, and have an opinion that counts. In the West, a woman can be all she ever hoped to be."

Magnes, standing nearby, turned at this remark and scowled, wishing his eldest had more tact. His daughter occasionally behaved with impertinence, but usually within reason. This chatter, which he'd heard many times before, had gone too far. McKennon, however, seemed charmed.

"Now, now, Miss Marg'ret. Philadelphia'll always be yer home. Ye can return anytime ye like an' yet be a part o' th' new frontier. I'm pleased that such a man as myself suits yer taste. Trust me, ye' wilna' regret it. Th' West is a grand way o' life, fer women *an'* men, an' so ye'll see. I'll look well after ye, o' that ye can be sure. But first, I'd ask ye tae call me Kerr."

It was then that Maggie noticed how beautifully his name sounded, rhyming ever so softly with the word "fair." "Kerr," she repeated to herself as she smiled back at him, allowing him to take hold of both her hands.

"Later on," he continued, "we can talk abou' lookin' back.

Fer th' moment, let us only go forward."

This he offered with paternal tenderness, reaching out and stroking her hair. Maggie stood stunned, not only with the thought of marriage, but by the sudden possibility of going West. McKennon seemed kind enough, she trusted her instincts on that, and getting better acquainted could always come later. Some things wouldn't wait, of this she was quite sure.

The pair strolled through the double doors into the soft spring air. Standing as close as politeness would allow, her shoulder barely touching his, Maggie searched his face for a sign of warmth. Discerning none, she followed his gaze to the clouds fading into the sky, wisps dissolving against the blackness like smoke after a fire. *Could he really want me—?* she wondered silently, *or was the sparkle in his eyes before only a reflection of the light. How will I know what he expects?* She struggled with the enormity of it, the finality. How could she possibly guess?

Ah, well, she assured herself, *he is older, wiser. A man of experience; he would have to know.* Excitement flooded her as one idea led to the next. She would learn to ride, and most certainly, how to shoot. She would become a ranchwoman, of course, and raise a family but, unlike her mother, she'd pray only for boys. Whatever was about to transpire, she knew for certain that nothing would please her father as much as finally seeing his eldest become a bride. She realized too that he might actually have been behind this sudden proposal from the start, possibly including his approval as part of a wider arrangement, perhaps a bank loan and a daughter all at the same time.

What if he had known about his client's intent, but simply not found the time to share with her the suitor's plans? Surely McKennon had to have approached her father first for his permission. If so, she concluded, all the more reason to be in agreement. Whatever this most daring invitation turned out to be, she would accept it, for her father's sake, as well as her own.

"Let us get on wi' it then," Kerr decided, bringing her back from her reverie. "See what ye can do. I'll speak tae yer father, o' course, an' make plans tae stay close by till arrangements are firm. There's plenty o' time tae talk abou' all th' rest: th' weddin', a new home, an' th' like. I'd like tae head out in a fortnight if it suits ye."

Nothing more. He'd made his offer and waited, expectantly. Kerr ignored Maggie's curious expression and looked away, his own eyes impenetrable, preoccupied with deeper thoughts. Then, a gold ring bearing a ruby in a Celtic knot appeared from his pocket, and he slipped it on her finger with the lightest touch, searching her face anew. Her father must indeed have spoken with him about her earlier: he had come prepared, hoping for the best.

Still standing by his side, her arm tucked through his, Maggie noticed that he seemed more tired and older than before. She shivered, feeling a chill, then reached for both his hands. "It suits me," she said softly. "It suits me fine."

Engraved invitations, the ink barely dry, went out quickly to immediate friends and family. Despite Anna Dowling's reservations about the older suitor, she took undeniable delight at the prospect of a wedding and proceeded to conduct the hasty arrangements with enthusiasm. She knew of more unusual couples much closer in age and did not try to dissuade her eldest from accepting the stranger's offer. Who could say when another opportunity would arise?

Maggie fit nicely into her mother's wedding dress, quickly updated in design. Circumstances dictated that the festivities be kept small, a mere hundred guests or so. The event would be held in the grandly appointed Astor Hotel that her father had recently helped to finance and construct.

The gala dinner included caviar, oysters and the finest carved beef. The four-tiered wedding cake, towering on a stand, consisted of white layers trimmed with creamy garlands and filled with a rich, red raspberry puree. Crowning the top, a cluster of hand-painted porcelain flowers shone in the snowy frosting. Emily had found them in an antique shop and arranged them there herself; elegant wildflowers, the perfect promise of a brand-new world to come.

Champagne and wedding cake ended the meal and elaborate toasts wished them well. After the final waltz, the evening wound to a close. The bouquet found its way to a friend and Maggie rescued the porcelain flowers from the cake, wrapping them carefully and tucking them into her bag. As part of their daughter's elaborate dowry, the Dowlings bestowed a sentimental gift, their own treasured English silver dinner service stamped with the family crest, to be shipped as soon as the couple had settled. Maggie could only marvel that she was on her way West at last. Surely, that was present enough.

Kerr saturated himself with spirit. Wren found him in the lobby near midnight outrageously drunk and wandering alone, reciting a verse by Robert Burns. The eloquent refrain to a "Red, Red Rose" echoed over the marble tiles as he bowed graciously to the applause of an invisible crowd. Wren brought Arlen and Charles who convinced him to return to the ballroom where a concerned Maggie anxiously awaited. Then, as the last guests departed, the family also bid their goodbyes, leaving Kerr and Maggie alone. A team of valets helped them to their suite, the very finest money could buy, and the exhausted couple escaped into its privacy.

Once behind the locked door, Kerr excused himself and disappeared into the bathrooom while Maggie unpacked a tapestry valise.

"Hello in there," she called, after nearly a half-hour. "Kerr, is everything all right?"

The sound of sloshing water muffled his reply. At least he hadn't fallen asleep. Reassured, Maggie combed out her hair and undressed partially, removing the train of her ivory dress, her crinoline underskirt, her petticoats, and her satin pearl-studded shoes. Plumping the great feather pillows and turning down the sheets, she lay down expectantly on the wide bed to wait. The high, carved headboard bore an Italian coat of arms and supported a partial ceiling canopy ornamented with grinning cherubs. Although the heavily furnished suite seemed appointed for royalty, Maggie focused only on the brightly lit electric chandelier and its spinning crystal tears casting bright rainbows on the walls, each an illusion of color and form. She waited for what seemed an eternity.

She cleared her throat. "Can you hear me, Kerr . . . ? You know, it's quite remarkable," she began, in spite of the silence. Maggie wanted to speak, even through the closed door. Events had been so fast, she still couldn't put herself in the setting. After repeating their vows, the couple had danced and greeted nearly all of the guests, but had hardly exchanged two words privately during the course of the evening.

"Here we are. I hardly can believe it. You are now my husband and I, your wife. I always knew I would marry someday, but never thought it would be like this. . . ."

She wondered, in fact, if this was how a new bride should feel: bewildered and confused. She needed to know that he wasn't feeling the same way. "Tell me now," she said, as he finally emerged, undressed except for a set of longjohns that covered his loins. "Are you happy?"

"If ye are, Marg'ret, then I am." He turned off the lamp and fell into the sheets beside her. "But happiness, I'll ha'e ye ken, is not th' only thin'. Nae, lass, happiness comes an' goes. In a marriage, 'tis stability that counts."

Maggie sat upright as if to better understand. "I beg your pardon?" She had expected a far different reply. With eyes half-closed and no further answer, Kerr simply reached for her, fumbling to pull off her gown, then groaning as he saw her full corset and lace camisole beneath.

"Take this nonsense off," he demanded. "Ye're mine now. I want tae see all o' ye."

His bold remark shocked her although she dared not show it. Maggie obeyed, shaking visibly as she began to remove her lacy drawers while sitting on the edge of the bed, turning away in the darkness. Kerr wrapped his arms around her waist, drawing the two of them closer, his bare chest pressed against her back.

"*Och,* my sweet lass, such a beauty, y'are—" He squeezed hard, practically lifting her up, turning her body towards him. His warm skin grazed her breasts, still only partially exposed, and she shuddered at the touch, both afraid and anxious for the consummation to come. Caressing her roughly, he attempted to untie her corset, the fastenings a confusion of delicate ribbons and stays. Kerr's hands groped clumsily, first tearing the frilly lace, then causing her stockings and garters to bind even tighter around her thighs. Maggie finally rose to undo the undergarments herself.

Naked for the first time with a man, she sat, shivering at the edge of the bed, hoping he would simply take her so she wouldn't have to pretend she knew what to do. She'd imagined her wedding night many times before and had spoken of it with her sisters, begging for the details she so desperately wanted to hear. None of what she'd been told by either of them even remotely resembled this. She'd always thought the encounter would be more romantic somehow. She had every reason to believe that it should.

As Maggie huddled next to the headboard, Kerr reached for her. She instinctively twisted away as he lurched across the bed, causing him to slide forward onto the thickly carpeted floor.

"My God, lass, where are ye?" Kerr bellowed, surprised and humiliated. Indistinguishable curses led her to him in the dark. As she leaned over to help him stand, her exposed breasts brushed the deep hair on his chest, and her nipples stiffened in response. Shaking, she pulled him up realizing he was too drunk to stand alone. Together they climbed back upon the mattress and lay down, his head over her shoulder and his left arm tucked under her waist. He began stroking her with his right hand, following the gentle curve of her back and on to the fuller rise of her hip, then turning the back of his hand to her skin, slowly caressing the opposite way.

"Fine ye are, Miss Marg'ret," he said, quieted, now more like his former self. "Like th' down on a sparrow. Smooth an' fine, just as a woman ought tae be." He pressed close against her and she could feel that part of him, that manly part she did not know, stir and begin to rise. She wanted to touch him there, to know how it felt, but did not dare. Kerr tried to kiss her mouth but she resisted, so he pulled her close and nestled his heavy head against the cradle of her neck, holding her fast. She lay perfectly still beside him, breathing shallow rapid breaths, rigid and tense as a post.

His loud belch took them both by surprise. As Kerr turned away for a moment, apologetically covering a second eruption, intent and desire seemed to seep out of him like the beaded sweat on his brow.

"God forgi'e me, lass, what ha'e I done? Drunk too much tae make ye my wife?" He stroked her face with his hand. "We best let it go then, there'll be time. . . . In th' mornin', Marg'ret, what d'ye say? Sleep. Let's sleep now. Ye'll need yer sleep. In th' mornin', there'll be time."

Kerr had ordered a carriage to arrive long before sunrise to take them to meet the seven o'clock train. There would be very little time for sleep. Maggie lay back and tried to rest, his heavy head a dead weight against her chest, his left hand curled around her shoulder, his right, lightly resting against the warm flesh of her thighs. Between them, Kerr's loud and sonorous breathing regularly split the night.

Outside, a huge clocktower chimed the hour, two single notes that echoed through the darkness, then faded to silence once again. Maggie lay awake, exhausted, yet exhilarated and, to her own chagrin, even somewhat relieved. She slowly slid her fingers over the carved shape of her husband's shoulder, then down the length of his arm, even exploring the precise circumference of his wrist. Age had stolen the lean abdomen of his youth and his broad chest muscles sagged, but he was still handsome and appealing, like a rugged weathered tree that had grown thick and strong. Maggie stopped her hand at his waist. She lay motionless, shy and still afraid, yet hungry to savor the revelatory feel of a man lying warm along her side and the very new sense of herself, naked beside him, wondering, in fact, if morning would ever come.

Margaret had requested that Kerr refer to her as Maggie by the time they reached Saint Louis. That was the first step. Trying one of Kerr's cigars had been the second. He laughed at her, amazed that a woman would try so hard to behave like a man. He watched her while she read, her neatly coifed head bowed, only occasionally looking out to the endless blur of flatland as they crossed the plains on the Union Pacific headed for Denver.

Kerr had known he liked her from the first moment they'd met, especially her boldness and quick response, figuring she would work hard too when the time came. He had hope she'd be nothing like his first wife, God bless her, a canny *cailleach* tight with a purse and sharp with her tongue. She never bore him any children but managed the farm well enough, wresting from it every penny she could. Afraid of being left without, she had saved and scrimped and squirreled their moneys away, although they always had more than enough, living a quiet and gentrified life that others openly envied.

But the first Mrs. McKennon grew snappish and bitter over time, complaining that she'd sacrificed herself to the bone. Then, one day, she quit the farm entirely, leaving Kerr to raise the cattle, mind the pastures, and manage the big house on his own, never to be heard from again. Townsfolk said she'd fallen into a *fey* trance, susceptible to the supernatural, and had taken her own life after she started hearing the voices, but he never believed it. To put the rumors to rest,

Kerr officially divorced her after a few years, a simple formality on paper that gave him a kind of peace.

He thought to himself that Maggie would never leave him that way; she appeared to have courage. Indeed, she was a woman with confidence, tall enough, broad in the shoulder, and she seemed strong and healthy as well. He liked the expression of her lips too, full, parallel petals that rarely smiled, but could drive away demons when they did. He liked the oval shape of her face and the hard line of her narrow nose, a sign of good breeding and intelligence.

He especially liked the way she walked and sat, her back straight, shoulders square, breasts high and firm against the fitted traveling dress. But her eyes troubled him. Large, hazel-brown, and moody, bottomless like the lochs. Her eyes confused him. Too full of questions and hungry all the time. He often looked away when she spoke, only answering when necessary.

"Could you explain it to me again, Kerr, just the part about where we'll live?" she began.

"I've told ye. Until th' factors confirm my loan, we'll be roughin' it on a staked parcel, that is if ye will, in th' aspen wood near th' ranch. I'm homesteadin', accordin' tae th' law. I'll be addin' that piece tae th' bank purchase soon an' just tae make things official, I need tae spend th' summer on th' property. It's a small *bothy* or cabin, just two rooms, but cozy an' decent enou'."

Maggie nodded.

"Now th' main house, ye understand, sits nearby on a hill, next tae a fresh water *burn,* where it's cooler with a nice view. Not quite a mile from th' homestead but away from th' herds. Ye won't ha'e tae put up with th' sound or smell o' th' beasts that way."

"I see," Maggie said.

"Mind ye, th' cabin will be just fer a month or two, then I'll let th' punchers take over. If ye prefer, ye can stay at th' ranch house wi' my foreman an' his family. Decent folk, they ha'e th' lower floor. Th' upstairs was adequate fer me, but I'm sure ye'll manage things tae th' better. They can find other arrangements soon enou'. Th' big house will be yers then tae do wi' what an' when ye' like. If ye're more comfortable there at first, then I'll join ye when I can. Fer this summer, I'll do what I must."

He squinted at the landscape, far-off windmills and flat-bottom clouds. "Just till I get my acquisition, then we'll see. There'll be lots o' bonnie choices later on, nearer tae town or further out. I hav'na decided yet where we'll build anew, so don't be *blatherin'*, askin' too many questions."

Smoke from his cigar obscured the lack of a smile. Maggie looked out the window trying to imagine the rest.

"Will we be by ourselves then? Out in the middle of nowhere? Or is there a settlement of some kind?" Gloved hands fingered a string bag while she sought his eyes through the haze. The tassel on the handle flopped this way, then that.

"Now, there ye go ag'in. Can ye nae leave a subject alone? Listen hard an' understan' me well. All o' South Park sits in a wide *strath* shaped like a triangle, wi' a sprinkle o' villages clustered at its center. It's a cattle range these days shared by many, over twelve thousan' head, near a thousan' horses at last count, an' great flocks o' sheep as well.

"There's a decent *clachan* na' more'n an hour's ride from th' ranch, th' town o' Jefferson, where at least a few hundred souls ha'e settled tae trade their wares. Na' far off, say three miles abou', a train depot in Como brings freight an' stock in two times a week, an' in Fairplay, another fifteen mile south, there's a courthouse, a school, an' a church or two, as well as a reasonably *guid* saloon."

Maggie nodded again, absorbing every word. Kerr looked at her briefly then back out the window. He continued.

"The ranch I named th' Cameron sits at the foot o' th' northeast rim in a small *dair* or *glen,* an' th' *tigh* itself is built plain an' strong, out o' heavy stone, th' way we do 'em back home. Na' like th' miserable shanties in th' lowlands wi' crofters on top o' each other, animals everywhere an' underfoot.

"There's hundreds o' grassy acres covered wi' wildflowers o' everra' description that grow all summer long, an' where we are, at th' edge o' th' wood, th' mouth o' th' sweetest river ye e'er saw flows right out o' nowhere an' down past our door. Aye, th' place is a godsend, a gift o' th' almighty, tae be ranched fer th' good o' all."

Patting her knee, he smiled, shook his head and closed the conversation by adding, "Ye'll have tae see fer yerself, my lass, an' soon ye fair will. So dinna be *haverin'* away. I'm tired, that's it. Let me ha'e my peace."

Kerr nodded off, the train rolling westward into the hazy afternoon. Maggie gazed out the window and did not press for more, understanding that tenderness was surely not his strength.

Gleaming railways divided the country and reached for its borders. The last branch of the Union Pacific had been laid as far as Wyoming with a juncture down to Denver, the booming miner's town at the foot of the Rocky Mountains. The prosperous frontier city flanked Auraria, a spreading settlement that meandered between the banks of the Platte and the muddy Cherry Creek, shallow rivers that ran through its heart. At the edge of the great wide plains, the two towns bustled around the clock.

Transfixed by the brilliant sunshine and cloudless morning, Maggie stepped from the train at Denver's Union

Depot and waited excitedly as Kerr disappeared into the crowd. The streets overflowed with the noisy mingling of cattlemen and ranchers, miners, merchants and profiteers. A huge demand for imported luxuries amid an atmosphere of new-found wealth created a vibrant pulse Maggie could feel from where she stood.

Wagons loaded with kegs of whiskey, aromatic crates of tea and coffee, rolls of Oriental rugs, and colorful bolts of dry goods passed before her. As she gazed from the platform, the brisk pace of the scene warmed her, even more than the summer sun.

Strangers surrounded the depot, many pausing to stare at the odd collection of bags and satchels the stylish traveler had assembled at her feet. She minded her belongings while Kerr sought out their subsequent arrangements, though she wished they could stay the night in one of the city's fine hotels. Kerr, however, had no time to linger and intended to begin the final leg of their journey as early in the day as possible. Undaunted, Maggie picked up her bags and followed him a few blocks from the station to the great Elephant Corral, the stronghold for livery near the train, where they would pick up their reserved mounts and dispatch the luggage to the wagoners.

Horses, conveyances, and passengers of every description flanked the stable which covered two square blocks, serving the residents as well as numerous stage lines carrying passengers further west. Maggie met the hard faces of local men and women straight on, ignoring their questioning eyes.

Since passenger trains left biweekly to population centers near and around South Park, the daily stage still provided the best transportation into the Rockies for those who preferred reliable passage. A good horse would be another. Long before his journey east, Kerr had arranged for his return baggage to be delivered through to Jefferson and a recently acquired saddle horse and pack animal to be readied in Denver, well shod and outfitted for the trail. Although their destination was a mere sixty-three miles away, a stagecoach with all its passenger stops, plus slow passage over Kenosha Pass, would have taken at least four days to make the journey. A horseman could make it in less time and far less cost. Kerr preferred to ride.

"Can ye handle a *cuddie* a'tall?" Kerr asked Maggie as they stood in the hosteler's line, hoping the answer was yes. Maggie couldn't see why not, since she knew something about horses, though it had been years since she'd been on anything more than a pony. She approached the huge pack mule with a smile and asked about its name.

"Ramon, or Ramona," the hostler replied, "either one'll do. Ma'am, a mule ain't exactly a male nor exactly a female neither. . . . Take yer pick."

Maggie laughed as the man hoisted her onto the animal's narrow back. She'd expected a sidesaddle and was intrigued to see that she'd be riding astride instead. The saddle consisted of a simple, narrow padded back frame anchored by a crupper that ran beneath the tail of the mule, with a breastband running forward around its chest, in addition to a leather cinch. Behind the back of the saddle were tied a slicker and a roll of supplies. Stirrups hung from the sides and thick upholstery cushioned the cantle. In all, the extra layer of blankets and bags challenged the rider to stay centered, but Maggie dared not complain. Like everything else, she figured even riding three days into the Rockies was more attitude than skill, and regretted she had not packed a stout pair of walking shoes in her saddlebag just in case.

"Ye'll be safe up there," Kerr declared. "Such a brute will carry ye tae th' ends o' th' earth, I warrant." Maggie hoped it would never have to.

Kerr's own mount was a rare find, a striking mahogany bay from Kentucky, expertly trained to both pull and ride. He'd purchased her on the spot when he'd found her in Denver on his way to Philadelphia and had arranged to have her boarded until his return. Sixteen hands high and sleek of coat with fine legs and a full mane and tail, she was the very best of her bloodline. Small boned, round in the muzzle, wide of eye and deep in the haunch, the horse was a good choice to breed, even better to show.

Kerr had named her Bonniedoon and she moved with the grace of a true aristocrat, stepping high and long. Fleet and finely made, the delicate mare seemed a questionable choice for range work but an elegant and proper steed for a gentleman. Kerr would keep her for his pleasure, harness her for driving, and even race her on a worthy bet, saddling up one of the sturdier cowponies when he needed to work the herds.

"She's a beauty, that she is," he marveled. "Worth everra' cent o' her price. I'll find me a stallion that can be her match an' we'll breed her in a year. Ha'e ourselves a fine pair. Once I get her on th' ranch, there's nae tellin' what she can do."

"I hope you're right, Kerr," Maggie answered doubtfully. "Seems a bit skittish to me. I wish she'd stop tossing her head and behave properly. Just look at her. Doesn't she ever wear out?" Maggie's questions died in the dust of the mare's incomparable walk, a fine prance of a gait that spirited Kerr ahead of her on the open westward trail.

Together they began the long ride out of town, finding themselves among a caravan of wagons, peddlers, and horsemen, all heading west toward the mining towns and settlements of the front range. They ascended into the afternoon, moving quickly out of Denver and toward the low-rising ridge, riding slowly up through the copper hills that flanked the edge of the plain. Heart songs rose inside Maggie from a sense of happiness deep within. For once, the world appeared gateless and welcoming. She hummed aloud as they rode, her spirits rising with each melodious bar.

"Things will be as they should," she nodded with each rhythmic step, reassuring herself that the future and the man leading her toward it were one and the same. She could see no further and could hope for no more. This experience would be the beginning of the new, the possible, and, finally, the rest of her life or so she believed. Before her lay the westward open trail, the beguiling Scotsman on his spirited horse, and the endless azure Colorado sky.

Maggie's thoughts were as much a promise to herself as a prayer, a dedication to the change, and a necessary step in the act of letting go. She repeated them to herself over and over again, hearing them in the deep staccato of the animals' hooves on the ground and feeling them in the wonders she saw along the way. That May morning, everywhere she looked she found a miracle, wild iris the color of cobalt, crested bluejays, bold and bright. Around them, cool groves of cottonwood, birch, and alder vibrated as birds and squirrels darted from tree to tree. Flowering fields of Queen Anne's lace, purple yarrow, and budding stalks of Indian paintbrush shone in the late spring afternoon. Tiny trumpets of miniature phlox grew wild along the road and the red earth of the mountainside glowed deep behind iridescent fields of mineral green.

Maggie felt drunk with the richness of it, a lush contrast from the harsh and empty views of the plains. Kerr, always a few lengths ahead, looked back now and then, pausing often to let other travelers pass, seeing that she was still close behind.

"That's it, lass," he encouraged. "Sit tight an' keep

astride. Behold now, we couldna' ask fer better weather than this, nor a finer, bonnier day."

Her pulse quickened each time he turned, smiling back at him as he did. She wanted him close, not admitting the mix of apprehension and longing she felt in her heart. She hoped the ride would give them both the time to grow into the closeness necessary to ask the right questions, if they dared. They had been fated to find each other, of that she felt certain, although she still wasn't sure exactly why.

Great gray and black Canada geese flew in formation overhead, the apex of the wide V pointed north. Riders and mounts looked up as the migrators darkened the sky, filling the air with their sound. Kerr pulled the animals to the side of the trail, shedding his mackintosh as the heat intensified, while Maggie rolled up her long cotton sleeves to cool herself in the late spring breeze. Bonnet thrown back, she let down her hair like a street girl and basked in the warmth of the midday sun. The light summer wind caressing them all would hopefully hold until sundown when they would stop to make their first camp.

After the unsettling incident on the trail, Kerr kept a tighter rein on Bonniedoon and a watchful eye on the woods. The ears of the mare flicked back and forth as she continued to foam at the bit and toss her head, ever reluctant to settle down, while the mule plodded steadily on.

They kept moving west at a strong and deliberate pace, stopping only for short rests. The second day brought them to the settlement of Pawnee just below Kenosha Pass, the final leg of the journey before dense wooded hills gave way to the lush flatland and majesty of South Park, home to the Cameron Ranch. From there they would turn into the mountains that lay below the great Continental Divide, the protective shelf that ran the full length of the east rim of the plateau, known for brewing or trapping wild summer storms, depending on nature's whim.

Though the weather held, tranquillity did not. The mule, as exasperating as it was slow, had developed its own mind about stopping and grazing, and sometimes reversed for no apparent reason at all. The mare, having never been a trail horse before, continued to start at unfamiliar sights and sounds. Maggie's legs ached from constantly coaxing Ramona. The two riders had slipped into a formal quiet, often saying nothing for hours other than to urge their mounts forward, listening instead to the clop of hooves and the faint sounds of the forest itself.

"Kerr, please wait," Maggie called. "Slow down. I can't even see you." She pushed Ramona on, pressing the mule to jog faster. Kerr pulled the mare to a halt and waited at the edge of a wood. Here, the aspen grew so close that unless one could find the paths worn by the deer, it seemed impossible to see through the maze. The restless Bonniedoon would now have to pick her way slowly, allowing the trailing animals to follow, nose to tail. At last Maggie would be able to talk without shouting.

"Do you know where we are, Kerr?" she asked, wondering what had happened to the once visible trail. As she gazed about, all directions looked the same. "It appears to me we are lost." She regretted doubting him but had no feel for the distance or length of the journey. She only knew she felt confused and could not fathom the way. Kerr seemed to know just where he was going, always riding ahead. He appeared to be fixed either on the past or somewhere deep in the future. Maggie lived in the moment, as it was all she really had. How would she ever reach him, she wondered, kicking the mule with her heels.

As if reading her thoughts, Kerr called out.

"Stop yer worryin', lass. We're na' too far now."

Not far, she thought. What did he mean? Far from what? Ten miles, a hundred? Little of what he said seemed to mean what she had first thought. Her initial optimism had been dimmed by their very first evening's camp when McKennon, having laid out Maggie's bedroll after dinner, proceeded to sit up most of the night alone by the fire. Despite the excitement of sleeping under the stars, Maggie had crawled into her blankets and fallen asleep almost instantly, expecting Kerr to join her. To her surprise, he was packed up and ready to ride when she awoke alone the next morning, looking as though he had never slept at all. They mounted and started up the trail barely exchanging a word, each absorbed in their own thoughts.

What in the world have I done? Maggie reproached herself. *And where am I going? Is it possible that Kerr McKennon can be such a stranger to me still?* Though she'd felt certain about their fated meeting, she'd begun to wonder about its purpose and price.

Who was this man who had already so altered her life and had talked her into a wedding put together in haste? There had been one unfulfilling night in bed with someone she now hardly recognized, and now this interminable ride into silence toward an uncertain future. She tried to put the humiliation of that one attempted union on their wedding night behind them, blaming everything on the short courtship, the strange room, and the quantities of liquor Kerr had drunk earlier in the evening. Time would have to dim that painful memory.

"Here," he pointed to his compass, "we're just north o' Jefferson. Th' view at th' top of th' next hill is a vision if I e'er saw one. O'er that crag an' we'll be there." He flashed a smile and picked up the reins of the mule, allowing Maggie to stay closer behind.

Kerr watched the horizon for a break in the terrain and a change in the color of the grass. South Park, that great vista soon to open at his feet, drew him like the Holy Grail, its unfenced expanses of rolling fields covered in knee-high, scented hay, the richest virgin blue stem mixed with the sweetest shortgrass to be found anywhere in the West. The valley was God's gift to the ambitious, a bounty for the taking. Hundreds of square miles of the finest feed, richest soil, and purest water in Colorado surrounded by gleaming peaks rising in every direction, still snow-capped and bright like so many jewels on a strand. A hardy herd of Highlands would spend the summer there growing fat and marketable. Each year they would mate and increase and cover the land.

As they came over the crest, Maggie stood in her stirrups, stunned by the view that lay below. She gasped at the intoxicating sight, filled with its varied beauty. The turquoise sky paled to white on the rolling horizon, randomly dotted with grassy knolls, velvet with whisper-green sage. The far-reaching pastures, dark with the forms of cattle, beckoned in the midday sun. Even the mule seemed intent on absorbing the scene, eagerly sampling the deep grass, long ears erect, capturing every sound. Maggie reveled in the sight, boundless and beckoning, an ocean of grassland ablaze with blooming color.

Despite the thrill of the view, Maggie felt faint with fatigue. Swaying in the saddle, the nearby tops of trees began to dance and her vision blurred as she watched Kerr dismount at the edge of a grove. Feeling nauseous, she found herself clinging to the saddle with both hands clenched tight.

While tying the mare to a tree, Kerr turned, saw Maggie slipping, and ran with both arms outstretched to steady her. Letting go, she slid into her husband's grasp and collapsed as he eased her onto the grassy side of the hill.

Numb with exhaustion, Maggie dozed while Kerr unpacked the provisions and set up what would be their last camp. She watched him with half-closed lids, amazed as always at his efficiency. Around his horse's forelegs he fastened a plaited leather hobble laced with tiny silver bells, a treasured gift from a tenant in Scotland. As he had the first two nights, he unpacked tins of beef and fruit and hung the iron kettle full of water over a camp fire. But to Maggie's surprise, she also watched him produce brightly wrapped jars of jam and packs of shortbread, small buttery biscuits that melted in the mouth. "A Scottish treat tae celebrate," he said. "We're nearly home."

Who could have imagined a man packing such delicacies for the trail? Sitting up, she rubbed her aching legs, only to find blood on her hands. Her stockinged calves under ankle-high boots were blistered and raw, her thighs, sore and chapped. Kneeling by the stream, she washed her hands and face, feeling the fatigue creep into every bone, and once again, lay back into the grass. The sounds of Kerr preparing the evening meal floated dreamily by.

"Close as we are, we'll take our time an' cross th' rest o' th' park in th' mornin'," Kerr announced. "We'll rest here fer th' night an' freshen up tomorra'? What d'ye say, Maggie? That be all right wi' ye?"

Maggie neither heard nor answered. She had fallen asleep on the ground.

Waking after sundown, Maggie found a blanket around her and Kerr sitting close by. A hearty porridge sweetened with berries boiled in a pot and hot tea steamed before her. She ate with enthusiasm and rallied brightly, preparing their bedrolls and rising to groom the animals as Kerr had instructed her. He would see that she was just as strong as he. She continued to wear her emerging independence like a new-found suit of armor.

Strengthened by the simple meal, Maggie sat by the fire, searching the sky for familiar signs. The brilliant gibbous moon gleamed seductively, stealing her untrained eye. Venus shone steadfast and bright to its left, while distant stars sparkled faintly.

"Look, Kerr! Orion, over there, and the 'Archer,' straight above. And the quarter moon—I can almost see traces of the old man's face. I think he's watching us."

No answer. She cleared her throat, wondering if he'd heard. Never mind. She returned to studying the heavens, not asking again for what might not even be there. Just why he continued to be so reserved was a mystery, but she did not press him. There were secrets perhaps, that might have held him back, reasons she might not want to know. Certain men simply could not give much of themselves, or worse—could not receive either. Maggie hoped she might reach him eventually, but sensed that only time would tell.

"Nae, I canna' believe it!" Kerr began abruptly, "I canna'! He can convince yer father but he'll ne'er convince me! That sorry *guiser* MacGregor built an empire fer himself in Wyoming before his profits e'er proved true." He tossed the rest of his tea into the fire. "An' now we'll both be caught short!"

Maggie looked around, expecting to see someone else her husband might be addressing in this way.

"Th' scallywag!" he continued. "I thought he was a cut abo'e th' remittance men, dandies, an' scoundrels. Look here, Maggie, I warned him o' his foolishness. He's trouble tae me now, nothin' but a *canny* rogue! Wastin' our reserves, in spite o' what I told him, time an' time ag'in. An' now we're caught, like th' rest o' them, in a bind, with th' market bein' what 'tis . . ."

The tirade came out of nowhere. He continued. "Th' beef's down an' th' costs are goin' up. Him an' his huge cattle *spreague* in th' middle o' nowhere usin' our credit like there be nae tomorra' . . . 'Tis not my taste, such extravagance, squand'rin' our money t'impress an' show." He rose and began to dig through his pack.

Maggie noticed that Kerr often started a conversation in the middle of a thought, as if he'd been talking to her all along and suddenly decided to make it audible. Amazed by the outburst, she credited it to the open flagon now in his hands.

"What did ye say about th' moon there, my little lass? Did I see th' face? Och! Tae me, that moon is *guid* fer nothin'.

Couldn't light a *kirkyard* fer a dead man. Better, wait fer th' full moon, fer th' grand glow it gi'es. Mind ye, on a misty night ye'll see th' moonbows too, rosy rays o' color sparklin' like a crown!

"Where I come from," he waxed on in the dreamy vision he remembered, "th' legends are full o' bright nights an' gran' cattle raids. Some swore a man could see th' color o' a newborn calf by th' light o' that pearly globe, even th' way th' hair curls. MacGregor's Lantern they called it, an' tales are long abou' the cattle plucked from th' darkest glens by only th' light o' th' moon . . . !"

Maggie mused at the intriguing thought.

"Back in Scotlan' th' *reivers* do their finest work by night, that they do. Believe it or not, cattle thievin' used tae be an honorable livin' before we lost our rights. Now th' English think they own th' livestock an' th' bloody hills they roam in as well. Back then, th' herds belonged tae th' clans, tae those who had th' strength tae catch them an' keep them. Aye, legend says that th' MacGregors, fierce as they were, were th' ones tae watch. As reivers, they were th' best o' th' best. I should ha'e seen it comin'."

Maggie puzzled at Kerr's rising anger. "Seen what?"

"Him cheatin' me out o' what's mine, what was tae be shared fairly! Only a fool would ha'e missed it. Well, 'tisna' too late." He took another swig and snarled viciously, "He'll hear from me yet."

Kerr sat across from Maggie, poking at the fire with a stick. "Nae, I ne'er thought 'twould come tae this." A tone of self-pity crept into his voice. "Riskin' th' whole operation wi'out my say. Hugh MacGregor will be my ruin, or I'll be his—sooner or later." Maggie listened somberly, guessing that she was to hear only part of what was wrong and wondering what was really behind his wrath.

"Listen here," Kerr hissed. "Gossip tells he's stocked th' place wi' enou' wine an' whiskey tae float th' Queen's navy. That, an' a houseful o' servants tae polish th' silver everra' single day. 'Tis too much! Why, I've heard he's e'en built sportin' rooms fer his friends an' their 'ladies,' th' rogue. That's a fool fer ye, wastin' his money instead o' investin' it in th' land."

The silver flask caught the moonlight each time it touched his lips, each draught of whiskey raising his voice another note. Maggie moved closer and snuggled into the rough bedroll against him, anxious in the black night, watching the fire lick the stones. When he finally lay back, quiet and motionless, she turned away from his loud snores, not daring to leave his side. Fear was a feeling still foreign to her, it kept her anxious and mute. But the familiar gnaw of loneliness continued to keep her close.

Around them the woods crackled with the occasional sounds of animals rustling in the brush, nocturnal hunters reminding her that the night hides much that may be known, but not always seen. Maggie drifted off and then awoke with a start as the sharp cry of a coyote sent chills up her spine. Then she lay awake for hours, listening for the answer to the coyote's lonely call. Lying on her back, counting stars, she thought about the great ranches Kerr had described, like castles, rising in the wilderness. They would be hers as much as anyone's she hoped, grand incarnations of a dream. The proud Scottish cattlemen of the West would be their keepers and their kings, and she would be the Lady McKennon of the Cameron Ranch one day. That much Kerr had promised her before he dropped off in the middle of a sentence into a drunken deadman's sleep.

"O' that," he'd said, "my little Maggie, ye can be verra', verra' sure."

6

The remains of the old cabin sagged in the light of a clearing at the end of the narrow trail. "Hold up!" McKennon called. "We're here."

Maggie stared, incredulous, and jerked the mule to a halt. The sod roof of the long-abandoned building grew wild with stickweed and brambles and the corral to one side had collapsed entirely, its wormy weathered rails piled askew. Crumbling and rotted to a silver gray, the remains of the cabin appeared to be just two rooms, joined by a chimney, the hearth of a fireplace still dark with soot. Between the rooms, a front door once stood, now a gaping hole caught the wind.

Through the opening, Maggie could see wide chinks in the walls and patches of light scattered across the floor. Miraculously, a small window in the south wall, still bearing four wavy panes of glass, hung like an unexpected star but did little to brighten the ramshackle interior. Maggie's eyes smarted with hot tears.

"You call this a homestead?" she hissed between clenched teeth. "You expect me to live here, in this shed, not even fit for a dog?" Nothing Kerr told her had prepared her for this, a horrible kind of joke—another test, perhaps, of her patience or her strength. He hurled his bedroll to the ground and dropped the reins where he stood.

"Get down, now, Maggie McKennon, right this minute, an' help me unload!" he responded. "An' hold yer tongue.

Th' ranch is but a half-mile further on. This miserable *sheiling* is only fer th' summer, like I said, *if* ye be willin' tae help. Now then, na' another word!" Tying the mare securely to what was left of the fence, he approached Maggie and looked up at her imploringly.

"Forgi'e me, lass. I dinna mean tae *skreich.* 'Tis all a part o' th' plan, lass. I need tae make this dwellin' look like a home, that's all. An' I will. An' be livin' here when th' land officer stops by. Till it's good an' ready, ye can be comfortable at th' main house down th' way. I promise ye, ye'll be fine. Bear wi' me now. Be a *guid* lass an' lend a hand."

Maggie sighed. She had wanted a challenge and she'd found one. Silently, she dismounted and began to untie the provisions that filled the bulging pack. Tired Ramona arched her neck toward the roof and sniffed, then her long yellow teeth tore a bramble off the fragrant grassy patch. Munching contentedly, she proceeded to pull a flowering weed from the top, prickly stem and all, a hapless black-eyed Susan dangling from the corner of her mouth.

A great cast iron stove arrived first. Next, came a wagon with the metal bed and mattress, Maggie's trunks, and a high chest of drawers. Help came from throughout the ranch, as cowpunchers welcomed the new bride and traded time off to pitch in, chink logs, lay the floor, and rebuild the small corral. Each day, new faces and hands appeared, filling up the homestead with unusual accents and smiles.

Two cowboys, Gus and Jon, cleared out the old debris and brought in new lumber to shore up the walls. A young Scottish drover, fresh off the Midland Pacific into South Park, worked endless hours near the woods, stacking and cutting the many logs waiting to be set. Like hundreds of other immigrants from the British Isles, he'd traveled to Colorado to meet the needs of the cattle companies that had so quickly populated the West.

Maggie noted that the young man arrived early each morning in heavy breeches and a full-sleeved shirt, and that, by midday, he often stripped to the waist as the summer sun bore down. The first time Maggie saw him thus, she pretended not to notice as staring would have been inappropriate. But she could not help herself, as she'd never seen a young man so firm and strong or quite so appealing and fair. She stayed inside the cabin discreetly, occupying herself with the arrival of their belongings, putting up the many goods necessary for setting up a summer home and peeking out the window now and then.

Maggie realized that the drover had been watching her as well. Whenever she looked in his direction, she could count on him staring back through a tangle of unruly hair. Then, as though guilty of something, she would avert her gaze to his crude workbench where his incredibly capable hands shaped rough boards into windows, doors, and frames, transforming the cabin rapidly into a shelter she could accept. She marveled at the man's energy and skill, and finally, decided to ask Kerr about him.

"That be th' new lad," Kerr said. "A landsman, in fact. He belongs tae Glasgow nearabouts or so I've heard. Come in on th' train a few weeks ago. Roundup an' brandin' he's hired fer, that's all. But he seems tae be a decent worker, d'ye na' think? Moves fast an' sure. Worth his pay if ye ask me. A *guid* find, that one. Aye, that he is."

Maggie and Kerr spent the first two nights at the ranch house after all. Kerr had not misled her, the two-story structure felt like a fortress, well constructed although simply furnished. And to her delight, she'd discovered an upright piano in the parlor, an unimagined luxury in this remote part of the world.

As Kerr had explained, the ranch foreman and his wife occupied the main floor and the second story belonged to Kerr alone. Maggie explored the space with its stark furnishings, and wondered how to arrange her things. A hand-made bookcase contained ledgers and books and an armoire held Kerr's clothes; aside from these, there were no nonessentials or empty cabinets in the spartan room. Disappointed at the barren interior, Maggie reserved comment, then reminded herself that the Cameron was a cattle ranch after all, and Kerr appeared to have the major necessities.

The Scot urged her to think of all the ways she could to make the home more civilized and Maggie promised him that she would. Taking her to his narrow bed the night of their arrival, he still did not favor her with any kind of intimacy, in spite of her expectations. Dismayed but not discouraged, she assumed that the long tiring ride and lack of privacy had to be the reason.

The following morning, Maggie met Kerr's herd of Highlands up close for the first time. She marveled at the powerful creatures with their long coats, short legs, and sharp curving horns. They stared back at her with beguiling faces marked by square, flat muzzles, heavy forelocks, and expressive eyes radiating peace and bovine contentment.

Numbering fewer than a thousand, Kerr's imported herd had grown steadily over the years, adapting well to the climate and surroundings. He had allowed them to rotate feed and locale, sampling that which matured first and grew most dense, finding that they grazed efficiently on almost anything that grew. Unlike the bracken-covered hillscapes of the Scottish moors, the diverse and fertile grasslands of Park County in summer provided a veritable moveable feast, one that rapidly put on weight.

Maggie found herself charmed by the creature's primitive but entrancing appearance. Red, black, cream, silver, brindle, or dun, each steer or cow appeared unique and memorable, the massive bulls positively majestic. She discovered firsthand that if one moved quietly around them, they behaved as gently as any domesticated beast.

Despite the security of the ranch house and the warm welcome by Kerr's foreman and his wife, Maggie insisted on roughing it in the cabin with Kerr. She realized that restoring the old ruin was as close to frontiering as she might ever come. The promised castles could wait.

"Th' way I see it," Kerr explained to her with his usual logic, "we'll clear th' south side fer a garden an' build a stone wall tae keep th' varmints out. We'll ha'e th' new lad make us a table an' a couple o' benches fer either side. Fer th' time being, that should do us fine."

Silva Antonio Avendano deReyes, a Spanish *vaquero* from Mexico and his half-breed wife, Maria, managed Kerr's house and taught Maggie the art of cooking on the upright wood stove. A small firebox on the left held the kindling and firewood while a removable pan below the grate took the ash. Maintaining the heat seemed simple enough, although Maggie never believed she would master it. She learned to watch carefully lest the fire grow too hot and a pot above be left to burn. Kerr, always patient, forgave her mistakes, learning to accept occasional blackened biscuits and even blacker coffee without a reproachful word.

"*Señora!*" Silva called to Maggie one morning, "*Buenos dias, Señora McKennon.*" The old *caballero* stood waiting outside the cabin door, his face aglow with expectation. The toothy smile, his trademark grin, spread over his face as he presented a sprightly roan mare, bright in her strawberry coat of heathered red and white. Maggie squealed with delight at the sight of the showy mount. "For me?" she asked.

"Si!" he responded, placing the lead rope in her hands. Kerr appeared at the cabin door nodding his thanks to Silva, who had delivered the surprise as directed.

"Fer you, my lass," Kerr beamed, as he stepped outside and handed her a leather bridle. "A little weddin' present."

Maggie marveled at the mare's peppered markings, full white mane, and frosty eyes that looked like they were dreaming. She threw her arms around the brassy pony's neck, savoring the scent and feel of her.

"How beautiful she is! My own little mustang! A living piece of the ranch!" Maggie gave Kerr a quick hug. "Thank you so very much. You don't know what this means to me, Kerr. Now I can ride along with you!" Turning to the old Spaniard, she offered her warmest smile and shook his weathered hand. "You too, Señor. *Muchas gracias!*"

Silva grinned back, bashful at the unexpected attention. *"De nada, Señora, de nada."*

Maggie returned to the mare and ran her fingers through its forelock. Billboard images of costumed trick riders prompted a giggle of joy. "She's just picture perfect, that's what she is. I couldn't have chosen a prettier horse myself. When may I ride her, Kerr?"

"Whene'er ye're ready. Th' sooner th' better."

Maggie reveled in the mare's curious exploration of her pockets and hand, all the while blowing warm breaths from her soft, velvet nostrils. A lick to Maggie's palm forged the final bond. "At last," Maggie sighed. "I feel like I'm here, truly in the West."

In just a few lessons Silva taught her how to catch and

bridle her horse and cinch the riding gear in place. The gift included a fine carved leather saddle with a high cantle and finely tooled *tapaderas* over the wooden stirrups. No sidesaddles in this part of the world, Maggie observed happily. A woman could ride the same as a man. Maybe even better. The gentle horse stood quietly and seemed to enjoy the attention, turning now and then to watch with curiosity as Silva and Maggie unbuckled and resaddled her repeatedly. "I think I'll call her Calamity," Maggie announced with a smile, not bothering to explain.

The rest of May and June passed quickly, full of endless discoveries. Each evening, Maggie and Kerr walked together about the cabin, gathering firewood and sharing the day's events. After sundown, the exhausted Maggie would retire early, hoping for Kerr to join her. But, as was his custom, he usually stayed away, working late, self-absorbed and restless, reading by lantern light or scratching out various calculations for the ranch. During these times, he often drank and occasionally smoked his pipe, then would slip deep within himself, sitting motionless for hours.

When at last he fell into bed by Maggie's side, there might be a hug or a kiss, or a stroke of a wrist or thigh, and then he would turn away, deep in sleep until dawn. Maggie hugged her pillow in the dark and wondered why he didn't seem to want her, wishing and waiting, hoping each night would be the one in which he'd finally turn to her, still his virgin bride.

She didn't dare ask about it; it was improper for a woman to bring up such things to a man. And she knew well enough that a proper wife would wait until her husband wanted her, no matter how long it took. In fact, she sensed she might embarrass him if he wasn't ready.

No, she chided herself, she would be patient and push the matter from her thoughts, a difficult task which grew more bothersome with every passing day.

Each morning took Margaret McKennon further from her past, each night made her more anxious for the next to arrive. She stood one morning in front of the small mirror above the chest of drawers and mused about the unfamiliar woman she had so quickly become. Her long hair, once fashionably styled and pinned, now hung loose or lay plaited in a braid to one side, a style she had previously thought unfitting for women her age. Her hands, tanned beneath her riding gloves, were callused and often rough. Since her arrival, the simplest blouses had become her favorite attire, worn with divided riding skirts tucked deep into her boots. These enabled her to step through horizontal fence rails or even better, to climb upon Calamity's back at a moment's notice.

On the top of the clothing chest lay the porcelain flowers she'd saved from her wedding. Their elegant shapes and colors delighted her and prompted her to wonder about the hands that had painted them, somewhere, far away. These, like many other niceties still packed securely, seemed not to belong to this simple life she now led, and Maggie was in no hurry to reacquaint herself with them. With the exception of this momento, other luxuries seemed to have diminished in value.

Once in a while, Maggie would think about the past and the members of her family who now moved through her memory like actors in a play. Though the sisters had been close as children, as adults they'd grown apart. Emily and Wren had married selfish men who seemed to dictate their very thoughts, in fact, their very lives. No longer able to share common pastimes or diversions, Maggie, Emily and Wren had discovered sadly that what had bound them together in the past had not been half as strong as what was now keeping them apart. There were days Maggie couldn't believe she had ever lived among them: her parents, her sisters and their possessive husbands, and even all of Philadelphia, an illusion once called home.

Dark rain clouds stormed over the hills and the wind railed at the new sod roof. "I'll be back before nightfall," Kerr assured Maggie, as he pulled on his boots for a ride in the brewing storm. "If we missed any o' these new calves yesterday, they an' their mothers might na' find th' herd now that we're movin' downstream. I just think I'll take another look around, Maggie. I'll nae be long."

Maggie looked out the window to watch Kerr ride away, his hat pulled down low, tented in the oiled slicker that swirled around him in the wind. She thought of a great centaur cantering into the sky.

He rode Calamity this day. Maggie's trustworthy mare had turned out to be a calm and dependable mount, indifferent to either the elements or surprise. Bonniedoon would have proved unsuitable for such a critical task and Kerr had thought the better of taking her.

He followed the cow trails across the *strath*, well worn by beasts in search of higher grass. The wind howled and heavy gusts pushed the thick branches of the pines like waves. Kerr hunched down into the face of the storm. Peering among an ocean of swaying branches, he glimpsed an old mother cow hiding in a willow patch. Next to her, curled up in the tangled depths, lay a tiny newborn calf, a frightened heifer with a pale apricot coat.

After lassoing the reluctant cow and tying her to the saddle horn, he dismounted. He picked up the calf in one arm and swung into the seat, carrying it under his coat as he headed home. When he arrived, he shouted over the wind, "Maggie, come quick! Look at what I've found fer ye. Hurry, gi'e me a hand."

Maggie stepped out to behold an unforgettable sight. Fighting the long rope, a thin, wet, scraggly beast braced herself against Kerr's taut lariat. Unlike most of the Highland breed, the ginger-colored cow seemed feral and unapproachably wild, panicked by the abduction of her calf. Long twisting horns bobbed in the air as the cow resisted. Her *dossan,* the bushy forelock unique to Highland cattle, hung tangled and dripping wet, shrouding frightened rolling eyes. She bawled for her baby that was still in Kerr's arms.

Kerr had discovered that the calf appeared to be blind, possibly because its mother was an aging animal too long off her feed. This offspring would be her last if he had anything to say about it.

"A sure meal fer a coyote, I figure," Kerr yelled into the wind. "Left on their own, neither would ha'e a chance. Couldna' leave them tae such a fate, nor tae th' herd neither. Ye can raise a calf, can ye na', Maggie?"

As usual, it was more of a statement than a question and Kerr didn't pause for her reply. "Here ye go, now. It appears th' little one canna' see. Go easy wi' her. We'll raise th' heifer till she's old enou' tae sell. Brand her, keep her, an' milk th' mother twice a day. Fresh cream around here won't hurt anybody. They're yers, Maggie. Treat them like yer own. I expect no harm will come tae either."

The wet, day-old calf had a strange infant perfume, drawing Maggie instantly. Its fuzzy coat and milky breath made it seem familiar and she picked it up, wrapping the creature protectively in her shawl while the mother continued to protest.

"Shush now, you'll have to share," Maggie soothed, tightening her hold. "I'm going to help you, not hurt you." The spindly creature sniffed her face and rested quietly in her arms as they moved on up the hill to the shed, their backs to the slanting rain.

Maggie loved the pale calf and taught the summer baby to answer to the name of *August,* her favorite month of the year. The heifer followed its mother dutifully, but learned to wait by the corral gate expecting Maggie's call, one that often included a welcome cupful of oatmash or porridge. The calf's downy face with expressionless eyes eagerly poked its pink nose toward her, seeking security and warmth. The pitiful creature reminded Maggie that nature could be cruel as well as beautiful, and she took careful heed.

Days turned into weeks as Kerr and Maggie learned to accept each other, while she learned the way of life at the Cameron. Kerr and Silva taught their willing pupil how to read the tracks of wildlife and identify wild plants and grasses. The area was rich with mint and wild berries as well as useful herbs and grasses. Most importantly, she learned how to load and shoot a Winchester, a basic requirement of survival in the wild. Though the thought of killing anything offended Maggie, she knew the day might come when she would not have a choice, and she practiced diligently whenever she had the chance.

She took each new lesson in stride and true to her calling as a teacher, wrote everything down for herself and Kerr's occasional meticulous review. In fact, she did all that she possibly could to please her ambitious husband. But despite Maggie's effort, willingness, and affection, she could never kindle his ardor. No matter how hard she tried, she continued to be met by McKennon's restraint and unfathomable reserve.

Perhaps too much time had passed since he had been with a woman, she deduced, and he no longer had the need. Or the humiliation of the wedding night had caused him so much pain that he didn't dare try to approach her again. Whichever it was, Maggie couldn't tell. Not a soul would imagine that their bed was still cold, as their outward commitment appeared to continue to grow.

Occasionally, McKennon revealed an endearing tenderness or display of affection that caught Maggie unawares, such as an unexpected hug or sudden squeeze of the hand. Accepting him as a man of few words, she eventually learned that a simple touch on the cheek or cluster of wildflowers on the table said more than any spoken word could express. Maggie McKennon learned to read the signs of a man who obviously struggled to love. She took what little he gave and waited, wondering how the nights, as he himself had said, could truly seem so long.

July and August passed with no particular change. One early September morning Kerr noticed that the glass in the window appeared loose and needed some repair. He took off his chaps at the door and, picking up his tools, said, "Listen here, Maggie, th' window's a'goin'. Why d'ye na' help me now an' stop what ye're abou'. A couple o' wood stays will hold th' panes, a touch o' mud will fill th' edge. Fer now, anyways. Stay inside, lass, an' steady th' thing in place."

Kerr began to work on the frame, motioning for Maggie to hold her side. She spread her fingers wide against the glass and in its wavy reflection, noticed her face as though she were looking at stranger. It appeared freckled, faintly lined and brown, and oddly, older. Not fully approving the image of her new self, she squinted intently.

"Is that it?" she called to him. "Is that enough . . . ?"

Outside, Kerr leaned against the sash, pressing his bearded face along the glass, parallel to her flattened cheek. Their breath in the cool morning air made a steamy fog on either side, like a captured lover's cloud.

He busied himself with the task and knelt to pick up some nails. When he looked up, Maggie was nowhere to be seen. A leather riding crop propped across the window had replaced her steady hands and nothing but a moist smudge spoke of her parted lips.

On the other side of the cabin, a determined but furious

Maggie gathered dishes off the table and stacked them in a washtub. Her jaw clenched, she wiped away unwelcome tears that burned hot beneath her closed lids, her brows a rigid line. Ignoring Kerr's tapping at the window, she merely paused, looked at him briefly, then turned away, beginning to rinse the breakfast plates. She took note that the floor boards still needed oiling and the bed had yet to be made.

Part Two

Kelsey Sculler hated America, Chicago most of all. Hated it as much as he'd hated Dublin before he'd taken a mind to leave the stinking fisheries and tenements where the poor like himself were holed up no better than sardines. Many were drunk most nights till they were glassy eyed and stiff, and most mornings, dead to a world that didn't care anyway.

In spite of his love for the *Guinness,* he'd been hired by a boatwright for whom he quickly took charge, ordering materials and supplies. He figured out how to make a little extra on the side by padding the orders when opportunity allowed. The boys had come to depend on his easy money. Decent quid made the bets more fun, especially on the nights when they played winner take all.

When the owner finally accused him of stealing, he struck the old man, knocking him out. Kelsey didn't wait to be fired; he quit before anyone could ask questions or call the police to investigate. There would be none of that, no trouble with the law. To hell with them. He'd deny everything or run if they put claims on. No witness had seen him, it was his word against another's.

Just a block down from the wharf he signed on to leave Dublin for good, to go to America and build rail lines along the Allegheny, wherever that was. Just in the nick of time too. Good pay, room and board, and one-way passage; he'd heard all about it. You couldn't be poor and Irish and not know about the fabled promised land across the sea. At that moment, a railroading job anywhere sounded better than the local jail yard, so he kissed his mother goodbye and set sail the very next day with a loaf of homemade bread and an extra pair of boots in his pack. It was the fall of '88 and Kelsey and a thousand hungry men hunkered down in a freighter to share their common dream—of becoming rich men in the new world and walking the streets of gold.

"Turn over, ye got the sheets!" he groused at Callie, a silky-bottomed whore whose narrow bed and tiny room he now shared. Kicking him in the shin, she rolled over and released the blankets, then swung her feet down, sitting up with a groan that hinted at the grueling night before.

"You're a fine bastard," she sneered. "Why don't you get your own bed?" She got up, throwing a robe over her bare body and heading for the washroom at the end of the hall. "I've had just about enough! I need my sleep, do you understand? It's over. I want you out of here. Tonight!"

Kelsey looked at his fob watch and figured he'd gotten by with one more reprieve from a cold night on the street. It was nearly two in the morning and he knew he'd been pushing his luck. Why she even let him stay at all was a question he never dared ask. After the first time, when he'd convinced her to let him have a second go right away for the same dollar, it just seemed kind of natural. She dared him to try and they'd tossed and turned until they'd spent each other, Kelsey feeling for all the world like a rogue.

The next night at the saloon, acting bold and familiar, he called out when he saw her. "Hey! Have ye had enough? Or are ye ready for a good time with a real man?" He didn't wait for her answer. "Come on, my pet," he tried once more, "the night's barely just begun."

"No, I'm quite done, thank'ee," she said, with a Cockney accent, her nose in the air. "I turn in at twelve, that's the rule. Don't never give a man my bed for the night, I don't. I send 'em home while they can still walk."

This wisdom she had learned back in London where the pimps watched over their girls with a vengeance. Clancy, the owner of the saloon, smiled in approval and continued wiping the long counter. When the girl looked around, she caught Kelsey staring at her with heat in his eyes and a fresh mustache of foam on his upper lip.

"Of course, I do break the rules now and then," she winked, a grin turning up the corners of her painted lips. Pausing on the second step of the staircase leading up to her room, she turned to him, brazen but coy, and flaunted her exposed breasts rising out of a too-tight corset. Her cleavage reeked of cheap cologne and her skin flushed pink from the walk back in the cool night air.

"According to me' locket here, I believe I got ten minutes, more or less." She snapped the little watchcase shut and put the keys to her room in his hand, reminding Kelsey that women found his burley, broad-shouldered body, smoky amber eyes, and square-jawed face as irresistible in the new world as they did in the old. He took the keys in one of his hands and pinched her rear with the other. It was full and round. He liked that.

That was a week ago. Since then, he'd taken to hanging around Clancy's Saloon every evening until she came in the front door from a night's work. Then he'd grab her arm, and mimicking the barkeep, ask, "So, what'll it be?"

"The usual," she'd answer. And that was it. Like they were old friends, school chums, or even, real lovers. He would follow her upstairs, no questions asked, and peel down while she freshened herself. She'd never given herself to him again, though. Too much of a businesswoman to give it away again for free, but he didn't mind. First time he tried, she slapped him so hard, he lost his stand in a second.

"Yes, ma'am," he apologized humbly.

"You pay like the rest, you swine," she hissed, "or you sleep on the floor."

He had no choice. From then on, he behaved like an obedient child, reminding himself he could take her anytime he had a mind to, and leave her begging for more. But for some reason, he never did.

"Look," Callie announced when she returned, her red hair up in a towel and her robe open to reveal full hips and slender legs. Her loose breasts beckoned him and he responded spontaneously.

"I'm about done with all this," she said. "Don't know what I was thinkin'. I need my privacy. You best get out of here before Clancy catches on or he'll throw me out. You're a decent bloke but I don't need no trouble. You're in my way. Find yourself a rooming house or somethin', but you can't be my affair no more."

Kelsey had known this moment would come. Nonetheless, he'd enjoyed the lavender scented comfort of her steel spring bed and the abundant feel of her next to him in the night. He wished vaguely that he could afford to keep her for himself but he'd been without a job for weeks, and he knew he'd be hurting before long. He'd discovered earlier (the hard way) that working for the railway could be very short term, six months and you're done. Once laid off, he drifted for awhile and had heard that west of the Missouri was where real wages could be made, but Kelsey had tasted enough of railroading to know he didn't like hard labor and wanted no more of it.

By spring, he'd ended up in Chicago, hoping he'd find work in a freight yard or railway office. Unlike many of

America's immigrants, he could read and write fairly well, but had never apprenticed anywhere, never learned a decent trade. Even in a big city like Chicago, he still had no work and no respect. The rot of the fisheries had merely changed to the stench of the stockyards and he was still as poor as before.

"Ye're right, me love," he crooned now. "Tonight and it's over. I'm on me way. Got me a new job starting tomorrow, though. I'll be back, ye'll see, with good money and plenty of it. Then we'll do it right. Take ye to dinner, uptown, like a lady. Ye can be mine and rich at the same time." He lied so convincingly that Callie broke into a wide smile that showed her missing teeth and sat down beside him, tenderly, proud as a mama cooing over one of her very own.

"A job! You don't say! Hello! Now ain't that somethin'! Why didn't you tell me?" She pulled out a small flask from under the bed and twisted its silver cap. "Let's drink to uptown," she beamed, "to a fancy dinner with my big boy." As she tilted her head to savor the first swallow, he snapped her down on the bed like a fisherman wrestles a mackerel out of the sea. She flopped and squirmed face down, but he held her fast, gripping both hands behind her back. The flask fell upon the pillow, saturating the feathers with cheap gin.

"One last time, ye little bitch," he muttered, tearing off the robe and forcing her legs apart. "Ye'll have dinner when I'm ready, but ye'll not throw me out on an empty stomach. Turn over, or I'll have ye just the way ye are." She resisted and bucked beneath him, until she could move no more. Then he mounted her with a force she had not known in any man.

"This one's fer the road, ye stingy wench," he snarled as he pumped her from behind. "I promise ye, ye won't forget me."

★ ★ ★ ★ ★

"Good evening, gentlemen."

Clancy himself greeted the two well-heeled patrons as they stepped through the double doors. Barrel-chested and straight as a stick, he marched through the bar like a soldier on parade, capable of throttling anyone who got in his way. He smiled a tobacco-stained smile and gestured grandly.

"Right this way," he guided the men to a small table near the bar, its mahogany top glowing red under the gas lamp chandeliers. "Best seat in the house. Coat hooks are over there." Arlen Beale and his brother-in-law, Charles Leeds of the First Bank of Philadelphia, sat down gratefully and extinguished their cigars in the cinderplate beside them.

"Two up, my good man," Charles pointed with two raised fingers to the barrels of stout behind the bar, "to start."

"And what would your friend be havin'?" Clancy chortled, prompting a deep belly laugh from the men, who eased into their seats another notch.

Arlen removed his woolen cape and undid the buttons of his vest, checking the time on his watch as he did. "Not bad for a day's work," he smiled and reviewed in his mind the flow of events since they'd left their office in Philadelphia twenty-four hours earlier. The meeting at the Illinois Savings and Trust had gone smoothly enough. Seamus Maginnis, Magnes Dowling's old chum, had had a few years experience in the cattle industry and promised that the Trust would take a look at the Colorado venture and advise them in any way necessary. The encouraging discussion ended early and left the men time to explore the financial district at their leisure.

Arlen had ordered a new top hat at the haberdashery on Second Street and Charles looked into bonds in the divesting Union Pacific, since government-approved ventures in land development was causing its net worth to rise by the hour. By late afternoon they'd found themselves in the local dance hall where the floor show came with the price of two boilers, one drink being enough for an entire brigade. For five dollars you could sip as long as you could stand and watch a performance that rivaled the *Folies Bergere*. Baby-faced dancers with mascaraed eyes and cupid's-bow mouths did cartwheels and mule kicks on stage, showing off rouged bottoms and wobbly breasts pushed up like pincushions. One of them even kissed Arlen, leaving violet lip marks on his cheeks and collar.

The pair ended up at last at the Cattleman's Exchange, checking the sales figures posted for the day. The numbers indicated that traffic had been brisk. By luck, at the same time they found themselves right next door to Clancy's Saloon as the wind began to rise. A favorite neighborhood establishment since the mid 1850s, Clancy's was well within earshot of the stockyard. When the piercing freight train whistles blew, drowning out every other sound, the afternoon regulars would pause in their discourse and then, after a few seconds, pick up where they'd left off. The evening crowd lingered long into the night, drinking and playing cards and greasing the wheels of the great Chicago stock machine.

"You think they have anything to eat in here?" Arlen queried of Charles. "I'm hungry."

Clancy set down their drinks and pointed to the bill of fare above the bar which listed: "Beef, boiled or roasted."

"Good enough! We'll have one of each," Charles told the barkeep and pressed a half-dollar into the big man's palm, gulping the beer as if it were his last.

Kelsey Sculler folded the Tribune on his lap and stared. The two dandies by the door intrigued him. They didn't look like local stiffs. They spoke like gentlemen, educated for sure, and maybe ready for a night on the town, or at least a few more drinks. Maybe even a whore. But he wouldn't share

Callie, not if he could help it. No, he still wanted her for him-self. If he could, he'd join them, get them good and sotted, then maybe nab a wallet or pocketwatch like the old days.

Kelsey glanced at the paper one more time, quickly fin-ishing the article on the Pinkerton Gang. It was a humdinger of a story. Two road agents posing as security men had made a heist that set the agency back fifty thousand dollars. The pair had applied for a job as delivery guards and after a rou-tine check, were hired out to deliver funds on a cattle sale. A hundred miles from Topeka, they were accosted by the local pettijohn gone astray, a dusty hooligan lawyer standing by the side of the road, waving his arms and shouting hysteri-cally.

When the stagecoach stopped, he told a wild story about having been robbed of his horse and arms, but when the driver let him up inside he produced a gun from his briefcase and proceeded to gag and tie up the phony guards, all three were accomplices, of course. He then exchanged his briefcase for theirs, jumped out of the stage near Lawrence, and made off on a waiting horse with the bank notes, cash, and silver, all without a trace.

The two agents claimed then that they were duped and blamed the stage driver for picking up a vagrant. No one could prove collusion so the guards went free, slipping out of town that same day, never to be seen again. The three of them would be hanging material for a mob, if anyone could catch them.

Kelsey folded the paper carefully, Yes, he thought, that was the kind of story he could really appreciate.

"Evenin' gentlemen," the Irishman ventured, mimicking the barkeep as he approached their table. "Welcome to the finest establishment in all o' the Windy City."

At that moment, a burley stranger attempted to remove

Arlen's bowler from the extra chair at their table, needing the seat for himself. Seizing the opportunity, Kelsey sprang forward and grabbed the man's shoulder with a fierce and powerful squeeze. The hapless fellow lurched backwards, yelping in pain.

"Not this one, ye don't! Yer mistake, ye lowly puddock. Ye'll not be taking these gentlemen's things!" He shook a fist at the cowering man. With that, he extended his beefy hand to Arlen and Charles. "Ye have to watch yer belongings around here, yer honor. Got to be extra careful. Allow me to do it for you, that's me job. Clancy's main man, for the welfare and protection."

Arlen glanced at his brother-in-law. "Well, thank you very much. But I don't think the man meant any harm." The self-appointed bouncer maintained his vigil over them until Arlen asked hesitantly, "We do have an extra seat here. Would you care to join us?"

"Don't mind if I do." Kelsey slipped his bulk into the remaining chair and placed his hands on the table, fingers thrumming the wood top, and waited for one of the two dandies to begin. Charles opened a silver card case and placed a finely scripted calling card before him.

"Charles Leeds, Investments and Counsel, at your service." Kelsey picked up the white card with the elegant print and held it approvingly.

"And I am Arlen Beale, importer and wine merchant. Domestic spirits and exotics. Pleased to meet you." He proffered a manicured hand.

"Kurt Skoll, that's me," Kelsey began, forming the words crisply in his mouth. "Call me Kurt." The new name bolted out of nowhere. He grasped Arlen's slender hand and watched his face grimace with the pain of his grip. "Kurt Skoll." He liked the sound of his new name, not bad for split-second thinking. "Pinkerton Agency. Chicago. Pleased to meet ye."

Incredible. He'd done it again, reinvented himself and come up with a crisp new moniker as well, straightforward and simple, professional sounding. Had a nice ring to it— English maybe. It would look good on one of those fancy cards.

"And what exactly does a Pinkerton man do in these parts, Mr. Skoll?" Arlen inquired, genuinely interested.

"Oh, ye know, the usual. Bank fraud, detective work, auction security. The town is riddled with crime from one end t'other. Never have a quiet day to me'self." The brogue slipped out in spite of his best efforts.

"Is that right?" Charles marveled. "But, of course, why hadn't I thought of it? A business district as big as this one must stink from tip to tail. Well, bless you, my fellow, keeping the law and order. That's fine work."

Two steaming platters of food arrived at the table.

"I say, Clancy, serve one up for our guest here," Charles insisted. The newly christened Kurt Skoll did not refuse. The night was growing brighter by the minute.

"By the way, do you have a card?"

"Not on me at the moment. Off duty, ye know."

"I see. Well, it occurs to me we may want to stay in touch. Though we're headed back to Philadelphia, we're in town through tomorrow working out the details on a little venture in the far territories. Cattle business, as a matter of fact. There might be a time we could use your services, in some fashion. What do you say?"

"What a coincidence."

"How does one find you?"

"Ye can always reach me when I'm in Chicago right here at Clancy's, best address in town. Just leave word and I'll get in touch. See, my whereabouts changes so often I don't keep a postbox no more, that's how it is. Montana one day, then Texas the next, Chicago, of course, just to visit the children when I can. But whenever I'm back in town, I'm here, sure as church on Sunday."

Raising his glass, he turned toward the bar. "Ain't I, Clancy?" The barkeep, who hadn't heard a word, nodded enthusiastically and set about filling three fresh pints.

"Headin' west me'self, just this week. Aim to do a bit of work for the railroad, ferrying securities to build feedlots for eastbound lines." Kurt liked to read the daily paper and had memorized that day's front-page news. He liked to imagine that the reporters had written the stories about him.

"Yessir, first to Kansas City, then Denver, I believe. Lots of cattlemen down in Denver now, though I hear the market's takin' a dive. Anybody for another?"

Arlen and Charles studied each other over the table. Was this fellow genuine? If he was, he'd be a find. Useful to the bank. Capable of adding up what was or wasn't going on, but with discretion, with necessary anonymity.

"You wouldn't be available for private hire by any chance?" Arlen asked.

"What's that?" Kesley pretended not to have heard.

"A bit of contract work," Charles explained, amazed at his younger brother-in-law's good thinking in such a short time. A result of his own influence in developing financial strategies, no doubt. "We have some interests that need protecting, you see. And while you're helping us, you can also give service to a good fellow who probably could use someone to count his cattle for him and make sure he always ends up with a few more!"

Charles chortled out loud, amused at his own cleverness. The joke prompted the three of them into shared laughter until Charles brought them to silence by tapping his glass with his large gold ring.

"Now then, Mr. Skoll," Charles continued in a low voice, "here's what's on my mind. Take this card. On it I'm writing the name of a ranch in Colorado currently funded by our principals but owned by a Scottish fellow named McKennon. Recent family addition. Our people would like to know if two and two still makes four, if you know what I mean. We'd like to think about hiring you on to see if our client there has all his ducks in a row, or his cattle in a *queue,* or whatever the hell it is they do when they take a tally.

"And then, we'd like to know what that tally is. Do you see? And while you're at it you can assess whether he has something else going on behind our backs. There's another partner we need to know more about, undisclosed assets and such. It may involve a bit of invasive observation, but with discretion and complete anonymity. Does any of this sound problematic to you?"

"Hardly," Kurt confirmed. "I do this sort of work all the time."

"We'll need reports, week in and week out. Would that be possible?"

"Well, I'm kind of busy, ye know. I'll just have to see. But if I can arrange it, it's best not to mention it to the Agency here in town or I'll lose my job altogether. Such things are frowned upon, us being security men and all. But seein's as how ye're such fine gentlemen and this work is right up my line, I can hardly say no. What's the pay?"

"Mmmm. Good question. Unexpected opportunity, we hadn't exactly come prepared. What say, three hundred, depending on circumstances. You might start with this."

Charles stacked two shining gold coins imprinted with an eagle, worth one hundred dollars, on the table before them.

"When you locate the Cameron Ranch in Colorado, go to the telegraph office in nearby Jefferson and send us a wire to the address on the card. We'll forward another payment when we get the information we're looking for and then pay the rest when we're ready to let you go. About six weeks surveillance should do the trick. Are you game?"

Kurt swept up the fifty-dollar gold pieces like booty from a poker game and grumbled, "Less than my usual fee, gentlemen. I'll do me' best but this here's dangerous work. Don't like takin' chances. Seems to me it's worth a lot more."

"That remains to be seen. Let's negotiate by wire. By the way, if necessary, can you use a revolver?" Arlen asked.

"Does a duck fly?" Kurt quipped.

"Good. Very well, then. We'll look forward to hearing from you within the month. We'll forward more instructions as we decide precisely what's to be done."

"All right then, but don't use my real name when ye do, if ye don't mind." Kurt's insides could barely hold back his delight. He had them and wondered just how far he could go. "When ye're usin' the telegraph, use me code name, 'Kelsey.' Remember, that's how I'll be known wherever I am and how I'll always sign."

"By all means," they nodded with misplaced confidence. Kurt drowned his exploding ecstasy in a huge draught and then spurted a mirthful spray of stout all over the sticky floor.

"Me' apologies mates," he offered, wiping his face with his sleeve. "Some nights, I just can't seem to hold me' own!" With fresh glasses, the three raised a toast and drank to cattle, the West, and the railway. But most of all, thought Skoll, to an important new partnership, as well as shining gold eagles and girls with bountiful breasts.

The fall drive to the shipping pens of South Park, fifty-five miles away in Salida, usually took place at the end of September. From there, the railroads transported the fattened yearlings, heavy after a summer of grazing, through the mountains and north to Denver, to the great new stockyards for auction or processing. All across the West, this migration would be duplicated on each range as cattle plodded toward the trains that sped their delivery to the tables of America and beyond.

Vast fields of hay waited to be cut, baled, and stacked, reserved to sustain the gestating cows left behind. With grass as fuel, the remaining stock would need every blade to remain strong and give birth to the fresh crop of calves due in the spring.

With the passing of summer, the aspen had turned to brilliant gold and the mornings bore a damp chill that often lingered until noon. A great deal of the work of weaning and sorting remained at the ranch before the driving of the herd to the railway, but this day, Kerr brooded silently and lingered after breakfast. Refilling his coffee cup, he finally reached across the table and took Maggie by the hand.

"Say, lass, put aside yer chores. I'd like tae take ye fer a ride. It's time ye understan' all I've put my name on here, all that'll be ours once final payment's made. Wi' luck, this ranch will stretch from Jefferson tae Como one day, all along th' south ridge, by th' time I'm done. Year last, I staked out another parcel that reminded me most o' my home in th' Highlands. A place tae give us everra'thin' we could ever need, an' I want ye tae see it, today, this verra' morn."

Maggie finished her coffee and waited for his next thought. He continued in earnest. "I want ye tae dream wi' me, lass, lie awake nights as I do an' think about this place when th' sun rises an' th' sun goes down. Ye must ken what good fortune we ha'e an' what th' Cameron is yet tae be. Look into those fields an' tell me what ye think, because they'll be yers one day as well. So tack up Calamity now an' I'll fetch Bonniedoon. An' bring refreshment; we'll be gone fer th' better part o' th' day."

As they rode, Maggie surveyed the outer realm of the ranch while pushing the roan to keep up with Bonniedoon. McKennon rode the mare with style, stirrups long, back straight, centered and firm in the saddle. A broad-shouldered man, still narrow in the hip, he rode in perfect balance, a handsome and athletic horseman. He and his horse moved with so much grace they'd become a well-known and admirable sight in the territory, gliding over the countryside as if they'd become one.

The mare had put on weight over the summer, her glossy coat a burnished shade of brown and her long legs nearly black as coal. Sometimes, in the sunlight, her full mane produced glints of brilliant violet, and at all times, her dark eyes fairly smoldered with intelligence. "She's got great heart," Kerr would say. "Bonnie Prince Charlie himself could ha'e ridden her into battle, so fearless is she. Just a wee bit o' a stranger tae these parts, still. She'll be fine, once she kens th' land."

True to her bluegrass temper, the horse flared up now and then, shied at suspicious branches on the ground and snorted at the yapping dogs that ran about the ranch. She reared or bucked whenever she was feeling ornery, just to let the fire out, and lifted a hind hoof at anyone who approached from the rear. But Kerr had learned to tolerate her bad habits and rode her firmly, with confidence and ease.

Maggie was amazed at Kerr's horsemanship and riding expertise. He seemed to fear nothing. She still found the mare terrifying and unpredictable and disliked the fact that the horse was difficult to catch and hard to mount as well. But Kerr had solutions to all her faults. Besides, training her was a challenge, and he liked that most of all—a horse that made him think.

Silva had developed a nice familiar way with the mare. When Kerr rode one of the remuda ponies, the Spaniard would come to the cabin and take "Bonita" as he called her, though her paces. He spoke to her softly with musical-sounding words, teaching her to halt, back, and follow, coaxing her into submission like a well-trained dog.

"All she needs is patience," Kerr said to Maggie. "Look how well she's doin' today."

Maggie nodded, then proudly patted her own even-tempered roan that jogged briskly beside Bonniedoon's extended walk. She admired Kerr's enviable find, but rejoiced that the Creator had remembered to provide a wide selection of willing horses for men and women to ride.

Off to the right, slopes of wooded mountains rose up into the clouds. To the left lay the greenswards of open grazing land, topped by undulating horizons and dried stretches of grass. Later in the season, freight trains would cross the golden channels of the wide basin ferrying cut and bundled hay to customers as far away as Nova Scotia. The finest bales put up in the summer were purchased by none other than the Czar of Russia to be used as feed at the Imperial Stables in St.

Petersburg. Long freight cars of the Union Pacific hauled the neatly loaded hay to New York where it was tagged and shipped abroad, rich Colorado grass, that was to some, far more precious than gold.

Maggie loved to hear about the ambitious ranchers of the Park and encouraged Kerr to tell her all he knew. Perhaps, by so doing, she could better understand the world of the cattle barons more clearly. With luck, perhaps even Kerr himself.

Slowly, she began to realize that it was neither the Highland nor the Hereford but the very grass itself that sustained ranch life in the Park. Its protection and nourishment required the flow of good water and proper management of the many growing herds. No wonder the cattlemen hated the encroaching sheepherders whose sharp-hoofed flocks had lately begun to erode the landscape like an onslaught of four-footed locusts.

Good ranchers like Kerr sought to protect and preserve the land in order to secure its future. Maggie admired his deep respect for nature and continuous attention to its demands. Every living thing under his hand seemed to blossom and thrive, with one notable exception—herself.

Pushing the painful realization away, Maggie ran her hands through her pony's mane, hiding her disappointment. She tried to look without reproach at this man who could make such a commitment of his life and create a special kind of balance in the effort. With this perspective, she knew she could forgive him, at least for the moment. She, Maggie McKennon, seemed merely an afterthought in his great plan. Nonetheless, she persisted, unwilling to be discouraged. What good, after all, was resentment or self-pity?

Kerr McKennon had brought her this far, given her a foothold in a brand new world, and treated her like an equal. For that alone she knew she should be grateful. She needed to push all that was imperfect aside and focus on that which lay before her, the endless possibility of change.

"Wait for me," she called to him, spurring Calamity forward. Accepting her new point of view, she felt more encouraged than she had in a long while. The future would still be hers to define. She urged the roan closer to Bonniedoon and came right up alongside McKennon. Standing in her stirrups, she leaned over and planted a warm kiss of approval on his weathered cheek, smiling as she saw his surprise. Together they rode through tall stands of pine, while underfoot, white columbine and daisies still bloomed among the sage. Finally, McKennon stopped, and Maggie saw the checkered town of Jefferson in the distance.

"There," he said, pointing to the right. A bluff rose from the rolling terrain, interrupted by a wide gouge in the middle. Protected on two sides by rising hills, the site faced south toward the great stretch of the Park. A small creek bubbled visibly, shaded here and there by groves of aspen.

"This is th' place, Maggie. It's got everythin'. Water, shelter from th' wind, an' na' more than an hour's ride from town. Ye can be a 'city girl' when ye want tae, that is if ye want, when, an' if ye like. Th' next ranch is only five mile off. Can ye see yerself here, lassie? Th' two o' us together in a fine house wi' a parlor an' a nursery too? Sooner or later, a wee one ye'll be wantin' . . . I ken how women are."

At this remark Maggie faced him squarely, pulling her horse's head. "What did you say?"

"Nae, lass, I hav'na fergotten. Just dinna' want tae rush things, that's all. I needed tae see if ye were up tae it—all of it. Who knew if ye wouldna quit on me, Maggie? D'ye see what I mean?"

"No, I'm afraid I don't."

"Last thing I needed would ha'e been a wife wi' a full belly runnin' home in tears, afraid o' th' emptiness, hatin' th' wild, an' leavin' me all alone. I needed tae know ye were here fer th' keepin', nae just on a lark. So, I'm askin' ye. Are ye, lass? Fer it's now I need tae know."

Stunned, Maggie processed what he had said. How simple. It wasn't that he hadn't wanted her. It was the risk of losing her and never recovering. Of being hurt, in case she changed her mind. How impossible and yet—how kind. Or selfish, perhaps. He had spared her and himself from what might have been a complicated end. If he had taken her, she might have conceived right away, and then turned on him, backed out, or headed home. Familiar stories about women deserting their men reeked of dishonor and scandal.

But what of this hopeful talk? Kerr's first hint at a future with children. Surely, that's what he had said. Children. Could he be leading her on, the way he had at the dinner table so many months before? Promises, backed by unspoken conditions, and then, frustration? No, not this time. This time his voice sounded honest, sincere. A kind of tenderness, a current of compassion hinted at more. Something in her stirred.

"The site is perfect," she said quietly. "I can see it all. What I can't see or understand is how you could have doubted me, Kerr. I told you I was willing. I meant it, every word." The corners of his eyes crinkled in a deep smile and Maggie returned his affectionate gaze.

"So now, d'ye promise?" he asked. "Are ye wi' me fer th' next step, whate'er it will take?"

She nodded. "Of course I am. The next step and the one after that. The new ranch, when can we start? May I help you lay it out, build it?" she asked.

"What makes ye think ye can?" Kerr suppressed a doubtful grin.

"What makes you think I can't?" Maggie shot back, eyes flashing.

With that, they broke into a canter and rode along the bluff for a clearer view. Far from the clutter of town and the noisy trains, the beauty of the setting made up for its isolation. They stopped to catch another look and let the horses rest.

"I can't wait till we begin, Kerr. We can build the most beautiful ranch in all of South Park. An estate, just like MacGregor's in Cheyenne. You can raise all the Highland cattle you can count and invite ranchers everywhere to our door. Even the experts in Scotland will come to measure your success!"

At the mention of MacGregor, Kerr's eyes narrowed. "Hold on. I willna' be competin' wi' a fool. Ye'll na' be comparin' me wi' him in any way. Lower yer sights, Maggie, I intend only tae live like a rancher, na' a duke!" They spurred their horses into a canter and moved up the hill toward the crest.

"I'm sorry," Maggie said, "if I made a foolish comparison. I merely wanted to say that I'm behind you, now, more than ever. There's nothing I wouldn't do if you asked. You can teach me to brand and herd and breed your Highlands. I want to help you and work with you and be by your side. I want to make the Cameron, this country, this ranch, my home just as you have, and stay here with you until we're both so old we can't remember our own names."

McKennon listened, captive to her song.

"Maybe you thought I was using you to get away from a world that bored me, and if so, you're partly right. But nothing in my life has ever really mattered as much as all of this. Nothing is as important as my place next to you, here and now. You have to believe that."

Maggie's words expressed feelings she didn't even know she had until she let them free, released in the now-diminishing space between herself and the man who had seemed a stranger until this very moment, when she realized that she shared his dream.

Their eyes met. The expression in hers was no longer a question, and his were burning with an intensity she'd never seen before. Maggie's gaze moved across the landscape, picturing the future they would build. She felt a new sense of security flow through her as tenuous strands of affection formed into stronger cords that she could trust.

"Ye're a *guid* lass, Maggie," Kerr said with a smile. "I see now that I can count on ye. Just pray all goes well, that we fetch th' best price for th' herd come fall. Then, together, we'll live our life th' way th' Lord intended."

Maggie didn't reply but vowed silently to love this strange and mysterious man, hoping that he in turn would love her too with passion and a full heart. Perhaps the time had come. Together they followed the woods along the face of the slope. The further they rode into the wilderness, the closer she felt to home.

11

Kerr McKennon valued his relationship with the hired hand Stewart Merrill, a man who had become his friend as well as foreman. Merrill left a farm in Oklahoma just about the same time Kerr took his first look at South Park. They'd met in the land office, shaken hands, and grown committed to each other over five long years.

Though Kerr paid his wages, Merrill looked up to the older man as a son to a father. He shared the Scot's passion for the Highland breed and his respect for nature. Kerr's sudden marriage to Maggie Dowling tickled the salty cowboy no end and he laughed out loud when he shared his thoughts with his wife, Sarah.

"To think the old man still had it in him, courtin' one so young! I wish him luck. As far as I can tell," he told her, "my problem's just goin' to be keepin' my cowpunchers a little cleaner and as far out of the lady's way as possible."

Stewart suggested that his wife plan a reception for the bride. "Why not invite your church group up from Jefferson and host a proper welcome for the Missus? Surely, McKennon would approve." There hadn't been a party at the Cameron since the stone house had been completed. This would be the perfect time.

Kerr's ranch house stood as a symbol of his success in the New World. Locals boasted it was the finest-built home in all of Park County. Constructed of fieldstone, the red-tiled roof had come from Scotland, saved in its entirety from a small church demolished in Leith. Hugh MacGregor had salvaged it and taken care that the tiles were loaded straight into a waiting ship, carefully packed next to a stand of his bulls in the hold. MacGregor, Kerr's financial partner in the Cameron, as well as everything else he put his name on in America, spared nothing if it appeared to be of sound business and pleased God.

The two had quickly abandoned plans to share equally in the expansion of the Colorado ranch when Wyoming appeared more profitable. MacGregor decided to put his greater investments in the north and so they parted early on. What started originally as a mutual business venture changed slowly into a friendly competition, and then into a rivalry neither wanted to admit. Usually Scots stuck by one another, unless personal survival or financial difficulties interfered. Regarding the question of how to utilize their mutual profits, the pair would never agree.

"One day, thanks tae my Herefords," MacGregor would often say to his partner, "I'll buy ye out an' make ye a rich an' happy man. Or, if ye're right, yer shaggy Highlands will pay me back, in full measure. Wi' what's left over, we'll be mor'en even." But until he paid back the debt, McKennon would secretly resent MacGregor for the advantage that the other man's greater wealth gave him, a resentment that would come to fester sharply between them like a sore.

Sarah Merrill fussed over the dinner preparations, unsure of what Maggie might enjoy. The two women were so different, after all. She treated the new head of the household with respect, but felt awkward around an educated lady, the "laird's wife," no less.

She watched with envy as the new Mrs. McKennon, hair neatly arranged and wearing a fine fitted dress, welcomed the evening's company to what was, after all, her own home. Like a gaggle of geese, the curious women exchanged introductions and then sat down together to gossip, far from the smoke and talk of the men.

"Have you heard?" Eleanor Soggett began, entreating her companions. "The picnic's been canceled." Her youthful face bore no traces of the five children she'd brought into the world, but the telltale tic that plagued her right eye was proof enough. Maggie couldn't tell her age but noticed her dry and wind-chapped face, and rough, worn hands. Colorado ranch life leaned hard on its women, she decided, stealing beauty as part of its price.

"What a pity," said Alma Dalton, as she took up her embroidery, knees crossed under her calico skirt. "The Ladies Auxiliary of Colorado Springs won't be able to take their final tour of South Park tomorrow. Wildflower season's just about over. Looks like the cattlemen need the roundhouse and the tracks so the whole event's off, including the luncheon reception we were holdin' in Como on our end."

"Who cares anyway?" Molly Squires, the eldest matron of the group, interrupted. "It's a bit late in the season for anyone to be gawking at wildflowers. Ain't worth anybody's ticket if you ask me."

"But they're society, you know. City folk. Women with nothin' to do but take a ride to see the scenery," Sarah commented. "Just time on their hands. They give their children to the nannies and gallivant about like they had no chores or a care in the world. I never took a day off in my life. Never had much patience for their kind."

"I've seen 'em too," Alma continued, "starin' from the platform like they never saw country before. I can't imagine anybody payin' to ride out this far for a bouquet of buckbrush and thistle anyhow."

Through the chatter, Maggie felt as though the ladies of Jefferson tried to be kind, but she accepted them with an air of cautious reserve. The chit-chat floated past her, little of it making much sense.

"Mrs. McKennon, I hear you're a school marm," Eleanor finally focused on the guest. "Going to take up in the primary here? There's always plenty of room for a good teacher, isn't there girls?" She scooped one of Sarah's daughters onto her ample lap.

Maggie hadn't considered the possibility of teaching again. Not at the moment. She had a ranch to build, but wasn't sure if any of them would understand. She nodded, answering vaguely. "Perhaps."

Excusing herself to check on Maria and the meal, she continued on out to the front porch where Kerr, Stewart, and the others sat, reviewing the details of the upcoming drive. Silva leaned against the front door, his back to them, watching gray clouds chase the glow from a crimson sunset.

McKennon led the discussion, calculating distance, water, and weight loss against rustlers, weather, and time. Maggie stood by her husband's chair, listening.

"Well, I guess you know the latest," Stewart Merrill offered, folding a brittle newspaper back upon itself. "Says here in *The Stockman*, 'The foreign cattle kings can't be touched; they think they're above the law.' " He laughed. "What law? Bit o' humor, these newspaper boys. Goes on further to say, 'The cattle barons pretend that they still own the west, thanks to big brains and a long purse.' Nicely put, hey, McKennon?" Merrill took a long draft from a flask and put it back into his breast pocket.

"But the foreign market looks weak at the moment,"

Merrill continued. "The demand for beef is shrinking and no one knows when it'll hit bottom. Latest sales show the local market's flooded and prices are at an all-time low. What do you think, Kerr? Can it get much worse?" He directed his comments carefully. He'd read enough to have his own opinion on the matter.

"I wouldna' say rockbottom is a level we'll e'er see," Kerr replied. "Demand doesna' equal supply, but rumors o' liquidation are only fer those wi' no financial support. Hardly th' case. Drive these *stirks* an' yearlings tae market an' get what we can fer 'em. We'll persevere. People still ha'e tae eat, don't they? Canna' be o'er yet."

The sweet fragrance of summer grass filled the evening air and cattle lowed far off in the twilight as the talk approached more critical issues.

"Your friend MacGregor in Cheyenne appears to be cashing in twice the dollars off his Herefords, Kerr. Wyoming's been good to those cattle. Out on the short grass plains, they seem to fatten up overnight. Twice the body, twice the muscle. Do you think these Highlands are still worth the trouble after all?" Merrill's unexpected probe provoked the rancher.

"An' what trouble would ye be referrin' tae?" Kerr pounded the arm of a split-log chair as national pride swelled within him. "Show me a better steer, *if* ye can. *Nae* bother! There isna' a one! Why, th' Highland practic'ly raises itself. Ye know that. The beast is mild an' mannerly, sticks tae th' herd, an' eats whate'er it will. Th' mothers be kind an' protective an' barely one calf in a thousan' needs a man's help when it drops. How else d'ye think they lasted this long?"

"They don't measure up, that's all," Merrill replied.

"Measure up? Just look at 'em. Should ye not see it fer

yerself, 'tis th' finest animal that walks th' earth. Strong, steady, straight in th' back. Nae, if my voice still counts, th' Cameron raises Scottish steers, th' only beast abou' that's worth th' effort. They were *guid* enou' fer my ancestors, they'll be *guid* enou' fer me!"

Merrill hadn't finished. A receptive audience urged him on and so he continued at visible risk. "I don't know, Kerr. I hear what you're saying but something doesn't add up. There are as many trains headin' west with fancy breeds of imported cattle these days as is going east. Every Texas rancher alive dumped the Longhorn for the imported breeds, Shorthorns, all of them. Your Highlands may not make the cut. The hide takes too long to clean with all that coat, and they just don't carry the meat on them that the bigger breeds do. Them damn horns are a nuisance on freight cars and you know it. Hurts me to say it, Kerr, but all that's gonna cost you at the end."

"Are ye goin' daftie on me, Stewart? Look here an' listen so I don't ha'e tae say it again. That coat is what keeps 'em warm, the fat laying deep in the muscle where it belongs. Because o' what they are, th' taste o' th' Highland beats all th' other breeds put together. What ye're sayin's nonsense! Highlands sell."

"I believe the market tells another story, Kerr." Merrill's expression conveyed his concern. "A costly one. They can't compete. I've seen the best of the polled breeds unload by the hundreds all around us. Shorthorns, polled Angus, the Scotch Galloway, and look around you, the Hereford, by the thousands. You're out of touch with the times, Kerr. Just run our numbers by MacGregor next time you see him and see what he thinks. I know it's your ranch, but I need to say what's on my mind."

McKennon seethed. Stung by what sounded like treason,

he retorted, "When I want yer miserable thoughts, I'll let ye know. Meanwhile, ye'd best keep 'em tae yerself." Kerr took a long puff on his pipe, trying to conceal his disappointment.

"I'll do whatever you want, my friend," Merrill said, "but I don't think your herd will count for much in this tough market." He hurried to change the subject. "Say, speaking of markets, a great big fella who says he knows you rode up this afternoon saying he's here representing the state stock growers. You know anything about that?"

"What exactly does he want?"

"Don't know. He looked to be a stranger to me, Kerr. Can't say I remember ever seein' him around these parts. Says he needs to talk to you before you leave on the drive, though. Took himself a room over in Jefferson. He'll be back in the morning. Sure was all gussied up and not much on manners. Rode like a greenhorn if I ever saw one. Here's his card."

McKennon squinted at the white calling card with the unfamiliar name. "Don't know 'im. He'll ha'e tae wait. Got nae time."

At that moment, Sarah appeared at the door. "Oh, there you are, Mrs. M." She looked reproachfully at Maggie. "Won't you come in now?"

"Looks like supper," Merrill said. "Let's eat."

Round, silver-plated ashets of venison graced one side of the table and a braised saddle of lamb flavored with honey sat on the other. Per Kerr's precise instructions, a savory Scotch broth bubbling with onions, carrots, and herbs melded the local harvest. Bright bowls brimming with pole beans and cabbage crowded the center of the table. Roasted potatoes with sage, oat cakes, and fragrant homemade biscuits rounded out the festive meal.

Maria served chokecherry jelly for the biscuits and reminded everyone to save room for dessert, Sarah's famous gooseberry pies. Maggie promised herself she'd learn how to make such a treat herself as she downed the last mouthwatering morsel. Dabbing the rich fruit off her lips with a napkin, she caught Kerr watching her, a twinkle in his eye.

A full bottle of Glenfiddich added merriment and a welcome fire to the dinner. "A wee bit o' refreshment, gentlemen," Kerr encouraged, now fully tempered by the meal. "Time to enjoy a touch o' Scotch hospitality." After each man made a toast, he continued to fill the glasses as they emptied.

"Drink away!" he rallied, his anger at Stewart's remarks now forgotten in the glow of the whiskey's amber warmth. For this was a most auspicious occasion, a formal welcome for his Maggie, and a hearty send-off for the drive. Nothing could be more worthy of his generosity.

"I understand there's a large British community not far from here," Maggie inquired, hoping for an explanation.

"You might say that," Merrill replied. "The way I've heard it, most of the English are here because they can't support their own population. They need food, so they came west, promoting the region as the ideal place for raising cattle and sheep. Emigration from the isles these days is approaching flood tide. Over two thousand British passports are registered with the county courthouse at the moment. That includes tenant farmers and cattle barons alike."

Sarah cut in. "It's quite the joke hereabouts. They say from Fairplay to Manitou, you can get your tea and crumpets in just about any saloon! I wouldn't know, myself. They've even written a song about it. Shall we sing it, girls?" Laughter closed the topic as Alma moved to the piano to play the tune.

By the time the dinner had come to an end, the good ladies of Jefferson had suggested a calendar of activities for Mrs.

McKennon. They'd even brought the handbook of the Caledonia Society in Colorado Springs, a community to the west but a three-hour train ride away, where Celtic events took place on a regular basis. Kerr had never found time for such displays of patriotism, but Sarah's friends thought that Maggie should at least be aware, for both their sake. Maggie found it curious that the cultured city and posh resort had such a predominant Anglo-Saxon culture. A mere eighty-nine miles away, "Little London," as it had come to be called, flourished in the middle of the frontier west, an incontestable British home away from home.

Maggie could only respond tentatively to the women's various invitations. "When I'm settled," she said. "You know, there's still so much to do. When I'm ready, I'll be sure to join in."

Kerr and Maggie rode back to the cabin, warmed by the meal, the malt, and a balmy September wind. Secure under the starry skies, Maggie, riding Calamity, took the lead, following the silver ribbon of the creek as it wound past the wooded trail.

Unsaddling the mares in the dark, Maggie found Kerr unexpectedly beside her. He took the heavy saddle from her arms and laid it over the top rail of the corral.

"Come tae me," he said. "Come an' put yer arms aroun' me, right this minute. I need tae tell ye, ye are a dear an' bonnie lass. A-feared o' nothin' an' wise. Why, I followed ye home through these woods just now, watchin' ye pick yer way. Leadin' me like a tracker, ye did. Ye make me proud, Maggie, verra' proud." He stood before her, his hands on her shoulders. "Ye're th' best thing e'er happened tae me, Maggie McKennon. There is nae one tae compare. After all this time, I still canna' believe ye're mine." With that he kissed her on the lips and drew her close.

Maggie stood in Kerr's embrace, moved and baffled by his tenderness. She kissed him back, then buried her face in the collar of his coat, confused by his unprecedented show of affection, but thrilled that he could express himself at last in such a way. He kissed her again, harder than before, and then, just as unexpectedly, let her go, turning to pick up Calamity's tack and take it to the barn. In the stillness of the night, they finished putting away the horses in silence, then headed for the cabin and to bed where Kerr fell immediately to sleep.

Dawn had not yet broken when Maggie, wakened abruptly, found herself in Kerr's grasp.

"Are ye awake?" he murmured. "I canna' sleep." Maggie lay as captive in his arms as a quail in a pointer's gentle jaws. "Listen tae me," he said. "I need tae speak my peace. An' I need tae do it now. Listen well, fer this be hard t'admit. I know I hav'na' been th' husban' I should ha'e been. I know I've let ye' down. Hear me out. 'Tisna' easy fer me tae say." Kerr touched her cheek with his hand. "It waren't you, lass, I told ye that. There's more. I was afraid I wouldna' ken how tae please ye, na' being strong an' sure like before. 'Twas wrong, I know 'twas. My own fear has caused ye hurt, I'm sure." Maggie held her breath.

"How can I tell ye how much I love ye? How much it's meant tae me, these weeks, these days? D'ye understand? I need ye an' want ye, lass, ye need tae know that. Tell me please, that ye want me too, just a wee bit, still?"

Before she could answer and with no further explanation, kiss, or caress, he took her then, climbing over her body, taking her up in his strong arms and holding her so she could barely move, a great bear of a man in a fury of needing and wanting and taking her. He slid her cotton nightrail up around her waist while he pushed himself between her legs, abruptly, crazily, eager for her at last.

Kerr grabbed her buttocks from beneath and pulled her closer to him, as he balanced himself on his knees. Maggie gasped at the shock of it, her hips in his great hands, her body anchored, impaled by his rigid sex. Turning her face to the pillow and then back again, she tried to silence the words screaming inside her head. *"Stop! Not like this!"* But she couldn't make a sound, except to gasp sharply each time he thrust himself inside her. It was as if he intended to make up all at once for the weeks he'd wasted, the months, the years.

Maggie knew she couldn't refuse him, but only obey, as her sisters had said. She would have to endure it, those were their words. But where was the pleasure that she'd heard of as well?

Now she knew that this thing called love had to be a lie, a demon that possessed men, but only repulsed her. She shrank beneath him, frightened by his insistence, overwhelmed by his brutal, indifferent force. Kerr pushed hard against her, parting and entering her not as though with an instrument of love, but as with a weapon. With nowhere to go, she could do nothing but endure until he was done.

McKennon panted and growled, moving in and out, swinging his head with the rhythm of his body, his eyes closed, his chest, dripping with sweat, hovering over her. With a guttural grunt and a final shudder, he let go and dropped his weight upon her like a stone. He rolled slowly to one side, exhausted and then dropped off to sleep, satisfied and spent. First frightened, then outraged by Kerr's insistent possession, bitter tears coursed down Maggie's cheeks, pooling onto Kerr's lightly heaving chest.

Was this what she'd been waiting for so very long? She shivered in the sweaty sheets beside him and felt the wet heat of his release melt and trickle between her legs. She loathed the harshness of the act, cursing the romantic dream that should have been hers instead. Her virginity had been taken, not given. Why did her sisters have to lie? Just so children could come into the world?

Waking with a start, Kerr took her hand. He kissed her wrist and said, "Did I hurt ye, lass? Was I in too much o' a rush?" Maggie didn't respond, lying limply upon her back and staring into the dark.

" 'Twas only a question o' time, my darlin', like I said. Nae way could I be leavin' in th' mornin' an' you na' yet properly my wife. A shame upon me. God, help me tae be young again. Tae be patient wi' ye. I'll be a better husban' from now on, my Marg'ret, I promise tha' I will." He hadn't called her Margaret since they'd left Philadelphia, months before. The sound of it unnerved her.

"I needed tae know ye loved me. That, an' I needed time. Ye gave me yer word, an' now I ha'e it. But th' time, curse th' devil, has fairly come an' gone. . . ."

Maggie exhaled, woefully. "It's all right, Kerr, say no more. Everything will be fine, you'll see."

She didn't believe a word of what she said. She felt sick and needed air but only pulled the quilt around her, closing her eyes. She tugged her long nightgown down around her knees, wondering if they'd soiled their only sheets. Finally, without a sound, she slipped out of bed to the wash basin and twisted the rough wet cloth between her legs, wiping away the baptism of their first union. Over and over she wrung the tepid water between her thighs, as if to make holy again her bruised skin, as if to restore herself for another chance, for one whose embrace might yet flood her with some kind of ecstasy and joy.

★ ★ ★ ★ ★

With the glimmer of first light, Kerr got up from bed to prepare for the drive, the busy sounds of drovers and cattle intensifying in the distance. Arranging the quilt around her shoulders, he kissed her gently on the forehead, dressed quietly, and began to gather his gear. Maggie feigned sleep, listening to every sound, including the soft jangle of spurs and the belled hobble he always carried as it found its way inside his pack. She felt empty but tried to imagine the next time he might come to her, hopefully, with the kind of tenderness she desired. She would forgive him this initial crudeness. Closing her eyes, she dreamt she saw a great white bird winging its way through the fog of an early dawn. Then, as it flew closer, it disappeared into the rising lofts of the clouds. Perhaps the bird had been an illusion. Perhaps she never saw it at all.

Kerr stood over her wanting to say goodbye, but hesitated to wake his sleeping bride.

"When will I see you again?" Maggie asked. Her voice startled him.

"If all goes well, in a fortnight." He knelt by the bed and took her hand. "I must be back fer th' cuttin' o' th' fields. I'll be takin' Bonniedoon fer th' drive. Ten days an' be done. Don't worry. Silva will check on ye an' I'll send word if anythin' goes wrong. Ye can move on down tae th' main house if ye like, but don't forget tae take care o' th' old *kye* an' her calf now. An' keep th' Winchester loaded an' handy, just in case." Kerr knew that he was missing her already but couldn't say a word, for he regretted leaving her there alone.

Maggie nodded sleepily and, in spite of her anger and hurt, reached out and took his hand. With no choice but to forgive him, she bade him a safe trip. "Godspeed, Kerr McKennon," she offered. "I'll be waiting right here. And promise me, watch out for that horse of yours."

For the following few mornings Maggie checked on Calamity, the mule, and the calf to make certain the animals were safe and secure. Slowly, the blind heifer had learned her way around, probing the enclosed pasture for grasses and weeds, eating whatever she found. If not near her mother, the creature usually stood alone, waiting by the paddock gate to be petted and scratched.

Each evening Maggie added to her diary. Though Kerr would only be gone a short time, she planned to share each day's activities with him upon his return, anxious to prove her capability and worth. The minutest details she assumed would be the ones that would please him the most.

Though kindling and firewood were abundant near the cabin, Maggie enjoyed gathering wood from farther afield, varying the initial scent of the stove's fragrant fire. This day she planned to climb the hill above Michigan Creek where the forests grew thick with pine. She waited until the cool of the afternoon to ascend the woody slope.

Crisp, dry deadwood lay underfoot and twigs broke easily as Maggie gathered them in her sack. Far too soon, the fiery layers of a summer sunset warned of the day's end, and with her arms full, she began retracing her steps. In the approaching darkness ahead, Kerr seemed very far away.

Coming around the last bend in the trail, Maggie's breath caught in her throat. The window to the log cabin lay shattered. The broken wooden frame, fractured into pieces, poked through the shards of glass which still reflected the last rays of light in a jumbled brilliant pattern. In the twilight, the house appeared unnaturally bleak and quiet.

Laying down her load of wood, Maggie approached with caution. She'd heard tales of the grizzlies that still roamed the Park but no one had actually seen the legendary bears in years. The few remaining Utes that traded with the ranchers were friendly, giving her no reason to suspect a renegade. Just the same, she crept toward the cabin slowly, prepared for the worst.

Peering above the edge of the window, she scanned the darkness inside, straining to make out an unfamiliar form. She saw nothing to cause any alarm. Edging toward the door, she stood outside for a few moments, listening for a sound that might reveal an intruder's identity. Nothing. Then, something rustled. She waited for several minutes but heard nothing more; perhaps, it was just her imagination. And yet, she was sure that whatever or whoever had broken through the window had not yet found its way out. Finally, she heard it again, a soft brushing.

She pushed the door open, fully prepared to run if necessary, and reached for the Winchester which Kerr always hung to the immediate left. Gripping the rifle, she eased back the hammer, preparing herself for whatever might come and progressed silently, holding her breath, her back pressed flat along the rough log wall.

The swoop of a bird knocked her down as it struggled to escape out the door. Though she could not see clearly, she was pinned momentarily by its violent and terrified escape. She realized it couldn't fly because of an injured wing, yet the frantic creature seemed airborne nonetheless, flopping and jumping, a feathered dervish gone berserk.

Maggie screamed as its talons ripped her arm, and in the dim light, recognized a great horned owl, attacking her in its fear. She instinctively covered her face, turning away to protect herself. The frantic creature hobbled past and escaped into the night, leaving Maggie stunned and bleeding, curled upon the floor.

After the terrifying whir of wings and the thud of their collision, silence enveloped the cabin. All Maggie could hear was her own breathing and feel the hammering beat of her heart. She was relieved to discover she was only slightly wounded but lay motionless for some time after she regained her wits and could no longer hear the owl's thrashing among the trees. She pulled herself up by the bed frame and lit a lantern to assess the damage, starting with her shirt. Blood-stained and torn, she was scratched from just under the armpit down to her elbow, bearing a gash as neat as any swordsman could deliver.

Reaching for Kerr's stash of whiskey, Maggie downed a gulp to calm her nerves, then, knowing the wound would be vulnerable to all that lay beneath the talons of an owl, poured the searing liquid on the cut to act as a disinfectant. She hoped that that would be enough. Shuddering with the pain, she cleaned and wrapped the wound, binding it as best she could.

Then, resolved to regather the scattered firewood, she managed to pick up the larger pieces and stack them by the stove. Famished, she managed to butter a chunk of bread and washed it down with another swallow of whiskey, then set about to find a bit of muslin or wagon tarp with which to cover the window. She succeeded in hanging it in place and finally lay down on the bed, exhausted.

Sleep came slowly, only to be interrupted by fitful dreams erupting through the night, images of terrifying raptors with glaring, yellow eyes, and twisted, fallen angels wrestling in the dark. The next morning, with a good deal of difficulty, Maggie recorded the event in her diary.

September 21, 1889
Sunrise:
. . . My right arm hurts terribly but doesn't bother me half as much as the breaking of the window. The glass is shattered beyond repair. Last night, I came home to discover that an owl had crashed through it and when confronted, nearly scared me half to death. It tore me up a little, but nothing life threatening.

Dear Kerr, if you ever read this, know that I didn't waste a bullet on him. He got away and I didn't have to shoot. In fact, I awoke this morning and found him, not more than a hundred feet away, sitting under the spruce, the one just to the left of the trail. He stared back at me, defying pity. One wing is possibly broken, hopefully just bruised. The other is folded along side, apparently unhurt. Thank God, I think he's going to survive and so will I. But who knows? Somehow this whole situation isn't fair. He never meant to harm me, I am sure.

I approached the bird earlier this morning and it didn't move. I don't know if I can feed it, but we'll just have to see. We fought. I guess you'd say it lost and I won. But the owl gave me something, Kerr, I can't explain what, precisely. It made the terror of the dark into a bird, last night and forever. Do you understand? And though I think the scar will eventually disappear, this amazing lesson, this secret, never will. It's an occurrance I'll not forget. I feel as if I mustn't, if I am to survive at all. And now, the owl is mine to care for if it intends to live, and it will have to do so with my help, whether it wants to or not.

Maggie's entry was cut short by the piercing sound of

Ramona's blood-curdling bray. Almost nothing can stop the universe so entirely as the abrasive cry of a mule, she thought. She jumped to her feet, grabbed the Winchester and headed for the door.

Coming toward her was a mud- and sweat-encrusted horse, Kerr's own dark beauty, Bonniedoon. The mare, winded and worn, stopped in her tracks when Maggie stepped outside. With her coat scarred, and her saddle twisted to one side, reins dragging, she paused and lowered her mud-spattered head as if embarrassed to come home.

"My God, whatever's happened?" Maggie gasped. Forgetting her own pain, she hugged the pathetic creature about the neck. "What's happened to you? And to him?" she demanded. "Just what have you done with him?"

The sobs that should have followed the terror of the night before finally broke through. Maggie wished she had stopped Kerr from taking Bonniedoon, but he believed the horse would adjust to the stress of driving cattle. He wouldn't have listened to her anyway.

Her eyes stinging with tears, Maggie unsaddled the lame mare and put her in the corral. Then she slung the Winchester over one shoulder and mounted Calamity bareback, urging her down the trail to the ranch. To her dismay, she found the house nearly deserted with only Maria in the kitchen preparing the evening meal. Silva and the few other ranch hands were out and Sarah and the girls had gone to Fairplay while Stewart was on the drive.

"Have you heard anything from Mr. McKennon?" Maggie demanded. "Kerr's horse has come back without him!" The old woman stopped kneading and looked at her with a bewildered expression. "*No se,* Mrs. McKennon. Everything here good. Silva no here. Gone."

"I can see that," Maggie said. "But hasn't anyone come

back looking for the *Señor* or his horse?" Exasperated, she wanted the woman to have the right answers, but instead she had none. "If Silva comes in, tell him to see me as soon as he can! Please, Maria. Don't forget."

Maggie rode home at a jog trot, hoping she'd see fresh horses tethered outside the cabin door. Someone. Anyone. As she rode, black clouds rolled in over the valley shrouding the mountain peaks in dark thunderheads. With a storm gathering over the range, it would be risky to follow Bonniedoon's tracks, although that would be her plan if no further news arrived.

Once inside the cabin, Maggie grew more calm. It was not up to her to act, she decided. After all, Kerr wasn't alone. Someone had to know he was missing. Perhaps at this very moment, Stewart Merrill was on his way with a logical explanation. Maggie surveyed what had become an unsettling scene, the eerie transformation of a tranquil, familiar world. It wasn't just the broken window, or the injured horse languishing in the corral, nor even the strange feeling of being watched by a furtive owl. It was something altogether different, intangible and new. She felt a suffocating sense of fear, like an invisible rope wrapped around her neck, a feeling she could not understand.

Perhaps Kerr was on his way to the ranch even now. He just had to be all right. But if so, then where was he, or anyone else for that matter? Why hadn't anyone come? She struggled with the thought of riding back to the house again or saddling her own horse to follow the cattle drive's earlier fading trail.

No, staying at the Cameron made more sense. Someone would have to know her husband's whereabouts. In the meantime, she intended to feed and water the animals and attend her wound. She tried to be productive, but didn't really succeed.

When Silva finally arrived and she showed him Bonniedoon, a sense of panic began to rise. Sensing her fear, Silva listened to her story and assured her that the horse would be fine. Concerning Kerr, he was baffled. He had heard nothing. Remounting his own horse, he uttered something in Spanish, then with eyes black with intensity, said, "Do not leave here. I will go. Take care of yourself; I will find him." As quickly as he had come, he was gone. Maggie resumed her vigil watching the clearing in front of the trail.

Sitting on the porch in a rocker, she rocked and dozed, and awoke again, remaining thus until evening. Still and listless, she lingered, surrounded by the ever darkening skies and a circle of nature's own. *How did I come to be the center of such a universe,* she wondered. A world filled with creatures that each, in their own way, needed her strength? A world inhabited by victims of chance and the hard will of man. What was it they were trying to tell her? That the way is hard and never just? Or that the wilderness is unpredictable and full of risks. Or, more importantly, that love, in spite of all its appearances, would still be elusive, a mystery and a promise yet to be fulfilled?

Brisk winds drove clouds of rain into the Rockies. The brooding September storm dropped the temperature by several degrees and Maggie felt chilled. She wrapped a tartan around her shoulders and began to write, watching the last rays of light slip away from the sky. Nearly a full day had passed and still no word; no sign of Kerr.

No matter, she would wait for Silva's return, or Stewart—or someone, to come. If Kerr McKennon, God forbid, were dead, then there would be important decisions to make and more. If not, someone would explain things to her soon enough. His whereabouts couldn't remain a secret for long.

A sense of loneliness crept into Maggie's soul, replacing the anxiety and the fear. She knew she'd have to fight that feeling too and would; she'd find a way. She picked up her pen with stiff fingers and returned to the pages of her diary to write. *"My dearest Kerr . . . I am waiting for you here. For some word, some news . . ."*

Wind gusts slanted a torrent of freezing rain onto the porch. Maggie scrambled inside the house and lit the kerosene lamp, shaking out her hair. Her wound throbbed and she was hungry, but these discomforts seemed to be the very least of her dilemma. Whether he came back or not, she had a future to think about. It was that simple. There could be no turning back.

Part Three

13

Father Campbell met the eyes of friends and mourners, sad, reverent, and confused. No one could believe that the Scotsman, Kerr McKennon, was dead. From over a distant hill, the skirl of a bagpipe floated eerily in the breeze. According to an ancient tradition, the piper walked in a circle as he played, tracing a spiral upon the ground. The *Flowers of the Forest* sounded over the assembled crowd and the preacher raised his voice so he could be heard over the melancholy dirge.

"As for man, his days are as grass; as a flower of the field, so shall he flourish. But the wind shall pass over him and be gone, and the place thereof shall know it no more.

"We will recite together Psalm One Hundred and Three, Verse Fifteen. And remember our friend, the dearly departed, who came with love for the land. He returned in measure what he took and on his way, did no one wrong. He shall be remembered among the good and the righteous."

Here the clergyman paused and cleared his throat, then, with deliberation, began again in a more somber tone. "We gather together in the name of the Lord who hath called our friend and brother, Kerr Kinkaid McKennon, this twenty-fifth day of September, unto his final rest."

A ripple stirred through the crowd followed by a hush as people stepped back to make way for McKennon's infamous partner, Hugh Redmond MacGregor and his manager, Ewan Peters, arriving to the service at last. They made their way to the front, to a spot nearest the grave. The eulogy stopped until they and all the others stood quietly in place.

"The Lord is our shepherd, we shall not want. He leads us to lie down in green pastures. From birth to death, our fate is cast. We come when He calls and our work be done, for He shall take us from dust unto dust. We ask only now that the dearly departed join those who have passed on, as well as those who wait in the great beyond."

Maggie noticed a redtail hawk curiously approaching the circle of mourners standing around the grave. Perhaps it had come for Kerr.

"May the Holy Father guide his soul," the reverend continued, "and return him to the Scottish Highlands he once loved. Bless him and grant him eternal peace, now, and in the hereafter. Amen."

Kerr's body lay in a closed casket. The burial site at the top of a hill overlooked what would have been the future Cameron Ranch. Maggie had selected the spot herself.

The drovers told her that her husband had been torn up so badly it would be a blessing not to have to look upon him. All they could salvage were his boots, his hat, and his wedding ring, a knot of gold like her own, delivered respectfully by Stewart Merrill who embraced her with tearful and deep regrets.

Before the coffin had been closed, Maggie had glimpsed only the covered body concealed by Kerr's own heavy Scottish cape, his clan's dark tartan draped across his chest. No one dared question the men who had found him, the men who had served him so well. They said they had done all they could, but in fact, by the time they'd found his body, they were all too late. The coroner's report read simply, "thrown, dragged, and dead of his injuries."

Hugh MacGregor had departed for the Cameron at first

news after telegraphing his sympathies to Maggie. He'd ordered the coffin as quickly as possible and arranged for the funeral while still in Cheyenne. Once on the train to Denver, he realized that a trip to South Park was long overdue and reproached himself that it took this disaster to remind him of his duties. He hadn't been back to Colorado since the spring count.

Kerr's Highland cattle were already a lost cause by then as far as MacGregor was concerned. The small herd of Highlands weren't creating much interest. Besides, he'd learned the hard way that sheer volume provided the most successful element in the cattle business, the odds of success being what they were.

He'd let McKennon's folly continue far too long and now this—his partner killed on a cattle drive. A gentleman rancher like McKennon had no business in the Rocky Mountain west in the first place, taking risks not only with his life but with other people's money. MacGregor had advised him against the recent expansion but then, agreed to the loan in spite of himself, co-signing at the end. If he'd only waited, talked Kerr out of it, Wyoming's profits would have pulled them both through. Now the debt on McKennon's outfit would be his to repay as well, a burden he did not need. If he wasn't careful, the Cameron could be his demise as well.

Vicious gossip preceded MacGregor's arrival. Local ranchers weren't sure what to believe of the man's famed success, but by many he was regarded with a sense of envy and awe. The rumored rivalry between the two Scots had fueled a flurry of questions that even now rumbled beneath the hush.

As a result of their relationship, Kerr's death took on exaggerated proportions. Maggie scanned the crowd and sensed that many who stood in respect were really neither friends nor hired hands, but curiosity seekers, there to see MacGregor in the flesh.

As the pastor's last words trailed into the wind, the close of the service brought forth a gentle aire from the fiddle of Paddy Rose. His famous bow had played many a reel or jig on happier occasions, but few in attendance had ever heard a tune as tender or sad as the lament which floated that day over Kerr McKennon's grave.

During the remainder of the service, MacGregor stood directly opposite Maggie. Under a broad-brimmed hat, his unkempt silver-streaked hair fell shoulder length, a style adopted from the frontiersmen whose independence he favored. Fifty years of age, he stood straight as a spruce and broad-shouldered beneath his long-fringed jacket, a sturdy beam of a man, over six feet tall. Reserved and quiet with an austere demeanor and dark heavy brows, he avoided looking at anyone directly. When he did, his handsome bearded face remained grim.

Maggie found Hugh MacGregor more imposing than any man she'd ever seen, as if he managed to occupy more space than he actually did. The very way he stood exuded a presence, like a monarch among his subjects. In the cattle world, his reputation confirmed that the man *was* Rockrimmon Ranch, the largest foreign held capital investment in the Western territories. No mere absentee landlord like so many other foreign speculators, people said he knew the feel and lay of the land and that he rode herd on the great ranch, not only as the company's owner, but as its vision, its heart, and its soul.

Through her hastily borrowed black veil, Maggie found her gaze wandering back to MacGregor repeatedly. At the solemn close of the service, she watched him place his hand over his heart as a sign of respect and for one brief moment, thought perhaps a glistening shone in his eyes.

After the last psalm, Sarah Merrill sang a rendition of Kerr's favorite song, "The Wild Mountain Thyme" and Maggie, arms folded and head down, wept silent tears, in some ways more for herself than the stranger she had called her mate. After the last prayer, Silva stepped forward, laying a wreath of woven columbine over the freshly turned earth. Then he hung a crown of twisted cattle horns upon a wooden cross, marking the spot where the tombstone would eventually be placed. Maggie thought Kerr would have approved.

The crowd began to disperse. Maggie and Sarah comforted one another, walking slowly behind Silva and Maria toward the carriage. Abruptly, Hugh MacGregor stepped forward.

"Mrs. McKennon, I belie'e? I'm so sorry tae meet ye under these unfortunate circumstances. My sincerest sympathies."

Maggie offered her hand. "Thank you, sir. I'm sure Kerr would have appreciated all you've done, as I do. Arranging the funeral was more than kind."

"Nae, I did what was needed, what he would ha'e done fer me. He was a good man, a friend. He'll be missed."

Maggie nodded.

"How can I be o' help tae ye?" MacGregor asked. "All o' this must ha'e been quite a shock. Ha'e ye made any plans fer returnin' home? I'd like tae suggest that that would be th' best choice under th' circumstances. Goes wi'out sayin' this bristly country is nae a place fer a woman like yerself. I'd be willing tae handle th' necessary arrangements."

"I've made no plans," Maggie answered, "it's been so sudden. I'm not sure what to do exactly, but I did telegraph my father and ask him to look into a few matters for me. I'm waiting for word regarding Kerr's affairs in Edinburgh. So many details to think about. It's a bit overwhelming and since there were no children and he left me no will, I'm not sure yet where I stand. Meanwhile, I'm quite secure here at the Cameron, Mr. MacGregor. Feel no personal obligation."

At this the cattleman laughed. "I beg yer pardon. There's nae such thing as secure on an unfenced ranch in th' middle o' nowhere in this part o' th' world. Take it from me. An' as his associate, I feel obliged tae see that ye're provided fer, which I shall do. Fer th' moment, that is."

"Very well. Until matters are settled," Maggie replied. "I appreciate your concern. Meanwhile, I know the Cameron well and I intend to continue to the best of my ability. I'm quite fond of South Park and will do whatever's needed to stay."

At this remark his dark eyes narrowed. "Nae, that won't be necessary. I doubt e'en possible. I've brought along my ranch manager Mr. Peters who will stay here tae manage things fer a while. A woman's place is nowhere near an operation as rugged as this. I'll be spendin' a day or two myself t'assess th' situation. Ye just take care o' yer own person now an' get where'er ye need tae be. I'll worry abou' th' rest." His expression changed at that moment from one of grave concern to contempt. Maggie felt sure of it.

"But I *shall* worry, Mr. MacGregor. This is my home. What happens here is of great importance to me. Nonetheless, I thank you for your consideration. You're most kind." MacGregor tipped his hat as they turned toward their respective buggies, the cattleman murmuring something to his foreman Maggie could not make out.

Imagine a near stranger attempting to tell me what I should do, she thought as she climbed up in the passenger seat of the wagon behind Silva. Such arrogance, and typical of a man who was practically a living legend: revered, successful, and she presumed, probably as cold as ice.

After Kerr's death, the cabin quickly lost its charm. Yet, Maggie had insisted on returning there to be alone, to absorb what had occurred. For two full nights she lay wide-eyed listening to the hoot of the owl, wondering what was going to be her next move.

She refused to move into the main house, reminding Merrill that she still had responsibilities at the homestead. Besides, she needed privacy to mourn. There would be time enough to move down and take her proper place. For now, she needed to define her sense of self without a man named Kerr McKennon by her side.

To her shame, Maggie felt both grief and sadness *and* the strangest sense of relief. Her short marriage of five months had been bewildering. Just as it began to grow more clear, husband and wife were cheated of a proper ending. In so many ways, they had never had a proper beginning, either. And yet, a good part of Kerr had been absorbed by Maggie, and she wanted to stay where she felt she belonged, to finish what he'd begun.

On the fourth day of her self-imposed isolation, Calamity pushed down a fence rail and disappeared, probably seeking fresh grass. Before the other animals escaped, Maggie wired the fence back together and set out to find the mare, bridle in hand. She knew Calamity wouldn't wander far without the others. As she followed the creek behind the cabin, the piercing sound of a bagpipe echoed sharply through the woods. Maggie hurried in its direction and came upon a piper who stood alone near the water, his back to her. He blew an insistent and singular sound, sliding notes trailed by a clearly separate line, a continuous haunting call.

Maggie remembered hearing taps once while attending the reunion of her father's regiment after the War between the States. Much younger then, she had never heard anything so melancholy until Kerr's funeral, or perhaps, until now. The piper's tune burned its way into the morning like a torch, while black-throated magpies startled and flapped away.

Maggie moved closer to see the player who had so successfully penetrated both the stillness of the forest and the numbness in her heart. As she stepped into the clearing, he turned toward her and then, as they saw one another, he released the chanter abruptly. The vibrating drones wailed to a stop.

Maggie recognized him as the drover who had worked at the cabin when they'd first arrived. She'd seen him now and again over the summer, often somewhere near the homestead, clearing the land or mending fences. He had become a reassuring part of the landscape, someone who, through no real effort on his own, had inadvertently lent a constancy to the shifting picture of her life. Now, with the bagpipes in hand, she knew he also had to be the same man who had played the dirge at McKennon's funeral only a few days before.

"Good morning, sir," Maggie said, circling around the aspen so she could see him more clearly.

A full head of flaxen hair tangled about his shoulders and a day's beard shadowed his ruddy face. Still wearing the same heavy boots and collarless shirt that had marked him as a crofter, he now possessed a new air about him. A black hat with a wide brim and a traditional red bandanna stamped his new identity as that of the cowpuncher, like so many others around him. Nearby, a gray mustang stood tied to a tree and a rumpled bedroll lay upon the ground. He'd probably spent the night in search of Highland strays.

"M'God, m'lady, ye frightened me!" he said in a heavy Scottish brogue. The deep flush of his cheeks confirmed his uneasiness. Greenest eyes sparkled, partially in excitement, partially in fear. He quickly laid down the bagpipes. "I'm a-feared ye caught me off my guard, Mrs. McKennon. May I wish ye a *guid* day?"

He doffed his wide-brimmed hat and combed back his hair with his fingers. "Please, may I also say how sorry I am t'have learn't o' th' loss o' a fine man like Sir McKennon. 'Twas a real shame. I didna' know him well, but I could tell he was fair an' honorable. Meanwhile, I hope ye'll forgi'e me if I appear tae be trespassin' in some way. I didna' realize how far I'd come . . ."

"No apology needed," Maggie said. "I'm sorry if I startled you, but I was drawn to the remarkable sound."

As she spoke, the piper stared at her with earnest eyes. She'd walked out in her long riding skirt and boots, a simple open neck blouse tucked in at the waist, and a fringed jacket about her shoulders. The bridle hung over one shoulder, her half-braided hair over the other.

"I canna' say I ever expected tae see a woman like yerself abou' in these woods first thin' in th' morn. This land's full o' surprises, 'tisna' now?" He smiled broadly, attempting to put her at ease. "So, may I ask what brings ye out so early?"

Billy liked the contrast of so feminine a creature in mannish clothes with a sun-browned face. From where he came, a laird's wife would never be seen without her hair covered or with her skin as tanned. Was this what women in America were about?

"I'm looking for a horse," Maggie answered, sensing the

creep of an intense blush. Looking away, she added, "She seems to have escaped. Have you seen a red roan here abouts?"

"Canna' say that I ha'e."

"Well then, tell me what was it you were playing? That beautiful tune I heard . . ."

"In Scottish we call it *piobaireached,* th' ancient music. That piece was a part o' *Lament for the Sword*. A piece that a friend taught me once, my teacher, long ago . . ."

"I'd like to hear it again. Would you play it for me?"

The drover shook his head. "Nae, I dinna think so. I best be tae work." He had seldom played the pipes around another since he left the sea, for the sounds that came from them were as real as his own breath, and when he played, tears often came to his eyes. Afterwards, the memory of the music made him feel strangely unsettled and wild.

"Nae, I think I'd best be goin'. There's cattle tae be found." He knew he wanted to go on talking, watching this woman whose hazel eyes were fixed upon him, but he didn't dare. Just being near her felt exhilarating, the sharpest pleasure, yet with each passing moment, he grew more and more sure he had no right to be there, conversing with McKennon's widow, alone.

Before Maggie could ask him again, he knelt to take apart the long pipe of the bass drone and roll the instrument into his bedroll which he then tied to his saddle. Swinging easily onto his pony, he gathered the reins in one hand and turned the animal round to face her. It gave forth a shrill whinny as Calamity appeared unexpectedly at the edge of the clearing.

"Ye must excuse me now. They'll be expectin' me soon. And it looks like ye've found that horse, Mrs. McKennon. I bid ye a good day."

Hugh Redmond MacGregor made Maggie a decent offer, no one could deny. Before the week had passed, she'd received word that matters were now out of her hands and would be handled by the Scottish head of Western Land and Cattle himself. A meeting had been set up to explain to her just what her options would entail.

Stewart Merrill and Ewan Peters, speaking on MacGregor's behalf, rode up to the cabin to present the plan, documents in hand. The recently arrived stock detective, Kurt Skoll, who had sought Kerr out earlier in the month, had asked permission to join them. He insisted he needed to meet with Mrs. McKennon, as well, to discuss details regarding her late husband's affairs.

While Peters and Merrill stood near the cabin steps, Skoll waited a safe distance away, giving them privacy, yet standing close enough so that he could still hear every word. Maggie met the two men guardedly.

"Ahhemm." Peters cleared his throat. "Thank ye fer seein' us on such short notice. On behalf o' Mr. MacGregor, ma'am, we be askin' fer yer co-operation tae discuss yer returnin' home, before th' values change ag'in, especially th' return on Kerr's holdings: land an' cattle, an' what he owned outright."

Their foreheads wrinkled with genuine concern as they unfolded their papers and reviewed a handwritten list. "MacGregor's sent me tae speak fer him since there be little tae concern yerself wi', ma'am," Peters continued. "I'll do my best tae explain everra'thin' just th' way he asked. So, 'tis like this: time's short fer seeing ye back where ye belong. A tough winter's na' far ahead."

Skoll watched from afar with more than obvious interest, trying to look unconcerned. The widow showed a bit of attitude in his opinion, an arrogance that gave her style. He moved in closer so he could better overhear what she was saying and determine better the color of her eyes.

Peters had been well coached by MacGregor before he left. But he was impatient, unused to dealing with women. He insisted on getting right to the point. He stammered as he reviewed the situation, while Merrill stood silent, hat in hand, waiting for his cues. Skoll followed every word.

"Th' investors are ready tae buy off Kerr's share o' th' herd," Peters expanded. "That's cash in hand fer th' remainin' Highlands still on th' ranch as well as those tae be sold at auction. They figure ye deserve a percentage o' th' estimated sale; 'bout half, I believe." Maggie nodded, confirming the figure.

"In addition, Mr. MacGregor is prepared tae gi'e ye one-half th' value o' th' house an' its surrounding land, once 'tis all sold, plus full passage home tae Philadelphia. A stagecoach makes th' run o'er th' pass where ye can take a narrowgauge tae Denver. Or ye may go by passenger train across th' park through Colorado Springs, a bit longer, then on tae Union Station by that route. Ye're welcome tae choose whiche'er ye like."

Peters presented the offer as if all were done and accounted for and Merrill followed along with a serious air, adding authority, if nothing else.

"An', oh, yes. Mr. MacGregor said tae remind ye that a proper gravestone, tae be chosen wi' yer approval, shall be erected here on th' ranch markin' McKennon's grave for all time. Poor soul, may he rest in peace."

Here he stopped, taking a long breath, and checking his list to see that he hadn't left anything out, added, "Does this sound acceptable tae ye? Is there anythin' ye'd like tae say?"

The offer seemed businesslike and generous to a fault. Few widows had been taken care of as expeditiously. MacGregor's holding company, Western Land and Cattle, had built a reputation that was definitely beginning to make itself known and this settlement was no exception. Maggie, however, had no intention of accepting.

"Sorry, gentlemen, I think you've forgotten one important item. As Kerr McKennon's widow, I have a right to be here and I plan to stay. And for that matter, I plan to personally manage his investment and increase it if I can. I'm sorry to disappoint you but you can tell Mr. Hugh MacGregor that, although I appreciate his generosity, I must refuse. Now, would there be anything else?"

Maggie then curtsied slightly, offering a thin smile, and moved back a step or two before turning her back on the two ambassadors who stood speechless in her wake. Without another word, she walked back into the cabin and closed the door.

Returning to their horses, Peters and Merrill wondered what they'd done wrong. Skoll, who had moved in for a closer look, wondered himself, and decided to postpone his own meeting with McKennon's widow, or more precisely, those hazel eyes, for a more private occasion.

Maggie noted that a letter from her sister had taken almost two weeks to reach her and had remained unopened due to the many upsetting events. She decided it was time to see what it said.

September 15, 1889
Dearest Margaret,

Reading your last letter, I couldn't believe all the news. You—still in a cabin in the wilderness. Mother cannot fathom that you've accepted such conditions and tells everyone you're still only "visiting" Colorado. She worries that you chose a strange man after all and went off in such a hurry. But I'm sure you knew what was best.

Maggie wondered what they must be thinking now. The official notice had been wired to the family by telegraph the day of the funeral so she expected to hear from them soon. In any case, she hoped her father, still Kerr's creditor, would stand behind her and she planned to contact him to discuss the matter. Returning to the letter, she continued.

"Wren and I read that President Cleveland signed new laws to control animal exports to Europe. Shipping lines don't know how to handle livestock. Have you seen the papers? An entire ship sank in the New York harbor due to too many cattle aboard. Animals panicked and drowned. Fortunes were lost. Now the government is trying to prohibit the shipping of anything that breathes. I couldn't help but think of you. Do Highlands know how to swim?"

Emily's humor had never really amused her, but between her two sisters, the younger was the one she preferred. Old feelings of attachment tugged gently. Outside, a loud bray from Ramona reminded her that the animals needed tending, and tucking the letter into the pocket of her skirt, she went out to catch the mule and Bonniedoon.

Walking the injured horse was the only therapy Silva suggested to keep the animal's sprained leg from stiffening.

Slowly, the mare would improve. Maggie knew she'd never be totally sound, but for the sake of Kerr's memory, she'd kept the horse alive, never blaming it for the tragedy.

Nuzzling Maggie's arm, the mare slipped her head willingly into the halter. But instead of following Maggie's lead, she resisted and stood her ground, ears pricked forward, fearful eyes opened wide. Maggie, standing along one side, could see the reflection of a form approaching her from behind in the shining convex depths of the mare's eye. Bonniedoon snorted softly at the scent of a strange mount. "Evenin', Mrs. McKennon."

The stale reek of alcohol came to Maggie's nostrils as she turned and recognized Skoll atop his buckskin ewe-necked nag. Decked out in a brimmed bowler, frock coat, and formal bow tie, he looked ridiculously out of place. From his coat pocket peeked a whiskey flask and a large pearl-handled revolver bulged from out of his belt. To Maggie, the man looked comical, not official, decked out in his pretentious city clothes and fancy firearm, except that his face looked threatening, his eyes a bilious yellow, and he grinned like a hungry fox.

"Mr. Skoll. What brings you here? I thought whatever business you had would be finished by now."

"You might say I came to find something," Skoll replied, winking and leaning over the pommel of the saddle.

"Well, I don't think it's here," Maggie replied curtly. "You best leave." Using the mare as a shield, she started back toward the corral. *Whiskey precedes a man by a mile,* she thought, remembering for a moment those special evenings in her father's library where well-dressed gentlemen drank and talked late into the night. Only there, the aromatic smell of whiskey wafted out of crystal glasses, along with the scent of fine cigars and men's cologne.

Skoll dismounted and tried to grab her over the horse's back. Terrified, Maggie jerked away and ducked from his grasp but the mare shied, bolting at a brisk trot, leaving her exposed and at a greater disadvantage.

"What do you think you're doing?" Maggie demanded. His huge hands reached again as she ran.

"Giving ye what I know ye want." He scrambled after her. "Ye can't fool me, Mrs. McKennon. I can see it in yer eyes. You be needin' a man and I can sure take care of that."

"Go away or I'll shoot you," Maggie threatened.

Skoll's voice softened to a coaxing tone. "Shoot? Don't ye play hard to get with me. I'm not scared. Come on now, ye got no reason to be afraid."

Maggie hissed. Did he think she was his for the taking like an unbranded heifer lost in the brush? Single women, even widows, seemed to be fair game, especially here in the West. To Skoll, having a female was just a matter of being strong enough or moving fast enough, without regard for who the woman was or had been.

Maggie reached the cabin just ahead of Skoll and slammed the new planked door just as he reached it. Quickly sliding the long iron bolt into place, she reached for the Winchester, then listened breathlessly as Skoll pounded on the door outside. Poking the nose of the rifle through a log chink, she shouted, "Leave me alone or I'll fire!" and levered a round into the chamber of the rifle, causing a sound she knew was unmistakable in its significance. Satisfied that he understood she meant just what she said, Maggie was relieved to see him mount up at last and ride away, an ugly scowl on his face.

The door to the cabin stayed locked until the next day. Maggie slept with the loaded rifle next to her bed, the hammer on its safety, yet still apprehensive to open the door even a crack. The cow and calf bellowed at the paddock gate and hungry Ramona brayed, demanding to be fed. Maggie paced about the cabin restlessly, unsure of her next move, except for the realization that it was time to make other living arrangements.

Skoll had helped her come to her senses. She'd move down to the Cameron and assume her role as rightful occupant of the house that very day if she could. With that decision reached, she moved cautiously out the door, chin up, carrying a bucket of feed with one hand and a Winchester in the other.

"Mornin', Mrs. McKennon. Why don't you let us help you with that?" Merrill and Silva appeared out of nowhere as Maggie approached the corral.

"Goodness! You gave me a start!" Maggie gasped. "But I'm so glad to see you. What brings you out here so early?"

"Bad news, I'm afraid," Merrill answered. "We rode over first thing. Looks like it's official. MacGregor and First Bank have agreed that the Cameron's to be sold. Shut down and readied for auction if necessary. The crew is to move up to Rockrimmon just as soon as we can. South Park can't support the big herds anymore anyhow. With those damn sheep in the valley, there's no room left to grow."

"You can't be serious."

"Afraid so and I'd say it's for the best. We'll move you on down to the house this afternoon, if you don't mind. Then you can catch a stage later this week. As I understand it, you plan to return east before long."

"I beg your pardon! Has anybody thought to discuss this with me?" Furious, Maggie decided not to show how hurt she felt. Obviously, she would have to take up the matter with MacGregor at once. Such a decision couldn't be left up to him unless there had been an arrangement made with Kerr of which she was unaware. As soon as possible, she'd send him the briefest telegram saying, "Don't do another thing/Take no further action regarding the

134

Cameron/Will discuss everything with you in person in Wyoming."

Packing took less than an hour. Maggie's belongings fit into the front half of the wagon, the pet calf stood secured in the other. The cow would follow behind. Silva who had returned to assist her, tied Calamity and Bonniedoon to the back of the lorry and left Ramona and the old cow to follow behind.

Taking a final look around, Maggie sighed. Would the owl survive without her? Sheltered in the woods near the cabin, the bird had become a dependable sentinel by night, responding to any sounds. Lately, it had begun flying and hunting on its own in addition to accepting her food, returning to the house from time to time, adopting the tall pines as its home. The owl had accepted Maggie as much as she had adopted it, and she wished she could take the great bird with her. Perhaps, in some unexplainable way, she would.

As she closed the cabin door behind her, she remembered Kerr's promise only a few months before. "It would only be for the summer," he had said prophetically. Uncanny how right he had been.

Silva drove the wagon without a word. He seemed solemn and angry, not at all his usual self. Maggie had grown quite fond of the easy-going *vaquero*. Over the summer, he had accepted and treated her like a daughter. Doting and proud, he had coached her in her adaptation to life on the range and enjoyed watching her as she mastered her new surroundings. Between them a mutual bond had developed and a true sense of respect. Next to the ranch itself, Maggie knew that if she had to leave, she would miss the friendship of the old Spaniard the most.

Both were silent during the ride down to the house.

Maggie scanned the landscape and couldn't imagine not ever seeing their fields again. She needed to convince herself that what was about to happen was temporary. She was determined to stop the sale of the ranch. Kerr would never have tolerated such a thing. As the wagon creaked its way to the main house, Maggie discovered the letter from Emily still tucked away in the pocket of her skirt. She unfolded it and read . . .

Finally, I don't want to alarm you, but you must know that father has taken ill. The doctors don't know how long he will last. Should anything happen, he says that you, myself, and Wren will inherit the bank with our husbands and guide it into the future. Father's attorney, as well as Charles and Arlen who are both growing more and more involved, shall assist us in the legal matters, of course.

The large loan to your husband's ranch worries him very much since the market seems to be plummeting. Your McKennon seemed so positive last spring, I'd hate to think he took you all the way out there for nothing. Please confirm that everything's all right.

By the time you receive this, who knows what will have happened? Things may have changed for the better. I hope so. I miss you terribly. Wren sends her best regards.

Love,
Emily

Maggie refolded the letter. This would explain everything. With her father ill, the arrangements with MacGregor might have been drafted by someone who simply didn't understand. If his health were to take a turn for the worse and she inherited control of the bank with her sisters, then surely she would have a voice in the disposal or protection of the

Cameron as well. This idea gave her hope. As the wheels of the wagon turned in the dust, Maggie realized that there might yet be another way.

Wasn't it possible she might be entitled to at least a part of the ranch according to Colorado's laws of inheritance? And if that were so, depending on that law, couldn't she therefore also become MacGregor's partner in Kerr McKennon's place? Why not, indeed! If only MacGregor would be in agreement.

MacGregor. How did that indifferent man dare suggest she return home? Perhaps he knew that she had full right to the partnership. Whatever the case, she had a stake in this decision and did not intend to be dismissed.

Rounding the bend toward the clearing, the ranch house came into view. A small crowd had gathered on the porch. Maggie recognized Sarah and her daughters, and much to her chagrin, Kurt Skoll, and Stewart Merrill as well. Other faces were obscured except for one profile she knew instantly, even in the distance. His tall form, long fair hair and full white sleeves caught the light. As the team came to a halt, he stepped forward and began to untie the mule.

"Billy, give the lady a lift, will you?" Merrill instructed. Before the command had been spoken, the drover's strong hands encircled her waist to lift her down. His eyes met hers briefly, then each looked away.

Sarah Merrill moved forward to help with Maggie's belongings. "Thank God, Mrs. McKennon, you're here at last. Let me help you take your belongings to your room."

17

"Seems tae me, a successful bank ne'er takes anythin' but calculated risks," Ewan Peters proclaimed. He checked the door to the dining room, then glanced out the window where the remaining Highlands grazed innocently in the field. "First Bank misjudged this one. Profit should ha'e been their only goal. Wonder why they e'er got involved?" he continued.

"Because McKennon's wife is the banker's daughter, remember?" Merrill answered. "The Scot knew what he was doing."

"Well, somebody should ha'e put th' brakes on sooner. Where I come from, banks don't like tae lose. This deal wi' McKennon's share o' Western Land an' Cattle may ha'e seemed like a sure thing at th' start but it's goin' to cost someone a pretty penny now if it fails. Who'd ha'e bet on prices droppin' like they did?"

As MacGregor's manager, Ewan Peters spoke with justified authority. Per the cattleman's instructions, he had called the informal meeting to obtain a better sense of the situation before returning to Cheyenne.

"That's really not the question," Stewart Merrill said. "How to get our share of this sale is. Kerr promised me a percentage of this ranch on top of my wages if he ever liquidated. Too bad he didn't put it in writing. After all these years, I may never see a dime."

The cattle detective, Skoll, leaned back in a wooden

rocker, taking a drag on a cigarette. He'd convinced both Peters and Merrill he needed to be in on the discussion in order to finish his report. This way he would learn as much as if it had come from McKennon himself. This Merrill fellow would have to be eliminated, he decided after a few minutes, one way or the other. He worried he might not get paid as well if the sale of the ranch involved honoring old debts or promises.

Peters turned to a more urgent topic. "What abou' McKennon's wife? Has she agreed t'accept th' settlement an' payoff yet? Her part in all this complicates matters."

"I don't think so," Merrill answered. "She refused a clean exit straight out the first time we offered and hasn't changed her mind yet, far as I know. Maybe we need to try another approach. Why don't you or MacGregor convince her that her share is worthless, and maybe she'll back out on her own."

"That shouldna' be too hard," Peters grumbled. "I heard McKennon ran through all his cash a'fore he died. But it's na' my place. We'd best advise her or she'll be in the way fore'er. MacGregor wanted this loan debt o' Kerr's resolved between him an' th' bank, a clean settlement. They can ha'e th' whole thing, as far as he's concerned. Ne'er figured on a woman in th' picture, though. What does she know abou' cattle ranchin' anyhow?"

"Not much. But I bet she knows what's hers. Who wants to tell MacGregor we couldn't talk her out of it?"

"I'd say ye're th' one, Stewart. Maybe ye'd better try again," Peters prompted, poking Merrill in the ribs. "She'll listen tae ye. Tell her she either changes her mind or she'll be packin' for Cheyenne wi' th' rest o' us. We canna' lea'e her here. Then we can let her an' MacGregor figure it out. I'd like tae do my job an' see this settled now."

At this remark, Skoll finally opened his mouth. "Same

here, gentlemen. I'd like to see m'self and the rest o' us get just what we deserve."

Silva, busy sorting out the remaining tack after the drovers left, quickly knelt and hid behind a saddle rack when the three men from Philadelphia unexpectedly entered the horse barn. His position allowed him to remain unnoticed. Through their cloud of cigar smoke, he could see that these were the same men that had arrived by coach the day before to call upon Maggie, saying they represented her father. He hoped he would understand all that they were saying.

"It's very simple, Charles. Unless we get Margaret's signature, the document's invalid. We can't sell and you know it." Arlen Beale puffed on his cigar while Charles nodded in agreement. "Furthermore, if Magnes doesn't recover, the ranch will be claimed by the family, then heaven help us. Could be years before we can liquidate while the three sisters battle it out. According to the law, a consensus will be needed on every decision. I'd hate to see that happen." Arlen inhaled deeply and rubbed his chin. "What then?"

"That would be the day," Benjamin Farrell cut in. "Emily and Wren can't agree on anything as it is. In spite of your helpful guidance, gentlemen, Magnes's daughters are incapable of dealing with such responsibility. You had best be aware that such a circumstance could complicate bank matters if they end up as its inheritors. I'll be damned if our board of directors will sit by while they make up their addled minds. With things as bad as they are here, it's clear we have to take charge. An audit must be made and an accounting for all assets and debts, now, in Colorado and Wyoming. We can't stand idle while MacGregor simply tries to dissolve this branch of the operation and take our money with him."

"The Scot seems like a smart man to me," Charles commented. "Smart and very strong."

"Indeed, he is. Strong enough not to be bowled over easily. He can blame the bankruptcy here on a careless partner and continue on as before. I'm sure the investors won't question him. They might be at his mercy, but we're not. It wouldn't be the first time Dowling's bank has had to assume a property to protect a bad loan. But we'd better do it fast. We're not national like a lot of those larger institutions and don't have the cushion of being chartered by the federal government. Not yet. Loans in excess of our actual deposits are extremely risky, especially when they default. Bank failures, gentlemen, are not caused by negative factors in the economy, but rather by drains on banks that are loaned out to the point where they have practically no reserves at all. I hate to admit the similarity here. Shall we say Dowling's business acumen has grown a bit short-sighted?"

Farrell pursed his lips and nodded at the two young men in his tutelage. "Enough said! Wire Philadelphia in the morning. Tell them we'll definitely push for foreclosure."

"And what about Margaret? Does she have any say in all of this?" asked Arlen. "Or do you think we can expect her to return home per Magnes's request?"

Silva, still undiscovered, strained to hear the attorney's answer. He knew he could never recount all that had transpired but realized Maggie was in some kind of trouble. Something wasn't right.

Farrell stomped his cigar on the tackroom floor, grinding the stub into a pulp. "Frankly, whether Margaret Dowling returns home or not makes no difference to me. At this particular moment, gentlemen, her wishes matter little either way."

18

An early October moon beckoned over the horizon. Typical of the season, it glowed the palest shade of gold, luminous and round. Across the rolling landscape, dark forms of cattle dotted the fields. A bull bellowed and a coyote yipped back. The Cameron seemed quiet and unnaturally calm, all but for the activities of the few drovers preparing to depart in the days to come.

Outside the barn, a lone cowboy secretly worked a long-legged horse on a lead, watching her circle around him, effortless as the wind. She covered the ground in springy, far-reaching strides, all the while holding her head aloft and watching the cowboy with a sharp, mistrustful eye. Round and round she trotted, the drumming of her hoofbeats the only sound in the night.

Billy Munro slowed her to a halt and approached with caution. He placed one hand gently on the horse's neck. She flinched, but stood still, quivering under the wrangler's gentle touch. Open palms smoothed over her back and down her sloping haunches, checking for hidden scars and injuries. The cowboy had noted a subtle falter in her gait and a stiffness in the right rear hock. Whatever it was, it appeared to cause her no pain, and so he urged her once again into an ever wider track, guided by his lariat and the teasing flick of a switch.

Horses had come and gone on the ranch, most just typical

of the stocky mustangs of the plains, a few worth looking at, others, plain. But this one . . . Billy whistled softly. He had never seen a horse as fine as Bonniedoon.

"Easy, lass," he encouraged. "Come on, give me yer best." The night wind ruffled her mane and her arched tail flowed long behind her, balancing the fine arc of her neck. She trotted briskly, yet still held something back, testing the long rope, as if to tease. Billy marveled at her light elongated gait and aristocratic grace. What kind of horse was she? From where had she come? He was as curious as he was charmed.

Although she responded slowly at first, the mare came to life at last, twisting her neck until she began cavorting like a filly. Finally, cantering the full circle in a relaxed easy lope, she floated past him, stretching her long legs for the sheer joy of it, testing the lariat to its limit.

Inside the ranch house, all was still. Upstairs, in Kerr's old room, Maggie Dowling McKennon, heiress and widow, Philadelphian and pioneer, turned and tossed, her long hair churning about her face, bed clothes tangled. Oblivious to a scheming world outside, she clung innocently to a fitful, dreamless sleep. Worn leather boots propped in a corner sat next to a trunk of clothes that had not seen the light of day since their arrival West. A rifle lay across a big valise. And, on the endpost of the iron bed, a fringed jacket hung beneath a weathered wide-brimmed hat, the long brown feather of an owl slanting in its band.

Billy looked up often to check the window of the house. He assumed Mrs. McKennon wouldn't be up for hours, but couldn't be too sure. The mare, standing by the fence, warmed and excited, flicked her tail and tossed her head, watching him warily. In the moonlight, Billy noticed a fine sweat had brought a sheen to her coat, so he coaxed her into a walk, cooling her as he did.

There would still be time to ride her, Billy decided. He definitely *had* to ride her before he lost the chance. Putting on her halter, he twisted its lead rope around his wrist, gripped the mane at her whithers and then swung deftly up onto her back. She stood quietly, then stretched her neck low, pulling the rope through his hands. He gave her a bit of slack and squeezed with his legs until she began to move in a swinging tango of a walk that vibrated through his very core. So pleased was he with the animal's response, he immediately asked for more, clucking softly, urging the mare into a fully extended trot.

Maggie awoke and went to the window, opening the shutters just enough to see out. There she saw the drover of the bagpipes riding Kerr's mare like he'd been born upon her, bareback, steady, and relaxed. The man seemed to be one with the animal. Although his muscular build spoke of his physical strength, Maggie could sense a hidden spirit within him that dominated the beast. No doubt, the wily mare never had a chance.

She wondered about his age. Twenty-five or six perhaps, maybe a few years older? And where had he learned to ride? Watching him work the mare, she wondered how he knew horses after all. Horses, and cabin building, and bagpipes too. She scolded herself for her curiosity. After all, they were both strangers here. Did she have the right to ask? Why did she even wonder?

The answers haunted her as much as the questions. But this stranger, unlike herself, already seemed to belong to this often untamable world she so much wanted to make her own. No longer alien or separate, he seemed to fit, like the very animals he tended, his senses linked to theirs.

How did this drover come to it all? And how and when would she? Watching him effortlessly ride the horse, she envied his belonging, the easy way he wore the West.

Opening the shutters wide, Maggie saw the rider lean back as the horse broke into her long-reaching canter, lifting him higher with each powerful forward stride. Shoulders back, boots rocking in the air, holding the lead rope with one hand, he let the pacer have her head. Bonniedoon snorted, arched her neck, and gave him a fully extended gallop around the corral, not slowing until she'd repeated the circuit again, and then once more, as if only for herself. Satisfied, Billy dismounted, smiling triumphantly. He patted the sweating mare on the neck, knowing that in claiming her, she had accepted him as well.

Seeing Maggie at the window, he turned away, too embarrassed to meet her gaze. Dawn's first light faintly lit the sky as the sun peeked over the horizon and in full view of Maggie, with nowhere to hide, Billy tipped his hat towards the window. "Top o' the mornin' tae ye, Mrs. McKennon," he called cheerfully. When Maggie returned his smile with a wave, he murmured softly to the mare, "Aye, and I must say, 'tis a braw' morn indeed!"

"She's doing well, don't you think?" Maggie called as she approached the corral. Billy was now walking the mare once more to cool her. "In fact, I'd say she takes to you. She hasn't been ridden by anyone since the accident, and yet there you were on her back without even a saddle and she behaving, as a proper horse should. Yes, I'd say she likes you fine."

Maggie felt self-conscious, ill-prepared for the unexpected encounter. She hadn't bothered to comb her hair or wash her face and had dressed quickly, so as to catch Billy before he finished. Now she wished she was more presentable and looked more like a lady. Then again, would it have mattered?

She felt warmed with the delight of watching him ride and couldn't suppress her excitement. Nor did she try. She envied the drover's skill and confidence, and only wished she had the courage to do as well. In this world of men and cattle and vast distances, horses took on great importance, real and symbolic, valued both for transportation and as part of a man's success. To be perceived as strong and equal, she would need to be as capable a rider as any, but that would take some time. Especially since the thought of mounting a horse like Bonniedoon still worried her.

"Say now, if I was doin' any wrong here," Billy began, "I meant nae harm. The horse is a beauty. I only wanted tae see her move, even more tae see her run." His voice felt stifled and hollow. Nothing sounded as it should.

"No matter," Maggie said. "The mare needs exercise. You've handled her well. Perhaps she's nearly recovered. I'm glad to see it." She stepped under the horse's neck, running her hand along Bonnie's sleek side, now damp with sweat. Billy backed away.

"Well, now, sir," Maggie began, to ease the awkward situation, "I don't believe we have ever been properly introduced."

"Right y'are. That's twice I must beg yer pardon. An' 'tis my fault entir'ly if I've forgotten my manners. My name is William Munro. Billy's what I'm called."

"No fault implied," Maggie assured him. "I'm pleased to make your acquaintance, Mr. Munro." She parroted the precise way he said his name, the accent on the first syllable, a very Scottish sound. "It appears I've got a horse that thinks she's yours. Meanwhile, I suppose you know that soon we're all headed to Wyoming, to Western Land and Cattle's northern range."

"Nae, ma'am, I've na' been told o' th' move."

"Well, it's no secret. And since I want that horse to go where I do, perhaps I can arrange for you to help me get her there. She's normally not easy to handle, but you don't seem to have a problem. Would you consider the job?"

Maggie wiped the dust and sweat off her hands by pressing them along the length of her skirt, inadvertently pulling the cambric taut around her hips. She stopped when she realized Billy was watching her, yet his eyes almost never left her own. They seemed to be speaking to her, drawing her near. She stepped back a few paces and tried to re-establish the distance she needed, but to no avail. Looking at him in the morning light, his eyes revealed a deep kindness. They captivated her.

"If I can be o' any help tae ye, well, ye can count on me Mrs. McKennon, fer anythin' a'tall."

"That's very kind," Maggie said. "But perhaps I've spoken too soon. I should check with Merrill to make sure this fits with his plans."

She pulled her shawl around her shoulders and turned to leave. Had she made a mistake? Been too forward? "We'll discuss this later then. I trust you'll put the horse away when she's ready. A good day to you, Mr. Munro."

Maggie returned to the house both excited and confused, though she wasn't sure why. Combing out her hair, she noticed the sweaty scent of the horse upon her hands: acrid, pungent, animal. She inhaled, deeply. The scent reminded her of Billy. In her mind, the young Scot and the horse had already become one.

For a moment she felt as though she had betrayed Kerr, then dismissed the thought as irrational. She needed Billy's help. Left without resources, Maggie had little to hold on to. For the moment, the mare was difficult to manage and she welcomed sharing the responsibility. A chance encounter had brought the drover close to her again, and now he was pledged to her, to helping her make her way. Each new meeting with Billy Munro seemed innocent and uncalculated, yet, together they had begun to add up to something unlike anything she had ever known. She wanted to see more of him and enjoy the giddy feelings elicited by a kindred soul. Rationally, she knew better than to further a relationship with one so far from the path she walked, yet, greater forces seemed to be bringing them together. Forces she could not explain.

Maggie tried to put the drover out of her mind, for the most part without success. Thoughts of Billy filled frequent moments, until she had to strive not to think about him. Then again, why shouldn't she? If she were not meant to know him, not to be with him, then how could she explain his constant presence? Or more importantly, why was it that wherever she found darkness, this compelling cowboy stood, lighting up the shadowed corners of her life.

Part Four

Billy Munro had always dreamed that one day he'd become a man people could look up to with respect. No one would ever have to know that in Scotland he'd lived as did thousands of sons of the poor, powerless tenants of landowners with little hope of escape. Exhausted by poverty, Billy had run from the emptiness—that, and the pain of a brutal childhood, a painful beginning that haunted him still.

"Get on wi' it. Finish yer chores or they'll be no supper fer ye this night," James Munro growled at his sons.

Billy remembered the cruel threats, though he could no longer recall his father's face. That visage had vanished. But the thought of him still tied a knot in Billy's chest. The fear that stalked him then had followed him to this day. Like slow heat, it had forged indifference, caution, and an unnatural hardness early on. But Billy ignored what he could not name and as a child withdrew into a distant and lonely world.

By the time he'd turned ten he'd learned to hunt squirrel and quail and could catch a rabbit with a snare. Once, he lived off the land for a week just to prove that he could. Truth was, even when they all worked hard, food was scarce and supper for the two hungry boys was often only gruel or *clapshot,* if anything at all. They could count on the anger and the beatings whether their plates were full or not. His mother wept while his father railed and Billy learned to survive. When necessary, he also knew where to hide.

Together the brothers worked the meager farm. They ploughed the furrows behind a lumbering ox and dug up turnips and roots with their hands until their fingers bled. Billy quit school at the age of twelve, lying to the constable that his mother needed him at home to care for her. Though the story was partly true, fear of his father kept him close about the place, as well as the need to look after young Rob whose welfare mattered more than his own. Billy could read by then, just enough to get by, and managed to hitch into Glasgow to steal fruit or chickens whenever he dared. But the very first time he got caught he swore he was done with crime, fearing the Lord would strike him dead if he ever did it again.

"Dinna' worry, Robbie," he'd say to his brother, "stay out o' Pa's way an' I'll watch o'er ye. Be *guid* an' no harm will e'er come." He meant every word, but couldn't promise what he said was true.

When the ox died, an aged horse took its place. Swaybacked and half blind, the old Shire soon became a dependable friend and helpmate to the boys. Patient Moll stood quietly while the children climbed upon her back, taking turns jumping off her broad and generous rump.

A great barreling barge of a beast, she plodded down the fields carrying the children who shouted commands like generals. They invented games to enliven their chores until they both grew too big and Moll got too old. They loved that Shire like nothing they'd ever known and in her instinctive way, the horse loved them back.

The lads learned about the seasons from the land and developed a sense of respect from the horse. With tempered patience and gentle care, they discovered how to wrest the most from a humble beast, one that put up with the elder Munro's brutal whip and mealy feed. Moll plowed and dragged no matter how heavy the load, ignoring the lowland mud as it sucked at her worn and splayed-out hooves.

"Ye must fear th' Lord," Billy told Rob. "Pa says if ye don't, th' Almighty will get us in th' end. If we disobey, our souls will be lost. He says th' bogs are full o' sinners, *boddach*, who canna' even go tae hell, right out there, waitin' tae catch us. If we're bad, they'll cast their spell an' we'll both go mad. Ye ken, like Mrs. Duffy down th' road, th' one who talks tae trees . . . Ye know how daft she is."

Robbie listened, wide-eyed. Fearing God worried him, but fearing their father, his fists and his drunken fits, worried him even more. So far, God had never come without warning, grabbing your hair from behind and pummeling while their mother pleaded with him to stop.

Billy never understood why his brother had to die that night when he'd found him laying crumpled against the shed. He had bruises about his head and neck and his shallow breath sounded like steam rattling in an old pipe. Billy carried him back to the house, his heart racing with fear, and hid him in their room. Afraid to tell anyone, he waited till supper but Robbie never woke up. Just drifted off until the sound of his breathing stopped completely. Billy guessed the Lord had come for him after all, just like Pa said He would. He cried and prayed for his brother, but nothing did any good.

Where was I, he wondered, *when Pa went after 'im? I ne'er heard 'im call. I should ha'e been there,* he thought, *stopped it, turned Pa's fists on me. Why did Robbie ha'e tae die?*

Billy never did understand. He knew only that Robbie was dead and that would never change. He decided then not to pray, ever again, figuring there couldn't be much use. And he never gave a second thought when he decided to run away the next morning, either. Only wished he could have taken

Robbie too. He felt sorry for his mum, though, when he finally showed her his brother's body lying stiff in their trundle bed. She sobbed and screamed and tore at the sheets till he thought the bed frame would surely break, but as far as he could tell, all that broke was her heart.

They buried the child near the trees in a stony silence like a tomb. Then, when his Pa came home and collapsed in a drunken heap, his mum began to weep, trying to cover the sounds of her sobs. Billy slowly gathered his belongings in a sack then emptied the pockets of his father's coat, taking the few coins he found and slipping them into his boots. With a heavy heart struck numb, he crept to the shed where Moll, the great horse, lay dozing on the straw.

" 'Tis a sin tae lea'e ye here wi' him, my friend," Billy said in a daze. "He'll *nae* feed ye; ye'll fair starve. *Nae,* old Moll, he shall na' ha'e ye anymore. Ye've served well. Little Robbie loved ye best an' I know he'd understan' what I ha'e a mind tae do." Then he took down the butcher knife hanging from the ceiling by a cord.

"When ye get tae heaven ol' girl, I hope ye can find him still, that I hav'na' been tae late. Forgi'e me, Moll. Ye know I ne'er hurt ye, an' wouldna'—till now."

The blade hadn't seen much use of late but old Munro kept it sharpened for the occasional hen or goose. With all the strength and courage a mere strip of a boy could muster, Billy closed his eyes and plunged the knife deep into the horse's breast. With an explosive kick and a spasm, the mare jerked back, twitched, and shuddered, heaving, until she threw back her great head one last time and her eyes rolled into oblivion.

Crimson blood flowed heavy until the straw grew dark and wet. Billy, determined to dignify his brother's death, cut away the Shire's mane and carried it to Robbie's grave. There he spread its weight like a blanket, covering the freshly turned earth. With tears streaking hot rivulets down his flushed and burning cheeks, he picked up his pack and fled, escaping the nightmare of the croft forever.

A wagon headed for Glasgow that night found room for an anxious boy and his bag. By the cool dawn of morning, Billy had arrived at the shipyard of the Clyde where it seemed an entire fleet of trawlers, ferries and freighters slipped in and out of the docks. Most harbor crews didn't mind run-aways, even those with blood on their clothes, and Billy wandered trustingly among them. Burley longshoremen waved now and then while he watched them lift their loads.

"Watch it, lad," a stevedore called, "ye best git out of th' way." Billy stepped aside, straight into the firm grasp of a captain who took his sack and extended a warm and reassuring hand. The boy followed him up a gangplank onto a waiting ship and nobody asked any questions.

Six years a ship's mate, eight more on the deck. Billy learned to survive at sea. He sent word to his mother at the start, vowing he'd not return as long as his father lived. She wrote back from time to time, but eventually, her letters stopped coming.

The first girl Billy loved was Erin Moore, or at least, he thought he did. She and her mother ran the supply shop near the dock and knew all the fishermen by name. Only fifteen when he saw her the first time, himself still a lad and too shy to look her in the eye, he still knew he couldn't forget her. But by the time he'd made first mate and had grown a half meter taller than she, he had no trouble asking for a walk on the shore, especially after a pint.

Erin made him laugh and taught him how to kiss—proper, hard and full. In no time, Billy asked her to be his girl and she swore she would, sneaking away with him behind the shop. "D'ye love me, Billy?" she'd ask, pressing him for proof.

"Dinna' know. Guess I do," he'd answer. He didn't know, let alone how to show her if he did. All he knew was that he wanted the feel of her body beneath him and needed to hold her, often, long, and tight. Once she gave herself to him under the tarps of her mother's boat, he knew he was lost for sure. Billy promised her a ring and planned to wed just as soon as he could get leave, and began putting aside his wages.

While still away at sea, Billy was shocked to learn that Erin had run off with the minister from the very church in which they were to be married. Crushed by her deception, the episode left him bitter and wary, but wiser, fortifying his belief that almost no one could be trusted. Erin's betrayal confirmed what he had felt all along: that the world was a lonely place, and neither the Lord, females, nor the running of the cod could be counted on when you really needed them most.

The bosun adjusted the awkward instrument gently in Billy's arms. "Lift th' bag so 'tis against yer left forearm lad, like this, an' hold th' chanter wi' yer left hand. Then, puff into th' blowstick till th' bag is almost full. *Guid, guid.* Now, strike th' bag wi' yer right hand an' start th' drone tae' vibratin'. Do ye hear 'em, now, do ye?"

Billy nodded, attempting to follow the seaman's instructions.

"When they're a-goin' *guid* an' strong, tuck th' bag under yer left arm, an' squeeze hard aginst yer ribs. There! That's it. Lovely! Lovely! That's th' sound o' th' chanter chantin'!"

As the small ship coursed through the waves under a salient summer sun, the bagpipes came alive in Billy's arms.

"Now, blow an' squeeze an' blow an' squeeze, keepin' th' bag hard all th' while. Dinna forget, ye've got four reeds a'goin', three in th' drones an' one tae make th' chanter loud an' full. Can ye hear 'em, Billy?"

His willing student smiled.

"There's no hidin' it. Ye can hear their voices, so sweet they are." The music swelled as Billy blew and blew and together the odd pair rode the waves in a soulful swale of sound.

"Play th' pipes like ye was lovin' 'em, Billy, like ye was squeezin' yer verra' best girl. That's th' trick! They'll come tae life fer ye, love ye back. Blow new life into ye too if ye do it right. Dinna' be shy now; let me hear ye play . . ."

Thomas Fey was the closest thing to a father Billy ever

had. Caring and concerned, he was full of surprises one day and predictable the next. The old sailor could find his way through the many winding inlets which linked the tangle of the isles or course the narrow channels that ran between the seas. An expert in all kinds of navigation, he could maneuver a dozen harbors "with his eyes closed," he liked to brag. The bosun knew the difference between the curlew and plover or the seagulls and the rills, the many seabirds that soared daily overhead. And he knew the pipes. Like a Scottish warrior he played, and like a lover too, his dulcet Highland tones sweet enough to bring tears to a grown man's eyes.

Thomas swore to Billy that one night his bagpipes would summon the Silkies up from the sea, legendary seals that were known to swim along the bow of the ship and lure lonely men to their beds. The Ancient Ones said that the Silkies, capable of transforming into beautiful women upon the land, always returned to the deep, breaking hearts and stealing their half-human babes back into the brine.

When the euphonious sound of Billy's pipes wafted over the roar of the waves, he often scanned the phosphor seaweed and the foam, both afraid and hopeful to find one of the tempting creatures there. With every lesson, Billy tried harder to play the chanter the way that he'd been shown, but the sound hung heavy between his shallow breaths. He practiced faithfully, improving with each attempt, yet something vital remained inside. Only he knew what was missing, that deeper passion that would force the simple melodies to soar into the breeze. He longed to give himself entirely to the pipes, but couldn't, never sure what might erupt, or what spirits lurked within, waiting to haunt him yet.

"Grace is free, my boy," old Thomas liked to say. "Find it while ye can." Religion was the sword he brandished, and he sharpened it as he preached alternately of salvation and doom. "Nae, ye canna' buy it fer a king's purse! Ye must open yer soul an' receive it, only then will ye be saved. Walk in grace, my lad, an' hope ye never falls into th' hands o' th' livin' God. Lord, ha'e mercy on ye then . . . ."

This image of the Lord stalking his own sons was the old seaman's favorite. Attrition would be harsh, repentance required. "On judgment day, there'll be nae time t'explain yer sins. Save yerself now, while ye can. That's th' secret tae redemption, boy. Ye must repent while ye can."

Billy never questioned these well intended thoughts, not daring to admit he didn't believe in God, anyway. Thomas worried him, though, for he suspected that the wise old man could see into his past, to a brother who had died through Billy's neglect. But that particular terror remained his alone, to forget or reshape, in some unforeseeable future.

Together the two argued and agreed, probing the prophets and the psalms. With the song of the bagpipes in their hearts they guided the vessel through the waves, hoisting its sunlit sails to the blowing ocean winds.

Winters on the North Sea drove hard. Churning squalls, lashed by driving sleet and snow, often left fishing boats helpless and adrift. Only four miles from port on a windy February afternoon, the *Dunkirk* foundered and started to sink, forcing the crew to throw over the lifeboats and call out to abandon ship.

"Everra' man fer himself!" was the cry as sailors dashed from their posts when the waves came crashing over the decks.

"Jump, Billy, jump!" Thomas threw him a lifebelt, attached by a line to the one he had already slipped on. "Put it on, jump near th' escape boats, an' I'll come after. God 'elp us, I will!"

Terrified, Billy stared at the churning water and the life-belt at his feet. He didn't dare leave the deck. To plunge into the icy sea seemed like suicide, so he clung instead to the rail. In that moment's hesitation, a giant wave crashed upon them both, sweeping the two men into the roiling depths. Billy surfaced flailing, but Thomas Fey had disappeared.

Every fisherman knows that the waters of a storm rarely return the bodies of men whose boats capsize or are tossed overboard in the wake. Sailors tell of the lucky ones that have survived, but these are very few. When the howling storm abated, three members of the *Dunkirk* joined the ranks of those legendary men: the captain, the cook, and the first mate, Billy Munro, all still alive but nearly frozen stiff.

The captain and the cook had lashed themselves to a life-boat while Billy managed to climb atop a buoy. A rescue cutter sent out after the wreck lifted him onto the deck, chilled to the bone and nearly blue with cold. As he lay on upon his side, he saw Thomas's bagpipes floating in the water off the bow. They bobbed and rolled amid fragments of ice, the inflated bladder holding barely enough air to keep the instrument afloat.

Exhausted but not too battered to feel the deeper pain tear through him like a blade, Billy struggled to save the treasure with a long whaling hook. It floated before him, its drone and chanter splayed out like desperate fingers reaching into the air. Rolling close to the edge of the boat, he pulled the pipe aboard and squeezed out the water, drawing the soggy mass to his breast with an icy gasp. Holding the last remnant of his beloved friend to his heart, he lay thus all the way to the shore, shivering under a pile of blankets, his tears for Thomas Fey hidden by the cold salt spray of the sea.

Want ads fluttered like gulls. "Jobs in America" they said,

along with a sketch of Texas Longhorns herded by drovers in the American West. The handbills drifted across the dock, papered the walls of the bar, and beckoned from the rooming-house door. Billy heard the bartender read a flyer aloud and figured he might as well answer the call. He had saved enough to cover the ship's passage, steerage class, and the overland fare West. The North Sea had betrayed him, that he knew for sure. But the Lord, the very one he had so sorely doubted, seemed to have spared him for something. Now, renewed in his faith and with nothing else to lose, he was determined to find out what.

The aroma of fresh coffee drew Maggie downstairs. Sarah had just fed her daughters, Patricia and Jenny, and scooted them outside when Maggie entered the kitchen. Small talk for the ranch woman was never easy, but the foreman's wife began with an exasperated sigh.

"Mornin', Mrs. McKennon," Sarah offered warily. She craved the friendship of the widow but kept her place, mindful of the distance before them. Sharing the house and the small kitchen made little difference, she being the employee of Mrs. McKennon now.

"Wished I could say *good* mornin' but it's such a shame about the news. Nothin' good a'tall. Heard the ranch is closin' down, just like that. But I guess you must know what's best. I hate to think of givin' up this place. Seems like the Cameron barely got started."

"I'm just as sorry as you are," Maggie answered, pulling up a chair. "The decision appears to have been made by the bank that holds the loan and Kerr's partner, Mr. MacGregor. I hope to reverse it if I can. Things have happened so fast— seems like there's just not much to hope for."

Sarah poured coffee out of a large enamel pot. "Depends on what your hopes are. Or wishes. Can't say mine count all that much."

Maggie sipped her coffee and considered a plate of griddle cakes. She should have been hungry, but wasn't.

"My own seem dashed at the moment," offered Maggie. "I'm not quite sure what I myself am going to do. There's so much I still don't understand. But what about you? You're being uprooted too. You and the girls have been here for over five years, and now what? You're off to Wyoming while Stewart hires on for MacGregor. Tell me honestly Sarah, how can you bear it, being pulled along like the cattle, following your husband, with no say-so at all?"

"What would you have me do, Mrs. McKennon? I do what any woman does, what I'm obliged to do. Stewart and I go where the work is. My husband's been a farmer, a miner, and a cattleman. He likes cowboying the best. But it's all the same to me. The cookin' and washin' never change."

Maggie wanted to say that there was more. So much more. That all across America women were attending schools and working jobs and not only following their men West, but venturing on their own too. How could she explain that she wanted her own life to be different? That she'd decided to run cattle herself, not just wash clothes for a cowboy. Sarah was not ready to hear such ideas. Maggie put one of the pancakes on a plate.

"Anyhow, where Stewart goes, so do I. Say now—with all due respect," Sarah willfully changed the subject, "might I say a word from one woman to another? Maybe it's not my place, but I have my eyes open. I do believe that the cowpoke with the gray pony, the drover, Billy Munro, has taken a fancy to you, Mrs. M." She held her breath for a moment to assess the effect of the remark, then burst into a wide smile. "I swear ma'am, I know it's none of my affair, but I believe he does."

"Please, call me Maggie, Sarah. And don't be silly. That drover is a hired hand. I hardly know him. No such thing." Sarah's comment surprised her. How could the woman know? Had she seen so clearly what Maggie was only beginning to feel?

Sarah wrung her hands in her apron and began again. "You might try, but you can't hide the truth from someone who remembers fallin' in love once. I can see it all over him. He looks at you like you was all he can see. I know it's too soon for courtin', but I say watch your step. Women are scarce out here and men are in a hurry. Course, that don't mean you're the right one for him. Or vice-versa. Still . . . it's so soon." She tied her bonnet under her chin and turned toward the door.

"Looks like we'll be leavin' in a day or two so I got plenty to get organized. I hear you're also headed for Rockrimmon. Is that a fact?"

"Indeed, I have matters to attend with Mr. MacGregor," Maggie answered, still flustered over Sarah's earlier remark.

"I hear that MacGregor's ranch is 'bout the biggest spread in Wyoming," Sarah continued. "They say you can't ride the whole range in a week! And Cheyenne! Heard the women dress there like they was on the streets of Paris! How about that?"

Maggie smiled.

"My Stewart says MacGregor is a generous and fine man, *if* you stay out of his way. Already give us an advance on the first season's salary. Can you imagine? And best of all, me and the girls are going to travel to the ranch by train. Stewart's bought the tickets, including a stopover in Denver before we catch the Cheyenne-bound. Time for me to dress the girls proper and maybe myself too! Ain't that something? Me on a train! And in a real hotel! Why, I've never traveled like a lady in my life."

"Perhaps I'll be joining you," Maggie smiled.

Suddenly, Sarah exclaimed, "Oh, listen to me! I nearly forgot. A gent named Farrell got here a few minutes ago and sat himself down in the porch rocker outside like he owns it. Says he came here to meet with you personally and that it's real important."

Maggie finished her coffee and got up. "Thank you, Sarah. I'll invite him in. And we'll have plenty of time to continue this chat later . . ."

Benjamin Farrell! Of course he had come. Why not? Magnes Dowling hadn't failed her. He'd sent his trusted legal confidant to clarify matters after all. Maybe she'd learn for certain why the Cameron was in ruins, why the whole plan seemed so final. Losing all that she loved was unthinkable. Farrell would help her make sense out of it. She wouldn't keep him waiting.

The attorney rose as she approached. "My dear Margaret, it's a pleasure to see you looking so well." Benjamin Farrell smiled gratuitously and kissed Maggie's hand. His bristly mustache tickled the top of her wrist.

"Thank you. I think the West agrees with me," Maggie answered. "By the way, you may call me Maggie now, Mr. Farrell. I've shortened my name a bit. Seems to fit better out here."

"Yes, well, you don't say? Quite the modern woman, aren't you now? May I offer regards from your family, Margaret? Let me see, hugs from your sisters, a reminder from your mother to . . ."

"Tell me please, Mr. Farrell," Maggie interrupted, "what brings you here? Do you have news from my father?"

"As a matter of fact, yes. Is there somewhere where we can talk in private?"

Maggie opened the door to the dining room and gestured

for him to enter. "Perfect," he said, wiping his brow with a handkerchief. "Look here, Margaret. Magnes is quite concerned about your situation at the moment, matters turning out the way they have." He checked his pocketwatch as if to anchor the comment to the time. "It isn't proper, a widow so young fending for herself in this rugged land." At this he turned and walked the length of the room, peering out the window, squinting as if to assess the terrain itself.

Turning abruptly, he blurted, "Mercy! Have I forgotten my manners? Please, accept my condolences on the loss of your late husband. So unfortunate, so sad. Horrible, really. Out here I suppose no one ever knows what's ahead. If it isn't horses, it's rattlesnakes, desperadoes, or acts of God. No end of possible ways to die."

"Just what was it that brought you here, Mr. Farrell?" Maggie asked, looking at the large clock in the corner and ignoring his inquiry. His sympathies rang hollow, even worse than the tinny sound of the clock chimes striking the hour.

"The truth is, my dear, your brothers-in-law, Arlen, Charles, and myself are here on behalf of the bank and the family to insure that you are protected. Provided for in your hour of need and not burdened with the unreasonable debt and calamity it seems these Scots have led you into. Nasty piece of business, this. A scandal really . . ."

"Whatever are you talking about?" Maggie queried.

"Everywhere we turn back east we hear of erroneous profit figures, false reports, debts incurred. Insatiable greed, I'd say. But, I digress. Allow me to get to the point."

"Yes, please do," Maggie said, already frustrated by Farrell's insinuations.

"This may take a bit of time, Margaret. I want to make sure you understand, clearly. Would you like to sit down?"

To be put in my place or to be made comfortable, Maggie wondered. "Thank you, but I'll stand if you don't mind."

The smooth arbitrator smiled, seating himself in an armchair at one end of the table. Then, uncomfortable with a woman still standing, he rose again. "Certainly," Farrell responded. "Whatever you like." He unfastened a large briefcase and placed a sheaf of documents on the table. "Before I begin, allow me to also express my concern regarding the current illness of your father. He appears to be in an irreversible state at this point; his condition's terribly grave. I've seen him ill before but never like this."

Maggie remembered Emily's letter. "I was only vaguely aware. Please, tell me more."

"The worst I've seen. Of course, your mother fully expected him to recover after the last bout. He's only taken this turn in the last week or so, just before I left. Pneumonia it seems. Of course the stress over this cattle business hasn't helped. He was in quite a state before the breathing became so difficult and could barely dictate the terms I've brought with me. Nonetheless, we're all hoping for the best. But should things not improve . . ."

"For God's sake, Benjamin!" Maggie's impatience with the man could not be concealed. "He's been sick before, and he's always recovered. In any case, I am still his daughter. I trust I'll be informed if he worsens."

She didn't remember ever using this tone before. She realized she detested Farrell and not being in Philadelphia anymore, felt like she could speak her mind.

"My dear, in the wake of your own loss, I would only like to spare you. I will gladly handle the proceedings against the corporate entity Western Land and Cattle and bring the partner, this MacGregor fellow, to task. We intend to recoup the loan made to McKennon by repossessing the land here in Colorado and freezing the assets of the Wyoming establishment. It would be of great help to have you with us in the matter. Surely you intend to return home at this point to offer moral support to your family when they truly need you most? Your mother is beside herself, thinking of you alone out here with the whole arrangement falling apart."

Maggie studied Farrell suspiciously. She didn't like his position.

"Honestly, Margaret, this dirty ranching business appears to be no life for a decent woman. I, myself . . . ," he said with a clearly incredulous tone, ". . . can't imagine how you've managed thus far . . ."

"So far, there's been no problem, Mr. Farrell. I came to live on this ranch by choice and have learned what it takes to run it, should I have the chance. There's nothing a woman can't do here if she has a mind to. I have! And you may tell my mother that I plan to return home only if necessary. Are you going to try to arrange that for me too?"

"Now, now, Margaret, you needn't be impudent."

"If I am, it's because you are, sir. Whether you realize it or not, I believe I have a future here. One of my own making. What you or my mother perceives as a proper life for a woman leaves much to be desired and I have no intention of discussing it any further with you. May we move on?"

Farrell now eyed her warily. This was not the Margaret he remembered but her added spice was not entirely disagreeable. In fact he found himself almost admiring her obstinance. He decided to share more than he had anticipated.

"Yes, well, of course," he acquiesced. "Let's discuss the future, shall we? How aware are you of the national state of affairs at the moment? The new regulations? Probably you aren't. How could you be? Let me see if I can make myself perfectly understood."

Maggie waited, her mouth set in a pursed hard line. "I hope you'll do your best."

"It's like this," he began. "In terms of cattle, shall we say there are a few too many? No one wants them in the old country anymore. All of Europe fears the spread of disease ever since that tick fever scare out of Texas last year. Imports overseas have never been this low. That's for starters."

"Go on."

"Prices for land are up, leases skyrocketing. At present, there's a bit of a range war out there and it's going to get worse. Three years ago, the last cattle count in Wyoming showed over one million, five hundred head worth close to fifty million dollars roaming those grasslands. Rustlers and poor management haunt every rancher, as well as the caprices of weather and fluctuating markets." He glanced at her to see her reaction. "But the real problem today is real estate. Ranch lands have been selling at four times actual value and new acquisitions by European investors are at a standstill. The current backers in Edinburgh are furious and refusing to pay the currently inflated prices."

"But Kerr owned this ranch, did he not?" Maggie interrupted, pacing the dining room floor. "With the exception of the recent expansion, I believe it's all paid for, free and clear."

"Indeed. He arrived here early when prices were reasonable. But the current loan for the expansion has created a number of difficulties, shall we say? Now, please, be patient and hear me out.

"Raising beef until now has been hugely profitable because sale prices have been high and land was free. In the last ten years, over two hundred cattle companies have operated in Wyoming alone. At least a dozen of these are owned by English or Scots and individually are worth well over one million dollars. Another seventy-five are owned by Eastern co-operatives. As you can imagine, the competition at the moment is fierce and the rules are changing by the minute."

"What are you getting at?" Maggie asked, pausing next to his chair. She hoped eventually he would get to what concerned her.

"It turns out that many investors bought into these herds by book count," he went on, "the standard range custom, and have paid for two to three times as many cattle as have actually been delivered. Nobody ever knew exactly how many head existed anywhere. Cattle detectives rule the range, a scurrilous lot. But I would have to say at this point even the late McKennon's records are suspect. No one is exempt. Many of the figures reported to investors were and are entirely false. Returns based on air, if you will."

"I see. Are you implying Kerr McKennon was not honest?"

"I'm not implying any such thing. Just giving you the facts. Now, the brigands who run these operations have chosen to do so on the public domain, that is, grazing open lands to get feed without cost. Settlement laws are changing, forcing the cattle barons off that range. That means selling cattle at low prices under pressure. Flooding the market, once again."

Farrell unbuttoned his coat. He was sweating visibly and searched for his handkerchief. "Terribly warm in here. Do you mind if we get some air?"

"No, of course not," Maggie answered. Anxious for him to say something she could relate to, she flung up the sash on the nearest window.

"Finally, many of the ranches hurt have suffered most because of bad weather, Margaret. The British may have ruled the seas, but they couldn't control nature. The blizzards of '86 and '87 left cattle frozen to death by the thousands. Many ranches have never recovered."

"The way you describe it, success would seem impossible," said Maggie.

"Improbable is a better word. But how they manage is exactly the question. Bigger has not proven better. The giant ranches like the Matador, the Hansford, and the Swan are in dire straits at the moment. McKennon sold off the bulk of his Highlands in the nick of time. This MacGregor fellow, of course, is another story."

"According to Kerr, they never did agree . . ." Maggie decided not to offer further information. She'd let Farrell tell her what he knew.

"Precisely. Most of them don't. The Scots are an irritable bunch, hot-tempered to boot. That brings us to the problem of management. Expense accounts show that the dividends in this relationship have been eaten away in everything from travel junkets to personal frivolities. We've been forced to take a closer look at real assets."

"I'm sure you'll find everything in order," Maggie stated.

"I can't agree with you. The Scottish company Prairie Land and Cattle in eastern Colorado has just announced bankruptcy. Not surprisingly, trading beyond the capital they possess and falsifying the numbers of newly branded calves. 'For appearances,' they testified in court. That ranch was at the top, Margaret. They set the prices for the rest. Makes the other ranchers a bit uneasy, to say the least. My duty is to see that all is as it should be on these premises. Scrutiny throughout is the order of the day."

Maggie could see that her perceptions of the cattle trade had been extremely limited. The Cameron was only a small part of a huge puzzle that appeared to be unraveling. Larger forces dictated whether the cattle would sell or not. Farrell's comments made sense, though she hated to admit it.

"Are you still with me?" Farrell asked, resting his portly frame at last in an armchair at the end of the table. If Maggie insisted on standing, he'd just have to let her.

"Now, it appears the western plains are overgrazed. It may take years to see decent grass again. Streams have been illegally diverted while public property runs dry. Back in Washington, policy makers have announced that the continued acquisition of lands by foreigners will lead to a system of landlordism, incompatible with the best interests of the United States. We don't want to see that, do we?"

Not waiting for her answer, the attorney continued. "It's common knowledge that boatloads of immigrants have been brought over as employees of foreign lords, competing with the rights of honest settlers to earn a decent living." Farrell unfolded his handkerchief and lightly blew his nose.

"Damn if the whole thing hasn't gotten out of hand. Washington's not too happy about it. Ironically, your husband, may he rest in peace, has been spared the showdown, but I'm quite sure there's a high price to be paid."

Maggie walked around the corner of the table and stared silently out the window at the fields of South Park. A flock of sparrows picked at the foliage searching for fallen seeds. The thought of the land being overgrazed seemed ludicrous. There were so many acres of grass she couldn't imagine it otherwise. Kerr, who knew the cycles of drought and the effect of constant grazing, always rotated pastures, seeing that his own herds never destroyed the natural crop.

"Moreover, the locals around here and in Wyoming are tired of outsiders. They object to the power these foreigners exert in the territories they now act as if they own. Their money won't protect them any longer. Congress is pushing for control."

"What kind?"

"Every kind. Land holdings are no longer free for the

asking. Texas has decreed that land not owned outright by the cattle barons, or leased, must now be rented for up to twenty-five cents an acre annually. Hundreds of thousands of acres. Can you imagine?"

"That sounds costly."

"Exactly. Only this past month, nearly two hundred thousand acres near Kiowa were abandoned by the defunct Prairie Land and Cattle Company. They just backed out, rather than test their dubious title before the U.S. officials. Pure chicanery, the devils. The way the government sees it, the easy ride is over."

"What exactly do you mean?"

"New restrictions, retaliation, prohibitions. Who knows, maybe even deportation. This past summer, petitions against alien landowners flooded Congress! A bill is now in place that would keep any foreigner from acquiring real estate on public lands in the United States ever again. That's a fact. And President Cleveland is in favor."

"What are you saying, Benjamin? That European investments here are over? I thought the government wanted to settle the West. Does MacGregor know this? Did Kerr?"

Farrell was finally moving closer to the real issue. "Do I need to be concerned?"

"I'm afraid you do." The attorney ran his chubby fingers up and down the edge of the table. "It means that being associated with such trouble is socially and politically out of style. Your father would like the details on this ranch to be tidied up. Magnes now knows your McKennon was a bit overextended. But we can take care of that with your help. Liquefy would be the swiftest course."

"Liquefy? That's ridiculous."

"Meanwhile," Farrell continued, not pausing to acknowledge her remark. "Current legislation proposes that America be owned by Americans. If the bill passes, and I believe it will, all future foreign investors will be prohibited from holding real estate in the territories, except by inheritance, or in the case of collection of debts. That means, no new acquisitions, and plenty of pressure on the old owners to release their holdings."

"How very unfair. Is no one exempt?" Maggie inquired.

"In a way, yes. The bill also says that only those corporations committed to the construction of railways, canals, and turnpikes may acquire or hold more than five thousand acres. A comfortable catch."

"How do you mean?"

"Well, the bill leaves the cattlemen out, but the railway magnates in. British chaps mostly. *And* their money. Europeans will provide for the expansion of select industries no matter what . . . but that's not our affair. Not directly. Cattle pirates are."

"You're calling Kerr McKennon a cattle pirate? He was a decent man."

"Perhaps. But this is the situation. People back east are angry. The banks smell fraud. They figure all the Englishmen are here to make a killing. Truth is, Washington intends to take a closer look at banks and the deals they've made. Could be uncomfortable when they do." He took a newspaper clipping from his vest pocket.

"May I refer you to this?"

Maggie read the news:

July 20, 1889
The New York Times
    In the spirit of the times, several territories including Wyoming, have passed Foreign Corporation Registration Laws whereby foreign held companies must now file charters of incor-

poration and provide detailed information about their capital structure, personnel and purposes, with both the territory and the county in which they operate. Company officers, agents, and stockholders are all made jointly responsible.

"That means full disclosure, Margaret," Farrell warned. "No more private arrangements between the huge corporations. The directors want everything to be presented before a loan committee. Bank boards. Accountability. Sounds fair, doesn't it?"

"I'm not so sure."

"Well, your father isn't sure, either. He doesn't like it."

Maggie studied Farrell. *What was he up to? What does he know about my father that I don't? What kind of deal did my father make with Kerr?* She was beginning to feel uneasy.

"I assume there's more?" Maggie said.

"Indeed, there is. And it's important you know the rest." He paused, as if considering how to proceed. "Take note, my dear. This is for your own good. Listen carefully. Three years ago a bill prohibiting aliens from acquiring land in the United States came before Congress. It didn't pass."

"It doesn't sound too American," Maggie mused.

"Exactly. President Cleveland himself said it was straight-out unconstitutional. But the Scots reacted badly and pooled resources to block the legislation. They hired lobbyists and set up camp in Congress hoping to insure protection of their investments. Now they're making quite a fuss. Embarrassing lot."

Farrell sorted his clippings and pinned them back in order. "The Scots out West and abroad became something of a nuisance at this point and accused Washington of favoritism and bias. And they do have a point."

"Which is?"

"Well, Union Stockyards in Chicago has just been sold to a London company for a mere nineteen million dollars. British pounds at work with no resistance. It puts the gents from the Isles at odds with each other again."

Maggie sighed. "I see what you mean."

"First Bank usually takes sides. They have to. They favor the winners. Your father's bank finances railroads, Margaret. Chicago is important to him. General Palmer of the Union Pacific met with Magnes only a few months ago regarding expansion of the Rio Grande right here in Colorado, with British money, naturally. You see, until his health began to fail, your father was quite busy. Interested in the future. Making sure, in fact, that there will be one."

Maggie smiled at the thought, remembering her father's great need to be in charge.

"It's all politics, Margaret. And these are desperate times. The cattle industry's on its knees. Crisis, depression, call it what you will."

"Where do you think it will end?"

"Can't say. But it's highly unfortunate for the cattle owners that the rail center is now in the hands of those who regulate the price of cattle. Ranching has become one with big business and tied to the railway. The newly formed corporations will eventually run the small ranchers into the ground. Ranchmen everywhere are talking about setting up additional stockyards and trying to get the processing centers closer to the ranges to cut costs, but that gets back to big money, again. All I can tell you is that Magnes believes he was lured by Kerr McKennon into a critical loss. One way or another, the bank plans to cash in."

"May we intrude?" an unexpected voice interrupted. Arlen and Charles, the family's dutiful watchdogs, stood at the dining room door.

"Nice to see you, Margaret," Arlen beamed, "in spite of the unfortunate circumstances. So sorry we're late, Benjamin, I see you've started without us." Stunned at their unexpected arrival, Margaret realized Farrell hadn't come alone. Both men kissed Maggie's cheek and seemed genuine in their greeting.

Arlen sat down, crossing one leg over the other, locking both hands around his knee. Then he leaned forward, feigning brotherly closeness. "I say Margaret, you do look smashing. A real western girl if I ever saw one!"

Maggie seated herself, eyeing him doubtfully. "What ever brings you two here?" she asked, warily.

"Charles and I are here on behalf of your sisters. We're all terribly concerned, you see, to insure that they haven't been overly jeopardized. Debt and bad relations have a way of spoiling credibility and ruining reputations. Along with your father, we've grown a bit worried about your personal affiliation and hope it's not too late for amends. We have our best interests to protect. And certainly, yours as well."

Maggie doubted their sincerity, feeling as though she'd never belonged to the Dowlings of Philadelphia at all. "As we understand it, you intend to stay out here alone." Charles used a sympathetic tone. "Perplexing, but we're not here to criticize. If you don't intend to return home, then we need to ask for your signature on this document." He held out an envelope.

"Unfortunately, it's a letter of forfeiture," Arlen interjected, "of your rights of inheritance."

"Only in the event Magnes does not recover," Charles assured her. "By his authority, this addendum would be attached to his will."

"Your father insists you choose, Margaret, for his peace of mind." Arlen cleared his throat. "Unless you agree to support the bank in acting against Western Land and Cattle, a relinquishment of your rights to any future family estate is necessary. It's a matter of principle. The board feels it's appropriate."

Maggie rose abruptly from her chair. "Is that so? How convenient. Well, I believe my rights still remain to be seen. As long as my father is still alive, my signature can wait. And so can you!"

Fuming, Maggie turned toward the door just as Stewart Merrill appeared outside the window and rapped on the glass. He'd been scheduled to take Charles and Arlen for a ranch inventory and field measurement. Arlen whispered a few words privately to Farrell and motioned to his colleague to rise. Charles overtook Maggie and standing in her path, took her hands in his own.

"Good luck, dear Margaret. I do think you're going to need it." With that, the two men bid her a cool goodbye, leaving her alone with Farrell once again.

"You know, my dear, I knew this wouldn't be easy. Your father has his right to be concerned and so do you." He loosened the bottom buttons of his vest. As always, the master of sentiment, he continued. "I understand your struggle, I most assuredly do. Do you truly stand firm in this refusal?"

"Absolutely," Maggie answered.

"In that case, I believe I see another possibility for your future here as well. Your future and mine." With this, Farrell looked out the window momentarily, then rose and reclosed the dining room door, turning the lock. Lowering his voice, he continued. "If none of what you've heard thus far appeals to you, I would like to make you an alternate and private offer on my behalf. Something altogether different, just between us, for our mutual benefit. Would you be interested?"

Maggie sighed with exasperation. "You seem prepared to tell me, regardless. What is it?" She folded her arms, waiting for him to continue.

With a gesture, Farrell reseated Maggie and took the nearest chair. "First Bank has promised me a decent percentage to close this case quickly. That includes bringing together all three sisters so that we might proceed. If your father should pass away, then a two-thirds consensus would be necessary. That is, at least two of you must agree on each issue. Young Emily seems the most uncertain. She seems to favor your side, Margaret, and has confided in me that she would refuse to sign anything until she knows where you stand. Dear thing. So loyal to your rebellion. But the situation could be troublesome." He coughed lightly and looked at Maggie with one eyebrow raised as if to question his own remark.

"But I digress. Aside from joining forces with your sisters, should it come to pass, the interesting point here is that I've discovered the stakes are actually larger in your case should you decide to stay on."

"Go on."

"Consider this, my dear. Should you prefer not to proceed with the family against Western Land and Cattle, not relinquish a thing, you might actually be just as well off. You see, your inheritance as a widow may include a portion of the Wyoming holdings, not just the debt in Colorado. Do you see what I mean? McKennon and MacGregor co-mingled debts and some profits. I'm still looking into it, but it's possible they had arranged to split everything they owned in America right down the middle someday. If so, that's a tidy sum, my dear, and not to be sneezed at. No, no indeed. In my opinion, this MacGregor appears to be able to pay back the Colorado loan, and then some. Seems to have quite the foundation, here and over there. More than one bank in Edinburgh stands behind him. Four or five to be precise."

Maggie's breathing slowed perceptibly.

"Now, assuming nature doesn't sabotage the cattlemen like it has in years past, he could sell off his herds and make quite a profit, if the market improves. So, depending on circumstances, I could privately assist you in assuring that you receive what is rightly yours. One half a cattle empire. A widow's proper inheritance, to include land, cash, cattle, and investments, according to the official laws of venue."

"And then?"

"And then? Next thing you know, you could stay in Colorado or settle in Cheyenne or wherever you like. I believe you're the one who reminded me that women in Wyoming actually sit on juries and have the right to vote. Terrifying thought, really. With all that money, you might just gain rights and access. Run for office. Become a cattle baron yourself, or baronette. It's a brand new world, my little Margaret, indeed it is. All of this, of course, if you were to make it worth my while. Very worth my while. Such a move clearly violates my professional standing with the bank, and would certainly mark the end of my career. But Magnes isn't going to last forever and should he pass on,

I'm afraid my position with the bank appears unresolved in any case. Tenuous, to say the least. My own needs are paramount. I believe we could help each other. Am I making myself clear?"

At this, Maggie nodded her head and answered. "Yes, Benjamin, you're making yourself quite clear."

Was it possible? she thought. *Could he be making any sense?* Unbelievable. An unexpected turn of events.

Farrell's eyes shone and a wide smile formed deep creases in his jowls. Margaret might very well be a rich woman, he thought, and was now also single and available. A dim quiver of desire disturbed his usual implacable self. He wasn't any older than her late husband had been. Oh well, he mused, if there was to be any of that, there would be time later. A small bubble of saliva moistened his lips. Farrell gazed at Maggie, his usually rough edges softening in the greening vision of money.

How unlike him to be my ally now, Maggie thought, *even for a price.* She decided to use his behavior to move forward cautiously. Knowledge would be everything, but she had to be careful. As one true to his calling, Farrell was capable of switching coats in an instant, depending on whoever was winning the war.

"Why don't you put your offer in writing and tell me your price?" Maggie said. "Furthermore, I'd like you to leave these documents for my own evaluation. I'll get back to you by this afternoon with an answer, but I'd like to know where I stand before I have to face Hugh MacGregor myself. I dare not know any less than he, wouldn't you agree?"

Sensing a deal, Farrell beamed. "Absolutely," he answered. "Without a doubt."

"I'm a fast learner. And I'm rather tired of being the last informed. Let's try to improve the situation the simplest way we can." She put a special emphasis on the word *we* and

Farrell winked. "Of course, Margaret," he said, "*we'll* do our very best."

Margaret rose and pulled her shawl about her shoulders. "As to your proposal, I'm very interested. You know, Benjamin, I think it's time for us to become a little more tolerant of one another. If it's possible, I'll protect myself and the ranch and fulfill Kerr's loan obligations until we've won our case. If I'm able to do my part and you do yours, you'll be rewarded handsomely. I'm guessing Mr. MacGregor may be in for a surprise. And by the way, if you are sending word to Philadelphia, you may tell either my mother or my father that Maggie McKennon stands in defense of the Cameron Ranch and Western Land and Cattle. Now, and forever."

"Indeed, I shall." Farrell stood up and tugged at his jacket with a satisfying shrug.

"By this afternoon then, I'll have your proposition?" Maggie asked. "Apparently, there's no time to lose. I expect that if I say yes that you'll tell me exactly what I need to do?"

"Indeed I will. You can count on it, Mrs. McKennon—that is, Maggie. Shall we say, four o'clock?"

23

"The arrangement's over," Stewart Merrill said to Billy. "You can pick up your wages anytime you like."

"Sir? I'm a'feard I dinna' understand." Billy stopped in his tracks and turned to the older man. The muscles in his jaw tensed.

"Whether or not you stay on with Western Land and Cattle is not up to me." Merrill's voice sounded gravely with regret. "The South Park operation's over. We're closin' down."

"O'er? Just like that? How can ye walk away from all this, Stewart? A man could raise anythin' here, cash crops, hay, grain, horses, anythin' a'tall . . ." Billy swallowed.

"MacGregor is in the cattle business, son, not farming. When he decides to diversify, he can ask for your advice. Until then, we're leaving Silva and a few of the boys to cover what's left of the herd and watch the property until matters are resolved."

Billy stood his ground.

"The plan is to bring MacGregor's stock together and sell what's not profitable. He's got thousands of head in Wyoming that need to winter through five months of ice and snow. By March, there'll be calves to brand. We'll not be needing you there. He's letting anybody go that's not essential. Sorry things turned out this way, but it's not my call. From here on out, I'm afraid you're on your own."

Billy took each word in slowly. "I dinna' come this far tae be let loose now, sir," Billy began. "I beg ye tae keep me on. I just got started." He looked Stewart Merrill in the eye, nearly his equal in every way. They'd gained mutual respect over the summer, Billy adapting each day to the ways of the range and Merrill's demands. Most of the time, the men felt like family, each looking after the other as well as the herd. How could Wyoming change all that?

"Nae, I willna' go," Billy began again, more emphatically. "I'll mind th' horses fer ye or mend th' fences. Nae tellin' how heavy th' snow will fall this year; another pair o' hands might save a calf. You canna' let me loose now. Surely, ye can see that."

"No, I can't." Merrill turned his back and continued to strip the tack room of all usable items, leather straps and buckles, chaps, and tools. The conversation seemed to have disappeared into the very chinks of the logs, so suddenly did it end. Holding a gunny sack, the foreman began to throw in the remaining saddle blankets left after the departing drovers had taken their gear. "There's no telling what MacGregor would say. The man's not prepared to pay you, doesn't even know you exist. As far as he's concerned, you're just another hired hand whose work is finished. Why not head down to Denver, Billy? There's plenty of chance for an ambitious fella like yourself."

The young Scot followed him about, testing pieces of leather for soundness, rubbing the rust off old bits.

"I can work wi' me' hands," he argued. "I can rig ropes an' mend a harness. If it matters, I can tell when a horse is sick or when a storm's about tae blow. More important, I've got nae place tae turn, sir. It's th' land an' th' animals I want. I know cattle. An' where they go, so do I."

Here he stopped, blocking the foreman's way. "And then,

o' course, there's the offer this morning from the widow, Mrs. McKennon."

"What offer?"

"She's outright asked me tae look after that wild mare o' hers." Billy rubbed his chin with his hand. "Seems like somebody has tae."

Stewart paused and proceeded to roll a cigarette, curling the fine paper around the tobacco and placing it between his lips. Cupping both hands to strike a flame, he leaned against the wall with one knee bent. "And just what precisely would she have you do with that horse?" he queried as he inhaled the first puff.

"Git it tae where she's goin'. The way I figure, I can pony th' mare along side my gelding, if she'll mind. That much I'm sure o'. I'll take my chances on th' rest . . . if ye'll only let me come."

Shaking his head, Stewart eyed the determined young man. "I still don't know. It's not my authority. Oh, all right, then. Hell, Billy—you and MacGregor, you're two of a kind. Scottish and stubborn as the day is long. You can fight it out with him. Pack your things and throw 'em in the wagon. We'll be leavin' in a day or two, soon as we can get things in order." Slapping a dusty saddle blanket against his knee, he watched as a scrabble of spiders scurried out of it and disappeared into a crack along the wall.

"Packed up and ready?" Merrill asked. Billy paused from grooming his horse which was tied next to a wagonload of supplies.

"Yes, sir. Loaded th' grain, th' grub, an th' beddin'. What else can I do fer ye?"

Merrill looked into the wagons and nodded. "Looks good."

"I've locked up th' bunkhouse an' checked th' barns," Billy continued. "Propped up th' rafters as well, against th' heavy snows when they come. I sure will miss 'er, won't ye, sir?"

Billy referred to the ranch, a place he'd grown more attached to than any place he'd ever known. He surveyed the rambling complex with its low-roofed bunkhouses, horse and calving barns, and two-story stone house. After so many years at sea, this landlocked stronghold had begun to feel like home. It hurt inside to leave.

"Check the harness for this wagon and continue to load whatever's left," Merrill directed. "I want everything ready to roll come morning. Hey now—what's this?"

Under a tarp, he discovered two of Maggie's valises. "I thought the woman was to send everything of hers by train," he grumbled, referring to the arrangements made for Mrs. McKennon's move to Rockrimmon. "There's way more in here than there ought to be. I don't need a wheel breaking on me. Distribute the weight more evenly and tie it all down if you have to."

Billy busied himself with the task. He packed his own gear and bedroll and checked his tack, adding an extra rope just in case. He planned to lead Bonniedoon beside his own calm and steady horse, depending on her behavior. The whole journey covered approximately one hundred and sixty miles from South Park to Cheyenne, with Denver the main stop along the way, an easy ride barring no complications.

The unexpected arrival of Kurt Skoll, leading his leggy buckskin mare, caught Billy and Merrill by surprise. The greenhorn stood out in his wide brimmed ten-gallon hat, chaps, and a fancy leather vest, sporting conchos and fringe. As usual, the pearl handle of a Smith & Wesson poked out of his belt.

"Hey there, Mr. Merrill. You the trail boss of this outfit?" Skoll came equipped for the trail, a bedroll and canteen slung behind his saddle. "Looks like I can't stay outta' your way. Orders say I need to see that ranch up in Cheyenne myself. Can't finish my report till I do. Sure thought I'd be done by now, but there's more to this business than meets the eye. Ye won't mind me tagging along now, will ye?"

The rank smell of alcohol told Merrill all he needed to know. Without turning from his horse, he snapped, "The hell I won't. I mind plenty. But you're on your own, Mr. Skoll. I don't understand the nature of your business, but if you need to get to Wyoming, the trail's open. You're free to get there anyway you want. You don't need my escort."

"Now that doesn't sound cordial to me. No, sir. I thought we were friends. Thought ye'd appreciate the company."

Skoll had no idea how to get to Wyoming but had been told he wouldn't be paid until he investigated Rockrimmon the same way he'd checked out the Cameron. Charles and

Arlen were more determined than ever to make sure that neither MacGregor nor McKennon were hiding anything.

"That settles it, trailboss—I'll just tag along for the ride." The Irishman mounted, kicked his horse in the ribs and circled behind the wagons, as though surveying the goods. "Don't tinker with me, Merrill," he warned, coming up behind Stewart. "I got no patience for arrogance. I go wherever I need to with anybody I choose. That includes you."

"Save it, will you?" Merrill retorted. "I'm not impressed. In case you missed it, I got a job to do."

Billy listened to the exchange, while continuing to check tack methodically. He wanted to confront the cocky Irishman and remind him that the West was where men treated each other as equals. Where respect was given until, by one's own reprehensible behavior, just as easily withdrawn.

Their eyes met briefly as Billy came around the back of his horse. Skoll glowered, squinting dully as a missile of spit landed at the tip of Billy's boots. The Irishman smiled.

"Not bad."

"You do what you come here for and stay out of my path Skoll," Merrill added. "And leave my men alone. We've got work to do and at least twenty miles to travel in a day on top of that. They all know the rules—there's to be no drinking on this ride and no trouble. That includes you."

Withholding a reply, Kurt's eyes focused on Maggie, approaching with a valise in her arms.

"Well, if isn't my favorite little lady . . ."

Maggie, clutching the bag to her chest, went to Merrill and took him by the arm. "Stewart, may I have a word with you?" She avoided Kurt's eyes by turning her back and pushing the foreman ahead of her.

"What is it?" Stewart looked concerned.

"That so-called 'cattle commissioner' is nothing but

trouble. He's not to be trusted. Dangerous might be more to the point. Why is he still around here?"

"I wish I knew," Merrill said. "Pay him no mind. Just be ready with Sarah to head out of here tomorrow right after breakfast. We're sending you and my family both on ahead. We'll get you to the depot in Como by ten. Your train should arrive in Denver by late afternoon and you should find your lodgings easily, nearby the station. I trust a few days ought to cover it. Mind you, you're scheduled to be on Friday's Union Pacific noon departure, bringing you into Cheyenne by supper." He patted her arm. "Until tomorrow, try to stay out of Skoll's way."

"I just hope he'll stay out of mine," Maggie snapped, retreating quickly to the house. Looking back as she stepped inside, she saw Skoll watching her and wondered what his connection to Western Land and Cattle really might be.

Maggie climbed the stairs to her room and stood at the window, where earlier she'd watched Billy. As she looked down at the nearly empty corrals and across the wide fields, deep feelings of resolve rose within her. She had slowly acquired a new sense of self-preservation, as if Kerr's death had been for one reason and one only, to force her into the awareness that she herself would have to take charge. Without knowing how or when it had happened, she understood that Kerr's dream had not only become her dream, but also her destiny, the definition of her own life as it stretched out before her.

Would she have strength enough to see it through on her own? And once in Wyoming, would Hugh MacGregor be able to unravel the troubles of Western Land and Cattle and the Cameron, or would he only add to them. Perhaps, he might even be at the very core of them all.

Heading downstairs for one last walk around the ranch,

Maggie discovered Sarah packing. "Let me know if you'd like a hand with anything or need me to watch the girls. Just call, I'll be nearby, outside."

"Thanks, I will." Sarah nodded, not looking up from sorting the children's clothes.

Normal activity at the Cameron had ceased. A herd of three hundred cows grazed, all that was left of the Highlands. Around her, nearly empty buildings lay quiet in the afternoon sun and even the ranch dogs were stretched out motionless on the ground, sound asleep, twitching silently.

Still overwhelmed by the rash of decisions made between Farrell and herself at their four o'clock meeting, Maggie couldn't settle her thoughts. The picture had changed dramatically. He'd been fair, though duplicitous, and she knew it. Whatever she had to work with would now be in the cards he dealt for her. They were in the resolution together.

After supper, she decided to walk down to the barn to bid farewell to Calamity whom she had decided to leave behind for the moment, until she knew whether or not she'd be coming back. In a stall stood the old brood cow and little August, already a strapping heifer. Frisky and playful, the calf had grown strong, her shaggy coat grown dense for winter, small horns protruding like bullets on either side of her blunt head, blind eyes showing no fear. The calf moved to the stall rails as Maggie approached.

"I'm going to miss you, my little Auggie." She reached through and stroked its fuzzy topknot. The young Highland had developed a new air of fierceness about her and mooed plaintively at the sound of Maggie's voice. The old cow turned a wide eye, swishing her brushy tail.

"An' I'm sure she'll miss ye too." Billy's voice cut in unexpectedly, as he appeared beside Maggie.

"Do you really think so?" Maggie answered brightly,

smiling in surprise. She moved over so that he could stand next to her, within an arm's reach of the heifer.

"Do you think a beast can become attached as we do?" Maggie turned to him.

"I'll tell ye this, Mrs. McKennon," he said, placing his elbows on the top rail and grinning as he spoke. "It wouldna' be unusual. Where I come from th' drovers know all their animals by name. An' e'en th' Saint's day upon which they were born. They say a cow that trusts gi'es more milk, an' if ye respect her, she has no reason na' tae like ye back. Truth is, in Scotlan', they warn ye na' tae get too attached. The wee ones grow up an' when they do, they can knock a man down just by lovin' him. Say, are ye leavin' these two Highlands behind?"

Maggie sighed. "Unfortunately, yes. I've asked Silva to feed and look after them, as well as my little mustang, until I return. Protecting them is important, as if they were my first teachers, given to me to learn about the land. A strange attachment and a stranger meaning. Odd I suppose, but these two have come to symbolize the entire ranch to me."

Billy understood just what she said, so well that it hurt to think of it. In his world, it was possible for any animal to be a gateway to the human soul. He remembered old Moll, the horse that had been a repository of childhood love, the only living creature he knew capable of receiving and honoring affection.

No, her attachment did not seem strange. Her confession moved him and he wanted to tell her so. But instead, he stood speechless. Pigeons, cooing softly, hopped about the rafters, showering straw bits and dust upon their shoulders. No other sound but the cows munching on hay and straw beetles rustling tunnels.

"Would ye believe, Mrs. McKennon," he said at last, turning to face her, "that this ranch has come tae mean th' entire world tae me?" He sought her gaze for an encouraging level of trust, wanting to tell her how much he loved the Cameron and the inviting look in her eyes. He moved closer, his shoulder briefly touching hers.

"The Cameron is th' very first place where I found I could be m'self. That is tae say, th' man I thought I'd be when I decided tae leave Scotland. A place where I could work th' land an' even own a piece of it."

Maggie nodded, encouraging him to go on.

"I've come tae know everra' square mile o' this ranch, an' the strange part is, it feels like I always ha'e."

Maggie tilted her head as she listened, lost in the melody of his voice.

"In Scotlan'," he went on, "they tell tales about what we call th' 'second sight.' The old ones think it's a trick o' th' sprites, but I think 'tis just a way of knowin' a thin' a'fore ye really can. I come all this way west an' findin' th' Cameron was like returnin' tae somewhere I'd already been."

Maggie smiled, encouraging him to continue.

"Right from th' start there were places I swore I'd seen a'fore. I felt then as I do now, that I belong here. D'ye ken what I mean?"

Maggie, touched by the rush of words that tumbled into the quiet afternoon, nodded in acceptance. Strange as it seemed, he spoke for her, mirroring her own thoughts exactly. Thoughts about her own soul's deep longing for a heartfelt sense of place.

"Of course, Billy," she said. "Of course I do."

"Sometimes," he continued, "when I'm alone, deep in th' woods or out on th' open plain, I feel like I know everra'thin' there is tae know . . . that th' good Lord meant fer us tae know. Then it seems like there's nothin' in th' world I canna' do. Just like that, everra'thin's possible. There's a kind o' magic, there is, Mrs. McKennon, an' I can feel that too." He stopped, embarrassed by his confession, but spurred by it as well. "Ye'll forgi'e me fer askin', but would it be proper tae call ye Maggie?"

"Of course it would, Billy. That would be fine." She blushed.

In the silence between them, she could feel his shy tension slipping away, like the imperceptible shifting of ancient rifts beneath the earth. Maggie thought she could feel him moving towards her but he merely leaned forward against the stall, staring out the window at the blue hills rising in the distance.

"I've been lookin' aroun' South Park," he continued, "an' when this ranch goes t'auction like I've heard it will, I intend tae buy a piece o' it an' return tae settle down. A couple hundred acres on th' south if I'm lucky. Another couple o' years on th' payroll an' I'll be able tae make a down payment, anyways. Bein' here is as close tae heaven as I ha'e e'er come. I canna' let it go."

"Then we have something very special in common, Billy Munro," Maggie answered. Her eyes met his and stayed. "It may sound odd, but it appears that the Cameron has taken us in as strangers, and now, seems to be holding us both."

Maggie steadied herself. She hadn't expected to give voice to such feelings. Standing in silence, her thoughts hovered between them for an intangible sliver of time.

Billy gripped the gate rails with both hands as he continued. "If 'tis true, then we are both th' luckier for it. 'Tis fine an' pleasin' fer me tae think that we both belong here, tae this exact place." He smiled and took a deep breath.

Maggie had never spoken as openly to a man and felt buoyed by the exchange. "So, you plan to buy two hundred acres? Why so few? You can't run cattle on so little land."

"Who said anythin' about cattle? 'Tis horses I want. Only

the finest an' the best. A few hundred acres should do, more'n plenty."

"I've just learned that a part of all of this is legally mine," Maggie volunteered. "I don't know exactly which yet, and I still don't know precisely how. But after today, I know for certain that I am a part of this ranch as surely as Kerr is buried on the hill above the creek, as solidly as the house itself. And I am going to fight to preserve what is mine. It's something I know I must do."

She believed the sound of her own voice, sure and determined. "It's just that clear at last. I don't have a life except that of my own making. And, if I am truly a partner to this property, which the law says I am, then I shall have a say in what's to be sold or divided, should that ever come to pass."

"And will ye speak fer yerself when th' time comes?"

"Time will tell. But if I succeed, and you'd like me to consider a part of it for you, for lease or purchase, then I should be happy to do so. Should I fail and the ranch be sold, then I might have to ask you to do a favor for me if you can. I leave behind these few creatures I care about. Should they survive the uncertainty ahead, I'd ask that you look after them for me."

Standing next to one so hopeful, Maggie found it easy to believe in success. Beside Billy she felt calm, confident, and as though everything at risk would turn out all right. Yet, the reality of leaving South Park felt final and terribly sad. At the thought of the upcoming departure and the uncertainty of her future, a mist welled up in Maggie's eyes.

"What's this, now?" Billy brushed away a tear from her cheek. "Ye canna' feel defeated, lass. The world's na' what it seems. Ye're na' alone." Here, he paused, choked by the doubt that stopped him from saying what was on his mind.

"I'm right here wi' ye, aren't I?" he asked, finding a measure of courage. "An' I've been here—all along. Always a'watchin' fer ye whene'er I could. I know this. Ye canna' know how th' story ends when th' story's barely begun. Please, Miss Maggie . . . let me go on bein' part o' what ye need."

Billy's words washed over Maggie like a warm wind. How could he know what she needed? And yet, she was sure he did. As she stood next to him, his arm barely brushing hers, the urge to touch him overpowered her. Instead, she reached up and pushed her wide brimmed hat off her head, allowing it to fall backwards on her shoulders where it hung by its braided strings. Billy studied it, relieved by the diversion. "What's this?" he asked, running his fingers over the feathered quill in its band.

"Just a souvenir from a friend. A great owl that came to live at the cabin by the creek. Still there, I suppose. A remarkable bird recovering from a bit of bad luck. I helped him, and he stayed on."

"Is there no one ye hav'na' helped, Miss Maggie?" he smiled, turning toward her. "No one creature ye'd turn away?" Billy held his left hand briefly to her cheek, the heat of his touch coursing through her. He knew he risked everything by being too forward, the laird McKennon not yet two weeks in his grave. But they were alone, a chance that might not come again. There was no time to lose, his world was so quickly changing. He pressed on. "Tell me now," he asked, desire driving him to his wildest dreams and all propriety cast aside, "is there a chance there might yet be a hope fer me?"

The inquisitive calf greedily nuzzled Maggie's knee, searching, as always, for a treat. Incredulous at Billy's boldness, Maggie remained silent and reached down to pet the animal instead. Finding Billy's hand immediately next to hers, she dared hold it briefly. "I can only hope to return,

Billy Munro," she said, turning her face toward him. "At the moment, that's all I know."

Billy could hold back no longer and pulled Maggie to him as he wrapped his arms around her waist. She resisted momentarily, stunned that he would take her so, ready to voice her protest and then, held her tongue. Instead, she returned his embrace and slid into his arms, his face next to hers, spirals of his thick hair carrying the scent of sun-ripened fields, horses, and the sweetest timothy hay. Minutes passed, their gentle hug closing the final gap between them. Maggie didn't want to move, unable to get her fill.

"God help me, Maggie McKennon, I want ye," Billy whispered. "All o' ye, an' the world I ha'e found ye in. Please say ye won't refuse me; fer I canna' let ye go."

Maggie responded to his endearment by leaning into his arms, pressing herself against him as a climber hugs a rock in the wind, seeking its hard warmth and stability, steady, and eternally strong. As she did, she rose up on the toes of her boots, placing both arms around his neck, burying her face in his hair, her own dark mane entangling with his. The setting sun slanted in through the rafters, sparkling motes of diamond dust, filling the barn with light.

Maggie held on to Billy as if she'd found life itself. She even dared think of having him entirely, there, that afternoon. In a strange, mystical way she wanted to become a part of him, in some brand new form. To both have him and love him and reclaim all that had been sought before. To recapture the dream of a perfect love, still innocent and whole. With Billy, she dared to explore that intangible wilderness she knew dwelled inside each of them, a realm free of boundaries and a spiritual wandering that might never end. Something incontestable told her that by loving this man of the bagpipes, the land, and the horse, she might finally know the meaning of home.

Drunk with the heady rush of his embrace, she found her balance in his arms. She inhaled him like a newborn takes its first breath, savored the touch of his skin and at last, met his lips with hers as if they would never part. Maggie felt what she had always hoped to feel. Nothing less than free, alive, and on fire. Joyfully she received his devouring kiss, and as she did, sensed a splitting deep within, the final, long-awaited opening of her heart.

25

Darkness had fallen by the time Maggie realized it was time to return. She had awakened to Billy's wanting her, yet at the same time resisted, knowing this would be neither the time nor place to give herself completely. For now she was content to hear his dreams and know the feel of his beating heart.

Passionate as he was, he too restrained himself. He wanted all of her, but dared not offend. For each of them, it was too soon, and yet, not soon enough. Maggie knew that women in her situation were vulnerable, suspect to scandal. She had to be careful. And although she trusted Billy, the possibility still loomed that he could somehow betray her. She might have misjudged, been too unguarded in the wake of events, or succumbed to her own enormous need, painfully admitted at last, that what she longed for most was to love and to be loved.

"My goodness! It's so very late. I'm afraid Sarah and Stewart will be worried and looking for me," Maggie said. In the dark of the evening dusk, she was surprised that two hours had magically passed. Billy took her hand, leading her out through the gate of the pens and away from the cattle barns.

"Don't be alarmed," Billy answered as they walked towards the house. "They might care where ye've gone, but that's all. Ye're on yer own here, Maggie McKennon. An' ye seem strong enou' tae do whate'er ye like, tae run this whole ranch if ye had a mind tae." Billy hesitated only a moment. "Or e'en better, tae spend th' rest o' yer life wi' me."

Billy regretted his words, wishing he could retract what he'd just said. How dare he ask for her hand? He knew he had nothing to offer, but his thoughts found their way to her nonetheless. "Maggie, I can only ask ye tae wait, if ye will. Till I succeed. Till times change. I know they will. Try tae look into th' future, as I do."

"And how does that future look?" Maggie asked, smiling. His optimism seemed naive, yet she knew he was right about change. The whole world seemed to be in flux. "I do hope it's brighter than it seems to be now," she added.

"Aye, o' course 'tis. All th' signs are there. But there's something I've been wantin' ye tae know, so listen now, tae what I ha'e tae say." Maggie stared, curious.

He spoke in a low voice. "Yesterday, th' horse I was ridin' stopped dead still near th' knoll by th' creek, na' far from th' grave o' McKennon himself, an' wouldna' go another step. Horses see th' spirit world they do, an' I knew he was a'feart fer us both. We remained there, I couldna' say fer how long, th' beast scared stiff, his head up, hooves planted on th' ground. Then, a raven, black as night, lit on a branch abo'e us. An' a'fore I could blink, th' horse moved up again, as if that bird broke th' spell, scarin' th' spirit off.

"Then wi'out ne'er a signal from me, th' pony broke into a gallop an' carried me back aroun' th' base o' th' hill, past th' grave, th' long way, toward th' ranch. In a few minutes we were home, so fast we flew. The spell 'twas broken, I'm sure. That horse knew, an' so do I, that th' evil, whate'er 'twas, will be chased away from this place. Maggie, th' Cameron will be settled proper again. I know it, I can feel it, inside me—here." He reached for her hand and clasping it in his own, pressed it to his heart. She could feel the beating pulse beneath his chest and also, the cool flat face of the medallion he wore, smooth against her open palm.

"What's this?" she asked. Earlier, she had felt it when they embraced.

" 'Tis my saviour, Saint Michael. In Scotlan' a sailor asks fer his blessin' everra'time he sets a-sail, an' a horseman, everra'time he takes a mount. Michael watches 'em both, one man catchin' th' wind, th' other becomin' a part o' it. He saved me from a sailor's death na' too long ago. I consider him my compass an' my friend."

Maggie took his arm as they walked back to the house. "When will I see you again?"

"In a week or so. Not long." He reassured her gladly. "You'll be all settled by then an' once I arrive, well—we'll see."

Wyoming had become a battlefront for Maggie. She had a mission and until completed, knew she would have little time for thoughts of love. The most important thing ahead of her once she arrived would be the confrontation with MacGregor to establish what was hers.

"No matter what happens, we mustna' lose sight o' each other. That is, if ye'll consider me. As if I had a right tae ask . . ." Billy feared to go on. Maggie had not answered him. But he couldn't bear to let her go, wishing his words could keep her close.

Och, my fair Maggie, if ye'd only let me, I'd care fer ye, love ye, like nae man e'er did. A promise from ye now would be all I ask. Then, I'd prove m'self. Ye can't imagine how much I wish tae try.

Instead of speaking his heart, he merely hugged her close and said, "I need ye, Maggie McKennon. An' have for a long, long time." Daring discovery, he nonetheless picked her up and lifted her to the porch step, her arms around his neck, her head against his shoulder like a child.

"Put me down," she whispered, laughing. "Someone will see us." Obediently, he lowered her to the step and stood before her, his forehead touching hers.

"Nae, Wyoming's too far away. I canna' wait so long. Let me be wi' ye again, tomorra', what little there is o' it. Why don't I ride wi' ye an' Sarah tae th' train in th' mornin'? I'd like tae see ye off."

"I'd like that too," Maggie said, wishing he didn't have to leave. Now that she'd found him, it was a struggle to part. She longed to hold him again, feel his warmth against hers. Shocked by the intensity of her own desire, she felt allied at last, supported, and sharpened with the wanting of him.

"In the morning, then," she agreed. "I'll be looking for you."

They said goodnight, standing a respectful distance apart. Maggie murmured, "Sleep well."

Then, in spite of what might happen if anyone should see them, Billy stole another, final kiss, encouraged by the umbrella of bright stars and the gleaming, opulent moon. And Maggie did not protest.

The ranch house stood quiet in the clear night. Stewart, Sarah and the children had retired to bed. In the long bunk house near the corrals, Billy and the few remaining crew members slept. Maggie lingered on the front porch, unable to let go of the tumultuous day, the brilliant night, and Billy—no longer just a presence, but an emotion, insistent and real.

Out of the darkness, a familiar figure approached, then stopped. Silva, on his usual evening patrol, stood before Maggie. The tip of his cigarette glowed in the dark and he inhaled slowly before speaking. *"Buenas noches, Señora. Esta tarde. It is late."*

"Buenas noches, Señor. Si, verdad."

Maggie answered in Spanish, knowing how much he liked

the fact that she'd learned a few words from him over the summer while working together. She wondered if he'd seen her walking out of the barn with Billy, then, felt foolish, believing it wouldn't matter.

The temperature had dropped considerably, a cool night for early fall. Maggie found a blanket hanging by the door, and pulled up a stool. Looking out into the dark valley, she noticed an alabaster tinge of moonglow lighting up the sky. Nearly full, the globe beamed wistfully this night, luminous and benevolent as a pearl.

"You have been a very special friend, Silva. No—more like a father to me. Ever since my very first weeks here," Maggie began. "You have taught me much. I owe you a great deal and will miss you. We'll all be together again soon. I believe that—I must."

Silva nodded, glumly.

"You seem sad. Is something wrong?"

The old cowboy, carefully forming his thoughts, said, "*Cuidado.* Be careful. I have heard strange talk. There are those among us, even your family, who would hurt you, take from you what is yours." He shook his head solemnly, his wrinkled brow furrowed.

"You worry too much," Maggie responded, wondering, in fact, just what he meant. She touched his arm in gratitude for his concern.

She hoped her reassurances would prompt his, that he'd flash his old smile and she would see a resemblance to the same light-hearted *vaquero* that she knew. "I am hopeful that the ranch won't sell at all," Maggie began, "or the bank will start up production again. Or maybe I'll come back and surprise you as your new *patron.* What would you think of that, Silva? Wouldn't Kerr be proud if I did that for him?"

"*Señora,*" Silva turned to her. "Do not speak of my *patron.*

My heart weeps for one who was so honest. *Señor* McKennon. He meant well, to make strong the land. Now, we must all suffer."

"Whatever do you mean?" Maggie interrupted, confused by his strange lament.

"*Señora* Maggie, we have been friends, *si?* We care for each other. It is time I told you what I know, what no one else knows, except maybe someone on this ranch. For now, this secret is between us only, *si?* I want to tell you, but if necessary, you will forget how you learn this."

"What is it, Silva?"

"The grave on the hill, *Señora*, it is empty. *Señor* McKennon is dead, but his body is not there."

"What? You can't be serious!"

"*Seguro.* He may be dead, somewhere, but to me, his death was no accident. *Comprende?* He go away but no come back. The body, only blankets. That horse, I think she knows the truth. She may be *loco* but she no killer. No, *querida*, he was taken by someone, somewhere, and we may never know why."

"*Por que*, Silva? Why would anyone want to hurt him?"

"*Quien sabe?* I can only tell what I saw. *Es verdad!* And now, McKennon's soul, *su alma*, it is lost. *Perdido, si?* Without a home. It wanders *muy triste*, looking for him, each night, of this I am sure. And this is a sin for the dead, *Señora*, this is the worst kind of sin."

"What about the corpse I saw wrapped for burial?"

"Like I say, *no existe*. Blankets. Many blankets."

"The service, the prayers?"

"The padre, I believe he did not know, he is innocent. You must be careful, Maggie. Do not be like McKennon. Do not be blind. Times are bad, but I believe you are protected. You are blessed by the *Madre*, by the Virgin herself. This I also feel. This I know."

Maggie was stunned, a thousand fractured thoughts cratering into a dark abyss. Silva had no reason to lie. Based on what he had just told her, she struggled to understand who could be behind this treachery. How did Kerr die? And where was his body? Stewart Merrill must have known there was no body. Why hadn't he told her? Was Stewart involved in Kerr's death?

"Thank you, Silva. For telling me that which must have been very difficult for you and caused you great pain." She felt numb, then nauseous, the sensation of bile rising in the pit of her stomach like a hideous force. She touched his arm and shook her head. "Dear Silva, now I see behind the sadness. Now I understand." Even as she spoke, his eyes showed bewilderment, as well as anger and pain. "I will share your burden," Maggie told him. "And this will stay between us for now. I will do what must be done, though I'm not sure exactly how or when."

"*Señora,* what shall I do?"

"Nothing. We will speak again when we can. I promise I will keep you informed." Maggie smiled, patting his hand. Her show of confidence was the smallest lie, necessary to ease the other's sadness, as well as her own.

"*Si, Señora* McKennon."

"Goodnight, dear Silva." Her voice already sounded far away. "I need to think."

Midnight hid all in empty blackness. The moon had disappeared behind heavy thick clouds and now, not even the stars could return the magic Maggie had felt just a few hours before. She sat on the porch where Silva had left her, trying to remember every conversation she'd heard since she arrived at the ranch, every move of every man, of every drover and every hand. Who could have benefitted from Kerr's death? If it was intentional, she hoped it was a bullet that took him, not a hangman's noose, or worse . . .

The slow chill of dread spread through her. Too tense to sleep, she sat shivering in the dark, waiting for what, she did not know. Silva had retired to the bunkhouse with the others. She wished Billy would join her now, still craving his warmth and tenderness. Perhaps he too, was awake, lying in his bunk, wanting her.

Snap!

An unfamiliar sound erupted in the dark. A shiver rippled up Maggie's spine. She heard the sound again, this time more like feet on rough stones. Rising out of the chair, she heard the scraping for a third time. The raw abrasion of a boot heel against a rock? Or the cracking of a twig in the bushes near the porch? The noise came from somewhere to the left of the entry, where thick branches obscured the view. Maggie tensed with fear.

Could it be Kurt Skoll! It would be like him, to attack a woman in the dark. She prepared to make a dash for the door and glanced around for something to protect herself. As she did, she hoped it might yet be Billy, coming back to join her, walking across the dry leaves and debris scattered everywhere. *Please, let it be Billy.*

One minute she had been paralyzed with dread, the next filled with the deepest longing. She could neither move nor breathe. She froze, voiceless in her fear. Then, determined to face Skoll, she seized a branding iron leaning against the wall and steeled herself for his attack. Brandishing the tool in both hands before her, she waited.

The intermittent sounds had been replaced by labored breaths. Maggie gripped the iron like a sword and stood her ground. Out of the murky shadows came the timorous calf, its head cocked slightly. Hesitant but inquisitive, the heifer approached and placed two cloven forehooves on the lower step. Its flat pink nose poked forward, sniffing the night air for a scent. The little Highland had finally found what it sought.

Clattering up the steps, the heifer scrambled onto the porch, emitting a deep muffled greeting as it located Maggie. The excited beast pushed a shaggy shoulder forward like an oversize dog, waiting to be scratched, rubbed, and hugged.

"Oh, my God," Maggie gasped, "Auggie, it's you! It's only you!" She put down the iron and embraced the animal with both arms. Sinking to her knees she clung to its thick coat.

"Thank you for finding me, little one. Thank you for coming. But how in the world did you get out?" The magic of the rendezvous with Billy in the barn and the unlatched door were temporarily forgotten. She laughed, then cried with relief.

She petted the calf and rubbed her ears, then the hard spot between her horns. Relieved yet troubled, she huddled against the contented animal standing quietly by her side. There in the forbidding darkness, Maggie meditated on the strange turn of events. She resolved for the sake of the Cameron, and herself, that she would find out who killed Kerr McKennon. And one way or another, she would also find peace for her missing husband, knowing that until she did, it would certainly elude her as well.

Holding her beloved Highland, she buried her fingers in its forelock. This was not the parting she had imagined. Later, on her way to Wyoming, she would recall this night of sweetest pleasure laced with the sharpest pain. For a long time, the last thing she would remember was the vibrant heat of Billy's kiss and the veil of a cloud fading against a cold, October dawn.

An exhausted Maggie climbed aboard the wagon the next morning and sat next to Sarah's sleepy daughters. The four of them would take the train out of Como and switch in Denver for the northbound to Cheyenne. Soon the Cameron would be nothing but a memory for Sarah Merrill and a source of on-going pain for Maggie. In the light of day and the departure, the hideous travesty of Kerr's funeral seemed more haunting.

Billy followed the wagon to Como and bid Maggie farewell as they approached the depot. Reaching for her hand, he took it briefly in his own. "Ha'e a safe journey, Mrs. McKennon," he whispered. "I'll be waitin' fer ye."

Sarah nodded mischieviously and smiled as Billy rode away. "Well now, like I said before," admonished Sarah, "that man's sweet on you."

Maggie blushed at her audacity. "Nonsense. But he's a great help. I've asked him to take McKennon's mare along with the drover's horses. I don't want to leave her here. Nothing wrong with that, is there?"

"Not at all," the other woman replied merrily. "You do what you like. But people notice, they talk. I'd just be careful if I were you, that's all." Maggie let the comment pass, hoping her own indifference would discourage any further remarks.

The mountains surrounding South Park seemed unusually vivid in the morning light, making it twice as hard to say goodbye. Looking from the train window while waiting to depart, Maggie took a long look at their majestic grandeur. She knew she would never forget them. "The Guardians of Paradise," Kerr had once called them. She would remember their significance no matter what Wyoming had to offer.

Early that same day, Billy, Stewart, Kurt and the rest of the crew headed out of South Park on horseback, due north, over the gentle pass that would bring them to the canyon winding toward Denver. The loaded supply wagons led the way followed by punchers, several who rode a cowhorse and ponied a second.

Skoll took a lead position next to Merrill as though officially in charge. He grumbled and cursed the horse he rode, the thick dry dust, and the chill of the overcast skies. Stewart regretted that he had not insisted the man travel alone, but he didn't have a choice. He didn't want to antagonize him. The first day out the party moved briskly, stopping to rest in Pawnee for water and then again in Bailey at the ranch Glen Isle.

The next evening brought them all the way to Pine where a hostler had agreed to corral and feed the horses, as well as put the travelers up for the night. By sunrise next morning they were off again, well ahead of schedule. Nearing Denver on the fourth day about mid-afternoon, Stewart put the driver of the supply wagon in charge.

"I'll be needing to take care of some business while we're in town," he said matter-of-factly. "Bring the boys on in and tie up near the railway. Then water the stock and head for the tavern on Osage. We'll feed the crew on the best steak and potatoes in town before we move north to make camp. That ought to make these boys happy. But it also means we have no time to waste."

Stewart stopped at the Cattleman's Exchange for the latest copy of *The Roundup*. Quickly scanning the front page, he could see the news looked bad. From the east coast to the west, the cattle barons had become the butt of cruel jokes as disillusioned investors looked for safer ventures. The cattle boom had become "the cattle bust," just like gold and silver before it.

The crew headed over to Zeitz's, fondly known as the Buckhorn, a popular bar and restaurant at the edge of town frequented by a diverse clientele. From roundup riders to bank presidents, the patrons of the busy watering hole came and went, exchanging stories and feasting on the heartiest fare west of the Mississippi.

"Ye wouldna' see this where I come from," Billy marveled to the wagon master, gawking at the smoky gathering. He listened carefully to bits of ranch talk coming from cowboys in dusty boots as well as businessmen in fancy suits. "In th' pubs o' Glasgow, common men an' gentry dinna' mix, much less share a table," Billy whispered to one of the boys. "Here, a belly up tae th' bar is served th' same no matter who ye be." Tempted by the smell of scrapple and fresh sourdough biscuits, Billy pulled up a bench and poured another glass of beer. All was well. At least, as well as it could be. America promised a blessing greater than he could have ever imagined. One day, with luck, he just knew he'd own land himself and have the finest woman he knew at his side—Maggie McKennon, a dream to drive him to greatness.

Thick cut steaks sizzling in a pan reminded him of the task at hand. Without hesitation, he attacked the first round with gusto, feeling more confident and satisfied than ever before. When Stewart Merrill arrived, Billy slid over to make room for him to join them.

"Looks like we have a little trouble, boys. The latest news

from MacGregor says First Bank of Philadelphia thinks we're moving stolen property. He says they believe this little caravan is part of their inventory, and they're demanding repossession. They might be tailing us or sending a sheriff out. Hogwash. According to my recollection, we didn't see no inventory when we left, now did we?"

No one disagreed.

"Any questions from anybody, let 'em take it up with MacGregor when the time comes. I'm just doing my job. He can decide what's his and what isn't. Anybody approaches who looks too curious, you point them in my direction with a warning—I ain't in the mood for interference."

That night, while making camp near Fort Vasquez along the Platte River, the horses spooked when a long train huffed past them in the dark. Two huge locomotives spewed out hot smoke and ash and the shrill scream of the whistle brought the exhausted cowboys to their feet. The tethered animals broke the line in a panic, but none could get far in hobbles. Within minutes, the drovers herded them back into a makeshift corral but hours passed before the horses settled down again. The worst among them was Bonniedoon, the dark mare stamping and snorting at everything and nothing, ready to bolt at the first chance.

"Why don't ye just shoot the damn thing?" Skoll hissed. "She's nothin' but trouble. I got me a dog wouldn't eat that horse if he was starvin' to death. I never seen such a sorry nag."

"Shut yer mouth," Billy retorted, resisting the urge to swing at him. "She's my responsibility an' nobody touches her. She's just nervous, that's all."

"She's not fit for carrion. Nag like that's a poor excuse for a cowhorse if ye ask me," Kurt continued. "Tell ye what, I'll do ye a favor and shoot her when the next train comes by.

When it blows its whistle I'll just put a bullet in her brain, if she's got one. That way the other horses won't hear. I'll make it easy for ye, boy."

Merrill snapped a leather rein so hard against his chaps it sounded like a bullwhip. Kurt jerked to attention, grinning, and took a swig of liquor as he straightened his long legs and laid back toward the campfire.

"That's enough," Stewart snarled. Kurt put down the pocket flask, eyeing the other man carefully.

"Whatever ye say, Mr. Merrill. It's yer party," Kurt replied. Billy untied Bonniedoon to walk her, talking to her in a soft voice. Behind him Billy could hear Stewart begin again.

"Did you forget you're supposed to mind your own business, Skoll? I want you to leave the boy alone. He's got enough of a job to do without you interfering."

The dark night grew uncomfortably cold as Billy walked the mare to calm her. He seethed at Skoll, kicking stones out of his path around the camp. The mare followed, blowing clouds of steam at Billy's back. He couldn't stop thinking about Maggie. Perhaps she'd been on that very train and would be waiting for him soon in Wyoming. He longed to see her. This was America, after all, where almost nothing seemed impossible. He continued to circle the horse in a wide track, but not too far from the rising voices of Stewart and Kurt as they continued to argue.

"Come on now, ye know the horse is nuts, Merrill. Look at her out there. She'll take this bunch with her when she goes. Anyhow, I was just teasin' the boy. Hell, I don't give two bits about that nag."

The rest of the men dozed off, bundled heavily in winter coats and blankets or bedrolls. Stewart studied the night sky, hoping the weather would hold for at least a few more days. Then he lit a smoke, anxiously awaiting daybreak.

★ ★ ★ ★ ★

Blowing a shrill long whistle, the northbound Santa Fe came by at dawn hauling coal, livestock, and passengers. This time the horses trembled and whinnied but didn't try to run. They and the wild creatures on the plains would have to learn to tolerate the great rumbling trains that now traversed the West in every direction.

"Only the rich travel by rail," Kurt complained as usual. "Don't seem fair. The rest of us poor bastards have to ride or walk. Isn't that just like MacGregor to bring the ladies in style? I bet that the widow McKennon and Merrill's wife can ride horses as well as any of us. And they'd a fit in these wagons fine too if they wanted to. But, nah, the ladies got to go up by railroad, fast and fancy."

He paused to check Stewart's expression, hoping he'd gotten a bite. No man alive had a right to feel superior to him, especially some cowboy. He remembered for just a moment the hostile brush-off he'd received from Kerr McKennon when he'd cornered him back in South Park. All he had wanted was a few minutes of Kerr's time to get the facts that morning before the cattle drive. Sonofabitch fairly threw him off the place, he got so hot under the collar. That didn't sit well with Kurt Skoll. Those transplanted westerners and big-shot cattlemen were all arrogant bastards. No one yet had given him the attention he deserved.

"Seems to me, we should'a all been on that train. It's too damn cold for sight-seein' this time a'year. Or maybe MacGregor jest wanted it that way, hey, Stewart? Too cheap to ship the goods. But not them pretty little ladies . . . Mrs. McKennon and your Sarah. Maybe he had special plans for the evening, wouldn't ye know? Wanted 'em all to himself, jest for a bit. . . ."

Billy, who overheard the remark, bristled, but remem-

bered Stewart's warning. As much as the insulting insinua-
tion riled him, he couldn't protect a woman's honor without
starting a row. The other drovers smirked at the ugly comment and smiles flashed between them.

Rolling a cigarette, Billy looked up just in time to see
Stewart's long-barreled Colt slide out of the holster. Merrill
spurred his big gelding over to Kurt's left side, pointing the
muzzle of the cocked revolver straight at the man's face.
"That's the last time you ever mention my wife's name, now
or ever, do you hear?" Stewart growled. "You're nothing but
scum. I've suspected you of no good ever since you arrived
but you couldn't stay outta' my way. No, you just keep
coming back, like boils and bad news. Well, I've had all I'm
gonna take of you, that's for damn sure."

Kurt grimaced, his head shrunk back into his jacket like a
snake retreating into its hole, his right hand seeking the butt of
his gun. "Take it easy, Stewart. I was just havin' some fun."

"Better not give me one more reason to shut you up. Another insult like that is all I need, do I make myself clear?"

With a dozen faces fixed on the two of them, Stewart
spoke quietly. "Boys, this is it. Looks like we got ourselves a
little problem. My friend here is gonna' ride ahead of me nice
and quiet and keep his mouth shut until we get where we're
going. One false move and we never knew him, understand?
Now pick up the pace and get these nags moving. I aim to hit
Cheyenne by Friday or else." Stewart shot a cold look at Skoll
who now found himself ahead of the foreman with a forty-five
pointed at his back.

The entrance to Rockrimmon lay only six miles over
grassy rolling terrain from the outskirts of Cheyenne. The
headquarters spanned over twenty acres square, including a
web of narrow loading chutes near the rail line, the smooth-

poled corrals, calving stalls, red-roofed horse barns, tackrooms, a smokehouse, and a tall grain silo.

Set back on the bluff away from the cattle pens stood the stone house, rising like a mystic mirage off the prairie. The interior had just recently been upgraded with the latest amenities including running water and electricity, as well as a fire hose that connected each floor straight to the well. Not a rancher in all of Wyoming could compete with such extensive arrangements.

Statistics detailing MacGregor's wealth fueled stories the cowboys loved to trade, each more outrageous than the next. The closer they got to Rockrimmon, the taller the tales grew about his infamous lifestyle and friends. Still, only a few cowpokes could brag about working for Western Land and Cattle. Among them an unspoken air of pride showed their pleasure in having been chosen to stay on.

Their curiosity rose as the miles passed, each rider now laying bets on the size and abundance of MacGregor's holdings. They didn't have to wait long. The jokes and speculation ended when Merrill's hand signaled they had arrived. Before them lay the impressive entry marked by the MacGregor brand, the outline of a thistle over MacGregor's own initials, fashioned out of iron and bolted to a stone arch that rose over a fieldstone gate. The compound beyond fanned out far into the distance, its scattered rooftops and fence rails radiating in all directions around the ranch house itself.

"I want the wagons up first," Stewart shouted. "Take the supplies and food down to the cook shack, the rest into storage. Unload in an orderly fashion. Move the horses to the west of the barns, in the corrals where you'll find the working stock. But don't let them loose yet. Put them in the smaller pens by themselves. They need re-branding and time to settle down. Then, I'll meet you boys at the bunkhouse once you've cleaned up 'proper.' You're on MacGregor's payroll now, and like you've all heard, everyone cleans up for dinner." Raucous laughter rippled through the bunch.

"Well, I guess I'll be seeing ye," Kurt interrupted, spurring his horse full circle. "It's been a nice ride, gentl'men. Would'nt'a missed it for the world." Wheeling out from under Stewart's guard, Kurt now faced the group, meeting Stewart's steely gaze head on.

"Might as well bid ye cowboys goodbye. But before I do, I'd like to turn over to MacGregor what's rightly his, personal-like. Part of my job, ye see, to deliver McKennon's mare. Ought to bring him a pretty penny somewheres. Yes sir, I plan to present that skinny nag myself. Hand her over, Billy boy." Before anyone could move, he grabbed the mare's leadrope and Bonniedoon shied and reared straight up, the end of the lead rope slipping out of Skoll's hand.

Billy lunged for the mare as she spun away. At the same instant, his right hand went for his pistol, a Colt Peacemaker. Stewart, still holding his gun, pulled the trigger with the revolver pointing straight up, sending a warning shot into the air. Risking a stampede, he nonetheless intended to frighten Skoll or at least divert his attention. Pandemonium broke loose as horses bolted and wagon mules reared. Thinking that the bullet was meant for him, Kurt pulled out his flashy Smith & Wesson and turned it on Stewart, now obscured by clouds of swirling dust. Aiming for the man's unprotected left side, he fired twice. One bullet hit the ground, but Stewart's left leg took the second, the lead finding its way deep into his thigh.

Rage exploding, Billy dove forward, throwing his body in front of Merrill. Too late, he realized the trail boss had already been hit. Reflexively, Billy opened fire, sending three bullets into Kurt's broad chest. As the Irishman's huge frame tumbled forward over his horse's neck, the big buckskin mare sidestepped and staggered. The wounded man hit the ground, then rolled onto his back in the dust, blood oozing from the dark stain spreading across the front of his shirt.

"Holy God, what ha'e I done?" Billy gasped in shock as he saw the body fall before him and cowboys scatter, the entire scene unfolding in slow motion movements of men and animals. Billy couldn't move, his eyes focused on Skoll, now silent, grotesque, sprawled before him on the ground.

"Stewart," he rasped, wrapping his arms around the wounded man who lay doubled over on his horse. "Skoll's dead! God help me. What am I going tae do?"

Stewart gritted his teeth over the searing heat in his leg. "He asked for it, the bastard. He deserved it. You're not to blame. MacGregor won't give a damn. If he does, I'll tell him it's not your fault. Tell him it was self defense."

Billy moved slowly toward his own mount, his right hand still holding his gun. His hands trembling, he slowly placed it back into the holster. Glancing around, he realized that Bonniedoon was nowhere to be seen. Only the stunned faces of the cowboys stared back as Billy moved toward the gray. The anguish over the loss of Maggie's horse added to his fear. The skittish mare had bolted and run away at the sound of the first shot.

"Nae, I willna' stay here an' be hanged. Who'd belie'e me? Skoll was one o' MacGregor's men. I wouldna' stand a chance in court! A pox on him!" He kicked the dust with his boot. "I canna' stay here now. I'll be run down like a dog!"

"Billy," Stewart said through his pain. "Calm down. Don't be a fool. We'll cover for you. Hey! Where are you goin'?"

His question faded in the pounding of hoofs as Billy

spurred the galloping horse back up the slope of the hill, heading for the top of the ridge. Within moments only his hat could be seen above the crest.

"Billy," Stewart moaned, clutching his wounded leg. "No one's going to hang you. Come back!"

Billy crouched low over his mount and squeezed hard, forcing the horse into a run. He hoped he remembered the way they'd come. With luck he would soon find the cover of trees, or better, a creek to follow. And if the mustang's speed and strength held, he'd be back in Colorado by nightfall.

Part Five

ROCKRIMMON

W.G.D.
© 2001

"What did ye say, Elizabeth?" MacGregor asked, turning toward his wife, pale and motionless against the back of the high mahogany bed. "Did ye call me?"

He was sure he hadn't imagined it, not this time. Staring across the rose patterned broadloom toward the bed, he studied her. "When?" he murmured sadly. "When will I e'er hear ye say my name aloud again? I thought I heard ye now. Speak tae me, Elizabeth . . ."

A porcelain doll had more expression than the wasted figure who stared past his face, past all cares, and past even the terrible awareness of her own isolation. The illness had gradually robbed her of her voice, her strength and her youth. Her condition, caused by a weak heart, worsened with the increase of fluid in her lungs, and even breathing had become more difficult. Her mobility hampered, depression had drawn her to her room where most days she lay quietly in her bed.

Hugh blamed himself for ignoring the early signs and now it was too late. Her health gone and their dream turned into a nightmare, Elizabeth's journey had become a slow march to a ghastly and inevitable end.

Dr. Jeb Taylor, a specialist out of Cheyenne, had seen no comparable case in his long career. "I tell you, Hugh, there's no prognosis I can offer. Her chances for recovery are slim. All we can do is keep her comfortable and free from further stress. Her blood pressure's low, color's weak. This kind of sickness sneaks up on you and then hunkers down and stays. Wish there was something more we could do . . ."

Doc went on sympathetically but MacGregor couldn't listen. His frustrated attempts to save his wife had thwarted his once amiable self. Powerless to restore her health, he cursed his lot, regretting ever having brought her to such a hard land. He struggled with his guilt, pushing it deep into a place he could not reach.

Furthermore, there was no one with whom to share his burden. At least, no one he would allow himself to approach. Even if he could speak of it, he lacked the words or means to express his fury and his loss. His anger came from his helplessness, his loss from feeling robbed. And so, he distanced himself from the source of sorrow, forcing himself to confront his wife only when necessary. He'd taken to sleeping in the next room and checking on her before he retired. Secretly he begrudged his impatience, the dry well of his self-pity, and the unbreakable chains that bound him.

"Mrs. Heiser, bring a pitcher of water, will you?" Hugh tugged hard on the bellpull and called down the stairs. When around the attentive housekeeper, he did his best to feign detached concern, hiding his pain.

Thelma Heiser, a vigilant caretaker, left him free to tend the ranch which, with its endless circle of activity, helped him cope. MacGregor buried the vestige of his marriage in the enormity of the work. Yet, like his father, and his father before him, he was not deterred by circumstance. He faced life with a mixture of spirit and courage, no less than any other son of the Highlands, that rugged part of Scotland that throughout history had fashioned martyrs and heroes out of common men.

Mrs. Heiser appeared at the doorway, as always ruddy-cheeked and crisp, a fresh pitcher of water and a washbowl in her hands. Without a word, she entered and began to attend to Elizabeth, moistening a cloth to refresh the woman's face. MacGregor distanced himself slowly, backing toward the window from where he could view the breadth of the ranch. He had sought refuge in the enormity of that emptiness before. Its solace reminded him of the legends of his ancestor, the great Rob Roy MacGregor, a man who had persevered even more than he and during far more difficult times. He too had lived by cattle and suffered at the hands of those who sought control.

In the old days in Scotland, when a man's wealth often consisted entirely of stock, the great Highland cattle were prized. Originally roaming wild in the hills, the clans regarded them as common property. By wit or might, rounding them up and keeping them was a job perceived as both precarious and challenging by clans in every generation. In spite of his eventual betrayal by the drover MacDonald and punishment by the Duke of Montrose, the great Rob Roy had left a legacy of strength and purpose, and a name which he, Hugh MacGregor, would strive to honor with all the power he possessed.

How little had really changed in two hundred years, he thought, gazing over his herds. Aggressive and bold, neither Rob Roy nor the MacGregor Clan had ever been known to turn away from fear. Proudly he remembered their creed, *"The Clan MacGregor; their greatness springs from great and glorious victories, and oft' remembered kings . . ."*

He knew well that until the conquest of Scotland by England, the MacGregors had dictated their own terms and tenaciously defended that which was their own. Only those lured by greed ran the risk of failing the clan, a family of fierce reivers and farmers who fought bravely for ancestral lands and values.

MacGregor missed them all. Not only his people, but also the land, the wide moors swept by the cold northeast wind, the graves of his clansmen in the vales of the lofty *Trossachs,* and the sense of past and pageantry that had given meaning to their lives. The Clan MacGregor, before the English reduced many in the end to desperate landless emigrants, would always be the "children of the mist," men of the mountain who would rather live free or die. Even in far off Wyoming, he would honor their memory and their success, disregarding any thought of failure until such time he would finally be forced to do so.

"There, there," he said tenderly. "It must o' been my imagination. Forgi'e me, lass. Rest, now." Disheartened, he returned to the window.

"Look, Taylor," he had said to the doctor only a week earlier, "there was nothin' I could ha'e done. It's been ten years since she joined me here, how could I ha'e known? She was only eighteen then, fully grown, but I confess now, weak beneath th' bloom. Ah, but what a beauty she was. I told her I'd take care o' her, I thought that I could. But she began missing her kin an' feelin' frail, wanin' an' faintin' like a wisp.

"I thought all she had tae do was lean on me, Jeb. Our life in th' West, th' sun, an' th' fresh air I felt sure would bring her health. We'd want for nothin', I promised, but she didn't last. Nae, she's gone tae ruin." The cattleman's eyes burned hollow, coffee brown pools of guilt and pain. He'd turned away from the doctor to hide his grief.

"I remember exactly what I told her, e'en on th' deck of th' Gunnar as it sailed fer New York. In this Scotlan' o' ours, I said, there's na' a MacGregor alive that doesn't yearn tae ha'e that which he may call his own. I was nae different. I had prospered well enou', but I wanted more. I told her that I made this move fer th' Clan, one an' all, an' fer th' children I hoped we'd ha'e. Fer their future. I dared na' admit my own greed. That's what I told her then, an' what I myself thought I believed . . ."

Young Elizabeth had been honored to think she might be a partner to a new generation that would live in America. She had married in full faith that her life would be better and for good purpose. Therefore, she followed her ambitious husband wherever he would take her. Joyfuly they culled the best bulls from his farm near the Glen Moore and shipped them with the finest cows as seed stock for a new herd. Packing with them a veritable household of goods, they left for the West carrying the hopes of his forefathers with him.

"With ye," he told Elizabeth, "our children will be th' beginnin' o' a great generation." And she believed him, striving to give him what he hoped for most. With each new pregnancy he dreamed of strong and sturdy boys. Then, through two miscarriages and one child stillborn, he stood by distraught, unbelieving, grieving for his lost babes and a future that was not to be. He prayed, reassuring his wife that the good Lord would give her healthy children by and by. Privately, he wept for those he never knew. After the last, doctors cautioned his wife to watch her health, that further childbearing would be out of the question, for her heart was frail and more pregnancies could be fatal.

Finally, at thirty years of age, in a body still young, her heart weakened even further, stealing from her the little strength that remained. It raced and fluttered one terrifying winter night and actually stopped, first for one second, then two, then four, taking with it her breath, her voice, and the rest of her normal life. When it started again, the damage had been done. Her heart had failed her, but refused to stop entirely, forcing her instead to become its prisoner. She lay at Rockrimmon in its isolated grandeur, waiting until her final hour.

Earlier in the month Hugh MacGregor sized up the situation. No point carrying two properties. He'd dismantle the Cameron and get the best men into his own outfit where he could use them. His telegraph message to Peters and Merrill made it clear.

"Need you and Cameron crew as soon as possible. Let the bank have Colorado. Saving Wyoming takes priority. Head north now."

A copy of the telegram lay on MacGregor's desk, already a week old. *Where were they after all? How much longer would he have to wait?*

Randolph Hunt, head of the Cheyenne Stock Growers Association, visited MacGregor weekly. The Scottish cattle baron's success or failure, he knew, would affect them all. Earlier that morning he had taken breakfast at the ranch and reassured MacGregor that they were all behind him, meanwhile hanging on to every bit of information he could use. Stirring his thick porridge slowly, he savored its strength, covering it with spoonfuls of brown sugar.

"Shame about your partner there, back in Colorado," said Hunt. "Lost a fortune, eh? I hear the banks are after you now, are they?"

"Hell, nae," MacGregor answered, defensively. "Nobody's after me. I'm surprised ye pay attention tae such rumor. Nae, ye can spread th' word. Rockrimmon will see a profit, as always. Meanwhile, I expect y'all up for th' Burns's

Supper after th' New Year. We'll be servin' dinner as usual fer anyone who can make it. Includin' th' Governor-elect, whether he gets my vote or nae." MacGregor smiled, showing rows of even teeth beneath a pewter mustache. Hunt smiled politely and made a mental note that the politician should be advised.

"I hate to bring up gossip," Hunt switched his tact, "but word has it that the English syndicates are in trouble. Land titles are in question across the board. A few of your friends from the old country seem to think that the cattle interests of the West are strong enough to defy the laws of this country. They've taken possession of millions of acres of land to which they've no more right than to City Hall."

MacGregor listened attentively. He didn't like what he heard.

"Thousands of pounds sterling in fencing and improvements in Colorado will now have to be cleared away," Hunt continued. "We know that these syndicates have attempted to control whole grazing areas with 'dummy' river frontages and the keeping of fraudulent records. What can you say to convince me that those in Scotland whom you represent really have a right to be here at all?"

MacGregor didn't answer. The implication was preposterous. He knew that the question of the validity of land titles and the position of aliens had been a subject under close scrutiny by the Wyoming Stock Growers Association for months. By 1888 the Association members themselves, many of them Scots, had over 1.5 million cattle on 500 square miles in Wyoming and the adjoining states, worth approximately 150 million dollars. The investment in America was extremely strong. English companies had also sunk sizable amounts of capital in the ranching industry and, although recent investigations had divulged that some foreigners had dealt dishonestly with the American land system, this was hardly MacGregor's case.

He understood the prejudice against the English and Scots rising throughout the country. In spite of the drought in the Midwest and failures on the northern plains, no American rancher had even a shred of sympathy for the cattle barons who, by the late 1880's, had lost personal fortunes everywhere. MacGregor had heard from his own sources that English investors had lost approximately ten million dollars, and the Scots, between seven and eight. The American Cattle Trust, a cartel formed by the biggest ranches out of Texas, Wyoming, and Montana, had recently collapsed as well, leaving the future of the cattle world up to a few determined individuals.

"I dinna' think I ha'e tae answer yer question, Hunt. Ye know well who I am. I am no stranger tae ye, nor those that fund Western Land an' Cattle. I've always paid my dues." MacGregor shifted in his chair, waiting for Hunt to continue, wondering what the man really wanted. His financial stability was no one's business but his own. Although the early profits to investors had yielded a high percentage, the margins were slipping. MacGregor calculated his operating budget to the penny. The recently acquired interest on the loan from the Philadelphia bank would alter his balance sheets enough to cause concern. He didn't need McKennon's debt at a time like this and regretted ever having co-signed on the loan.

Neither he nor Kerr McKennon had expected the Wyoming herd count to be cut in two by the hard winter of '86. Although the cattle seemed on the increase again, the animals had spread far and wide over the land and now mingled like never before. Without fences, not even his drovers knew whose cattle were whose anymore. Wide-spread rustling had become an alarming problem as well. Accurate figures would be hard to reckon and the fall roundup difficult. But these problems he did not feel he needed to discuss.

Looking back, he realized that in a period of five years, nature itself had seen to the end of free-range ranching. Sadly, only those with land blessed with abundant water and the rights to use it would continue. The rest would fail; speculators and opportunists deserting the range as fast as they had descended upon it.

"Nae, Randolph, ye surprise me," MacGregor rallied cheerfully. "All these years, we're still th' biggest an' th' best. Would ye doubt my prosperity? If th' Lord would grant me real abundance, he'd help my poor Elizabeth, see her tae smile ag'in. That would be a gift. Th' ranch will take care o' itself."

Hunt made no comment, gulping the rest of his coffee and staring at his empty cup.

"By this week," the Scot continued, "wi' my additional crew, we'll divide th' main herd by age an' gender, still o'er twenty thousan' strong, an' drive the cows tae fenced pasture. The steers we'll sell off. Th' best bulls I'll pen here at th' ranch. Then we'll hang on like e'erybody else until th' reserves run out or new grass appears, whiche'er comes first. Just like we've always done. Only now we'll ha'e tae pray a bit as well." A hollow chuckle followed.

Hugh MacGregor never believed that the end could arrive in any other form but glory. A bad winter or a bad market would not be his demise, not now or ever. He had never learned how to lose.

"The dream has nae eluded me," he assured his skeptical friend, although he knew in his heart he had surely awakened from it. " 'Tis only th' task tae reshape th' business tae th' times, bend it, make it fit. 'Tis too late tae go back t'Edinburgh empty-handed. We'll succeed. Ye'll see."

No one doubted his down-to-earth optimism but Randolph Hunt shook his head skeptically, wondering whether or not the Scotsman would survive. So many others had already pulled up and returned home, penniless, or worse, overwhelmingly in debt.

Though faithful to his original plan, MacGregor lived in private torment with the thought that he might have been wrong from the start. The future had lied. The Hereford would never be as hardy as the wild buffalo or the Longhorn, nor the plains as fertile as the farms he'd left back home. Now the railroads would dictate the course as the beef market shifted to feed lots in the Midwest. Competition loomed everywhere, all at once. Foreign demand continued to decline as America's plate filled. Although starting over seemed impossible, secretly MacGregor dreamed of one day returning to Scotland, to the simpler life he'd once known. But the firm grasp of Wyoming held him fast. That and the vestige of his wasted wife, the barest remnant of the woman he had to remind himself he once loved. With the world changing around him, he clung to Rockrimmon with a blinding commitment, convinced that all would bear out as planned if he would only stay the course.

"I'm sure you'll be fine," Hunt reassured his host. "Work things out like you always do." He slapped MacGregor on the back as he said goodbye. "Keep in touch if you need anything. I'm always glad to be of help. And look for us at the Burns's Supper. We'll be there."

MacGregor watched Hunt's black surrey pull away and retreated to his study. Deep inside him burned a current of pain he rarely allowed himself to feel, a pulse charged at opposing ends by shifting images of Scotland and those of Wyoming itself. Closing his eyes, he remembered the sounds and scenes of a life that beckoned him still. Like wraiths, these rogue memories materialized during unsuspecting moments of the day, haunting his thoughts and likewise inspiriting his dreams. From half a world away, the scenes of his childhood came to life, at once both comforting and close, yet unreachable from where he stood.

MacGregor dreamed of returning to the family farm, Glen Moore, near Killin, to roam the steep-sided glens and follow the ribboned emerald lochs from bank to bank as he did in his youth. To return—as if to do so were an obligation by which one could finally close a life. Like the well known refrain from Burns's fabled song, *"You take th' high road an' I'll take the low, an' I'll be in Scotlan' a'fore ye . . . ,"* he knew he would one day put his feet on Scottish soil again, even if coming home also meant never leaving again. But to take the high road, to travel that path of the spirit and the true heart, he would have to beat the persistent dark angel whom he also knew traveled the other, quiet and unseen, forever intent on taking the weary traveler unaware as he makes his final journey home.

Scanning the window for riders, MacGregor worried that his men heading up from Colorado were late. Another day out would put them in the heart of the approaching storm. Earlier that week, inquisitive auditors had already advised him of McKennon's debts, past and upcoming. He needed the informant Skoll to tell him more. The man had approached him after Kerr's funeral and offered to look carefully into the Cameron's affairs. He himself had no time for such detail and didn't know if he could trust the foreman, Merrill, who would surely be looking out for himself. Certainly, he would never believe the bank's reports on what was or was not. Not that Skoll had impressive credentials, but his arrival was not surprising. The cattle detective had surfaced just at the right time, and seemed to ask very little for the service.

Only the unexpected business of McKennon's widow, an intrusion by a woman to whom he felt he owed nothing, seemed to be the problem now. The news astonished him; that by the terms of her husband's death, she assumed she would take McKennon's place as his partner. Annoyed by the thought, he wrestled with the fact that no precedent existed, of this he was quite sure.

Concerned, but cautious, he waited to contact his lawyers in Edinburgh in order to examine the terms of the original agreement with the late McKennon. For the moment, he would confront the audacious lady face to face and try to bring her to her senses. Or, failing that, his infamous temper and a hard line of refusal would conclude the matter instead.

Joining Elizabeth in her bedroom with its grand western view, he seated himself at the window ledge. Behind the rolling hills, a slate-colored sky had begun to absorb the fog now forming low to the ground. Pale mists, churning one layer above, pulsed with a soft reflected glow. There could be no doubt that the moisture-laden clouds of an early Wyoming winter hovered, menacing and cold.

Squinting, MacGregor searched the horizon for riders. There should be at least ten of them if he remembered correctly. Eric, Weston, Val—some of his very best, the lot of them having wasted five good years on a gamble in the Colorado mountains. He could use them now. Good horse wranglers, cowpunchers, and trail cooks were scarce. He pressed against the window ledge, searching for a sign.

Still nothing and the hour grew late. Suddenly, from the far distance, the unmistakable ring of gunfire broke the silence. MacGregor bolted to his feet. What could it have been? Within moments, his eyes focused on a small speck moving in the distance. Whatever it was, it appeared they'd arrived at last. He was sure it had to be them.

Yet the sound of gunshots concerned him and he strained to see what could be the cause. Against the gray landscape, a luminous halo of dry winter dust encircled the speck as it moved, but he saw nothing else that followed. His eyes narrowed as he tracked the approaching form, impossibly just one lone figure, streaking across the plain.

Squinting sharply, he leaned far out of the window, his fingers gripping the sill, his anxious heart pounding at the sight. Behind him in the shadow of her canopied bed, Elizabeth lay still, staring and silent. He looked at her briefly, then back through the great leaded-glass window that opened to the bleak unnatural light. MacGregor blinked hard, trying to discern better the fast moving form, now streaking along the distant edge of the ranch. It was a horse all right, that he could tell for sure, but the animal was running free, alone and riderless, galloping instinctively toward life itself, flying like the north wind now blowing so hard at its head. The heavy gusts whipped its long black mane and tail into a line, urging the animal on, and driving with it the stinging beads of a cold unwelcome snow.

By the time the horse had reached the paddock area, MacGregor had thrown on his heavy coat and stood directly in her path. He'd picked up a lariat on his way and whirled it slowly as he waited, expecting to toss a noose around the dark horse as she cantered by.

"Whoa there," he called out, throwing the loop wide. He missed by several feet and quickly dropped the rope, attempting to block her bodily, his arms spread out to each side. She veered around him without losing a step.

"Halt, my beauty, just where d'ye think ye're headed?" Bonniedoon found herself stopped by a fence and pulled up short in a cloud of dust, tossing her head warily. Having skirted MacGregor, she side-stepped and pranced, defying him, nostrils flared wide.

"Calm yerself," he coaxed. "No sense actin' like a damn fool. Easy . . ." He reached for her bosal and the dragging lead. Bonniedoon shied away, rearing out of his grasp and cantering off toward the cluster of saddle horses at the far end of the big corral. Ewan Peters walked out of the bull barn just as the scene unfolded. Surveying the pair, he laughed out loud.

"Looks like ye've lost yer touch, sir!" he said with a smile. "Ye used tae ha'e such a way wi' th' ladies. Can I get her for ye?" MacGregor, not amused, stamped a boot in disgust.

"Fetch th' damn thin' a'fore she hurts someone an' lock her up by herself," he shouted. "And check her fer a brand,

234

will ye? Hey . . ." He stopped short as he realized riders were approaching. "Look there, up on th' ridge. I reckon 'tis abou' time."

A small party of travelers, about a dozen cowboys and half that number of wagons, had assembled on the low rise above the ranch. Someone waved. In a short while, the convoy rumbled up to the main gate in a cloud of dust, including two cowponies being led slowly, one bearing the body of Skoll tied across the saddle, and the other with Merrill, still seated, but bent precariously over his wounded leg.

The dark mare, continuing to canter through the compound, ran herself straight into the loop of Oscar Hill, MacGregor's finest roper. He'd seen her coming and quickly mounted his own mustang to cut her off. But on she came, thundering through as though the devil himself was after her. She never saw the lariat sail over her head or the cowboy at her rear, but found herself in a deep slide, back on her haunches, head jerked up in a tight noose, hooves rasping against the earth. Struggling to her feet, she tested the rope and only then, stood still at last, terrified, trembling, snorting fear into the air.

"Good job, man," MacGregor called out. "Take her on down." He would explore the mystery of the mare later. There were certainly more pressing matters to attend to. It was then that he noticed that a large buckskin horse supported the lifeless body of a man. Another bore a rider doubled over and obviously in pain, one hand clutching a blood-soaked thigh.

"What-th'-hell? Anybody want t'explain this?" MaGregor demanded, swinging wide the entry gate for the lead rider. No one said a word, fearful of saying something wrong. The last wagon through bore MacGregor's old acquaintance, Ripp Robart, a camp cook who'd been on many a roundup at Rockrimmon and elsewhere. Grizzled and greasy, he looked like a part of the load itself, tattered and covered with dust.

"Morning, MacGregor. Long time no see."

"What's goin' on here, Ripp?" the Scotsman demanded. Taking a hold of the lines near the bit, he drew the pair of mules to a halt. MacGregor leaned closer and said quietly, "Give it tae me straight an' simple. Who's th' dead man an' how d'it happen?"

"That piece o' dog meat?" the wagoner answered. "Nothin' but a varmint and a skunk. Got caught in a bit o' gun play, but the sonofabitch had it comin'.."

Crossing over to the body, Hugh took a closer look and recognized Kurt Skoll, the man he'd met only once, weeks earlier, at McKennon's grave.

"Who fired first?" MacGregor queried.

"Couldn't say . . ." Ripp drawled in reply. MacGregor shook his head. "All right then, where were you when it happened? What did you see?"

"See? All's I know is what I see now. Ain't a purty sight, neither. That leg of Merrill's gonna take real expert fixin.'" Ripp gathered up the lines, flicked his whip, and the team and wagon creaked on through the huge gate.

MacGregor knew he'd have to ask Merrill himself to get the whole picture. By the looks of things, Kurt Skoll hadn't been of much use after all. Unless, there was something of value in his saddlebags. He only hoped they held the records he needed. Without those documents, he would never know what Skoll had learned about his late partner's affairs. After all, the distance between he and Kerr had grown great. Something in those records might prove that the Cameron was worth hanging on to after all. Then again, maybe it wasn't and wouldn't be for a long time to come. The truth remained to be seen.

★ ★ ★ ★ ★

"Yes, ma'am," MacGregor confirmed, shouting into the long black receiver. "We need medical help out here right away."

The new telephone system had been installed for just such emergencies, and MacGregor was proud to have been one of the first ranchers to buy into the idea. Of course, not everyone had been hooked up yet, but the operator promised to try to track down a doctor as fast as she could. On most ranches, minor broken bones from a horse kick or the effects of a snake bite required only home treatment; you couldn't be a cowboy if you couldn't handle the aches and pains that came with the territory. But acts of God, or worse, acts of men, often went beyond the average rancher's medical expertise.

Merrill had been brought into the kitchen and a rough tourniquet applied to stop the bleeding. The phone vibrated with a shrill ring, causing everyone around the wounded cowboy to jump.

"Hey there, Doc," MacGregor shouted into the mouthpiece, "Where've ye been? We've got trouble here. One shot in th' leg, another dead. Come as quick as ye can, will ye?" MacGregor put down the receiver, calculating that Doc Holland, the local medic who treated emergencies and common colds, would take at least a half an hour to arrive from the clinic in town.

"Mrs. Heiser, would ye boil some water, please? An' someone get that mule skinner in here an' tell him tae wash up, just in case," the Scot said with authority. "If th' Doc does'na' get here soon, we may ha'e tae perform a bit o' surgery." Merrill was handed a draught of whiskey while they waited. Ripp looked at him skeptically, then rolled up his shirt sleeves as Mrs. Heiser brought him a pot of water and a chunk of soap.

MacGregor pulled up a chair next to the table as the freshly scrubbed wagoner began to cut away the stiff trousers caked with blood and clean out the wound. "Well, Merrill, how goes it? Can ye talk?" he asked, wondering if the man was still conscious. The wounded foreman meanwhile looked fuzzily at MacGregor through half-closed lids.

"I'm sorry, sir. Did my best, tried to anyway. Has my wife arrived yet? And the girls?"

"Nae till this afternoon most likely. Ye'll be up an' dancin' by th' time they get here. Just tell me what happened. Yer boys don't seem tae know much. Should o' been a simple trail ride, a Sunday outin', not a rollin' gunfight."

"He's a horsethief, MacGregor," Stewart gasped. "I was just doing my job. Believe me, it was self-defense. Skoll had a hot temper . . . I was protecting your property."

"Is that so? I wouldna' thought." MacGregor guessed that Merrill might be lying, but let it go for the moment. Old Ripp started to dab at the wound, and Merrill writhed in pain with each touch. Finally, to everyone's relief, Doc Holland arrived. He surveyed the crude preparations underway and nodded approvingly. Putting down his bag of instruments, he bent over for a closer look, then patted the crusty driver on the back. "Nice work, old boy. I'll take it from here."

"Thanks, Doc. Honors are yours . . ."

"Don't mind if I do. Lest I be out of a job soon," Doc replied, taking off his coat.

"Think ye can fix him up?" MacGregor asked.

"I believe so," smiled Holland. "He ought to make it."

MacGregor gripped the wounded man's hand to steady him. "Hang on, Stewart, not tae much longer now. Just tell me what you know abou' th' dead man an' th' runaway horse?"

"The man's a thief . . . and the mare," Stewart winced as Doc Holland gently swabbed his leg in search of the bullet.

"The mare . . ." Stewart started again, recoiling as the Doc probed deep into his groin. He grabbed MacGregor's arm and jerked up into a sitting position.

"Jesus Christ!" he screamed, staring at his bleeding thigh and then into the implacable face of the medic. "Do you have to do that?" Sweat drenched his face, already contorted with pain. Doc Holland injected a syringe of morphine into a vein.

"Sorry, sir," Stewart said as the drug took effect. He looked imploringly at the Scotsman and started once again. "That damned mare . . . half-crazed bitch of a broomtail . . ." This time he rolled to one side, grimaced, and collapsed on to his back. "The mare is . . . Mrs. McKennon's."

MacGregor glanced at Doc Holland for sympathy. He found none. Instead, Doc showed him the end of a long-nosed pair of forceps that gripped a two-hundred grain bullet from a .38, still glossed with blood. The man raised his eyebrows in response, then dropped the find into a small tray, and proceeded to close the wound. Stewart Merrill lay still, unconscious.

Billy pressed the lathered pony until it began to stumble, wheezing loudly as it slowed to an exhausted walk. Nostrils flared, it sucked for air while thick foam dripped from its mouth. The winded animal was bathed in its own sweat.

Concerned, Billy dismounted. He unrolled his poncho, threw it over the gelding's back, then led the horse slowly, hoping it wouldn't catch a chill. As the temperature dropped, a stiff wind rose that made Billy's fingers ache and his body shiver. All around him the empty swells of dry grassland seemed deserted and safe, but each time he looked back, he felt haunted by the lonely indifference of the landscape, featureless and plain.

Horse and rider had galloped nearly four miles, a considerable edge on a posse if there was one, but Colorado still lay far ahead. The icy wind meanwhile brought tears to Billy's eyes, reminding him of his last violent brush with death at sea and the loss of his friend. He dabbed his eyes with the back of his hand.

Instinctively, Billy veered west, toward the cover of Wyoming's Black Hills, up and over "the gangplank," that great lift of earth that swelled up from the plains. The quickest route back would have been due south over the grasslands toward Greeley, but he knew that the prairie there lay bare of cover, as flat and dry as a desert. So he sought the twisting paths through the distant hilly buttes south of Laramie,

240

seeking the valleys of the Laramie River where he assumed there would be water and places to hide.

In the twilight he could see no horsemen in pursuit. Why hadn't they come? Surely he was being followed. He looked over his shoulder until his neck began to hurt, staring as long as he could into what felt like a black hole behind him. Just thinking about the scuffle started waves crashing deep within, as though the world had come to its end. Imagining the horrible consequences in the hands of the law, all that loomed before him seemed a maelstrom, a swirl of doubt and worry, like a storm within the sea.

Sundown came early. In what remained of the cold afternoon light, Billy wished for nightfall so he could move unseen toward the river, to lose himself and the tracks that marked his trail in the dry dust. All around rose strange silhouettes of rock, deeply carved windswept formations thrusting upwards out of the earth. He remembered hearing about similar outcroppings in Scotland where the foggy mists in the northern heath spawned strange apparitions. Northerners always teased that you couldn't tell if the shapes were real or not, but those around him now were real enough and seemed to speak to him in hushed cries and desperate whispers.

In the distance a grayish fall haze faded to white near the sun. Though low in its arc, the pale light warmed, but the haze told him that a cold front wasn't long in coming.

Following an old stage trail, Billy led the horse along a ridge of jackpine and conifer until he reached the waters of Box Elder Creek. To his left, he continued to count the red sandstone sentinels in what he had now nicknamed the "Valley of the Goblins," a wide-reaching passage of the half-eroded stone outcrops, rounded by the wind, like beasts crouching against the earth. Spirits must linger there, he guessed, but whose?

The gray gelding sought its way through the cottonwood and forged downward toward the creek to slake its thirst. Plowing through thorny branches of mountain mahogany and scrub oak, the horse headed past the sandy scree of the bank, dragging Billy with him. Above them on either side, the red walls of a ravine cut the wind, but its veined and layered strata left Billy uneasy, reminding him of an unnatural open wound in which he was now trapped. Surrounded thus, he felt vulnerable, not hidden. He preferred the inviting length of the river, rimmed with screens of cottonwood, wide banks, and easy getaways.

He found his way through patches of cattail growing along the creek bed as the sun slipped behind the peaks. With nightfall ahead, he needed to find shelter. Horse and rider continued to move south and west, toward the looming crests of the Rockies, their dark profile and hidden depths luring him with the promise of safety.

Before long he would cross the Colorado border at Owl Creek where he could follow the stage roads to Denver and trade his horse if necessary. From there, he would continue on through to Jefferson and back to the Cameron Ranch where every glen and valley was familiar, to hide, for as long as he needed. That was his plan, to reach South Park, without getting caught. It was just outrageous enough to work. The Cameron had to be the last place on earth they'd think he'd dare to go. At present however, his stomach told him he'd have to find something to eat, and he knew he had to let the gelding rest.

Billy tied his horse to a willow near the water. A cottontail hopping into the brush froze for an instant as he hoisted his rifle, then took off with lightning speed. Billy aimed, then stopped himself, wondering how he could be so foolish as to give himself away with the sound of gunfire. The rabbit stopped in a little gully, melting into the landscape as it considered its next move. Billy picked up a sharp edged rock, and flicking it like a whizzing disk, managed to crease the rabbit, wounding it. The small creature bucked and twisted in the air, then dropped to the ground, and after a moment, lay still. Walking toward his prey, a feeling of nausea rose in his throat as he recalled the shooting of Skoll. The blood that flowed from the dead animal's neck seemed no different than that of the man he'd left lying on the ground. But because of Skoll's death, his hands would be stained forever.

The smell of roasting rabbit meat increased Billy's hunger and while it cooked, he busied himself rubbing down his horse with the saddle blanket and checking its hooves. So far, the pony had managed the getaway well. Sitting to eat before the fire, he imagined he saw Maggie's face, pale but serene, hovering before him. Her eyes filled the space above the flames, gazing at him with that bold straight-forward look he'd seen the very first time they'd met. Though the rabbit filled his stomach, he still felt an emptiness inside and yearned to hold his beloved once again. Somehow they would find each other and she would forgive him his crime. She was his only reason to go on.

Billy watered his horse and tethered it once again. The tired animal nibbled on grasses nearby and then stood quietly, head down, dozing off, its hindquarters to the wind which now riffled its charcoal mane. After his supper, Billy placed his bedroll against a rock outcrop which protected him from the wind. He propped the saddle up for a pillow and lay down before the fire to ponder his grim circumstances, staring up at the night sky now hoary with frost.

Nothing made any sense, not the feeling of losing Maggie or the spectre of killing a man. Not even the grand vision he'd seen from the hill above Rockrimmon Ranch. Too much, too fast. Was this to be his curse, to run forever just to save his life? To grapple with death? Or was death going to continue to be there alongside him, at the birth of each new phase, like some cruel midwife to everlasting change, a recurring ghost haunting a nightmare that never ends? Perhaps the evil eye yet stalked him ever since his brother's death so many years before. About his fate he did not know.

For now he tried only to recall what good things he could and trusted that Maggie would not forget him. Somehow, he believed, through the journey he would find his way and then, start over again, a new man, with a new name if necessary. For once, something was important to him and he wasn't about to let it go.

Edging closer to the fire, Billy dug into his bedroll and tried to escape into the numbness of sleep. The medallion he wore slid sideways onto his neck, both the circle of silver and the chain as cold as ice, and startled him briefly. He wrapped his bare fingers around them before sliding them inside his shirt and, as he did, pondered the power of Saint Michael for his guide.

In the silent darkness, Billy felt as alone as he'd ever been. Not a soul would ever know if he lived or died that night. The pain of such a possibility stunned him, and prodded him into staying alive all the more intently. Shallow breaths made bright clouds of steam in the air each time he exhaled, only to evaporate as they neared the heat. He reveled in these signs of his own existence and blew the vapors into the chilly night with a vengeance. Afraid of being found, he added the smallest amounts of wood to the fire, and hoped that he wouldn't freeze to death before morning.

After a few hours, Billy awoke with a start. The darkness was entire. The fire died out and the temperature had dropped below freezing, but to his amazement, he felt a greater heat warming him. A pungent equine smell filled his nostrils while the cold air assailed his lungs. Turning carefully, he felt the heavy mane and weight of the gelding, his own horse, along one side. He laid down again slowly, so as not to disturb what he understood had been his salvation, the gray pony was sound asleep, its back full against him like a shield.

"Hey there, young feller—wake up! Better get off the ground before yu plumb freeze ta death!"

Billy looked up to find a red face peering down, woolen layers stacked all the way to its nose. Blue eyes twinkled under white eyebrows dusted with snow and a thatch of knotty yellow-white hair stuck out like a pinecone beneath a wool cap. The man sat atop a thick coated burro not much bigger than himself, dragging a *travois* of firewood. His worn leather boots nearly touched the ground as his legs dangled to either side.

"Name's Sven Solvaag," he said brightly. "No cause fer alarm. In the mornings, I ride out ta empty my traps and saw yur horse first thing, all by himself, pawin' through the snow. Now, what's a stray doin' this far off and me not knowin' whose it is, says I. I'll be durned if it waren't yur'n. Yah! So here I am. Didn't mean ta scare yu."

At this he poked at Billy with a long whip, his only respectable piece of riding equipment. "So I says ta myself, I'm not losin' my mind. Nope, not this early I'm not. But what's a man doin' sleepin' on the ground like some kinda' durn fool in the middle of a snowstorm anyways? Ain't yu got no sense?"

Billy brushed at the mantle of white covering his bedroll. Sitting up, he noticed a bare patch of ground filling up with fresh flakes. No, he hadn't been dreaming. He scrambled to his feet and stammered sheepishly.

"Yes, sir, it dinna make much sense," said Billy, "ye're right abou' that. Just got caught in th' storm here on my way south."

"South yu want ta go?" The blue eyes crinkled up with laughter. "Yu don't say? 'Fraid yur a bit late. The geese took off a couple a months ago. Yu'll be lucky if yu get as far as my shack a'fore this storm blows in. There's more ta come, sonny. Nah, if yur askin', I wouldn't be goin' nowheres t'day, 'cept with me."

Sven picked up a long black instrument hanging around his neck and peered through the narrow end, focusing a large round lense. Billy gaped as he recognized a mariner's scope. Taking notice, the older man placed it back inside his coat, protectively. "Sure enuf," he confirmed, "there's a big 'un brewin'. By noon the flakes gonna be comin' at yu so thick yu won't know which way is up. Where I come from, not even the caribou would budge. Come on, boy, yu best come along."

Needing a friend, Billy quickly saddled the gray and rolled up his bedding, glad that this night he'd have a roof over his head. Setting caution aside, he followed the Swede without a word for a half-mile or so until they came to a hut planted at the edge of a creek bottom. A few barren cottonwoods formed a small hedge against the wind. Here the old man slid off and limping noticeably, unhitched the travois, sending the burro off to a corral with an affectionate slap. He piled the wood outside his door and turned to look at his guest.

"Well, come on now," he said with a wave of a fingerless glove. "No questions, yah? Put yur horse in the shed, an' foller me."

Billy surveyed the hut. A small keg of whiskey, a table, two handmade chairs, and a bed anchored to the wall filled three sides of the simple room. To the right of the raised hearth stood a wooden counter topped by shelves for supplies and cooking utensils. Various animal skins lay stretched across the mud-covered walls and the full antlers of a six-point bull elk provided hooks for hats and coats.

A sturdy plank well above the fireplace, spanning the entire wall, held a large selection of books with titles Billy couldn't recognize, barely visible beneath their coats of dust. Off to one side, a kettle of water sat on a stand and a cast iron pot of tasty looking stew hung cooking over the coals.

On top of the mantel lay assorted drafting tools made of brass or steel; an angle, compass, a straight edge with a sliding scale, and a sextant, the one tool necessary for maritime navigation. Next to these, an old pewter cup held pencils and the feathered tops of crow-quill pens, along with dusty bottles of ink, their labels faded and worn. Billy resisted the temptation to pick up the tools and examine them one by one, wondering about their purpose.

It didn't take Sven long to stoke up a roaring fire, throw a couple handfuls of coffee into a pot which he placed on a small grate, and then pull up a bench for Billy and a small three-legged stool for himself. He proceeded to light a pipe that filled the cabin with a pungent aroma.

A pile of skins and pelts lay stacked loosely on the floor, tagged in a numerical code. Sven noticed Billy studying them and said, "Simple: animal, location caught, and date. Want ta be sure I get me another." Billy nodded and examined the skins with interest. The largest he laid over his lap for warmth.

"Yu just set tight," Sven mothered, "and let me lay out some hospitality. Been a long while I ain't had any visitors." A brindle sheepdog that had been lying by the fire rose stiffly and sat down in front of Billy. It nuzzled his hand, blinking bright brown eyes at the stranger.

"Yer more than kind," Billy said. "But is there nothin' I can do, sir? Fetch water maybe, or bring in a bit o' wood?"

"Nah, wouldn't think of it. And don't be callin' me sir. Yu just set quiet and toast those feet. Durn if yur boots aren't wet. Might as well take 'em off. Nothin' worse'n wet boots!"

Sven puttered about, drawing cups and plates magically out of a cupboard while the dog sidled closer to Billy, enabling him to scratch his scruffy coat. Sven poured the steaming coffee into two speckled china mugs, and Billy drank gratefully, starting to relax for the first time in two days. He could feel his stomach growl in response to the fragrant dish cooking over the crackling fire.

The afternoon grew colder as the snow continued to fall. Sven talked almost continuously, having had few occasions that year to exercise his love of conversation and, in Billy's mind, obviously demonstrating a need to make up for lost time. An endless source of information, the man rarely stopped to wait for an answer to a question, or even long enough for Billy to comment now and then.

"What I dinna' understand," Billy finally interrupted, "is how an old rover like yerself came tae be here, so far from everra'thin'. If I may ask . . ."

"No secret. Where d'yu want me ta start?" He tamped his

pipe and inhaled deeply. "Act'ally, we don't have enough time ta start when I was born," Sven chuckled, "so let's pick up with me leavin' Malmo, down off the strait near the tip of Sweden. Yu know where that is?"

The old man unfolded a map of Europe tucked deep in a leather bag, then sat across from Billy, leaning back, causing the stool to creak. Sven's story began. He'd come from Scandinavia in 1866 seeking fortune in a timber area of Wyoming known as the Big Horn Range. Hard weather discouraged most of the pioneers, scattering men to dry land farms in the Dakotas and Montana but Sven stuck it out, resisting the long winters like a bear, holed up and lonely for months. After a few years, he'd gotten a reputation as a trustworthy guide and ran timber crews until the logging company offered him an easier job in town.

Married to the wilderness, he refused to relocate. He banked the last of his pay in Laramie and slipped back up into the woods to forage and hunt and live by himself. Eventually, he drifted on down to the ranches of Wyoming where so many new immigrants made their living off the land. More than a few offered him a bed in exchange for his capable help but fences and farms hemmed him in. Having become instead a renegade range herder, he worked for all and for no one in particular. Ranchers paid him by the head for whatever cattle or sheep he found and brought in alive. He knew every brand and breed in the region and fondly christened the lost mavericks with names like Otto, Anders, and Olga.

Slowly, he accumulated a few head of his own as payment for his efforts. These few cattle and sheep he tended loosely on the banks of an uncharted creek with the help of Rolf, his crossbreed dog, a runaway like so many others he had rescued or found. He figured he had everything a man could want. Sven liked best the fact that he accounted to no one, and yet knew every range and rancher for a hundred miles or more in each direction, many miles of the same territory that Billy now needed to cross.

The two men viewed the heavy snow as it accumulated along the window ledge and Sven shook his grizzled head.

"Still early. This 'un won't stick. Course, if the deep snow don't getcha', then the ground blizzards will. I been so lost a'ways back I couldn't tell which way was up and *up* was the only direction it weren't snowin' a'tall!"

Billy looked skeptical.

"Wyoming's version of a hurricane," Sven explained. "If yu ask me, I think this'n will melt before long. The one that stays till springtime is still a ways off."

"I hope ye're right," Billy said. "I need tae get home before I get caught in bad weather." He used the word home with the certainty of men who have lovers waiting in ports, or of fathers with children tucked in familiar beds.

"An' where might that be?" the Swede inquired.

"Uh—up in th' minin' country near Leadville," he lied, hoping to cover himself with details. If he were too vague, he might be suspect.

"Yah, that's a hell of a ride fer a loner this time of year. Tell yu what; I got nuthin' t'do. I'll take yu part way. I need ta make one more trip that a'ways ta stock up on supplies. We'll tie that horse of yurs ta the old wagon and yu can ride with me far as Lyons. How's that? From there I can show yu a shortcut up over the front range that'll steer clear of towns and take yu on into South Park. From there yu can get ta Leadville easy. That'd be my choice under these conditions. Sound good?"

Billy couldn't believe his good fortune and nodded his confirmation with a smile. Rubbing his hands together, now warm from the radiant fire, he dug into a plate of squirrel stew, one of Sven's year-round specialties. The hermit liked the furry rodents best in the fall, when fat and ready for winter. Black coffee washed down the strange taste of the wild meat and juniper berries, along with the unidentified musty vegetables that floated in the gravy.

"I'm a man with no country, boy," Sven stated proudly. "I don't keep secrets cause I cain't remember 'em and I don't keep promises, so I never make 'em. You got somethin' on yur' chest yu wants ta unload, yu can tell me and it waren't go no further than this." With that he threw a squirrel bone into the fire and watched it burn.

Billy leaned back against the pile of pelts that covered his makeshift bed on the floor. "Nae much tae tell," he said guardedly, "but maybe later. And I'm kinda tired, tae be honest. Mind if I sleep a bit first?"

"Not at all."

With that he rolled over to face the earthen wall, dark with soot and time, desperate for sleep to take him far away. The snow continued to fall, sifting silently into the night.

"Where'd ye get th' telescope?" Billy asked the next morning, pointing it toward the window and adjusting the focus.

"Oh, I left that part out, did I? Yur Royal Swedish Navy. Second mate I was, finest little fleet ta sail the archipelago. Just a boy then; went fer the fun of it. Never did see a battle but had a hell of a good time learnin' ta tie knots, hoist sails, and make maps. Here, have a look at these."

Sven pulled out a bulky sack full of wrinkled papers from under the bed, the most remarkable of all being a series of night maps, the constellations clearly drawn in each of the four seasons. Over the years, the hand-held telescope had served the old man well. By using the north star as a guide, he had created a kind of celestial calendar that could tell a person what month of the year it was.

"Would ye look at these?" Billy exclaimed. "They're th' real thin'. I canna' belie'e my eyes."

"Do yu think an old man just sleeps during all those months by himself? There's plenty more where these come from."

"In all my days at sea," Billy said, filled with nostalgia and wonder at the tracings and figures that brought the constellations to life, "I ne'er saw nothin' as sharp an' beautiful as these. I've sailed from Oban as far as Brisbane, an' ne'er met a captain who could navigate th' night sky worth a tinker's damn. If he'd only had one o' yer maps, he would ha'e known where he was, clear as a bell. Here ye are, ye old landlocked salt, hidin' 'em away from th' world. Could ha'e saved a ship or two if you'd ha'e shared these wi' th' men on my sea." He stopped and folded the maps neatly, just as he had found them. "Maybe," he paused, " 'tis nae tae late."

"Too late for what, boy?"

"Fer a sailor tae use 'em . . . tae travel, by night, I mean . . . that is, fer me . . ."

The words slipped out before he could stop them. Then, nothing. He looked up with a face so troubled that Sven put down his coffee. "Better tell me the real story, boy. Where yu been, and where yu goin'. It's time ta tell. Otherwise it's gonna eat yu alive and somebody will be blaming me for a dead man. Come on," he said, putting his hand on Billy's shoulder, "I want the whole thing from the start. Yah—yu gonna talk now. Most of it I'll forget by tomorra', anyways."

Two days of wind bursts and flurries and then, a bright dawn sparkled in the wilderness. Like so many high-country November mornings, this one opened balmy, dry, and filled with light.

Downing a breakfast of jerky and hardtack, Billy hitched up the burro to a small cart and tied the gray gelding behind, burying his saddle under a pile of furs.

The pair traveled slowly, south towards Lyons with the ease of trappers on a familiar trail.

Billy, wrapped up in a chieftain's blanket against the cold, now wore a lumberjack's cap with fleecy ear flaps. His blond hair hid under the massive headgear and his cowboy garb disappeared under the woolen cover. There remained no resemblance to the runaway drover who'd left Colorado a week before.

The gray mustang wore a cavalry blanket with a slit cut through, leaving only his dark head, neck and legs exposed. To any passerby, he seemed like a black horse protected from the wind. Together, the odd pair might have passed for a couple of drifters if anybody cared to look closely. But no one did. The way was long and sparsely settled and news had not yet traveled. Nor would it. The true code of the West, still unknown to Billy, but laid down hard and fast in a world where lawlessness often ruled, prescribed that death usually came to those who summoned it.

By the time they reached Lyons where the two would part, Billy understood precisely the way to travel. Passing the foothills west of Denver, he was to ride south along the old MacClellan stage trail which followed earlier paths cut by the Utes, now nearly invisible through the pine.

Bearing the papers of a trapper who had left his pack with Sven one night and simply disappeared, Billy even had an alias if he got stopped. He could protect his identity and procure a night's lodging if he needed it.

"Just behave like yu got a reason ta be wherever y'are," Sven advised. "Trust me boy, Cheyenne's a long way off. Ta those folks, yu're already history. But I'll keep a weather eye out and my ears unplugged and listen fer news, not that I'd know how ta find yu if I heard any. But if I did, I'd make sure yu got what yu needed ta know. Yu want ta make it easy for me? Why not tell me where yu're really headed?"

Billy looked at the old man in silence and felt his heart grow full. He never dreamed on finding such friendship with a stranger.

"That's okay," Sven said when receiving no reply. "Yu just do the best yu can. I'll find yu if there's a reason. And, son, I thought yu might be needin' these." With that he drew a bundle out of the cart and put it in Billy's lap. Inside were four maps of the night sky, one for each season, the telescope, and a week's worth of beef jerky.

"Yah, I thought yu'd get more use outta' this stuff then I ever will. Truth is, I don't see so good no more anyways. Yu can return 'em ta me someday if yu don't need 'em." Then he dropped two gold pieces into Billy's palm.

"Use these if yu need ta. And be careful. Now, git on outta here! Winter's comin' fast."

Billy dug his gear out of the buckboard and saddled up the gray with new confidence. The striped woolen blanket he wore as a poncho now covered him and his mount against the cold. "I'll ne'er be able tae thank ye," Billy said, his voice cracking. He urged the horse into a jog trot and then turned once more, calling out, "If ye come tae find me, look fer th' Cameron Ranch, near Jefferson, in South Park." A lump rose in his throat and he swallowed hard. The old man smiled and waved goodbye then turned back toward Lyons to purchase his supplies.

32

"Stop fussin'," Sarah scolded her daughters. They turned and squirmed and pressed their faces against the glass until it became clouded with fingerprints and fog. Neither she nor the girls could wait for the journey to end.

The trip from Jefferson to Denver, followed by three nights in town while Sarah and Maggie shopped, had been extremely tiring. The women outfitted the girls with new clothes, shopped for books and paper, bought themselves each new boots and hats, and managed to arrive at the Union Pacific bound for Cheyenne on Friday on time with all their additional baggage.

Once the novelty of train travel wore off, Maggie engaged the young sisters in a variety of games and riddles, braided and rebraided their hair and told them stories until they fell asleep in their seats. Nonetheless, the last few miles into Cheyenne could not have come too soon.

"I swear, all this movin' around isn't my style," Sarah complained. "I want to settle down on a place of our own." She squinted at the flat brown prairies where dry tumbleweeds rolled in the wind or occasionally stuck fast in the spiny low growing yuccas. Shy herds of pronghorn sometimes appeared along the tracks.

"Maybe this'll be the chance we're waiting for," Sarah went on, smoothing the pinafore of her youngest daughter who now lay sprawled across her lap. "The MacGregor

Ranch is big enough to need an army to run it. Stewart says there's cattle strung out from one end to the other. Could use a dozen foremen. Sure hope it's so. I'd like to stay awhile, raise these girls proper, get 'em in a school, and teach 'em how to be ladies, like yourself, Mrs. McKennon."

"Sarah, please. I've told you, you needn't call me Missus," Maggie responded. "And I wouldn't bet on the size of that ranch, either. Everything about MacGregor sounds like a bit of an exaggeration to me."

Maggie felt awkward that Sarah continued to call her Missus or ma'am. Nearly the same age, they'd been acquainted for months. She hated to admit the difference that her own education and marriage made to a woman who could have just as well have been a sister or a friend, but who could never see herself as equal.

True, Maggie had pursued her schooling and prepared herself for a teaching career, one where women were respected. But Maggie had betrayed herself in a way. She hated to admit that, like her sisters and so many other women before her, she'd accepted an offer of marriage that provided not only a way out, but also a social position. Married women usually demanded and received more respect. She didn't begrudge the trade-off, but merely doubted its worth.

Despite all the education a woman could acquire, society dictated that a female might not be perceived as successful until she had married someone of stature and means. Maggie had hoped she would be the exception. She'd watched the shift in her own sisters' lives as whatever ambition or independence they might have had shrank away. She promised herself she would never be like them.

Still single at twenty-eight, Maggie had resented that in the clearly defined world she once occupied, a man shaped a woman's destiny. And she could see that this would continue to be the case unless the woman changed the perception of her limits or her choice in men.

Sarah Merrill had married young and assumed the role of devoted mother and wife. She'd probably never considered the idea of a potential beyond her immediate role. She took her place and stayed there, dedicating herself to making a home for a man who might never have considered whether his wife had ideas of her own. Stewart, a contract cowhand, worked hard at his job, doing his best to provide. Like so many others, their relationship evolved in keeping with the times.

Maggie suspected that she and Kerr might not have succeeded as well. Over time, she might have slipped from standing by his side to living in his shadow. Or would she even have stayed at all? The searing memory of Billy burned in her memory and clouded her thoughts. What if Kerr had lived and she'd been drawn to Billy just the same? What then?

Who can I possibly be in this shifting world of cattle, politics, and men, Maggie wondered. *Especially in this West, where women are so few, and so easily absorbed into its vastness. How can I find my place or be judged on my own merit,* she pondered. The jumble of her thoughts put her head in a spin and she wished there was someone like Billy with whom she could discuss them.

Will I go on forever defined by Kerr's name, or my father's, or the burden of my widowhood? Maggie didn't share her torment with Sarah. How could she? She anguished silently over her options. The lines in her forehead creased and deepened, a sign of the doubt which now plagued her since Kerr's death. Retaining the Cameron and exposing the truth behind Kerr's disappearance consumed her, even more than her thoughts about Billy Munro. Yet his smiling eyes returned often in her thoughts to delight and tempt her.

Very well, she reasoned. *If Maggie Dowling McKennon is a stranger to these parts, she won't be for long. I'll use all my powers to make myself heard and establish my presence at Rockrimmon. This MacGregor will have to hear me out and accept me for who I am.*

She wondered if the information from Benjamin Farrell would be waiting for her, as promised. She still didn't trust him, but knew he was a necessary ally. Before she could distress herself further, the great four-story clocktower of the Union Pacific depot rose into view as the train approached Cheyenne, the crossroads of the cowboy and the cattle baron, the cultural metropolis of the western plains.

Cheyenne had grown to be a rich and lively junction, bringing together railroad gangs, soldiers from Fort Russell, and employees from Camp Carlin, once the great supply center for all the northern posts on the Indian frontier. By 1875 the town boasted nearly 5,000 residents, among them ambitious men from the east and Europe who brought with them wealth, power and influence, as well as a host of impeccable social amenities. Many were graduates of the top English or American universities, sharing an elite camaraderie similar to the fraternities found in those revered institutions.

Although Denver, a mere hundred miles away, had by this time grown to nearly 100,000 residents, no more than 40,000 persons occupied all of Wyoming. More than three hundred of these were registered stockmen and a third of them lived year-round in Wyoming's young cities or towns. Fifty or more had settled in Cheyenne. Twenty-nine such cattlemen hailed from Britain and nine among them were Scots, including Hugh Redmond MacGregor, proud to be included in their midst.

In the heart of town, one could find a fully-appointed opera house, a boarding school for girls, and enough saloons to wet a man's throat not more than half-a-block's stroll in any direction. The railroad itself tied this remote region directly to the east, enabling the residents of Cheyenne to acquire the very latest styles in furnishings, art, and architecture, the most recent magazines and newspapers, and the most fashionable apparel from the big city salons as well.

Maggie learned from the conductor on the train that the town was not only well planned with many of the finest homes in the Victorian style, but was one of the first cities in America to be lit with the new and novel incandescent light. In 1882, the public square had been fully illuminated for the very first time, creating a new standard nationwide.

"Even a woman could move safely through the town center at night now," he said proudly, lowering his voice as if not to offend. "Of course, that's if the drovers aren't in town. Then, nobody's safe, nowhere."

The Cattleman, the monthly paper reporting transactions, growth, and change within the western cattle industry, made it clear that Cheyenne enjoyed a glittering social life unique to the West, on a par with numerous cities of similar size in the east and surpassing many of them.

Maggie couldn't compare all this to the high country wilderness she'd so recently come to know, the Colorado mountains with their lush meadows and small hamlets. Everything from the flat horizons of the prairies to the ornate buildings around her gave her the distinct impression she'd gone farther than a few hundred miles. Scanning the view as they rolled the last few miles northward, the treeless land seemed bare and exposed, vulnerable to change, clearly riveted by the hard steel railways cutting through it. The land had no choice but to succumb to the hungry and the new.

Wyoming's emptiness frightened her. She couldn't imagine a ranch like the Cameron anywhere in this environment. The Cameron, her first home in the West, her stronghold, now lay fixed in her memory as nothing less than a spiritual retreat hidden at the edge of an Elysian field.

"Halloo, halloo!" The bearded driver showed a gloved hand as the women and children stepped from the railcar. "Over here, this a'way, ladies!" Reggie Wilcox waved both arms about, motioning the party to a matched team of bays and a fine leather-trimmed brougham.

"Mrs. McKennon, ma'am! We'e been expectin' ye. Hope ye had a pleasant journey." Another hint of a Scottish brogue, gently softened by time.

"Step this way. Nae, nae . . . dinna' touch those bags, musn't pick up a thin'. I'll take care. Ye' jest gather th' lassies an' step aboard." He tipped his hat and bowed as he introduced himself. "Reginald Wilcox at yer service. Seventy-Ninth Highlander Regiment, *an'* the MacGregor's secretary, roustabout, an' occasional driver." The military identity was a reference he'd maintained for more than twenty years, still a loyal Scotsman at heart and a member of the Union Army forever. Tall and thin with a pot belly and an elfin, long gray beard, he wore a jacket with military decorations that fascinated Maggie and the girls.

"MacGregor's been waitin' fer ye', hopin' ye'd get in on time an' early enou' tae miss th' storm. Even th' Union Pacific ain't figured out a way tae keep th' snow from fallin' on these train tracks. The cow catchers on those big engines make darn good snowplows when they ha'e tae, but still, there's been many a train stuck dead in th' middle o' nowhere in a drift. Ye've arrived just in time!"

Maggie studied the enormous wedge of steel that jutted out before the leading locomotive and imagined it plowing through the heavy snow, grateful they weren't sitting aboard a train car while it did.

"Come tae visit, ha'e ye? Sure do wonder if ye'll find Rockrimmon tae yer likin'," he said, screwing up his weathered face, as lined as a Tartan plaid. "This time o' year, canna' be tae comfortable, 'specially fer a lady like yerself. Once th' wind get's a'goin' an' th' snow's knee deep, kind'a limits yer activ'ties."

Wilcox lashed the luggage in the back and helped Sarah and the girls aboard, then turned and offered Maggie a hand. "No, thanks," she said. To his surprise, he discovered Maggie reaching for the passenger seat in the driver's box next to him instead. She climbed up, unaided, with a smile on her face. "May I?"

Sitting next to the old soldier, Maggie anchored the long silver pin on her hat more firmly, then tied the underscarf securely in a bow. The cold dry wind blew briskly across their faces and heavy clouds scudded across the sky. Sarah, sitting behind on the passenger seat with the girls to either side, buttoned up their coats and wrapped a traveling blanket over their knees. Reggie then drove the rig through the station on a brick-paved traverse created just so that transport could move through the depot's center rather than going around it.

On the other side of the impressive building, the town square boasted a small park with a large concrete fountain in its center. Composed of three tiers, the lowest basin watered dogs, the next horses and mules, and the highest was for people. Water still spilled over its sides despite the cold weather, and the charming structure looked no less grand because of the empty flowerbeds and brown grass that surrounded it. The unexpected charm and humanity of Cheyenne intrigued Maggie, none of it seeming to belong to the prairie stretching out as far as the distant horizon.

"How far to the ranch?" she asked.

"Na' more'n five mile tae th' gate. Then it's just another three or four tae th' front door," he teased. Maggie pulled on her leather gloves. Over the summer, she had learned to drive Kerr's two-seater cart and loved the feel of a hitched horse in her hands. Surely, this set of leather lines couldn't be much harder than one.

"Well then," she said, scanning the roadway, "with such a distance ahead, would you mind if I took a turn driving? With your directions, I bet I can get us there in no time." With a smile, she took the long reins from him, making a sharp clucking sound with her tongue. Then she pulsed the whip and flicked the horses into a trot, leaving the old sergeant stunned, but smiling, his scraggly beard flying in the wind.

The fancy carriage sped out of town and onto the rolling flats of grazing land. The drove road, formed by cattle being brought to market, dipped and rose, following the subtle swells of the landscape. To Maggie's eye, the ride was akin to sailing, for the horizon never stayed within view, but became obscured now and then by a swale of dusty brown grass rising ahead. Forward or back, the illusion created a strange sense of vertigo, a kind of seasickness that caused Maggie to release the lines at last and hand them back to the old cowboy. She closed her eyes to steady herself. When she opened them Reggie Wilcox was staring at her like he'd seen a ghost.

"Ye all right, Missy?"

"Yes. I'll be fine. It will pass."

She mused about the variety of Scotsmen she'd met in such a short time. Coming West had almost been like crossing the Atlantic and arriving in Scotland instead.

Noticing Maggie staring at his coat, Reggie stammered, "Somethin' wrong?"

"Not at all, Mr. Wilcox. It's just your jacket. The uniform

of the Union army, is it not?"

Though Reggie had gained a few pounds over the years and could no longer button the fine garment, it was indeed the very same jacket he'd worn on the march to Knoxville in 1863. A double row of silver buttons still gleamed on the front and four rows of stripes curved toward the shoulder from the elbow. Among many other Scotsmen like himself, he had fought in the famed kilted regiment—immigrants who had gone to battle against the slave owning South, playing "The Campbells Are Coming," and blowing their pipes as part of the battle cry.

"Aye, 'tis an' I thank ye fer askin'! I wore th' gray an' red 'till McClellan himself ordered us tae switch tae trousers at th' end. But we were th' stalwart Scots o' Fort Saunders, we were. Damn if me brawny knees dinna' come near tae freezin' durin' those long winters on th' front! Ye see this?" He pointed to a hole under the right arm from a bullet that had pierced it. "That's my medal. Reminds me everra'time I put it on how close I come tae givin' my life tae this country. I was lucky; I survived. An' prospered, but that be thanks tae Mr. MacGregor, an' a fine man he is. D'ye know him well?"

"Somewhat." Maggie liked the old man, yet she would keep her reasons for being there private. "Considering everything, your jacket is in remarkable condition; you must take very good care of it," she continued, anxious to hear more of what he had to say.

"Aye, that I do. Only take it out fer special occasions: Hogmanay Day, pickin' up th' ladies, an' dancin', when I can!" he said, daring to wink a squinty eye. Then he sat up straighter and stroked his long beard with his hand. "Willna' be long, now. Nearly there."

As the wheels rolled over the last swell, the gate came into view at last, and Maggie gasped at the size of the sprawling compound. Before her, a large herd of white-faced Herefords fanned out to the left, a few hundred gathered around a low-lying water hole, and the rest foraged in bunches as far as the eye could see. As they neared the rambling two-story house, Reggie steered the carriage toward a second hitching rack. Tied to the first he saw Dr. Holland's canvas-covered phaeton and to the second, the Sheriff's bald-faced bay. With a look of grave concern, Wilcox brought the team to a halt and, in a flurry of white flakes, tied the horses to a post and began to help the ladies down.

Part Six

33

A portly woman with a welcoming smile greeted them cheerfully at the door. "Thank goodness you're here! Good afternoon to you, ladies. Mrs. McKennon, I assume? And you would be Mrs. Merrill, isn't that right? And these are your daughters, of course. Won't you come in, please?"

They stepped into a stone foyer trimmed in dark wood paneling. A wrought iron chandelier gleamed overhead.

"I am Thelma Heiser, Mr. MacGregor's housekeeper. We've been expecting you, but have had a bit of excitement, I'm afraid. Mr. MacGregor sends his regrets. He's awfully tied up at the moment . . ."

She bustled ahead holding Sarah's daughters by the hand, one on each side. Looking every bit like the domestics Maggie remembered in her own childhood, the matron wore a full apron over her long skirt and a crisp white cap over tight gray curls. Her lined face was tempered by an apple-cheeked smile. She guided the guests swiftly away from the front of the house to a back parlor where a pot of tea and a tray of Scotch tassies sat waiting.

"You just never know what's to happen with these cowboys and their tempers," she said, her voice strained with apprehension. "Some kind of a fracas, I guess, some-body hurt. Landsakes, it's just one thing after the other." She chattered while she hung their coats on a rack made of steer horns, then proceeded to serve the tea.

"You must all be quite exhausted," Mrs. Heiser continued, cupping the children's faces and looking into their tired eyes. "You needn't tarry a moment longer if you are. We can draw hot baths for the girls and turn down the beds in the spare room. What do you say? Twin beds and the best view of the ranch!

"Mrs. McKennon, you and the lady can have the guest quarters all to yourselves, just the next building over, through the breezeway, there. Tell me, how do you like your tea?"

As she spoke, she pointed a plump finger toward the leaded window where one could make out the edge of a stone portico outside linking the guesthouse to the main building. "Nice and private," she prattled on with barely a moment's break. "You'll be quite comfortable, I'm sure."

"Of course, we'll all be fine." Maggie's educated eye noted the fine furnishings in the elegant parlor, but Mrs. Heiser's remark worried her. "But may I please ask what happened? You said someone was hurt." She hoped Billy wasn't involved.

"Who's to say?" Her expression clouded perceptibly and her cheery smile disappeared. "It's the crew from the Colorado ranch. They were due in yesterday but straggled in just a few hours ago with one man dead and another barely alive. Oh my, now I've gone and told! Until the sheriff makes his report I was told not to discuss it with anyone. But how could I possibly keep it from you?"

"What do you mean, Mrs. Heiser, who's dead? And keep what from us?" Maggie demanded, putting down the tea.

"Well, you have a right to know. It seems that one ruffian was murdered and the other is lying on the kitchen table this very minute with a bullet in his leg."

Sarah approached Mrs. Heiser with an anxious look. "Someone died? Do you know who?"

"Oh, my dear, I cannot keep such a thing from you. Mr. MacGregor will have to forgive me. Indeed, the wounded man is your husband, Mrs. Merrill. The dead fellow was a stranger, I don't know who exactly."

Sarah stifled a cry of alarm. "How badly is he hurt?"

"Doctor Holland's with him, says the worst is over."

"Oh Sarah, I'm so sorry!" Maggie put her arms around the other woman who gasped and grew visibly limp. She collapsed in Maggie's grasp, and the girls rushed to their mother with frightened cries.

"Quick, Mrs. Heiser," Maggie urged. "Help me, please!"

MacGregor had left word with the staff that he would be occupied until the following morning. Assigning duties to the new crew and explaining the geography of the ranch would detain him until after dark. To his regret, the roundup of the herds, spread out over many fenceless miles, was already late. He'd gambled on the market improving and had held back both the gathering and the weaning until the last possible opportunity, hoping the prices would improve.

By giving himself an edge in a tough economy, he'd also gained some ground in shipping schedules and market demands, but just as well risked approaching bad weather and a shortage of help. If he didn't gather the animals destined for ship-out, and move the rest to ranges with accessible water soon, the majority would never survive the winter.

Sarah Merrill wasted no time joining her husband once she herself revived. As a result, Maggie found herself left to her own devices and decided to explore Rockrimmon on her own. Although it tormented her not to know where Billy Munro was, she didn't dare ask about him. Such bold interest would be misunderstood. She certainly had every right to know if her horse and extra luggage had arrived, but that wasn't what concerned her now. She had expected Billy to be at Rockrimmon and now his absence alarmed her.

Who was the man who died, she wondered? A stranger, Mrs. Heiser said.

The large ranch house formed the hub of a gigantic wheel around which radiated storage sheds, a root cellar, chicken house, milk barn, blacksmith's shop, carriage barn, tackrooms, and bunkhouse. A separate structure consisting of two bedrooms with a fireplace and a cozy sitting room provided guest quarters.

Built originally in 1864 by an earlier settler, the home, English Tudor mixed with Victorian, had been rebuilt by MacGregor into its current splendor, one lofty wing at a time. Its grand stone portal welcomed one into a great hall, inset with etched glass and leaded windows. Imported carpets from Belgium and India covered the polished wood floors, and dark paintings of Scottish landscapes graced the walls. The rambling mansion included a large formal dining room, a grand salon with a dance floor and a piano, MacGregor's private office, the master suite with a private bath, and sleeping quarters for the cook, housekeeper, and other staff.

The back half of the kitchen served as the mess hall for the bunkhouse while the front part catered to the family. That way, the continuous heat of the central fire never went to waste, even if it was just keeping coffee heating for cowboys working twelve-hour shifts. The house had recently been upgraded with all the latest amenities including indoor plumbing, steam heat, standing showers, and electric lights. Comfort and convenience often marked MacGregor's way of life.

Maggie bundled up, draping a full cape over her long riding skirt and wrapped a rabbit-trimmed wool scarf around her neck. She laced her boots up tightly and secured her hat. While the afternoon light held, she intended to canvas the ranch to see what she could learn. Reggie Wilcox spotted her and offered her a guided tour of the grounds. She accepted, hoping she could pump him for information regarding the whereabouts of Billy Munro. Together they walked towards the corrals, heads bowed against the wind.

"Watch yer step an' stay close, Missus. Th' snow be fallin' fast now, enou' tae co'er yer tracks," Reggie cautioned paternally. "I'd sure hate tae lose ye. An' after th' wild ride home ye gave us this afternoon, I see I need tae keep an eye on ye!"

In the horse corrals a small herd milled about the hay troughs waiting to be fed. Maggie looked for a black-stockinged gray but didn't see one. Perhaps Billy had ridden out to work as a line cowboy and was already far off in a remote part of the ranch. But then something caught her eye. Behind the mass of bushy manes and tails, to one side in a small paddock with an attached shed, the mare Bonniedoon paced and trotted, snorting angrily.

"That's th' new one," Reggie said. "Come in this very day all by herself, runnin' like a sprite had landed on her back. Half-crazed she was. No saddle, no markin's, nothin! Just a rip-snortin' dustmaker wi' a bug up her tail! Canna' make no sense o' it. I figure she's a part of Merrill's bunch, somehow. If not, she's one hell of a maverick."

"Yes, indeed!" Maggie could barely contain her excitement. Bonniedoon proved that Billy had made it to the ranch after all. At least, it appeared so. "That's my late husband's horse," she explained. "She's mine now and I'd like to see her, if you please."

With that Maggie climbed through the corral poles and moved toward the mare who trotted about nervously, tossing her head with a jerking motion. Her long tail twitched back and forth and her ears lay flat against her head, eyes opened wide with fear. She shied as Maggie approached and scrambled to the far end of the corral where she continued to pace. Maggie had never seen the horse so agitated. She called the animal's name softly, and taking off her right glove, held out her hand. One step at a time, she edged forward, closing the distance between them. "Here, Bonnie, here . . ."

The mare stopped, pawed the ground, and turned to look at Maggie, twisting her neck over her long back. She moved away, and then, turned full circle, facing her pursuer, as if in a stand off. The horse took one step forward, hesitant at first, and then slowly began to move toward Maggie with a visible confidence as she recognized the familiar human scent. She must have remembered the sweet offerings that always came from that hand. A low nicker broke the silence, then another. Finally, she sidled up, lowered her frosty muzzle, and rubbed her magnificent dark head along Maggie's wool coat.

Maggie rubbed the mare's neck with her bare hand while the flabbergasted Reggie looked on. "She's yers all right," he gasped. "Ne'er seen nothin' like it, Mrs. McKennon!"

Maggie didn't answer. The story Reggie Wilcox had told her was one more piece of a strange puzzle that had been forming ever since she'd arrived at the ranch. An uneasy feeling rippled over her and she couldn't let go of it. She patted the mare one more time, spoke a few words in Spanish, and looked at Reggie, saying, "I think I'd like to return to the house now. I'm really very tired."

"Sure thing, m'lady. Ye can see th' rest tomorra'." As she climbed out of the corral, he gave her his arm. "Allow me," he said as they turned around. "Shouldna' been keepin' ye out s'long. Anyhoo', supper will be on th' table a'fore too long; we mustna' be late."

No point questioning him, Maggie thought. Appearing to

know little, she wanted to avoid arousing any suspicion. But what had happened to Billy and why was Kerr's horse here without him? As they walked, the rising wind wuthered fiercely, producing an eerie moan as the snow swept over the barns and rooftops. Unnerved by the lonely sound, she stopped to listen, and then closed her eyes, suddenly blinded by a hot surge of emotion that obscured everything in her path.

Hugh Redmond MacGregor strode into the dining room, freshly bathed and changed. He smelled sharply of mint, with a brace of fresh glycerin and talc, and appeared younger and more striking than Maggie remembered. He had combed his dark hair, evenly streaked with silver, back off his face and its length lay in dampened curls around his neck. A white collarless shirt with crisp full sleeves billowed out from beneath a woolen vest while his broad forehead and finely chiseled nose created a regal profile. Maggie felt his presence as one feels lightning in the air, with a perceptible hum and a crackling. She took a deep breath so as not to reveal her reaction.

"Mrs. McKennon, please, excuse me fer th' delay." Intense brown eyes met in friendly recognition as MacGregor took his place at the table, nodding warmly to Sarah Merrill, the children, and Ewan Peters, invited for the occasion. He scrutinized Maggie for a moment, as though trying to remember the details of their first introduction a few weeks before during the brief meeting at the grave of Kerr McKennon. Maggie smiled politely through closed lips.

MacGregor didn't normally dress for dinner but had decided that tonight would be an exception. He intended to use his unquestionable authority in resolving the pending matter and didn't want the dust of a day's work to diminish either his luster or his message. The sooner he could impress his unwavering position upon his unwelcome guest, the better.

"No apology necessary," replied Maggie. "It is I who owe you, for we came in rather late today. I do like to be on time and dislike keeping a gentleman waiting." Maggie smiled again, this time broadly. Her provocative remark did not go unnoticed, its tone as perceptible as the aroma of the wine, a fragrant French Beaujolais which MacGregor uncorked before them. The Scotsman turned toward her, his mouth set sternly, while Maggie glanced at the fine painting above the sideboard, a pastoral of curly-horned cattle composed in dark greens and curried golds.

"I have heard it said," Maggie began, "according to my late husband, that wherever a MacGregor sits, that's the head of the table. Therefore, I would assume that whenever Mr. MacGregor is ready to eat, that is also when supper is actually served. Would I be correct?"

Her attempt at humor escaped the others completely and Maggie felt unexpectedly embarrassed by the remark. Trying to set a friendly mood, but entirely off course, she had taken the lead, perhaps too boldly. Early on, she'd decided that this battle would be one of the sexes, if necessary, and feminine wile was a force she thought she intuitively understood. Furthermore, she felt that her best defense was attack. If possible, she planned to make the first move and try to stay ahead. For the moment however, she resolved not to say another word.

"Well now, ye've heard right. At least partly," MacGregor countered. "But I must defer t'a real authority when it comes tae supper. What would ye say, Mrs. Heiser. Is th' lady correct or nae?" MacGregor poured the wine.

"Absolutely. Supper on this ranch might be anytime from sundown to midnight, depending on the day and the circumstances," chuckled Thelma. "That is, if you don't care if it's served cold. But I won't be kept waitin' on a Sunday, mind you. They either show up on time, or they starve!" She winked at Maggie, her gray eyes dancing amidst a fan of fine lines.

"And now it's time to serve the soup before the whole meal spoils." She disappeared into the kitchen, leaving an uncomfortable silence hanging over the table like a mist.

Maggie noticed that the place opposite MacGregor's, set with china, glassware, and silver, remained empty. For whom were they waiting, she wondered? She glanced toward the darkened doorway to the hall.

" 'Tis fer my wife," MacGregor said, observing her stare. "Out o' respect, and if she feels like joinin' us. One never knows, so we set her place in case she does." He spoke with difficulty, his voice dry. Maggie nodded.

"Well now," MacGregor brightened, "allow me tae welcome ye tae th' ranch properly, Mrs. McKennon. I do hope ye had a safe trip an' that ye've found yer quarters comfortable enou'. I regret I was occupied when ye arrived but I'm sure ye've been in capable hands. In fact, I hear ye've made yerself quite at home already. Wilcox tells me ye've discovered a renegade horse here that belonged tae Kerr. The wild thing that found her way in this morn' an' damn near ran me down when she did. Ye' must tell me abou' her, if ye dinna' mind . . ."

Tureens of hot broth appeared on the table and Mrs. Heiser filled their soup bowls with matronly confidence.

"Oh, yes. I took the liberty of arranging to have Kerr's mare brought up with the drovers, but it looks as if she had her own plans. According to my late husband, the horse is a special breed, what they call a pacer. Kerr had great hopes for her. I didn't want to leave her behind.

"It's a shame about all the trouble she's caused. She was my husband's favorite, even if she was also the cause of his . . . demise. The mare behaved well with him, just a little skittish now and then. In fact, one of his drovers had been assigned to lead her here. He told me before leaving that she followed nicely enough, gentle as a lamb . . ."

Maggie stopped. She'd thrown out a hint that fell flat. No one followed up on the horse handler. She couldn't explain to MacGregor why the horse had become an obsession in her life, why she wouldn't part with it under any circumstances when she'd left her own little mare behind. She couldn't even explain it to herself. Instead, she complimented Mrs. Heiser on the succulent dish that followed, a braised rump roast, and decided that MacGregor surely knew what he was doing. The Hereford beef was richer and more delicious than any she'd ever eaten.

"After the incident, the mare actually found her way home without him," Maggie continued, "in terrible shape, but still walking. She's been recuperating from her injuries sustained in the fall and is nearly sound again. I believe she has great value. Bonniedoon is truly a fine and willing animal and has never acted wild with me, although I confess, I've never actually ridden her."

MacGregor listened carefully to every word. The sudden arrival of the dark horse, nearly running him down, had left him troubled. He didn't know why. Such a thing had never happened before. Yet the elegant creature appealed to him, filled him with a sense of awe. He couldn't understand what a practical and conservative man like McKennon ever wanted with such a flashy mount. In Cheyenne such horses were big business for races, driving, and competitions. In town, horse fanciers would pay a pretty price for her. The wilds of the Cameron would have been no place for such a high-strung and temperamental animal. Perhaps he didn't know Kerr McKennon as well as he thought. Obviously, the man had a hidden side, one with a weakness for expensive high-steppers and outspoken women.

Aside from Maggie's straight-forward account, most of all he was struck by the young woman's unwavering loyalty to an animal she had every right to fear. He urged her to continue.

"On a practical side," she said, "I do feel there is an investment in the mare and I didn't want to let her go. My personal circumstances being what they are, I need to retain what I have, as well as what Kerr and I came to Colorado to build. I realize there is much I do not understand about his arrangements with you, sir, but I am sure that in due time I shall. Sooner than later, would you not agree, Mr. MacGregor?"

Hugh considered her remark in silence, then closed his eyes briefly. He was tired, and more over, completely bereft of the patience required to tolerate either sarcasm or impudence. When he opened them, his facial expression had become dour and strained. This last remark was in excess. Maggie had moved too fast. In fact, she had crossed the wire.

"We'll not discuss that matter except in private, Mrs. McKennon." He opened his piercing eyes to a half-squint. "I would beg ye hold off till we can find an appropriate time tae review th' matter. It's been a long an' difficult day. If ye'd be so kind as tae meet me first thing tomorra' in my study, say eight o'clock, we can review yer position at that time. I'll be at my desk by first light. And, I wouldna' unpack more than necessary if I were ye. There be two trains a day headin' east from here. Until then, I bid ye goodnight." With that, he picked up his glass of wine, pushed his chair away from the table, and stalked out of the dining room, leaving a half-finished plate.

Maggie, shaking, steadied herself against the edge of the table. Her face reddened to crimson and she busied herself folding her napkin, tense and tight-lipped. Obviously, she had provoked him. She had lost her lead by taking it. Now she'd have to do as he said and begin the tack anew. Just as well. She would be in his study early in the morning and vowed to herself not to leave until she had just what she wanted. Simply everything Kerr McKennon had a legal right to, not less.

Mrs. Heiser informed her discreetly that a packet from Philadelphia had arrived and was on the dressing table in her room. Farrell had, as requested, outlined her rights and terms of inheritance so that she would be fully informed in her demands. Maggie decided to review it all, even if it took the rest of the night.

"Just a moment, Mrs. McKennon, please, before you retire, could you help me in a small way?" Mrs. Heiser appeared with a large tray in her hands loaded with a bowl of broth, a pot of tea, and a small cup with two handles. "I hate to impose on you, but we're short-handed tonight. I've just been told I'm needed to help Mr. Merrill and someone needs to carry a bit o' refreshment to the Missus. Would you be so kind as to take this and leave it on the butler's table outside her door? I'll be straight up to take care o' the rest. Careful now, don't burn yourself. It's just there, off the first landing. I'm much obliged."

Maggie felt uncertain. What should she expect? The Missus? MacGregor's wife? What was all the mystery about and why? Maggie was beginning to sense that all was not as it should be. The meager meal on the tray hardly comprised a proper supper. "Gladly," she agreed, and took the tray from Thelma's hands.

Meanwhile, MacGregor had shut himself behind the heavy doors of his study, withdrawn from the present company with obvious rancor. Maggie felt embarrassed that she had caused his angry mood, but perhaps whatever kept his wife from joining them probably peeved him as well. She could only imagine the dilemma of a man married to such a moody and capricious creature who, on a regular basis, might or might not appear at supper. No wonder he angered so easily.

An ornate brass knob gleamed on the mahogany door at the top of the winding stairs. Maggie set down the tray and realized that the door was ajar just enough so that it could be nudged open. She knocked, twice, but hearing nothing, decided to announce herself and deliver the supper to the room. She opened the door a crack. The interior was dark with a quiet and oppressive stillness broken only by the low crackling of a fire. A huge canopied bed hugged the far wall and two gas lamps burning dimly stood on nightstands to either side. Maggie stood at the doorway transfixed as she made out the figure of a small woman lying in the bed. A black and white border collie curled before the hearth jumped up, growling as Maggie entered.

Inhaling the scent of rosewater and orange, Maggie recognized a combination of fragrance intended to disguise the scent of illness, especially of a body confined too long to bed. The large room, filled with a myriad of Scottish collectibles fairly danced with an assortment of bric-a-brac, feminine treasures, costumed dolls, figurines, and small paintings on easels. They crowded together like an odd museum of fantasy, childhood and memory.

The light of the fire in the grate warmed a tapestry of rich pastels reflecting a strange and artificial sense of spring; a man-made, endless spring. Withered nosegays rested in ribbon-tied bunches and dried florals in heavy crystal vases proved evidence of a woman's passion for a season which, in such an arid climate, passes almost before it has begun.

Clusters of wildflowers, desiccated and dry, seemed to suck the air from the room. Someone had collected a full display of formal garden flora by drying them, thereby retaining their beauty the only way possible. A room full of flowers, preserved, but utterly dead, fading like ghosts.

Maggie inhaled deeply, as if struggling to breathe, and felt dizzy trying to separate the patterns that met her eyes; cabbage roses on papered walls, festoons of dried garlands above the windows. Even dried corsages lay on the dressing table, a vanity covered with petal-edged runners of hand-made flowery lace.

Maggie put down the tray on a console near the fire and stood before the woman propped up against large pillows. Erect but limp, Mrs. MacGregor appeared to be a waxen figure inside a cream-colored bed-jacket, silken auburn hair streaming from beneath a cotton nightcap. She seemed youthful, but terribly frail. Not much older than herself, Maggie thought, though hard to tell. She appeared to be awake, but unseeing. Maggie, wanting to be sure she had not frightened her coming in thus, hesitantly placed her own hand upon the other woman's.

"Forgive me if I startled you, Mrs. MacGregor," she said softly. "My name is Margaret McKennon and I am visiting your home. Mrs. Heiser will be up soon." No real sign of recognition but a flickering of her eyelids and a slight parting of the lips, as though the woman wished to speak, but couldn't. Maggie took her hand in both of her own. It didn't feel real. She warmed it between her palms.

"My goodness, your hands feel cold." It was the only thing she could think of to say. Her words expressed only part of the pain tearing in her heart, not only for the woman in the bed, but for MacGregor as well, and even for herself, as the task ahead loomed much more complex.

How can I add to MacGregor's burdens? Why didn't someone tell me? Then again, why would they? How many other secrets does Hugh MacGregor harbor in this place? To this poor creature, there seemed no reason to say anything more. *My God,* Maggie withdrew her hands gently, *how much must a person endure? Behind the legend of MacGregor's success, lay this tragic illusion of a life.*

"Ah, there you are, Mrs. McKennon," interrupted Mrs. Heiser who had entered noiselessly. "Thank you, my dear. I'll take over from here." The housekeeper pulled up a stool and placed the large tray upon the bed, then pushed back Elizabeth's hair and tied a napkin around her neck. "Her heart, you know," she whispered over her shoulder. "Has good days and bad. We're doing our very best."

"Of course," Maggie answered. "I understand. I'll take to my room now unless you need me. Goodnight, Mrs. Heiser. And goodnight to you too, Mrs. MacGregor."

Maggie closed the door behind her and stepped into the dark hallway, turning at the landing to look out through the window at the glittering Wyoming night. She exhaled a deep breath she didn't even realize she'd been holding. In the distance, the prairies appeared luminous with their first real blanket of white. The snow had stopped, and the cobalt sky seemed deep and clear, maybe even more brilliant than in Colorado. The moon, nearly full and oddly elliptical, floated above the horizon, impossibly huge and glowing an ominous amber gold. Smiling to herself, Maggie imagined it might yet fall to earth and dissolve like the yolk of a giant cosmic egg.

As everything else this night, it was not what she had expected. An illusion perhaps. A paper moon. She shut her eyes, then opened them and looked again. The giant orb listing over the horizon seemed distorted, a crude mockery of the ideal. Standing there alone, she felt sure she saw it scowling back at her and anyone else that night who dared look up and doubt its existence, or ability to ascend, eventually, into the dark Wyoming sky.

Benjamin Farrell had performed as promised. Better in fact than Maggie expected. The packet he sent held two separately bound presentations, one consisting of a list of Kerr's holdings in Scotland, and the other, of all the Colorado assets and liabilities. In addition, she found a letter summarizing First Bank's loan for the expansion and the deed to the original thousand acres of the Cameron.

The difference between Kerr's assets and his debts turned out to be in Maggie's favor. If Scottish law would deem her brief marriage valid and she was legally Kerr's heir, then Maggie had a right to one-half his property, a sum which appeared to be substantial, clear, and unencumbered. Therefore, no further entitlement could be discussed without a will and prior provision. Kerr's old farm near Edinburgh might be worth a great deal, but at the moment she didn't want his land in Scotland, whatever it's value. She wanted the Cameron and the means to keep it.

In addition, Maggie found a brief note from Farrell and a check from an Omaha packing company for three thousand dollars, the value of the sale of the yearling Highlands, not a small amount considering the market, but still below expectations. Had Maggie not intercepted the sale through Farrell, the check would have been endorsed to MacGregor, based on the arrangement he had made with Kerr long before he died. She slipped it into her purse with a clear sense of relief and security.

★ ★ ★ ★ ★

"Well, don't just stan' there. Come in," MacGregor said, looking up from his desk as he motioned for Maggie to enter. His dark eyes, shadowed beneath thick peaked brows, looked tired and somber.

"Good morning," she said cheerfully, glad to be getting on her with mission. "I hope I'm not late." The clock read two minutes to eight and she had stood before the partially opened door of MacGregor's study for several minutes wondering if she were too early. MacGregor looked as if he had been up for hours.

"Not at all. Thank ye fer bein' prompt. I have a great deal tae do Mrs. McKennon. Please, ha'e a seat—there." He motioned her to a leather chair with a footstool and a table beside it. She walked across the oriental carpet, glanced at a portrait of a lovely woman which hung over the fireplace, and finally gathered her skirts to sit down, her back straight, hands folded.

"I'm sure ranching involves a great deal of paperwork," Maggie said. MacGregor was, in fact occupied with examining Kurt Skoll's saddlebags, which were draped over a chair. The contents of one side spilled across his desk, the other still bulged with the proof of Skoll's various enterprises.

"Aye, th' load even surprises me sometimes." He laid the leather pouch over the mound of papers before him. "Breedin' records, expense accounts, payroll fer th' staff, feed an' buildin' maintenance. Would ye like me tae go on?"

"Only if you wish to." Maggie had learned her lesson and would tread lightly until confident she stood on steady ground. She propped her feet, clad in soft black kid boots, on the ottoman, crossing her ankles in a gesture that indicated she felt relaxed, comfortable and ready to begin.

MacGregor stared, speechless. His eyes traced the shape

of her from the tips of her feet to the twist of her upswept hair, combed severely for the occasion to great effect. He contemplated his charming guest far too long for propriety's sake, but found her entirely arresting in this innocent and seductive pose. Why had he not noticed how attractive she was?

Maggie had chosen a simple ankle-length dress with a flared short jacket, its design effective in accentuating her square shoulders and narrow waist. Made of the finest wool in a rich mocha brown, she looked serious, but feminine as well, in the understated outfit. She didn't want to seem provocative or too conservative either, since this encounter with the cattle baron was the first in her limited experience as a "businesswoman."

What she didn't realize was how much its brown velvet collar and trim accented the auburn in her hair, its broad shoulders enhanced her waist and the skirt, swaying fluidly when she walked, revealed her lean hip and firm derriere.

"I beg yer pardon, Mrs. McKennon. I occasionally ferget myself," MacGregor offered. "Too many things on my mind. Now, where were we? Where would ye like tae start? I've accepted yer insistence fer an inquisition regardin' th' sale o' the Cameron ranch, but I ha'ena' a lot o' time."

Maggie noticed how clearly he spoke, his use of the language tempered by his formal education in London and later years at college in Edinburgh, or perhaps his life in Wyoming. His accent, cultured and rich, was nothing like Billy's which had the rough sound of the country in it.

"I'd like to start with whatever happened to our cowpunchers yesterday," she said. "I understand there's been some serious trouble."

"Everra'thin's under control. I don't quite see why that's any affair o' yers," MacGregor snapped, as he pushed his chair away from the desk.

"And why not?" Maggie answered. "If Kerr were here he'd demand an explanation. Those were our men. We knew them personally. I'd like to hear the details, who got killed and how Merrill got injured, and how my horse escaped and ended up here on her own." Her voice took on a hostile and caustic edge.

"Would ye, now?" MacGregor's mouth formed a hard line above his gray beard, his chin jutting forward in defiant frustration.

"Absolutely. Why, the mare might have disappeared altogether," she continued, "taken a fall or been hurt. Indeed, I think I have every right to know. Besides, to Kerr, those drovers were friends. And by the way, our foreman, Stewart Merrill returned to his wife and daughters last night. I know you hoped to protect yourself from gossip, but did you think you could hide the man's injuries from his own family?"

Maggie couldn't hold back the tide of emotion that had gripped her since she arrived. This elusive cattleman had quickly become the target for her anger, the reason everything had gone awry. In her mind, he was a selfish mercenary who had no sympathy for anyone. Despite his sick wife, Maggie no longer felt sorry for him.

She also suspected that he might be responsible for Billy's disappearance and, just possibly, have had something to do with McKennon's death as well. Such a possibility frightened her. Rivalry surely might even include murder. But if she suspected MacGregor of Kerr's disappearance, then her own plan might as well be abandoned. She might as well fear for her own life. No, MacGregor's sad dark eyes expressed a long-suffered pain. Maggie remembered Elizabeth the night before and decided he could not possibly be Kerr's killer. She had to be wrong.

The morning sun streamed through the window behind

MacGregor's desk, filling the room with refulgent light. Maggie shielded her eyes against the glare. Losing eye contact with the man made her feel lost, as if slipping blindly into an abyss. She changed her position so she could see him more clearly.

"Mr. MacGregor, of just what exactly are you afraid? I'd still like to know what has happened. So, please—I'm waiting."

"And wait ye will, but ye won't have tae wait fer long, M'lady! Ye test my patience. I find that ye are rude, intrusive, an' arrogant. I'll nae ha'e ye interrogate me or insinuate that I am hidin' a thing, nor that I ha'e anything tae fear. Kindly change yer tone o' inquiry or I shall ha'e tae ask ye tae leave."

Maggie flushed. "My apologies, sir. Forgive me if I've angered you. It was unintentional, to be sure. It's only that I will not be put off. I don't," she searched for the right words. "I don't know how to wait anymore." She wanted to say she didn't know how to be a proper lady, either, to bury her feelings, hold her tongue, and look the other way. But this he would never understand.

"All right then, I'd appreciate it if ye'd not interrupt me. Fer yer information, th' dead man wasna' an employee o' mine. Supposedly, he worked fer a cattle brokerage out o' Chicago an' came tae validate th' counts before shippin'. Some new regulation. Trust me, he wasna' someone o' importance tae us, though God knows, he might ha'e been tae somebody, somewhere. His death appears tae ha'e been th' consequence o' his own actions, accordin' tae th' crew.

"Next, just how yer banshee o' a horse broke free is anybody's guess. From th' looks o' things, I'm sure 'tisna' th' first time. That she's here is what counts an' ye may take her whene'er ye like. So much fer what's passed. Now, what say we get on tae th' real matter?"

Maggie took the story without batting an eye. At last the details were hers. Fortunately, Billy was not among the injured. Maggie rose and stepped to the fireplace where she stood quietly, collecting her thoughts. She needed to swallow her anger and appeal to the man's feelings, as one who had once been Kerr's trusted friend. She needed to make him understand that he was the only person left who could help her. And by helping her, he would be helping himself as well.

"This *is* the real matter, Mr. MacGregor. My being here is real enough to me. A ranch in Colorado has both our names on it and I'll not let First Bank of Philadelphia take it while you look the other way. Kerr might be dead, but I'm not, and I'll not be shipped out of here by the order of any man. Not you, not my father, not anybody." At this MacGregor folded his arms and looked skeptically at his guest, hardening his handsome face.

"Like my husband, I believe completely in the Cameron. I understand there are payments that should have been made, months overdue. Not surprisingly, my father's bank is greedy. They want their money back and plan to collect by foreclosure and sale. I am powerless to stop them unless you work with me. If they don't get what they want from the sale of the Cameron, you know very well they'll come after you for the amount still due. I need you to help make the payments and allow me to keep things running just as Kerr had planned."

"Y'astound me, madam!" MacGregor interrupted, furious. "Unless I'm verra wrong, ye know little o' Kerr's operation, an' furthermore, I know nothin' o' ye a'tall. I choose my partners carefully on th' basis o' common ground. Nae offense, but so far, I'm nae convinced. I take risk enou' in my own business."

Maggie began to pace the room, the folds of her skirt

moving about each time she turned. Then she faced him. "Just listen to me, whether you want to or not. You may be a legend in these parts, but you had to start somewhere. Well, so shall I. You may not know me, but that gives you no right to doubt me. There is little a man can do that I can't." She spoke intently, from her heart. "I'm sure I can make the Cameron profitable. I've thought about expanding the herd, crossbreeding if necessary, adding new lines altogether. There is too much that's right about that ranch to give it up now. I don't understand why you can't see that."

MacGregor rose and moved past her, toward a side window looking out upon the snowy windswept prairie, his broad shoulders hunched, his thumbs hooked into the pockets of his breeches. He turned to look at her directly. "Mrs. McKennon, there's much ye do na' see. Th' whole world has changed since Kerr began. Nae one can afford tae take such risks anymore. The cattle business is in shambles. Ye have no idea what ranchin' has become. I'm shocked by yer proposal. I have my own hands full an' unfortunately, things are not what they appear. I have other problems ye wouldn't begin tae comprehend. Besides, ye ha'e no experience, no conception o' what it takes. I'm afraid ye're quite naive, in fact. Though I must say, ye ha'e a strong will." His demeanor softened. "I admire yer tenacity. My old friend chose well."

Maggie was defeated for the moment, a fine sweat causing the down along the nape of her neck to curl. She stared at him, pleading with her eyes. Her shallow breathing quickened as she considered her final appeal. Head bowed, she looked up at him through lowered lashes and said softly, "Your old friend would be proud if you'd take me in his stead. Do it for him. I promise you'll not regret it."

A smile spread over MacGregor's face, though he tried to

suppress it. He smiled because her assumption was so absurd he could only see the humor in it. He smiled too because she pleased him, immensely. The color in her cheeks had risen to a high flush and her eyes burned with intensity. He couldn't remember when he'd last seen a woman look so attractive, so alive. Tempting. He struggled within himself. He hadn't looked at another woman in years, not seriously. Elizabeth's illness had destroyed something inside. He looked at Maggie incredulously and she looked right back, unafraid to meet his gaze.

"So? What's your position?" she asked. "Do I have your support?"

"I thought I made myself quite clear, Mrs. McKennon. Were ye not listenin'? Th' answer is nae. What's this abou' support? In what way?"

"In *every* way. I want you to think of me as a partner you can trust. I need your experience and your financial backing for at least a year. You must know exactly what it will take to pay off the note. Can you cover it?"

Maggie knew that the recent sale of the Highland cattle would cover a few of the payments but she was afraid to mention the check for fear MacGregor might claim it.

"If you cover the loan payments," Maggie added, "then I only need ask you for one more favor—the most important one of all."

"An' what might that be?" he asked in exasperation. He wanted to know, partly out of curiosity and partly because he couldn't take his eyes off her and wanted her to go on talking, begging him, needing him. Needing him and yet dictating her own terms. She provoked him, her demands a stimulus to a deadened soul that yet longed to feel. She revived him, made him feel warm and alive. He could not ignore the strange mixture of anger and lust that boiled up within him, that made him want to strike her one moment and caress her the next.

"I want you to make me into a real cattlewoman," she said with fire in her eyes. "Teach me how to run a successful ranch, like the great Swan Cattle Company, the Matador, or better, like yours. I want to know everything; how a steer thinks, or doesn't, when to breed and when to sell, how to deal with the punchers, where the markets are, what to feed . . . everything!"

Her pent-up plans poured from her. "I'm willing to stay in Wyoming for as long as it takes and not a day longer. Although it's the slowest time of the year for ranchwork and I know winter can be the most difficult for man and beast, I'll try to help you anyway I can. Hopefully, there will be plenty of time for you to help me. I trust my hardy Highlands will fare well enough on their rough winter pasture. But when the calves start to drop, they'll be needing me back at the Cameron. And a new crew as well. I'll have to return by then, early spring at the latest, so we have to work fast. In the meantime, I promise to listen to every word you say and not be any trouble. I know the Cameron Ranch is nothing compared to this, but someday it will be. I can do it, trust me, I know I can."

MacGregor stood beside her, emitting the invisible field of electricity she had sensed the night before when he walked into the dining room. His powerful magnetism seemed to pull her toward him, and she leaned on the mantel to steady herself. She focused on the portrait above the fireplace and noticed that he shifted his weight so that his left shoulder barely touched hers.

"Your wife?" she asked, ignoring the brush of his coat.

"Yes."

"She is very beautiful." Maggie felt a wave of sadness for the now frail woman.

"How well I know." It seemed difficult for him to look at Maggie.

"Oh, please, don't you see?" Maggie began again. "I can do this for *her* too. She wouldn't want you to lose something you had invested so much time and money in. And I can surely do it for you. You *have* to give me that chance!"

"Ha'e tae? Fer her?" He moved back to the desk. "I'll ask ye tae please stay out o' my personal affairs. She has nothing tae do wi' ye an' I'm na' askin' ye fer help. Give me more credit than that. Ye're a canny woman who's had an unfortunate loss, an' ye have my sympathies. But I canna' pick up yer burden, I've got enou' o' my own." He wasn't sure he meant what he said but his temper flared easily. He was known for it and for feeling sorry afterwards.

"But why should you risk losing anything?" Maggie retorted, undaunted. "You're part owner of the Cameron. You could take an even bigger share. When I can, I'll buy it back from you.

"If we keep the ranch operational, you and I together, we can save something we both know has real value. Let me transfer a herd of your Herefords to Colorado and turn things around. It will bring you profit in the end, Mr. MacGregor, I'm sure it will. In any case, I know you have your hands full. I am aware that you have someone here who desperately needs *you*."

She paused, then went on bravely. "I could even help you with her if you'd let me." Maggie's eyes met MacGregor's at the same moment that his sought hers. Each plumbed the depths of the other, wanting something, needing to connect for reasons beyond their own understanding.

"In fact, I'd *like* to help," Maggie said softly. "I'd be honored if you would allow it."

MacGregor's eyes grew moist, for he was moved by her spontaneous offer, the very mention of Elizabeth. He trembled with repressed energy that appeared close to being set free. Words were no longer enough. He wanted to reach out and take her in his arms, thank her for her sensitivity, for her beauty, for her vitality, but couldn't.

"Look here. I need time tae think this o'er." His voice husky, he cleared his throat. "I need tae see if there can be any other answer, save nae."

"If I may go on, Mr. MacGregor, there's more."

"I'm na' surprised. Go ahead, lass." He caught himself using the endearment, so familiar in Scottish. What was he doing? How did he dare call her thus?

"The real truth is," Maggie sighed, "I don't just need *someone* to help me. I need *you*. The world I came from doesn't make any sense to me anymore, not any of it. If I look back, I guess I have to say it never did. I can't return to Philadelphia, and I won't. No one I ever cared about really knows me there anymore. More than anything else, that's what's at the heart of it. I'm in love with this frontier and everything in it. The Cameron is the first place I've ever felt at home and I'm not turning my back on that."

Hugh nodded. "Yes, I suppose I ken what ye mean tae say. The exact words were mine ten years ago. I canna' return, 'tis what I said. An' I meant it. Smarter people than myself at th' time told me I should leave while I was ahead. But I was stubborn an' could see nothin' but this land before me, what I thought was endless opportun'ty. I've stayed too long perhaps, longer than I should've. An' I've paid th' price. Indeed, Mrs. McKennon, yer story strikes home."

MacGregor gently put his hand over hers, still resting on the ledge. A hot branding iron might have left a cooler touch. Maggie startled at the shock of it and withdrew her arm instantly, catching her breath. He ignored her surprise and embarrassment.

"Honesty is somethin' I can respect, Mrs. McKennon. I believe I understan' how ye feel. If I were tae say yes, tae help ye in any way, it would have tae stay strictly between us. I might well become th' laughin' stock o' th' Cattleman's Association here, or worse, th' Cheyenne Club. In Wyomin' women don't do men's work. Unless they ha'e tae."

"That may change in time." She laughed, still feeling the heat of his touch on her hand. He excited her, but she blamed it on the moment and pushed the sensation away. A stranger's touch. Anyone would react to one so powerful being so bold.

"No one in Wyoming has to know," Maggie said, encouraged. "I could stay on to teach Sarah's daughters if you need a reason for me to be here, or to help Mrs. Heiser with your wife. Whatever you think seems best. I'll live in the guesthouse and stay well out of the way. The financial arrangements are between you, me, and the bank. Tell me you'll say yes, Mr. MacGregor, please. I promise you won't be sorry."

"My God, woman, ye ha'e no mercy." The vulnerable man could not continue nor resist her any longer. He closed his eyes for a moment, searching for a new defense, another reason to refuse. His mind had gone blank. All he could see were her lips, her eyes, the curls along her neck.

"Then we have a deal?" Maggie asked, her heart racing.

"We ha'e a deal." A warm smile spread across his face.

"Partners?"

"Very limited partners, Mrs. McKennon. An' don't crowd me." The smile vanished as quickly as it had appeared. "Furthermore," he forewarned. "If yer goin' tae be learnin' from me, I advise ye tae always be on time."

Hugh Redmond MacGregor couldn't admit defeat. She had made sense, he told himself. She was right about the ranch, and he did fear becoming the bank's next target. His obdurate heart had thawed with the sheer intensity of her, an honest woman demanding to be heard, and he could not doubt the merit of her quest.

He knew what Peters would think, as well as Wilcox, McCall, and the whole lot of them. But how could he turn her down? How much risk could really be involved? And why did her hands have to look so appealing, sunbrowned and strong, yet so feminine, with fine narrow fingers and pale oval nails? Those hands could probably do any task they set out to do. He wanted to know them, to touch them, hold them.

How was it that he had not noticed she was wearing an intoxicating fragrance, one that had finally released its scent in the heat of the fray. He inhaled its sensual aroma, like Scotch pine in the high country, and just as well inhaled her, that mix of female, damp wool, perfume, and passion.

Closing his eyes to savor the memory, he knew he wanted her. All of her. She was the first woman to awaken a desire in his heart in so very, very long. Too long. Impossible, but she did. Before his marriage, there had been a flame or two, a few nights to remember, none really even close to being right. And then, after his wife's health deteriorated, he couldn't even look at a woman that way. The frustration was too great. Everything changed as he withdrew further and further into himself. Since Elizabeth's collapse, even chance encounters with other women inevitably evoked pain. But this woman was different. He found her irresistible. He would not let her go until he'd had his fill of her, whatever the purpose, however long the time.

May Kerr McKennon forgi'e me, he thought, even from his grave. With all respect, he could not deny what he felt when he shook Maggie McKennon's hand to conclude their private arrangement, then politely bade her goodbye. He'd actually trembled with excitement. He knew then, at that moment, and in every fiber of his being, that she had won him over. The odd partnership loomed vague and complicated, but they would work through the ambiguities and manage to find a way. Much more importantly, in spite of his earlier resistance and doubts about her, the unfamiliar heat coursing in his veins told him that he undeniably desired the late Kerr McKennon's wife.

Part Seven

W.G.D.
© 2001

36

Billy entered the canyon above Turkey Creek one week after leaving Sven. Heavy snows had given way to days of dry, sunny weather typical of November in Colorado, allowing for easy and fast travel. Once he felt reasonably sure he wasn't being followed, he kept his mount at a steady walk, rising early and seeking shelter before dark, avoiding others.

Knowing he'd be over the pass in a short time, Billy began to rehearse his homecoming. Only one person out of the few left behind would ask any questions, and he deserved the truth. Billy had seen the way the old one, Silva Avendano deReyes, moved among animals and men and felt that he alone could be trusted.

A lace of frost covered the aspen at the foot of Kenosha Pass, an ascent that began abruptly at the end of the canyon. All along the hillsides, deep stands of pine bravely bore their frozen snow-laden branches, shadowing the well-worn trail. When Billy realized the rocky path up over the top had become slick and treacherous, as well as ribbed with ruts of ice, he dismounted and led the mustang through the woods until he reached the summit. From there he could see clearly down and across the winter grasslands to the blue snow-capped peaks in the distance. Although he might have only imagined it, he was almost sure he could smell the sweet scent of wood smoke wafting through the air. Heading down the steep pass toward Jefferson with his horse trailing behind, he was cheered by a distant spiral, dark against the sky, a fire in the Cameron's chimney, not more than a few miles away.

Approaching cautiously, Billy cupped his hands and hooted loud, mimicking the sound of the great horned owl he knew frequented those woods. He stood a safe distance from the house, hidden in the trees, hoping not to be seen by anyone save the old *vaquero*. Nearby, the herd of Highlands stood, each carrying a small blanket of snow on their backs, shaggy faces clouded in rising billows of steam. He hooted again, this time even louder, hoping to attract Silva's attention.

To his amazement, a real owl returned his call, a sure promise of hope. He kept his eyes on the door, shut tight against the wind and cold. Then it opened and a cautious man stepped out, carrying a rifle. He shaded his eyes with his hands, turning slowly as he peered into the bright sunlight. Billy was in luck. Clad in a heavy woolen poncho and a wide sombrero, Silva, standing motionless, studied the fields and trees. Billy called once more, and then, stepped forward into the clearing. His gray mustang whinnied, and Silva turned, surprised by their appearance.

"Ola! Mi companero!" he called out, waving his hat. "Billy, where you been?"

The young Scot stumbled towards him and grabbed the old cowboy in a rough embrace. Still smiling, they put the horse away in the nearby corral, then returned to the house and to the welcome warmth of the fire. Over a meal prepared by Maria of tortillas, beef, and beans, Billy regaled Silva with the events of the past few days. The man listened respectfully. "And now, what you goin' to do?" Silva asked, after hearing the whole story. Somehow, he was not openly disturbed by any of it, or at least didn't let on if he was. "They come back," he predicted. "They find you."

"Nae, I dinna' think so, na' fer a while," Billy answered. "From what I understan', th' ranch is fer sale. By calvin' time, someone else'll be in charge. Someone who's ne'er heard o' me. Then, I can show up like I'm lookin' fer work an' stay on. Unless I'm wrong, there's still money tae be made off these Highlands by someone. Maybe me. I'll wait an' see. Got nowhere else tae go."

"*Si, si.* You may be right," Silva answered. "I don't know . . . My job is to make sure we lose no cattle. Nothing more. You can stay if there's no trouble, Billy. You want to live in that old cabin up by the creek? Just to be safe? *Porque no?* Nobody ever fixed that broken window, though . . . Must be a foot of snow in there by now. *No importante.* Tonight, you stay here. Tomorrow we fix, get settled. Don't worry, *compadre,* everything be okay."

The heavy snows of an early winter locked the valley of the Cameron ever deeper in nature's grasp. Passage in or out had become nearly impossible even on horseback. No one would attempt it unless absolutely necessary, but Billy planned to stay well out of sight of any intruders, just in case.

With supplies in good reserve, Silva helped Billy pack essentials to take to the cabin and agreed to warn him if necessary. They decided to use the hoot of an owl to serve as a signal should they have sudden unwanted company.

The next month came and went without incident. Days melted into nights while Billy hunted, tracked and watched the stars. Lost in his haunting sense of shame and imprisoned by his own fear, he ventured out cautiously. Though his days had sequence, they had no chronology and any real sense of time eluded him.

He visited old Silva occasionally to share a smoke or talk

and slowly began to release the weight of his crime, his fear abating that he might be caught. Then again, he never slept without his gun or his knife by his side. He often went for days without combing his hair, bathing, or changing his clothes. Not speaking for long periods, he tried in his own way to simply disappear into the woods, either by stalking game or simply moving through the trees like a ghost. Without realizing it, he had become pale, haggard, and gaunt, his face disguised by a full, reddish beard. One day, he looked into the water at the edge of a fast moving stream and discovered he hardly recognized himself.

The long hours alone gave Billy the eerie sense that he'd fallen from the edge of the earth, a forsaken traveler on the cusp between two worlds. He knew he needed to forge a new sense of himself, one based on purpose and hope, not guilt or fear. He'd had so few successes to count, so little to draw upon. Life had cheated him of any positive means by which to measure his own worth and he wished he could start over again entirely, entering the world belonging to someone or something he admired. Some days he awoke, cloaked in darkness and self-damning, loathing his own insignificance.

Billy found that he could not sever the past. No matter how hard he ran, fear always managed to stay by his side. When he'd taken to sea and then sailed to America, he had wanted so much to leave the Old World behind, the one where landless men became paupers and wealthy men became lords. But Scotland, his birthplace, would always be a punishment. The very name evoked misery, hunger, and hurt. His hatred for his homeland and himself caused him to suffer the deep, soul-searching pain of one who, by severing his roots, grows wild and ungrounded, adrift, and disintegrating by bits.

Time passed without incident. Most of the brood cows

had started to show, and sufficient nourishment and water to sustain the new life within became crucial. The majority stayed close by where Silva and Maria broke the ice in the creeks each day and put out enough hay to keep them full and satisfied. And yet, a few always insisted on foraging far along the banks, needing to be rounded up by the sparse crew and driven home.

If the snows weren't too severe, the small herd would nearly double in the spring. When at the ranch, Billy kept an eye on the stragglers, for losing even one animal was a loss the ranch could ill afford.

Hunting took most of Billy's time, searching out game that would add variety to his diet and insure he wouldn't come empty-handed when invited to Maria's table. Often, he thought he saw Maggie's face among the trees, or heard her voice in the murmur of the brook. He missed her and hoped she would forgive him for deserting her.

One afternoon, his keen eye led him to climb down a rocky shelf at the base of a snow-covered knoll. He'd been in pursuit of a snowshoe hare for more than an hour, moving farther and farther away from camp. Though several miles from the ranch, he was still on the Cameron range and noted how the wildlife seemed to be more abundant the farther away from the herd.

The pointed tips of two white ears could barely be seen against the snow, and Billy followed them until they disappeared into a burrow whose entrance was covered by fallen rock. Scrambling over the pile, he loosened the rock enough to cause a small slide and found himself looking into the mouth of a dark hole. The opening wasn't a burrow at all, but more like a large animal's den. Carefully he lifted the stones away, until he'd exposed a clearly man-made opening, approximately three feet high by as many wide. Peering into the entrance, he could see it led into a narrow space, and finally, into a cave large enough for a man to stand.

Laying down his pack, he crept in and tried to focus in the dark. Sunlight scattered along the floor, highlighting broken rock and bone shards left by some carnivore. Billy blinked and rubbed his eyes. Slowly, he was able to make out a dark mass huddled against the earthen wall. A bear or wolverine? About to make a hasty retreat, he stopped and looked again. The mass had a familiar shape to it, bent over and rounded as it was. He thought it might be a man.

Nae, impossible. And then again, maybe it was. Billy inched closer. Lighting a match, he saw in the flare a human form frozen stiff, a grim, extraordinary spectacle, but familiar. He searched his memory for a mere second, puzzled by the sense of recognition.

Then he knew. It was Kerr. The body of Kerr McKennon, lain on his side, knees bent, arms crossed, slightly decomposed, but recognizable nonetheless and still clothed, save for his jacket, boots, and hat. Billy lit another match and discovered precisely where a bullet had pierced the back of Kerr's skull, shattering bone. He touched the corpse and saw that the front half of the man's face had been partially destroyed by the bullet's explosive exit.

Stunned and repulsed, he recoiled in horror, then forced himself to look again. He felt humbled by the sight of one who had commanded so much respect, now lying so indecently, bare feet, shriveled hands, body rotted by decay, and frozen thus until the years would return his remains unto the ground.

"Mother o' God, bless this man an' spare me Satan's wrath." He bowed his head and murmured a prayer to both hold back the evil and purify his soul for he knew this had to be the great secret that had haunted the ranch for so long. Now he realized that this is what he'd felt in the hush of the whispering trees, heard in the piercing call of the ravens that flew over the fields, and felt in the wild, moaning wind at night, so sad and lonely as it wailed.

He lit another match and caught a glimmer of silver gleaming from beneath Kerr's shirt. Billy hesitantly closed his fingers around the object, barely dangling free, and pulled forth a fine chain of tiny silver bells strung to a leather lace. It was the jangly charm Kerr always tied to his hobbles, his signature means of keeping track of a horse.

The killer had missed it, whoever he was. Billy put the chain of bells in his pouch. In too damn much of a hurry to do the deed right, and now he had proof that Kerr had been found. Though uncertain of his next move, he knew the belled hobbles were important. "God save 'em," he whispered. "The bastards can blame this when th' crime sees th' light o' day."

Riding home through the snow-covered fields, Billy knew that his life had been changed by what he'd seen. Finding the corpse of Kerr McKennon would give him the chance to do the right thing, to bring justice into the world. He had to laugh at the perfect irony of it all. He, Billy Munro—a wanted man.

It was clear that in the light of this discovery, there would be everything before this time and then, everything after. As in the meaning of an omen, this too was like the passing of some larger force, a part of some more complex pattern. For Billy had learned long ago that an omen cannot only predict the coming of an event, but can reinterpret everything that went before it and integrate all that follows.

The more he considered his responsibility, the more he sensed the burden of the horrifying truth. He knew the discovery of McKennon would be of great importance, but didn't know exactly who to tell or how. A victim of his own witness, he rode to the homestead anxious and grim. Unsaddling his horse, he went into the cabin, his head swirling with doubt, worry, and finally, even hope, a dim light shining where none had been before.

Kerr McKennon had been murdered and his funeral a fraud. A hideous, unimaginable act. Why? he puzzled. And who was the culprit? Who among them would have done such an act and for what gain? Confused and distraught, he climbed into his heavy bedroll and lay thinking, staring blankly into the dark. Nothing made any sense. He couldn't believe any longer in what he thought was a utopian dream. He doubted too the hollow words of men. Both hid secrets, both lied. Finally, he realized that the new world hurt just like the old.

Indifferent to the increasing cold, he closed his eyes hoping to still his troubled thoughts, but couldn't. He wished he'd never seen the corpse, but its memory refused to fade. Even as he lay still, its distorted remains floated eerily before him, a spectre of betrayal and sin. Trembling with the vision before him, he threw a few logs on the fire and buried himself under his blanket. Sleep, his only escape, ushered him gently into a frozen dream.

The soft clop of hoofbeats faded in the loam, a gentle lonely universe of sound. He rode in that time of year when autumn glows to a pearlescent frost, along the Bowden Moor where curtains of light dance off the polar cap and the sky pooled in shades of pink, vermilion, and absinthe green. It was eventide, many hours before the dawn.

Gazing at the heavens, he saw reflections of Maggie through the veil, her smile a ripple of color beckoning far and away. The beaded dream dressed the night like a shimmering snake wearing time.

"Billy," she called, her voice echoing off the moors. "Tell me what you've found. Tell me—tell only me, and I will guide you home."

He listened for more but like a meteor she was gone, absorbed into the shower of light, melting into the stars. Billy cantered the gray horse into the void and saw the great constellations linked above like sparkling roskeles, the connected spirals of life that spring from an ancient Celtic source. Inchoate, formless, but intertwining, they spoke to him, pointing the way to his past and future and the single perfect truth that would finally set him free. Silently, they cast their spell, awakening his slumbering soul.

The blazing star dust rays coaxed courage from the weak and thanks from the lost and violated dead. Soon, the sky reverberated with the jingling of a thousand silver bells, while the hoofbeats of the gray were drowned in their thunderous ring. Billy pushed the pony on, arms opened wide, his face heavenward against a gale force wind.

"Maggie!" he cried, shouting through the din. "My dearest, dearest lass. When will I e'er see ye again?"

The hoot of an owl split the night and Billy awoke with a start. He crawled out of bed to relight the fire for his body shivered with the cold. Tomorrow, he decided, he would show Silva the cave and Maggie would have to be told.

As the heat warmed him, his thoughts began to crystallize, a daring plan that might just accomplish what was necessary without giving himself away. Before him, in the bright blue and orange tongues of the fire, he swore he saw Maggie's eyes dance again, and longed to close the distance between them. The finding of Kerr McKennon had given him another chance to reach her, another reason to live. He smiled at the irony of the strange gift of life that came in the wake of Kerr's death. If Kerr only knew. Would he have entrusted his wife to one as worthless as himself? *Nae,* he thought again, *maybe as worthy.* For he knew he could love her no more than he already did and could do no less for her than Kerr had aspired to, perhaps even more. He only needed luck to be on his side and finally, to believe in himself.

Following a hearty breakfast, Hugh tarried briefly. He put on his coat, then stopped, studying Maggie who was still seated, outfitted in her favorite riding skirt, lace-up boots, and a heavy sweater. Around her neck she had tied a jaunty white bandanna; a shade of white the color of pearls, silken and pale, like the underside of her wrist. His eyes full of her, he felt an uncomfortable feeling gnaw at him, until he forced it back inside.

"I say, Mrs. McKennon. Enou' talk. Ye canna learn much abou' ranchin' from this table. If ye want tae really learn th' way things are done aroun' here, it's time tae saddle up an' get a better perspective, get th' real lay o' th' land."

"Why, that would be fine," Maggie answered.

"There's much ye need tae know; how tae spot a stray, read an earmark, e'en th' way th' herds scatter an' drift when they graze. We'll cover what we can an' make sure ye're back fer th' noon lesson. I'll take my range horse an' ye'll take th' pacer, I assume. Will ye be needin' a sidesaddle?"

"I'd be more than delighted to join you," Maggie said with a wide smile. "But, as I said earlier, Bonniedoon was always Kerr's horse. I've never ridden her. I'll take any mount you have to offer, but no sidesaddle for me. I sit astride. I prefer it that way."

MacGregor's eyes widened in surprise. "Fine. Ye can ride a horse anyway ye like. Take yer pick from th' stock that's

well broke. Would ye not mind then if I take th' dark one?"
She wanted to say no, that the mare was Kerr's, or belonged
now in spirit to a wild dreamer named Billy, but she couldn't.
She didn't dare. She decided to leave the answer up to
Bonniedoon.

Down at the corral, no one said a word when MacGregor
saddled the mare and she lashed at him with a rear hoof. And
no one reacted either when, with the force of a geyser,
Bonniedoon exploded under the saddle as the Scotsman
threw his leg over her. Both the first time he was thrown, and
the second, he got up silently, holding his anger. He brushed
the snow off his chaps and picked up his hat, screwing it down
with a curse under his breath. The last time he attempted to
climb upon her, he had Wilcox tie her tight with a lead rope
dallied around a post. The trembling mare eyed him nervously as he approached.

MacGregor reached for the stirrup with his left foot and
Bonniedoon began to back up, pulling the rope until it
snapped in two. She jerked hard, throwing him off balance.
He hung on to the saddle horn and hopped alongside, until
the mare boxed herself in. With nowhere to go, she stood
trembling and tensed as MacGregor pushed her against the
fence while he reached for the stirrup again.

Then she went for the sky, rearing straight up, twisting as
if she could come right out from under him. When she succeeded in losing her balance, downing both MacGregor and
herself, she seemed unfazed, if not triumphant.

Snorting, the mare scrambled to her feet, hooves flailing
inches from where MacGregor lay, too stunned to get up.
The impact had knocked the wind out of him and he remained flat on his back, helpless, while the angry mare crow-
hopped and bucked around the corral in a fury, trying to dislodge the saddle as well.

"M'god man! Are ye all right?" Wilcox hoisted MacGregor up under both arms and dragged him out of the way. "I dinna' think she takes tae ye, sir."

"Tae hell wi' her! Strip th' saddle." MacGregor sputtered and stood up, shaking his head. He couldn't even look at Maggie who'd been sitting aboard a calm cowpony watching the episode, trying her best to maintain a straight face.

"Tack up ol' Rob an' let's get on wi' it. That's th' last effort I waste on that she-devil. Damn shame. I ha'e nae th' time nor th' patience tae break her. Th' way she is, she's worthless as far as I'm concerned."

"She is not," Maggie cut in. "She's willing and ridable sometimes. I just don't think she knows you, that's all."

"*Guid*," MacGregor said with a grin, "I'm glad tae hear that 'tis only because I'm a stranger. Next time, be sure we're properly introduced. Now, let's be on wi' it. There's work tae be done."

Pulling his collar up against the wind, MacGregor turned to Maggie who rode alongside, bundled in a full coat that covered the saddle and half the pony as well.

"Cattleman must adapt, ye see," he told her, "an' be prepared fer whatever comes."

"Like what?"

"Like changes in th' weather, fer instance. Open winters one year, hard ones th' next. Or cows that drop an easy calf one season an' struggle wi' breech births th' following. Ye just ne'er know. That's th' challenge."

"Sounds like more than a challenge to me," Maggie responded. "It sounds a lot more like a gamble. How do you ever come out ahead?"

MacGregor laughed. "Ye don't. The wager defies math'matics or logic. Keep at it long enou', ye'll end up

311

either bankrupt, rich or crazy." The horses plowed through deep drifts past a gully where strays had huddled to get out of the wind. "Or dead," he added with a somber note, glancing at Maggie.

"Why are you here, Mr. MacGregor?" Maggie asked, changing the subject. "Here, so far from your real home?"

" 'Twasn't so much tha' I came here, lass. 'Twas mainly tha' I left there. Even wi' all I inherited from my father's estate, there was no certainty o' a better future. Scotlan' is a poor an' fragile land. Th' English took th' best fer themselves during th' clearances, forcin' many off their farms so they could graze sheep instead. Many like my grandparents were forced tae seek their fortunes an' independence elsewhere. I broke away completely. With th' support o' others who still had large sums of money, I chose t'invest fer them an' settle here, in th' West. Start anew. What I had there I knew might na' last."

He pushed his horse slightly ahead of her to break the trail. "I'd hoped fer more fer my wife an' family. Promised a better life fer Elizabeth an' th' children who ne'er survived. I guess God gives just so much. Ye canna ask fer more. Hardly matters now. There'll be nae trace o' this marriage, nae issue, nae gran'children, nothin' o' substance a'tall."

"I'm sorry," Maggie said.

"Ye needna' be. I'm na' askin' fer sympathy. I had high hopes in my youth. Twenty years ago, th' great banks o' Edinburgh gave me th' courage tae think I was invincible. Though they may be, I daresay I'm na'. We made a go o' it, but ye cannot control change, ye can only adjust tae what it brings ye. I learnt that lesson late. Now, all that ye see here ends wi' me, sooner or later."

MacGregor rode on, stone faced, stiff in the saddle. Maggie wished she hadn't asked. Knowing she had exposed a tender wound, she returned to the subject of cattle.

"Let's assume, sir, that I'm starting from almost nothing. Like Kerr did when he first arrived. Say I've got a few good cows. Then what?"

"Ye add th' finest bulls money can buy. Breed fer form, strength, an' temperament. Whatever th' kind o' beef, ye want calm creatures ye can count on. Turn yer bulls out th' first o' June. That gi'es ye three months fer th' job tae be done. With luck, th' cows will each be wi' calf by th' next spring, gi'e or take a month or two, an' th' wee ones will start tae come as early as March, late as May."

They circled their horses up toward the draw where MacGregor showed her the watering holes that made the land so valuable. Then they headed south toward the house, turning their backs to the rising wind. Her face, barely exposed between the fur hat skimming her eyebrows and the high collar of her coat, stung with the bitter cold, but she'd never let MacGregor hear her complain.

"Come fall, wean th' young ones an' sell or ship th' yearlings off tae fatten," he continued. "They go by train these days, but I guess ye know that well enou'. Th' feedlots at th' stockyards like tae finish 'em up, addin' bulk 'til its time fer slaughter.

"Separate the bulls in pens an' winter them on grain feed if ye can. Ye'll need 'em strong an' healthy tae be any good come spring. The point is, lass, ye must follow nature's course, not try t'alter it. Ye learn tae repect yer limitations an' work wi'in 'em. Do I make myself clear?"

"Indeed."

"The rest o' th' cattle ye must protect. Fence enclosures so ye can feed when th' snow's tae deep an' provide hay enou'. We've all learnt th' hard way that winter fodder is necessary. Come spring, ye plan yer roundup tae move th' herds off th' winter range, followed by th' branding o' new calves. Th' young males ye cut at th' same time. Fast work an' hard it is, takes good men tae do it right. But tae talk about it, lass, 'tis na' tae ken th' job. Nae, ye must live cattle, day in an' day out, fer in time these animals become a verra' part o' yer soul. They swallow ye up in th' dust an' the blood an' th' stinkin' sweat o' their hides till ye almost become one of 'em yerself. 'Tis only then that ye'll understand th' life. When ye do, it becomes *yer* life. Still interested after all, Mrs. McKennon?"

"Did you think you could scare me off with the plain facts?" she laughed. "I understand the seasons and the cycles, but I do not have a clear sense of the task. How many men will I need, for instance, to manage calving, branding, and roundups?"

"That depends." MacGregor appeared to be enjoying the instruction of his apt student. "Depends on th' men, th' size o' yer herd, an' whether or na' ye ha'e dogs. At least, where I come from. One smart dog is worth two cowboys any day. In Scotlan', we move both cows an' sheep wi' th' fine border collies ye see here. Oftimes, there's no way e'en a man on a horse can keep up wi' a straggler that doesn't want tae come home. But wi' teeth an' fur at her heels, ye'd best git out o' her way. These border collies were th' best part o' Scotlan' I brought wi' me. Come tae think o' it, maybe th' only part . . ."

Maggie remembered the beautiful animal, Queen, that kept vigil over Elizabeth. The dog had continued to keep her distance, yet guard her bed-ridden owner by watching Maggie's every move. Even now, an obedient and tireless male, Bruce, followed MacGregor everywhere about the ranch, trotting through the snow alongside him, ignoring the wind and ice in his paws.

"Know yer horses, Maggie. Get th' best ye can find, those wi' good sense an' a lot of heart. Ye canna' run a ranch wi'out 'em. They be yer tools an' often, yer best friends as well. Cuttin' a cow out o' a herd, once yer mount knows th' one ye want, ye best let th' horse do th' job. A good puncher just goes along fer th' ride. I say, never argue wi' a smart cowhorse."

"Do you own the horses, or do they belong to the drovers?"

"That's up tae you, but ye'd best keep enou' tae get th' job done. Come winter, ye'll need a work team too, horses or mules, a strong hitch tae haul feed fer th' herds, fer where ye are, ye'll have t' sled th' hay tae where they stand. That is, if ye still plan t' return tae th' Cameron. Are ye sure ye want th' hardship, th' isolation, there in th' Rockies?"

"I do." She tried to suppress a sudden shiver but couldn't.

"There, in th' high mountains, th' snow's so deep, th' cattle canna' reach th' grass beneath. So far, since I've been here on these plains, Wyoming winds ha'e kept th' cover light. A couple o' winters ha'e been verra' bad. But our Herefords manage tae survive on th' feed that they find or th' fodder we provide. If they couldn't, they'd starve."

They rode over a ridge and the ranch house appeared once again, its eaves and gables covered with snow. To Maggie it looked like gingerbread trimmed with icing in a festive holiday display.

"Hey, now," he turned in the saddle, his gloved hand pulling the gelding to a halt. Maggie's horse stopped accordingly. "Are ye gettin' all o' this? Ye ha'ena' been able tae write a word o' it down, an' me goin' on so."

"Absolutely," she shivered, her teeth chattering. "I'll remember everything, I'm sure. But I'd be pleased if we could conclude the rest in the house."

MacGregor grinned at her spunk. The tip of her nose stung and snowflakes dusted her eyelashes, but Maggie rode with resilience. He liked the way she often remarked on things about the ranch he'd long overlooked himself. Like how the early morning fog rolled in, a pale blanket over the prairies, softening the harshness of the land until the sun burned the haze away. Or the wind, so often biting and cruel. Maggie could hear the different sounds it created whistling off the roof or blowing through the sage and took note of them, like one traces birdsong, she said. Even in the faces of the cattle, she saw courage and an innate dignity, more than just beefsteak on the hoof with neither heart nor individuality.

Maggie's fresh view helped MacGregor to fall in love with Rockrimmon all over again. The vastness of it, the sheer beauty of its rolling grasslands and endless plain. He marveled anew at the ingredients that had created his success, the strength of his herds and the gifts of nature, those things he could not measure.

Rockrimmon had become his world. The one place where he, Hugh Redmond MacGregor, had the last word on everything that came or went and lived or died. Everything, except the woman he'd loved. She had broken the circle of his power with the pain of her living death, and there wasn't a damn thing he could do about it.

Tempting MacGregor's reserve, Maggie tilted her face at him and prompted, "I'll race you back to the barns if you feel up to it," and positioned her mustang next to his larger horse. She smiled over one shoulder. Taking both reins in her gloved hands and leaning forward, she gently pressed the right heel of her boot toward the flank of her mount before MacGregor could answer. The cowpony lept forward, surging through the snow, heading straight for the corral and kicking up a cloud of white spray as he went. Bruce, the border collie chased after them, barking joyfully.

MacGregor let her go, amazed and delighted at the dare.

How long had it been? He couldn't remember. Maggie McKennon could make him laugh and see miracles in the ordinary. She cheered his desolate heart after long and difficult years. He couldn't imagine now why he'd ever resented her at first; how he'd thought her presence would be intolerable. Instead, sharing the morning ranch work over the past few weeks had begun to lighten his heart and force him to think more clearly about each day's tasks. He found himself thinking up ways to describe things he had never shared with anyone, things he'd never known he felt so deeply about.

As had been agreed, each day at noon Maggie would tutor Sarah's daughters, an assignment devised to avoid local gossip. MacGregor made sure his own tutelage ended in good time before her lessons with the children began. Today would be no exception.

As her snow-spattered pony skidded to a stop in front of the corral, Maggie looked back to see who had won. "Coward!" she called out as she saw MacGregor still far behind her. "You didn't even take the dare! Afraid I'd beat you, and so I have!"

"Aye, and so ye ha'e, fer t'day anyway . . ." he called out, urging his horse into a canter, his usually stern expression breaking into a smile. His horse galloped powerfully through the deep snow, quickly closing the distance between them. She had those children to teach after all, and he didn't want to keep her waiting.

After tutoring Sarah's daughters, Maggie usually looked in on Elizabeth, hoping to help her pass the long and empty afternoons. Sometimes she read aloud or told her stories, always searching those vacant eyes for a change, a sparkle, or a small sign of improvement. Sadly, since Maggie's arrival, Mrs. MacGregor seemed to have gotten worse, not better.

Late one afternoon Maggie climbed the stairs with a small package under her arm. "I've brought you something, Elizabeth, that truly reminds me of you. I want you to have it." The stricken woman's eyes focused intently on her new friend.

"Here, let me show you." Maggie opened the package and took out three carefully wrapped objects. These she carefuly untied while Elizabeth watched. She lined up the three porcelain flowers, the precious souvenirs of her wedding. The small elegant sculptures were delicate but very realistic with their painted petals and fine, curving green leaves. Elizabeth broke into a wide smile and reached toward them with a timid and trembling hand.

"Oh, you do like them! I was sure you would. Here, feel how perfectly they're made." Maggie placed a fully blossomed rose in the center of the woman's palm.

"Careful. They're very fragile."

Without warning, Elizabeth's open hand clenched reflexively around the rose, unintentionally breaking off one petal.

The sharp edge sliced into her palm and a bright line of blood erupted.

"Oh, my goodness, what have I done?" Maggie examined the cut, confirming that it wasn't too serious. "Don't be alarmed. You'll be all right." She rose quickly, reaching for a nearby linen towel next to the wash basin and, after quickly cleaning the wound, bound the cut. "I'm so sorry, it was my fault. Don't worry, dear," she reassured the bewildered Elizabeth. "It was just an accident." Elizabeth's eyes filled with tears.

Sitting on the edge of the bed, Maggie took the pitiful woman in her arms and held her, trying to erase the pain.

"I meant well. You know I only wanted to please you. You'll forgive me, won't you?" Maggie asked. Tears rolled down Elizabeth's cheeks and Maggie gently wiped them away. She didn't know if they were tears of pain or those of thanks as well.

She released her embrace and lowered the woman gently onto the pillow. Elizabeth lay back and closed her eyes, curling her fingers into the cut palm. She needed to rest. The trauma had upset her. Without disturbing her further, Maggie placed the porcelain flowers on the nightstand and slipped out, wishing she hadn't thought of the gift.

"You and I will be suppin' alone this Sunday," Mrs. Heiser advised one morning, checking the shirred eggs every few seconds. "Mr. MacGregor says to tell you he'll be gone for the evening. There's a celebration at the Cheyenne Club, campaign gala I believe, and he has a mind to be there. Him and Mr. Peters." Maggie looked up from her notebook, surprised at the news.

"The governor, Mr. Carey, is pushing for statehood," Thelma continued. "It's about time, I daresay. Everybody that's anybody will be there to hear him. How the times have changed! Can't believe we've come so far."

"Why hasn't he told me?" Maggie wondered aloud. "He can't possibly leave me behind. I intend to go too."

"My, my, I imagine you will then. I'm quite sure I wouldn't stop you. But what will people say?"

"Whatever they like. No doubt, they're probably saying it already."

MacGregor accepted Maggie's request to be included in the affair. It didn't surprise him, but he knew that appearing in public with her would set tongues wagging. Talk had already begun to filter through town, conjecture about her extended stay, her purpose, and intent. The time had come to clarify her position in the community as his partner, if in fact, it wasn't too late.

"Look here, Maggie, any questions, lea'e th' answers tae me," MacGregor advised. "Keep yer distance an' I'll see tae it that ye'll be looked after fer th' evenin' by someone I can trust."

"I can handle myself," Maggie assured him. "But I do appreciate your concern. I know at the moment women are only allowed in as guests, but one of these days I intend to become a member of the Stock Growers Association and the Cheyenne Club myself."

MacGregor smiled. He didn't doubt for a minute that she would.

On the festive night, Hugh MacGregor, Maggie, Ewan Peters and Reggie Wilcox arrived together at the Club. Reggie, dressed predictably in his finest military regalia, tied their carriage and squeezed by the crowded hitching posts, jam-packed with fancy broughams, shiny buggies, and wagons trimmed with lanterns and brass. Drivers chatted or dozed, equipped with blankets and coffee for the long night ahead.

Passing the tennis court and lower verandahs, they entered the three-story building by ascending one of its wide staircases. Inside, in the marble-floored central foyer they checked their wraps.

"Good evening, sir." A doorman in polished boots and top hat stared at their assembly. Maggie could feel the eyes of other bystanders upon her and tried to ignore them.

A woman in mourning was expected to dress in black for a full year after losing her husband, but Maggie had come west with no such provision in her wedding trousseau. With no time to consult a dressmaker, she had chosen her most conservative outfit and hoped for the best. Evidently her feathered black wool hat, dark crimson two-piece dress, and black velvet trimmed cape were not conservative enough. More than one lady's shocked expression confirmed disdain.

Maggie, daring to wear jewelry as well, had fastened her cape with a fine brooch, a polished oval lapis surrounded by seed pearls, a gift from her mother when she turned twenty years of age. Mrs. Dowling claimed that Queen Victoria had one just like it. Adorned with pearl earrings and elbow-length gloves, Maggie felt that if she were going to show up as MacGregor's partner, she'd better look the part.

Studying the rich wood-paneled walls and gleaming chandeliers, she whispered to the Scot, "Who'd have ever thought to see all this luxury for cowboys and cattlemen?"

"Cowboys an' cattlemen," he answered, leading her past the library with a smile. "This place was supposed tae feel like home fer a British aristocrat. A gentlemen's club, designed tae reflect th' old tradition o' comfort an' privacy while indulgin' in th' very best." He winked at her. "Act as though ye've seen it all before, lass."

"I have," Maggie confirmed with a smile. "That's the whole point."

"Follow me now an' be serious," MacGregor admonished and led the way down a gleaming hallway hung with photos of cattlemen, race horses, polo teams, and prize winning steers.

By the time dinner began, an elaborate buffet featuring oysters, pheasant and standing rib roast, Maggie had learned the club's entire history. The prestigious organization had opened in the spring of '81 to much fanfare and criticism, since the charter membership was by invitation only. A shocking twenty-five thousand dollars had been collected to build the posh clubhouse which included a smoking parlor, a billiard room, and a well-stocked library.

Interiors with waxed wooden floors, tiled fireplaces with quotations by William Shakespeare around the hearths, and imported carpets adorned every salon. Six sleeping chambers on the upper floors welcomed visiting guests with fine hand-carved furniture.

"My dear," explained Mrs. Phillip Dater, the club president's wife and gregarious hostess of the evening. "Of course you're surprised. Everyone who visits here is. No one gives us credit for civilizing Cheyenne the way we have. Why, we just might be the richest city in America! My Phillip says he can sell more cattle sitting right here at the bar than he can at any market and usually does! The club is the very heart of the industry."

Maggie nodded as the woman prattled on, struck by her lack of discretion. Success seemed to have loosened the woman's tongue, she observed.

"We townswomen take pride in our commitment to art and culture," Mrs. Dater boasted. "Did you know that Lily Langtry herself performed at the Cheyenne Opera two years ago? She told me I received her more graciously than the

Queen. At the reception in my very own parlor she gave us a lengthy private recitation. Quite impressive, really."

"Oh, it must have been," Maggie confirmed, scanning the hunting trophies and game heads on the walls. "I'm sorry I missed it."

While waiting for dinner, MacGregor explained that the club was only open to member cattlemen in good standing. A strict code of behavior kept a certain number blacklisted and the current miscreants' names were displayed on a coded chalkboard at the end of the bar. Swearing, spitting, extreme drunkenness, or dues in arrears were all reasons for temporary expulsion. Certain gentlemen seemed to stay on the list semi-permanently, bribing their way back in when the occasion called for it.

Mrs. Dater attached herself to Maggie and continued to brag about the charms of Cheyenne, especially the fine homes in the Rainsford district where she and many other fine families lived in the heart of Cattlemen's Row.

"Over there," she said to Maggie, nodding in the direction of the bar, "stands his Honor Judge Joseph Carey. His house, right in the middle of town, has twenty-five rooms. And he swears his livery barns are every bit as nice as his own home. Next to him is John Clay, manager of the Swan. When Clay was hired, they imported four-hundred Hereford bulls and cows all at one time. They not only run the biggest operation in all of Wyoming, but boast that their cattle barns are lined in redwood, steam-heated, and lit with Edison lights!"

A sigh of adoration heaved Mrs. Dater's bejeweled bosom. She fluttered her eyelids and looked Swan's way, fanning herself as she did. "According to Mr. Swan," she continued, "the Scots have single-handedly civilized the world and shall continue to do so, even in Chugwater!" The comely matron shook her head approvingly and winked at Maggie. "I would never disagree with him."

MacGregor stopped one of the waiters and ordered a whiskey for himself and Peters. He waited to sign the bill as was his custom, but the waiter returned and asked him to step over to the bar.

MacGregor asked, "What's th' problem?"

"Just following orders, sir. I can't put this on your account. You'll have to pay cash for the drink tonight. You can check with Mr. Dater if you like."

MacGregor stared through the cloud of smoke across the room where Dater stood talking with Hunt and the rest of his inner circle, all members of the Wyoming Stock Growers Association.

The manipulatin' bastard, MacGregor muttered. As expected, the long anticipated shift of power had finally begun. Alliances changing overnight, friends bending for money. He had seen it coming. For the moment, he wouldn't mention the insult to Maggie.

Instead, he took his seat, complimenting Mrs. Dater on her elegant gown. Maggie sat across from him, the debate for statehood scheduled to begin. Without any introduction, the portly Shubert Teschmacher, a noted member of the Wyoming legislature, stepped up to the podium, ready to discuss the upcoming campaign. The current Governor of the Territory and manager of the shaky American Cattle Trust, Francis E. Warren, stood just behind. A hush fell over the crowd as the speaker began.

"I ask you, ladies and gentlemen, to look around," Teschmacher began in a pompous tone. "And as you do, you may smile. Before us lies the beginning of a new era—yes, indeed! We have finally reached the population of sixty thousand, thanks to those who have settled here with an eye on the future and can qualify for statehood in every way. Unless someone can prove otherwise, I hereby proclaim that the forty-forth state of these United States is about to be ours!"

The audience stood up in unison and broke into wild applause. "With statehood and your help, we will gain control of the use of water, land, and minerals within our borders. As a state we will take back our coal from the federal government. As a state we shall determine our own development, as well as our own priorities. And in the future, we shall measure our wealth in men, not in cattle." Then, waiting for the din to subside, he added coyly, "And in women, as well!" Another round of applause broke forth. "But most of all, we will be measured in leadership," he shouted, raising a fist, "in manpower, not in profits alone." Hoots and whistles pierced the applause.

"As a state, we shall speak to Congress on our own behalf, not through officers appointed by the President. Remember, only those elected from within can give us the power we deserve. Yes, dear friends, I am speaking of independence, nothing less. A voice in our national government; the voice of our own people." Pausing as if to emphasize his next thought, he drew a deep breath. "Now, before I turn this podium over to our Governor, the Honorable Francis Warren, let me say, and I believe I speak for a solid majority, that this Wyoming has been a territory long enough!"

The holidays passed uneventfully, the great plains layered weekly by snow, then swept nearly clean by Wyoming winds once again. MacGregor struggled with his cattle and his ailing wife, sensing the colder front of politics changing the territory he had once loved into an alien and hostile world. Only Maggie seemed a constant, a light in the increasing darkness. He came to rely on her optimism to rally him as much as his first cup of coffee woke him each morning into action. He began to include her in nearly every aspect of his life.

The chilly month of January could not pass anywhere in the world without Scots marking the anniversary of the birth of Robert Burns. Traditionally, the commemoration of Scotland's beloved national poet was celebrated by a traditional dinner, marked by recitations, music and sentimental toasts. This year would be the 89th occasion since the tradition abroad had begun.

Several years earlier, the Cheyenne gathering had been moved from town to Rockrimmon Ranch and had become a cherished tradition in the MacGregor home. Although Elizabeth hadn't been well enough to participate in recent years, MacGregor enlisted the help of numerous friends for the planning. The dinner, replete with the presentation of the *haggis,* a national Scot's dish made with oats and sweetmeats and cooked in a sheep's stomach, was always the highlight. The talents of local musicians, pipers, and dancers helped create a true *ceilidh,* a get-together where everyone took part. In spite of the apparent shift in power, MacGregor saw no reason why this year's event should be any different. That is, until confirmations of the invitations began.

Checking the dinner list, Thelma noted that several responses remained outstanding. People that MacGregor had counted upon. Most obvious among them, Randolph Hunt and the Governor-elect.

He knew then that circumstances had changed for the worse. "Bah, tae hell wi' them," MacGregor growled. "We'll ha'e th' party anyway."

Though a light snow had fallen earlier and the temperature hovered above zero, candelabras sparkled inside the warm house and a cheery fireplace blazed. A genuine feeling of elegance glazed the great hall like a sweet shimmering sauce. Guests arrived in gracious attire, weather-beaten cattlemen in what were fondly referred to as "Herefords," (traditional black and white tuxedos), and their wives in full-length gowns, beaded, trussed and tucked.

Most of the Scottish men proudly wore the tartan of their clan ornamented with elaborate *sporrans* or pouches, boldly anchored over the kilt. Maggie delighted in the traditional costumes which included frilly jabots, knee-high leggings with the blades of short daggers or dirks tucked inside, and long pointed claymores or swords fastened at the waist. For the most part spirits ran high and whiskey flowed, this being the one time each year that rivals forgot their arguments and joined in sentimental reverie about their homeland, as well as its favorite poet.

This year, Burns's beloved poem, "Tam O'Shanter," a favorite of MacGregor's, would be read in its entirety, preceded by the downing of the *"quaich,"* the two-handled silver cup filled to the brim with Scotch whiskey. As usual, all would sing *Auld Lang Syne* to close the evening.

MacGregor acted the perfect host, concealing the disappointment that had embittered the night. In the same way he had dealt with other private sorrows, he had grown adept at disguising his angst. Proudly, he continued to smile and chat with his various guests, wondering how many others would prove to be traitors to an empire he thought they had built together.

When MacGregor disappeared during the Burns reading, Maggie had a hunch she'd know where to find him. Above the roof of the mansion, battlements around a small lookout framed a dramatic view of the stars, the only access a winding staircase with a hidden door. By day, the grand view inspired, but by night it was simply dazzling. On a clear night, especially after a snowfall, the sparkle of the constellations lit up the void, the multitude of stars a dazzling canopy with no beginning and no end. The immensity of the night sky only served to shrink a man's view of himself, MacGregor had told her once. Occasionally he went there because he himself needed to be reminded of precisely where he stood.

"Hugh MacGregor," Maggie called softly from the landing. "Are you here?" She hesitated before stepping out into the night air, cold but refreshing. "Come back in. You'll be missed."

"Nae, I doubt that."

"Of course you will. But not if you come now."

"As usual," he sighed, shrugging his shoulders. "I canna' argue wi' ye. I suppose I must." Reluctantly, he followed Maggie toward the door. She was right. Why give them reason to suspect weakness? He would not be daunted, but he himself could not hide from the truth. It waited for him downstairs and in every hour yet to unfold. The only thing that cheered him was the transfusion of Maggie's boundless energy into his deteriorating world. She made all this bearable. He would continue to act the part and not expose his torment to anyone. Western Land and Cattle would persevere, even if it meant risking everything he possessed.

"Listen tae me, Maggie," MacGregor said sternly. "In th' end, th' secret's water. That's all." He looked at her somberly, his eyes red from a night without sleep. She carefully titled and dated a clean page of her notebook and underlined the word "WATER." Then waited for him to continue.

"Mark my words, lass. Ye canna' raise beef wi'out it. Nae, ye canna' raise a damn thing. The inability o' range cattle tae find water is th' cruelest an' surest way tae failure. At least four times as many cattle ha'e died for th' want o' water than fer th' lack o' food. Ye must provide fer 'em as they canna' manage fer themselves.

"When I started this ranch, I was lucky. I had ground water, well water, an' full creeks with enou' runoff tae sustain forty thousand head. But I didna' own th' land; I laid claim tae it like everra'body else. It came free fer th' askin'."

MacGregor paced his study like a caged lion while Maggie listened, as she had for weeks since their liason began. "Homesteaders ha'e changed all that wi' their fences. Overnight, I'm bein' forced tae buy th' land th' water flows through or lose access. Th' way things are, I'm a bit squeezed tae make th' purchase. If I refuse tae buy up at least a ten-mile stretch o' Crow Creek, an' soon, I won't be able tae use any o' th' water that flows there." Maggie put her pen down and listened attentively.

" 'Tisna' that I don't ha'e th' money, though cash is tight. It seems my money isn't good enou' all o' a sudden, Scottish notes bein' suspect. Furthermore, such a purchase must come from th' investor group out o' Scotland through th' banks that carry th' ranch. I only act on their behalf. Such a transaction takes a bit o' time. I've been told I don't ha'e it. An' told wi' rudeness an' disrespect. Certain people forget I helped build this community. Now I'm hearin' 'twas all at their expense."

His dark eyes smoldering, MacGregor ground his teeth, causing deep muscles in his cheek to flex beneath his beard. "I dinna' want tae worry ye, lass, but while ye're fixed on savin' th' Cameron, I'm afraid things aroun' here are beginnin' tae go tae hell. It looks like I've got tae clear na' only Kerr's debts, but a few of my own as well, or we might ha'e tae sell off th' ranch in Colorado after all. We wouldna' want that now, would we?"

"Oh, come now," Maggie answered. "Surely you can afford to purchase a few hundred acres to control the water rights you need? Can't you use livestock or property as collateral?"

"That's na' what's holdin' things up."

"I'm afraid to ask what is," said Maggie, remembering her conversation with Farrell, almost afraid to hear the rest.

"Unfortunately, there's a nasty piece o' legislation in Washington that says th' problem just might be my name. Foreign investors at th' moment may na' make new purchases o' government land fer personal use. Senator Oates thinks such acquisitions promote Eur'pean power, weakenin' American control. He has a wide circle o' friends. As ye know, Wyoming will become a state soon. Our new candidate wants tae look good. If he an' his people follow Washington's lead, they'll want tae white-wash this territory fer th' new America."

"Does that mean what I think?"

"It's a freeze-out, Maggie. A move tae put American

money first, what there is o' it. Kerr an' I were partners, financed by investors who wanted a piece o' America's prosperity. Our profits bypass th' local economy. Domestic banks want tae handle th' expansion now, forcin' Europeans tae return home. My signature's no longer enou'."

"Are you saying that an entire herd of cattle will die of thirst this winter because you can't get access to the water that runs through your own property?"

"More or less."

"I can't believe it. There has to be a way."

"The Stock Growers Association wants th' future held by American businessmen. I'm grateful that Kerr McKennon has been spared th' humiliation o' such politics. It would ha'e cut him tae th' core." Maggie winced at the mention of Kerr and once more, thought of the hideous truth she still shared with only the Spaniard. Did she dare tell MacGregor that Kerr's funeral was a mockery? Once more, she wondered if, in fact, he knew. And even though she was now sure he had nothing to do with such skullduggery, this was not the moment to bring it up. She pushed the thought aside. "How much money are we talking about?"

"For the moment, nearly three thousand dollars, there abouts."

"Good," said Maggie, rising up from her chair with an air of relief. "Consider it paid. The signature on the check may say McKennon, but they'll have to look more closely. It will be Margaret Dowling McKennon. Do you think anybody will have a problem with that?"

"What can ye mean, lass?" One did not joke about matters of money.

"I mean I intend to help you. After all, that's the only way I can help myself, isn't it?" Maggie pulled on her coat, fastening the hood around her neck. "I'm sure time is precious.

Do you think Wilcox could drive me into town today?" She peered out the window at graying skies and wind squalls swirling up wisps of snow.

"Would ye mind fer just one minute staying where y'are an' explainin' yerself?" MacGregor demanded.

"Let's just say we're going to solve your problems one at a time. I have had for several weeks a check from the sale of Kerr's Highlands that will buy you just what you need. They sold for top price before the market crashed, fifty-two dollars per steer. Six hundred and fifty prime beeves to one customer. First Bank's attorney Benjamin Farrell was kind enough to send the draft to me personally. I've refrained from drawing on the fund until now hoping I would eventually figure out how best to utilize it. By covering this land purchase, I hope to assure that I'll be back at the Cameron by spring. Is that a fair arrangement?"

MacGregor stood stunned by what he heard.

"Furthermore, I suppose it's time to tell you that according to Mr. Farrell and the legal statutes in the new state of Colorado, I actually have full rights to act as your bonafide legal partner since McKennon had no living family or other heirs. My signature is as good as his would have been. But I do want you to know that I appreciate having been accepted by you for my own sake."

MacGregor sat back upon his desk, arms folded, gazing at her in sincere admiration. "Ye confound me. Is there anythin' else?"

"You tell me. Hopefully, the Stock Growers Association won't turn down a McKennon that happens to be a native-born American. My money should be good enough."

"I guess they wouldna'. But don't take this lightly, Maggie. My place here is not secure. Yer effort might be a waste. I canna' guarantee 'twill buy me anythin' but time.

The Stock Growers Association has grown so powerful they ha'e gained control one way or t'other over who can sell cattle an' where they can be sold. Already certain settlers an' ranchers ha'e been black-balled because o' their 'alleged' rustling. Many ha'e been driven from th' territory. My instincts tell me that my hands will be tied an' soon. If ye're tellin' me th' truth now, then there's a wee bit o' hope where there was none before. Do ye really mean ye'd sacrifice yer holdin's?"

"I do." Maggie wanted to conclude the conversation and get on with what was necessary. She did not fully fathom what he was describing but felt ill at ease with his unfamiliar humility. She prevailed in a businesslike tone. "Well now, we had better take care of it without wasting any time."

"Not so fast." MacGregor moved towards her and gripped her shoulders, looking stern yet tender. "I'm na' sure I understand yet what ye're up tae, but if ye're tae make this one thin' work, then God help ye. If it's Kerr's money ye're usin', or rightfully yer own, I'll get it back tae ye soon as I can. I don't feel right, takin' from your inheritance, th' price ye paid was dear. But by this alone, if ye can delay th' beginnin' o' the end, then there may be a reason beyond my understandin' as to why ye're here after all." He drew her to him in a fierce embrace. Maggie resisted, momentarily.

"Nae, I will na' stop ye anymore than tae say this." He looked lovingly into her eyes. "That is, that I give ye my deepest thanks. Thanks fer bein' on my side, fer bein' here. Fer what it is you're about tae do, fer I am deeply in yer debt."

"Please don't," Maggie protested, but found his arms incredibly calming. Calming and exhilerating as well. She wanted very much to hug him back but stopped herself.

"Please don't what?" MacGregor's eyes pooled with desire. "There be nothin' wrong in my wantin' tae hold ye. Don't turn me away now, Maggie. I need ye tae know ye're th' only thin' left in this world I can trust. I've wanted fer a long time tae put my arms around ye," he said. "To hold ye, like this." Sliding his cheek across her hair, he held her close. Maggie stood breathless, her resistance disintegrating in the furnace of his hold. She felt dizzy with the intensity of his embrace, inflamed by his body against her.

He has so much passion, she thought. *And so many needs. He is so much like Billy, in fact, and yet, so much more. A cattle king perhaps, but a king dethroned. A victim of the times and even, of his own success* . . . God, how she wanted to help him hold on to what he was about to lose. She closed her eyes and allowed herself to feel the strength of him about her. But the thought of Billy returned. Where had he gone? Why hadn't she heard from him? How could she betray him by allowing MacGregor to move her so? And how could she possibly be there for them both?

The Scotsman looked into her face once more, with new light behind his usually sad eyes. "I owe ye much," he said. Hands clasped tighter round her waist, he moved his cheek alongside hers and whispered, "And I need ye, more than life itself. Tell me that ye'll na' turn me away . . ."

Maggie searched her heart for an answer but couldn't find the right words. Finally, she pulled free from his embrace.

"Please. I'm not what you need. I would never disappoint you, but I'm still not what you deserve. My dreams aren't yours. I don't even know what yours are. Don't you see? Right now, there's a ranch and a future to protect that's more important. So give me a few minutes and I'll be ready to leave for town, if you are."

A gentle squeeze and a kiss upon her cheek was all the agreement he gave. "So be it. I'll be ready. An' ye dress warm, now. Th' winds are up ag'in."

Although Billy had resolved to tell Silva about finding Kerr's body, he postponed sharing the news for several days. Instead, he returned to the cave to make certain he hadn't been dreaming. Nothing had changed. The corpse remained very real, as was Billy's fear, which squeezed his heart like a vise.

No longer imprisoned by the discovery, he wasn't entirely free either. To be free he sensed, even in the wilderness, one had to be free within oneself. The incriminating knowledge of Kerr's true whereabouts had him feeling as trapped as any animal. He wondered if he should risk his own safety to reveal his grisly discovery. And if he were to do so, how would he go about it? For more than a week he struggled with the decision and at last decided to tell Silva and instruct him to carry the news to Cheyenne from there.

"First," Billy rehearsed outloud as he rode through the woods, "ye must take th' news tae MacGregor, an' tell him ye found th' body yerself. Ye must never mention my name. It's as though I dinna' exist." Billy's voice trailed through the trees, only his pony listening, its ears flicking.

"An' then, ye must find Maggie an' see tae it that she learns th' truth as well. Tell her th' real story. Tell her I ha'ena' forgotten her. An' canna' wait tae see her agin." Billy realized that MacGregor might not tell anyone about Kerr's body once Silva brought him all the facts. He might notify the authorities or he might not. But at least he would understand that someone else also knew the truth. A truth MacGregor might have known all along.

The gray mustang slipped through the silvery aspens, an attentive audience of one. It seemed as though the platinum trunks of the trees and the dark thick needles of the spruce also absorbed every word. Billy spoke louder, addressing the woods and waiting, as if someone would answer. Then he repeated his instructions again, clarifying his thoughts.

"An' ye willna' mention how badly wounded Kerr was. Only tell Maggie that he was shot. Ye must spare breakin' her heart any further." Billy rehearsed his conversation first one way, then another. He needed to be sure that the old horse handler would understand what was expected and what Billy himself had seen. It made sense that Silva deliver the news while Billy stayed behind at the ranch, whatever the risk. Sending a letter might also work, but Billy wasn't sure if either one of them could write well enough to tell the story the way he wanted it told. No, if delivering the message in person were the only way, then Silva would be the one to do it.

The light snow falling throughout the day grew heavy, filling in the gelding's tracks. If it didn't stop, Billy would probably end up spending the night at the Cameron, which didn't seem like a bad idea. He felt like he needed company. Emerging from the woods into the clearing where the house stood, he pulled his horse up short and gasped. Ahead of him he saw Silva, splitting firewood, and not more than fifty feet away crouched a large, tawny form, a full-grown cougar. The big cat lay low to the ground and nearly motionless, its tail twitching back and forth, studying its prey. For one moment it caught wind of Billy and turned its head.

Billy dismounted quickly, his Winchester in his hand, hoping the wind would cover him. He wanted desperately to call out and warn his friend, but was afraid that by doing so he would trigger the attack. He closed in cautiously trying for a better shot and hoped to get the cougar before it got to Silva.

The cat might have been after the Highland cow or her calf in the nearby corral, but whatever its prey, the hungry animal would not succeed. Afraid of catching its attention again, he cocked the rifle and carefully crept forward. The lion heard the click and turned to face him. It snarled and hissed, curling back lips that revealed gleaming sharp teeth. One huge forepaw lifted as the animal crouched and Billy could see taut muscles ripple outward on its shoulder. He fired. But his aim was off and the bullet only grazed the top of the cougar's back. The cat screeched in pain and Silva whirled at the sound.

"Run, Silva! Run!" Billy shouted but the cry came too late. The cat lunged, its anguished snarl echoing through the woods as it hit the old man with the full force of its charge. Billy ran forward, knowing there'd be no stopping the wounded animal. Silva fell to his knees, the cougar on his back. The man's screams pierced the air, as gnashing teeth sought flesh.

Realizing that firing a bullet might mean hitting Silva if he missed, he threw his rifle down and drew his knife instead. Now there would be no other way to finish the cougar. He assailed the lion from the back and locked his left arm under its neck, while driving the point of his knife downward into the animal's chest. The cougar arched and twisted beneath him, trying to dislodge its attacker, snarling and raking his arm with its extended claws. Thrashing together, Billy managed to plunge the blade in again and again until the cat collapsed and finally released its deadly hold, leaving the battered Spaniard unconscious on the ground.

The cougar's last rasping breath vibrated like an ill wind as it turned its head upwards, emitting a foam-flecked, guttural hiss. Billy watched it die, feeling numb and frozen inside. It had all happened so quickly. Now, he stood dazed as the blood pumping wildly through his own veins turned to water, his legs buckling like wet rope.

The old man was bleeding badly, his coat torn, his neck and shoulders slashed. Sheathing his knife, Billy wrapped his jacket around Silva and picked him up in his arms. Every minute was precious. Maria would have to attend to him immediately or he would die from his injuries.

Billy staggered with his load to the house, but began to lose hold and sought to lay Silva down by the step. Maria rushed to meet him. She picked up her husband's shoulders as Billy raised his feet to carry him in.

A low nicker caused Billy to turn around. It was then that he saw the strange saddle horse tied to the corral. Just as he feared, the law had undoubtedly come for him at last. Ignoring the rising sense of panic, Billy carried his wounded friend into the house and looking into Maria's anxious face, tried to reassure her. "He'll be all right," he said, trying to sound convincing. "Just a bit scratched. Help me get him on th' bed."

Within seconds Maria had removed the torn clothing and begun to clean and bind the areas that bled the most. Billy stepped aside, willing to let Maria take over while he prepared to face another front.

From the moment he entered, he had sensed the presence of someone else in the house, somewhere beyond the door in the front room. He braced himself for the worst—jail, or deportation, then thought better of any compliance. He could be on the back of his mustang and gone, deep within the forest in seconds, or—whatever happened, he'd resist. No one would take him now, not if he could help it.

Was it to be that I have just saved a life, he thought, *only to go to prison for also having taken one?* Clearly, in his mind, one man had deserved to live, but not the other. The forgiving God whom he had doubted, but who had remembered him so long ago at sea, surely had to know that now.

Still numb from his ordeal, he quickly removed his bloodied shirt and slipped a poncho over his head. Then, taking a deep and resolute breath, he pulled out his knife and holding it beside him, entered the room beyond the hearth. The stranger still sat motionless in a chair, looking out the window where the cat lay in the snow.

Sonofabitch, Billy thought, *he must have seen the whole episode.* The man, who had heard Billy enter, got up from the chair at last, though with difficulty, and standing with the help of a cane, turned to face him.

"Nice work, young'un," his raspy voice sounded familiar. "Step closer so's I can see yu. Imagine that—jest rode on up ta these parts ta be sure yu got where yu was goin' and yu swagger in, bringin' me a pelt for my efforts. Git over here, Billy, and greet an old friend!" The stranger was none other than Sven Solvaag.

Relief drew Billy to the old Swede. Placing his knife back into its sheath, he said, "Ye had me worried there fer a bit. Next time, could ye let me know yer comin'?" He wanted to embrace the old man but reached instead for his wrist, squeezing it with the force of a bear, as if to playfully test the other's strength.

"Yu don't need ta wrestle with me. Yu done enough o' that fer one day. But I could'a beat the pants off yu in my prime."

Billy collapsed into the chair next to Sven and closed his eyes, waiting for the pounding in his heart to subside, and for the tremor in his hands to settle. Now and then a shiver of pure energy shook him and brought back the picture of the fangs and claws which had come so close. Sven watched as

339

Billy cleaned his knife and turned it over on his lap, watching the metal reflect the flicker of the fire.

The old man sat expectantly for a few moments, then glancing to the far side of the house where Maria tended her husband, said, "It's high time we took a look at yur friend there. Mebbe we can help."

As they entered, only the soft shuffle of Maria's moccasined feet could be heard as she moved protectively around the bed where Silva lay.

"Do ye think he'll recover?" Billy asked, staring at the wounded man.

"Why sure," said Sven. "Look at what a fine job she's done." Maria had stopped most of the bleeding and sewn up flaps of skin that lay ragged along the old cowboy's back. Billy sponged off the man's forehead, then knelt down and felt for Silva's pulse. It beat rhythmically and steady.

"Still, I believe I'd better fetch him a doctor from Jefferson tomorrow," Sven concluded, " 'case any infection sets in. He won't be much good ta nobody till he heals up a ways, but he'll live. Now then, what about yu?"

Billy, not realizing he was injured, followed Sven's gaze to a long gash gaping across his right forearm. "I'm okay. Nothin' tae bother. I'll be fine."

"Yu best have Maria take a look at that," Sven said. "But let me say that was a right nice piece a work there. Who taught yu how ta kill wildcats?" Sven cocked one eyebrow up and looked hard at Billy.

"Why, no one."

"Didn't think so. But yu jumped in like Geronimo, I'd say. Wished I could'a helped yu, but my eyesight's too far gone ta shoot worth a damn and my hip's so far out'ta joint I kin hardly walk. So I jest said to m'self, if me and the Devil was layin' bets on who was gonna win out there, I wouldn't have laid two bits on that mountain lion. Figured you'd get 'im and sure enuf, here yu are. Thanks fer not lettin' me down. I sure hates ta lose a bet."

Billy grinned. Just as quickly, a clouded expression stole his smile. "There was nae time tae be scared. All I know was, I couldna' let a man go that away."

"Uh huh. And what about yerself . . . ?"

Billy ran his left hand over the swelling gash and wiped the blood away that had trickled down to his wrist. The touch of his own fingers on the open wound triggered a sensation like wire snapping, something ripping away that had long held him fast. Up until now, he had always been too late or too frightened to act. He looked out the window at the body of the cat. By his bare hands he'd taken its life and it had surely given him back his own. With luck, old Silva would live and walk again and know that another had met death in his stead. Billy now understood how it felt to flaunt danger, to act selflessly, and move as though it did not matter if one lived or died.

So many years before, when still a student of Thomas Fey and his self-styled catechism of the sea, he had learned that to fear God enabled one to find strength in himself. What he had not understood was that to fear death didn't prevent one from dying anyhow.

He knew now, as he stared out beyond the blood-stained snow, that something vital had changed. He saw into and beyond the darkening pines and that wide plateau separating him from the meaning and promise of the rest of his life, and sensed that somehow, he had become the cougar. He had taken it in. In his own way, he had sought his demons, and annihilated his prey. And now understood with full acceptance, that he would not, nor could not, ever be ruled by fear again.

The bulky-looking envelope addressed to "Mrs. Kerr McKennon, Rockrimmon Ranch, Cheyenne, Wyoming," arrived at exactly the same time as the documents from the Wyoming Livestock Growers Association, addressed to "H. Redmond MacGregor." Thelma Heiser delivered both packets to MacGregor's study after the pair returned from their morning ride.

The package to Maggie bore no return information and was as odd a parcel as Thelma had ever seen. It was a homemade brown envelope with a strange bulge along one side, tied securely with string and fastened with a series of snug interlocking knots. The elaborate classical script adorning its face was written in a curious and foreign hand. She turned the packet over again and again, as if by so doing she could decipher its contents.

Mrs. Heiser had deduced by this time that Mrs. McKennon was no longer merely a guest. Three months and the widow had slowly become a part of the ranch and MacGregor's daily life. She observed the way the Scot looked at Maggie across the dinner table, taking note of how the usually somber cattleman had changed. His mood had brightened in a way she had not seen since the early days when she'd first come to Rockrimmon while young Elizabeth was still a blushing bride. He appeared to stand taller, seemed more relaxed, and even treated them all in a more kindly and patient way. Everyone noticed that he spoke to Mrs. McKennon with the unmistakable warmth, tenderness, and eagerness of a man in love. Anything therefore concerning Mrs. McKennon took on considerable importance.

"Look here," Hugh said to Maggie, "a letter has arrived fer ye. Slow down an' bide a' wee. Ye need na' be in such a hurry tae meet yer students everra' time." Maggie put down her things and picked up the strange package.

"Perhaps it's from yer family," the Scot continued. " 'Tis time ye heard an encouraging word from home." Taking out a small pocket knife, he offered, "Shall I open it fer ye?"

One glance told Maggie the letter wasn't from Philadelphia. She deduced that it had to be from Billy. It could have come from no other. Her heart racing, she answered hastily, "No, that won't be necessary. I'll do it later. I hate to keep the girls waiting."

"Verra' well, then. I'll see ye at supper." He reached out to stroke her cheek and turned to his own affairs.

Closing the door to her room, Maggie pulled out a small pair of sewing scissors to cut the twine on the bulky pack. The envelope open, she found a folded letter written on the same fine parchment Kerr himself used when he had contacted his factors in Scotland. She must have left some behind at the Cameron. The unusual script began thus:

Dear Mrs. McKennon,

On behalf of yer late husbin and as one who feels partialy responsible fer yer welfare I regret to be the bearer of bad news.

Thanks to a mutual ackquaintaince (and trustworthy source) it has been recently proved that the true and acktual remains (what's left of em) of yer recently deceesed Kerr

McKennon lies not in the grave where he was so-called buried months ago, but rather, in a cave herebouts, on the very premises of the Cameron Ranch near Jefferson Colorado!

Furthermore it appears that the corpse bears proof of a bullet, sum several signs o' which have been the actual cause of death in my humble opinion. No other persons save your <u>Entrusted Servant</u> (merely a scribe) one drover by the name a Silva d'Avendano deReyes, and he who dictates this letter are privvy to the awful truth.

Prior to informing the authorities(which we have a mind to do) we send this news to you with the enclosed proof found upon the body. We trust you'll mind this information and use it as you see fit.

Someone wants you to know that you have not been forgotten. You may telegraph any message care of the depot in Jefferson to the attention of "The Trapper."

Most sincerely,

Your servant,
S. Solvaag

In place of any further name, Maggie found the brown feather of an owl which had been affixed with a touch of pine resin to the bottom of the page. Signature enough to cheer her heart and soften the grim truth of the message. She inhaled the scent of the piney substance and rotated the delicate feather against her cheek. It was from Billy, there could be no doubt. She smiled to herself with the knowledge that Billy Munro was indeed safe, obviously back at the Cameron, and thinking of her still. About the rest she was not surprised, only more determined than ever to find out why Kerr had been murdered.

The small bumpy pouch, rolled and tied inside the envelope, weighed almost nothing. Made of fine lambskin with the curly wool on the inside, she unrolled it to reveal a fine leather lace with the silver bells Kerr used with his hobbles on the trail. The dense batting had served as a muffle for the bells, but now they tinkled with innocent gaiety as she held it before her.

The silver ornament had been among Kerr's most beloved possessions and he almost never rode without them. How could she have forgotten them at the time of the funeral? Now, the Scottish bells would be proof enough of their owner's true identity.

Maggie slipped the whole packet into her bureau and buried it beneath her clothes. With half the mystery solved, she resolved to conclude the rest, if not by herself, then with the help of someone who could investigate the truth for her. Benjamin Farrell would do. It would be enough to contact him by telegraph and tell him that she now knew where McKennon's body lay. She felt sure he would know how to explore the rest. She'd ask him to come to Cheyenne at once.

The more she thought about it, she could see no reason why he couldn't take the problem of the discovery of the corpse off Billy's hands and look into it quietly, without revealing much to anyone. For a slightly adjusted fee, he could be talked into almost anything.

For the moment, she would keep the news to herself except for the telegram to Farrell. Perhaps a simple confirmation to Billy, via "The Trapper" as well, although such a telegram might cause questions when received in Jefferson. She'd have to think about that. But Farrell's message couldn't wait. Despite the storms that had been blowing off and on for days, Maggie decided to take the chance of going into town that very afternoon.

MacGregor and Peters sat across from each other in the

study behind a closed door. Maggie rapped gently. "Forgive me for intruding, sir. May I come in?"

"Certainly," he answered. The men had been studying a series of pages laid out across the wide desk.

"Have a seat, lass. There are no secrets here. Word's out that th' blizzard that's hit every territory north o' here has struck west o' Laramie County. Looks like we're next. Reports from Montana tell that th' drifts there are killin' off th' herds. If th' winds willna' stop, there's na' a one of us will ha'e a live cow next spring."

"The storm's that serious?" Maggie too grew concerned.

"Might be. But that's just tae begin wi'. It also looks like Rockrimmon is abou' tae be devoured by vultures. Th' Stockgrowers claim that th' water on this ranch was first filed in another's name. They say that there's a record of that earlier filing, which I canna' disprove. Tae make matters worse, homesteaders want what has been mine by the right o' public domain, an' it looks like these open lands 'round me will be fer sale by year's end."

Maggie frowned, taking in the grave situation.

"I either reduce my herds an' become somebody's tenant, or stake out a property line an' buy up this ranch from th' Federal authorities. And all this at a time when everybody knows th' property is good for nothin' without th' streams feedin' it." The Scot rubbed his forehead, kneading his heavy brow.

"Och, 'twas no different fer another MacGregor na' so long ago. History tells that th' lairds reduced th' great Rob Roy ta a mere steward o' another till th' end o' his days. Nae, I dinna' come this far tae be turned into a serf fer th' local politicians."

Peters interrupted, casting a long glance at Maggie. "Do ye think ye should be discussing all o' this, right here?" He began stacking the documents as if to indicate they had concluded the topic.

"An' why not?" MacGregor answered, forgetting how well he and Maggie had concealed their personal arrangement. "The problem is soon tae be shared by us all. But I will na' run from it. Perhaps I can buy some time." A loud knock sounded at the door.

"Who's there?" MacGregor asked.

"It's me, Mrs. Heiser. Oh, please, sir, come quick. It's Elizabeth!"

MacGregor opened the door to the distraught woman.

"I called the doctor the minute I found her. I didn't even realize you were back. I was just trying to change the bedding I was, and I left her sitting in the chair there by the window the way she likes, you know, and went out to the closet in the corridor for just a moment to get another—"

"Hush, will ye!" MacGregor cut her off as they hurried up the stairway toward the master bedroom door, followed by Maggie.

Elizabeth lay partially upon the mattress, one arm still hooked around the bedpost, the lower half of her body sagging toward the floor. Her head, turned to one side, rested against the bed, her face partially covered by her hair. Her china blue eyes stared vacantly through the long strands and the faintest curve of what looked like a smile played at the barely visible corner of her mouth.

"At long last," MacGregor sighed, shaking his head in disbelief, and approaching her slowly. "Look there . . . e'en a smile fer me, saved fer th' very end. My bonnie Elizabeth, my sweetest flow'r. My beautiful Scotch bluebell . . ." He lifted her gently onto the mattress as easily as one gathers dried heather from a field.

Maggie took the housekeeper's hand and stepped hesitantly into the room. Mrs. Heiser buried her face in her kerchief with a sob and uttered a prayer. Then she stepped past MacGregor to the foot of the bed for a closer look and realized Elizabeth had been dead for several minutes. The woman had to have been so grateful to finally succumb, she thought, staring at her in shock.

Queen, the isolated woman's ever-present companion, now stood between Maggie and the body, her teeth bared, growling protectively. Gently, MacGregor hushed the dog and then reached over to close his wife's eyes and cross her limp hands across her chest. As he did, he leaned forward and placed his lips on her finger tips, kissing for the last time the hands of the fragile woman he had struggled so long to save. Then he removed her gold wedding ring and lightly drew a blanket over her.

Steadying himself at the edge of the bed, he placed his open palm, hand shaking, upon the head of the dog whose muzzle now lay against Elizabeth's lifeless arm. Queen whined and wagged her tail feebly. One firm stroke along the dog's back and MacGregor turned away to hide the tears that filled his eyes. A sob of grief escaped as he hurried from the room and down the narrow stairs.

Maggie stood for a few moments by the bed until the persistent whimpers of the dog tore at her heart, then she too retreated. Mrs. Heiser and Maggie returned together to the foyer where Peters waited. Their faces told him all.

"I'll get th' word out," Peters said, putting on his coat. "We'll need tae dig a grave soon while we can. If we can."

"You'll forgive me, Mrs. McKennon," Thelma said to Maggie, "but I'd appreciate a moment to myself, if that's all right." She dabbed at eyes, her chest heaving. "Let me know when the coroner arrives, would you?"

"Of course," Maggie assured her. She embraced her

briefly and then turned down the corridor past the library toward her own room. She saw MacGregor standing alone at the far end of the library, gazing out the windows. A heavy snow had started to fall. Maggie stood respectfully at the doorway, waiting, she knew not for what. When he finally saw her, he began to speak.

"Can ye see th' plains out there?" He drew his arm across the void. "Elizabeth loved this view. I did too, once. Now, look at it, would ye? It's nearly March an' He had tae save th' worst fer last."

The predicted blizzard had begun to sweep across the landscape with a fury, thick snow clouds blotting out the morning light. The wind howled around the eaves. "I knew this day would come. Sure as I'm standing here, Maggie. This day an' th' fact that there's a whole new world out there before me an' I canna' see a goddamn thing!"

"How can I help you?" Maggie asked in a low voice, almost hesitant to speak. "Or would you rather be alone?" She hated to admit that she herself needed someone, that the sadness in the house felt too overwhelming, the horrific image of Elizabeth's lifeless body too upsetting to forget.

MacGregor turned to look into her eyes, his own reddened with grief. "I loved her," he said. "God help me, I did." Maggie put her arms around him and he bowed his head to rest upon her shoulder.

"I wanted her tae live, d'ye understand?" he asked, his voice cracking. His broad shoulders began to crumple and he surrendered to the pain so long buried within. Maggie held him close, his weight against her, her arms supporting him as a buoy bears an anchor in the sea.

"She was all I had, fer all this time, fer such a long time. An' she ne're e'en knew it. I turned away at th' end, a coward I was. Couldna' be wi' her, couldna' e'en tell her." His tears moistened the silk of Maggie's blouse, his arms tightening their hold, and he pressed his damp cheek against her own.

Her heart ached in response to his pain. "It's all right," she said tenderly. "It's all right. You did what you could. I'm sure she knew." There was nothing to say or do but to hold him, still and close.

"Nae, nae one knows how much I really loved her, Maggie," he whispered, struggling to speak as he wept. The sound of the wind and the gathering storm outside rose all around as if to express what MacGregor felt, deep within. Looking into Maggie's misty eyes and searching for the confirmation of his thoughts, he repeated, almost inaudibly, "I loved her. D'ye hear me? I loved her, Maggie. Almost—an' may God forgi'e me fer sayin' it—almost as much as I now love you."

Benjamin Farrell left for Cheyenne after receiving Maggie's wire. He wasted no time packing once he heard the remarkable news and arrived just in time to attend the funeral services for Elizabeth. A small gathering of friends and cattlemen had responded, braving the freezing temperatures.

"Wasn't that your father's personal counsel I saw at the church this morning?" MacGregor asked.

"Indeed," said Maggie, not looking at him.

"I remember him clearly from our meetings with Mr. Dowling early last year. I wouldna' thought First Bank would send a representative on such short notice. Did ye notify them o' Elizabeth's passin'?" MacGregor persisted.

"Yes, I did. I sent word to my family the day after she died. In a way, your loss touches us all. Father sends his respects and Mr. Farrell has come west to see if he can be of any personal assistance to me. After all, the ranch debt isn't the only thing that concerns my father, you know."

Maggie wished that what she said were true, but since her move west she had begun to realize that to her family, little else mattered except banking and business. And she was still not ready to complicate MacGregor's life with the news that McKennon had been murdered in Colorado, or that she needed Farrell to help her find out who was responsible. Not yet. But Farrell's appearance needed a decent cover. When the time was right, MacGregor would also know.

"Where can we talk?" Farrell asked, smiling through closed lips as he passed by her in the church foyer.

"Stay here," Maggie responded, "and I'll find a reason to remain behind. I know Wilcox has errands to do. I'll remind him to come round for me in an hour or so."

Assisting Mrs. Heiser into MacGregor's carriage, Maggie announced she needed to stay in town for a short time. With no further explanation, she waved goodbye and returned to Farrell who waited inside.

"The worst part," Maggie explained, after reviewing the letter written by Billy and Sven, "is not telling MacGregor what I know. Somehow, I still actually suspect him. I feel torn between what I see and feel for him and these hard truths. Isn't that awful?"

"Not at all," Benjamin assured her. "You are wise to be cautious. He had every reason to get rid of an unstable partner. It just seems out of character based on what we know about him."

Maggie nodded.

"Stewart Merrill must have some insight into what was going on," he continued. "He may be on this ranch for a reason, stationed out on a line camp trailing cattle, but he's not far enough away that an arrest warrant can't bring him back. I'd like to ask him a few questions. But I'd also like to handle this quietly for the moment. I don't think I need to involve the sheriff in Colorado just yet."

"Good," Maggie cut in, "because I have a feeling that Billy Munro isn't ready to meet up with the law. I've been trying to make sense out of all the pieces to this story and am thinking that he's not stepping forward himself because he might be connected to that horrid cattle detective's death. Why else would he be contacting me through a cover? I've asked the other drovers and no one will talk about the details. Also very suspicious. Maybe Skoll deserved what happened to him for some reason. Who knows? Oddly, MacGregor never pursued the matter. In any case, Billy's hiding out, and I'm sure the only explanation that makes any sense will be his own. I'm sure he's as far above cold-blooded murder as I am. He has to be innocent, at least of intent."

She dared not say more and reveal her special relationship with him, but as she spoke, her emotions flared as she sensed the magnitude of the drama in which Billy now played a part.

Maggie never believed for a moment that Billy's motives could be anything but honest and that he had probably been trapped into the circumstances that now held him fast. Her belief in him solidified, her yearning tempered with a sense of protection and loyalty. There was so much still to be realized, so much to become.

"Fine," Farrell continued. "My first suspect in Kerr's death is Stewart Merrill. If he's not the guilty party, I'm sure he has a degree of involvement. I think it's time I had a talk with him, one way or the other."

"Be careful," Maggie warned. "There are those here who would like to see MacGregor eliminated. Even long-time friends have let him down. Randolph Hunt has been supportive, but I suspect he might align himself with whomever has the most influence at the moment. A hearing has been called to investigate water rights and disputed claims on portions of the ranch. It's scheduled for two weeks from tomorrow. Can you work that fast?"

"Is there a decent hotel in town with a reasonable kitchen?" Farrell smiled his familiar, obsequious smile.

"Certainly," Maggie replied.

"Well then, let's find it so you'll know where to find me." He took her arm and together they stepped out into the chilly afternoon.

"Over there," Maggie said, pointing to the nearby Albany Hotel on Central Avenue. "Indoor plumbing, steam heat, and," she teased gently, "a dining room with a Swiss chef." Farrell patted her gloved hand and led the way.

The hearing was to take place at the Cheyenne Club at two in the afternoon, the third Wednesday of April. Notice to the public had also had gone out to any members of the Stock Growers Association who might be affected by the outcome. Maggie assumed there would be a full house, weather permitting.

"I'd appreciate it if ye'd stay at home," MacGregor told her. "This meetin' is a man's business an' ye ha'e no part in it. I'd ha'e a hard time explainin' yer presence there. When I return, I'll share wi' ye whatever transpired."

For once Maggie couldn't argue. "Very well. I'll not insist. You have my support, whatever the result."

"I'll be leavin' Wilcox here in charge if ye need anythin'. Peters will ride wi' me. We should be home by sundown."

He looked at her the way a condemned man looks at freedom. "Should things fall their way, Maggie, the ranch will be run dry an' me run off it, ye'll na' be a'goin' ahead with yer fool plan, will ye?"

"Why do you ask?"

"Because it's clear ta me that my time may be up here, like it or nae. I'd fight them all, but I admit I'm tired. Ten years too late. The whole thin' may na' be worth fightin' fer. Ye'd have nae way o' knowin', but there's more muscle behind this charade than ye can see. By th' looks o' their claims, this ranch has been divided while I'm still standin' on it." He paced angrily.

"I've been thinkin'. Maybe its time ta sell out an' finish wi' all this business before it finishes me. Part company, like a gentleman. I used tae be one, if I remember rightly."

"You can't be serious."

"I can. After all, na' much glory goin' down wi' a sinkin' ship if th' lifeboats are empty. Keep this t'yerself, Maggie, but I've been approached, as o' yesterday, by th' Two-Bar spread. They made me a cash offer. Look at me, lass. I could sell out an' be done. An' my point is, if it comes tae that, could I count on ye, still?"

Maggie could no longer avoid MacGregor's eyes and their desperate need of her.

"I cannot turn my back on my own dream yet," she answered. "You've lived yours, Hugh. But Rockrimmon's still here and I believe that things will work out for you if you persevere. Meanwhile, I know I can't stay in Wyoming any longer. I can feel it. What I've learned from you here I need to be putting to use. I need to be heading home."

What she did not say was that a piece of her heart belonged to another who's future seemed full of promise, wherever he was. And that it was her job to discover the truth of her husband's final end. MacGregor's glory lay behind him, and although she was sure he could provide her a new start with style and substance, she could not see herself in any part of it.

Maggie forced herself to repeat the vows that had been guiding her through the past few months. Returning to the Cameron had become her destiny and she was determined to see it through. But each day at Rockrimmon made leaving more difficult. She had quietly accepted MacGregor's affection for her, never encouraging him, but never denying him either. Had it not been for Billy, she might have been more receptive, but for more reasons than she cared to admit, to return MacGregor's tenderness seemed impossible. Although she admired him and cared about him, both her haunting suspicions and her affection for another kept her in check.

"Whatever the outcome," Maggie continued, "you will do

what you want, and I will do as I must. And since there were no buyers for the Cameron over the winter thus far, First Bank is stuck with a ranch to run, like it or not. As I said when I first came here, I intend to run it for them. I'll claim the half that's mine as I should have at the first, and deal with my obstinate family on my own."

"Are ye sure, lass?" MacGregor asked. "Are ye so stubborn that ye won't consider any other way? I'm askin ye Maggie, could ye nae picture comin' wi' me, if I pulled up now an' returned tae my roots, tae Scotlan', tae start a new life?"

Maggie took both his hands. "You honor me, my dear Mr. MacGregor," she said with a gentle smile. "But you're well aware what the answer has to be. You do what you have to do. I intend to return to Colorado . . . and the Cameron."

MacGregor framed her face with his hands. "Ye're as stubborn as I am, God love ye. Nae matter, then. I'm na' abandonin' ship just yet. I told the bastards no."

Farrell had arranged for Stewart to be summoned the day after the hearing to inquire into the death of McKennon. Since the investigation would have to involve MacGregor as well, Maggie begged Farrell to schedule inquiries after the hearing, not before. If MacGregor were innocent, then he surely had enough to deal with for the time being.

Through the Sheriff in South Park, Farrell had discovered that the town coroner in Fairplay had been paid to issue McKennon's death certificate without ever looking at the body. Who actually paid him was still undetermined, but the gruff undertaker, tanner, and sometime gravedigger confessed it took little encouragement at the time. Busy that week dressing out elk and mule deer, he didn't mind not having to inspect the corpse. He took Stewart Merrill's story on its own merits, plus the twenty-dollar gold piece that went with it. Being a sheep rancher himself, cattlemen alive or dead were all the same to him. Regardless of who they were, he had no passion for either.

An unexpected meeting took place at Rockrimmon just hours before the convening of the Stockgrowers Association. Maggie watched a black carriage approach over the icy road and counted three male passengers, two members of the XIT Ranch, and the third, Randolph Hunt, now secretary to the governor-elect.

Hoping to keep the afternoon hearing short, the self appointed "committee" wanted MacGregor to concede the ranch based on written claims alone. No one wanted a scene. Hunt felt it was politically a bad time to be ousting a fellow cattleman in any case, but personal sentiment would never prevail. There were more urgent matters at stake, such as the statehood of Wyoming and the loosening of huge tracts of land near Cheyenne for more profitable developments.

Maggie, watching the trio enter the house, decided she needed fresh air. Whatever was to happen at Rockrimmon seemed beyond guessing, but she felt confident MacGregor would know what to do. She laced her boots, put on her gloves and, as had become her custom in the late afternoons, headed down to the corrals to check on Bonniedoon, whose exercise and safe-keeping had become her responsibility.

After a thorough brushing, Maggie usually haltered the mare and led her around the branding pen where the snow was packed and smooth. Still isolated, the pacer seemed to crave human company and always greeted Maggie with a whinny. The animal followed so willingly it seemed unnecessary to hold her at all or even use a halter. It was hard to imagine that this docile creature was the same one who had run away with McKennon, thrown MacGregor in a fit of fury, and given Billy the most exhilerating ride of his life.

Anxious about the proceedings back at the house, Maggie patted the mare's cheek and continued to walk her about. As she turned toward the gate, she noticed Randolph Hunt leaving in his black carriage. MacGregor and Peters rode behind on their own horses. She didn't like the feel of it and really didn't know why.

In the light of the late afternoon, Maggie paced about the house, watching the clock. At a quarter past five MacGregor had still not returned from the hearing and Maggie grew concerned, then reminded herself that he and Peters could take care of themselves. She had no real reason to worry.

In spite of the cool weather, spring sweetened the air. The lengthening days, wet snows, and the first calves nursing at their mother's flanks offered proof of the approaching season. Whatever the verdict for MacGregor, life would still burst anew all around and, water or none, the prairies would continue their endless cycle, greed and politics not withstanding.

The clock chimed half-past six with still no sign of MacGregor and Peters. The ride from Cheyenne normally took no more than an hour. What was taking so long?

"You mind yourself, now," Mrs. Heiser tendered. "I'll put away the tea." The two had poured a fresh pot and discussed gingerly the distressing state of affairs. Maggie reached to pick up the tray before the other woman could do so.

"I'd like to do it for you," she countered. Thelma folded her arms over her broad stomach and frowned, as if being deprived of an essential duty but sat down just the same. The two women had begun sharing this comforting ritual since Elizabeth's death and hadn't missed a day. Somehow, they'd made a silent commitment to one another, as well as to the one man they both cared about, each looking after him in her own way and recognizing that they were a vital part of what kept the lonely rancher at ease. Each tried to give him what Elizabeth could not, both holding fast to an invisible net of ropes that would hopefully catch him in his fall.

As the sun began to set, a spring snowstorm briefly brightened the sky and the wind rose just enough to make the snowflakes dance and swirl. Maggie had stepped outside to check for riders once again when she smelled smoke. Something was burning, there was no mistaking it.

Maggie whirled to see flames curling above the wooden roof of the barn. A mere hundred feet from the house, the wings of the cross-shaped building spewed roiling plumes of smoke. Somewhere inside, the bawling of cattle could be heard. Her heart pounding, she ran to Mrs. Heiser's room and knocked on the door. "Thelma! There's a fire in the barn! Hurry! I'm going to find Wilcox!" The ashen face of the frightened woman appeared at the door. Then, her coat thrown about her shoulders, slippered feet racing down the hall, Thelma shouted, "I'll be out in a minute but first I've got to get Queen. She's upstairs!"

"There's no time!" Maggie screamed, but the housekeeper scrambled up the steps to the bedroom where the dog had lain for over a month, loyally vigilant for its lost mistress. Maggie ran to the bunkhouse behind the kitchen and pounded on the heavy door. "Reggie! Come quick. The barn's on fire. Help me get the animals out!"

Cowhands in for the night hurriedly assembled by the water tanks to begin a bucket brigade. Others ran for the ladders. A ranch hand clanged the triangle to summon anyone still out with cattle. Then, lining up with big leather buckets kept for such emergencies, the crew began to throw water toward the roof of the barn. They struggled to hold back the flames which sped along the edge toward the house. The fire glowed bright with the rising wind.

Inside the barn, the breeding stock milled in panic. Five Hereford bulls, the best sires of the herd, bellowed and strained against the stall gates, lowering their massive heads to butt and push. Two stallions and four brood mares confined to the stalls on the south side whinnied and thrashed, kicking the walls of their enclosure in terror.

Wilcox started on the north end, releasing the wagon teams. Maggie ran down the south corridor, unlocking stall doors to the right and left, hazing the animals out into the center aisle. The bulls stampeded for the doorway, two abreast, but the horses, wild with fear, stamped and reared where they stood, unwilling to be coaxed into the smoke-filled hall.

"Oh, God, help me," Maggie shouted, "don't leave them trapped like this. Run!" she screamed at the horses, helpless in their confusion. "Run, run for your lives . . . !"

Bonniedoon, frantic with fear, reared and pawed in the very last stall. Maggie flung open the door and stepped inside. "Come on now," she urged, flicking a lead rope at the animal's flank. "Get out, girl! Now!" The mare laid back her ears and pressed against the outside wall which was already hot from the flames. A fore hoof lashed out, narrowly missing Maggie's knee.

Realizing she had only seconds before the glowing rafters and the huge timbered roof would collapse, Maggie untied her scarf and wrapped it over the mare's eyes. Blindfolded, the mare nervously allowed Maggie to attach a rope to her halter and lead her into the corridor. One by one, the other horses stepped forward, warily willing to be led by one of their own. At the wide doorway, nearly obscured by smoke, Bonniedoon pulled back against the lead, neighing in terror at the sound of the fire popping and sizzling all around. She trembled and snorted in fear.

"Don't stop now," Maggie screamed, pulling the horse forward with all her might. "You'll trap us *all* in here. Come on Bonnie, you can do it. Come on out and bring the others with you."

"Mrs. McKennon!" a voice called from somewhere outside the barn. "Can ye hear me? Fer Godsakes, are ye still in there, lass?"

The roar of the flames and the shouts of men drowned out Maggie's answer. The smoke-filled air had grown too painful to breathe. Coughing, circling behind the mare in search of a whip, Maggie felt a shove from behind. One of the mares, heavy with foal, was now crowding behind Bonniedon, willing to find a way out. A second terrified horse followed.

"Get out of the way or lead them to safety!" Maggie screamed, pulling the mare by the mane. Bonniedoon, blocking the passageway, neighed and began to back up, the halter rope dangling free. Unable to see and trembling with fear, the horse stood still, unsure of what to do next. Grabbing the lead once more with a firm grip, Maggie squeezed alongside the mare and climbed up on a grain barrel, mounting the frightened animal right where she stood. Grasping her mane with shaking hands, she urged, "Come on girl, don't let me down. Please, please! We're not going to die in here if I can help it . . ."

If Bonniedoon would not be led, then perhaps she would obey. Heels, calves, a whip, anything that meant run—run for your life.

Just as the very first smoking timber fell, searing the back of a stallion that shrieked in pain, Maggie ripped the scarf off Bonnie's head and dug her heels into the mare's sides. The animal leaped forward, through the smoke and over a low burning wall of flame, exploding in a gigantic surge out the barn door, now as wild as the fire itself. Following close behind came three mares and a stallion screaming in fear, bits of burning manes and tails glowing like torches in the night.

Bonniedoon cleared the burning debris and hit the ground at full speed, intent on putting the terror behind her. Maggie, still astride, gripped the halter rope with both hands, struggling to keep her balance. The pumping of the mare's long legs as she flew over the ground challenged her best riding skills and Maggie knew she would have to stay on or risk a devastating fall. Finding her breath at last, she took a tighter hold on the mane, higher up, knowing she had no other choice than to ride the runaway out.

Clasping the mare's lean sides with her knees, Maggie's legs swung in rhythm to the rise and fall of the pounding hooves, now flying across the frozen snow. Eventually, she found it easier to wrap both arms around the animal's outstretched neck, her head tucked down, cutting the wind. Daring to look behind her, she saw the flames had reached the house, a scene like a biblical Armageddon, smoke reaching high into the night, a great beacon of fire and brimstone glowing in the sky.

There was no stopping the fear-crazed mare, no telling how far she would run, or for how long. Maggie closed her tear-filled eyes once more, and held on as the horse ran headlong into the night across the prairie, past the dark masses of the herds strung out like islands in the white snow, and past the invisible perimeters of the ranch.

The horse ran because instinct had taught her that when in danger, only flight would save her life. And Maggie held on because there was nothing else she could do, and because she sensed, even in her terror, that this escape would somehow also be her own—an escape from the prison of doubt into soaring certainty, and from the strangle of fear to freedom.

Slowed by the swells of the prairie and the great drifts looming out of the darkness, Bonniedoon began to tire. In staying with her, Maggie felt as though she and the mare had become one. Now, able to control the horse with either the lead rope or her heels, she understood that they had not only run out of danger, but also into an inevitable, inseparable belonging of one to the other, no longer fearful or afraid. They had become partners at last.

Turning the exhausted mare homeward, an anxious Maggie headed for the glow on the horizon. In the darkness, the burning ranch house could be seen for miles. As if in a trance, Maggie rode toward it, numb to the freezing cold. Grateful for the warmth of the animal beneath her, she hoped MacGregor had returned in time to protect whatever could be saved. Shivering, she feared the worst.

The now docile horse was responsive to the slightest squeeze. She even stood quietly when Maggie pulled her to a halt a quarter mile from the ranch, to watch the glowing frame of the master wing crumble against the sky. Half the mansion still stood intact, but the barns had burned to the ground. Incredulous at the devastation, tears rolled down Maggie's cold cheeks.

Somehow, Hugh MacGregor will survive this, she thought, hoping what she said was true. *His kind always does. And I can be of no further help to him,* she convinced herself. *Nor he to me.* She tried to muster some courage as she approached the nightmare before her. *No matter what happens here next, it is time for me to leave. It must be. What else is there?* Patting the sweat-lathered horse on the neck, she urged the mare into a jog. "Yes," she said out loud to Bonniedoon, relieved that the horse was still under control. "I guess you can feel it too. I believe we're finally ready to go home."

43

"Easy girl," Maggie cautioned as they continued toward the house. During the course of the night, help had come from neighboring ranches and in the aftermath of the blaze, a crowd watched as the house smoldered on the hill.

Maggie approached the men standing where the corrals had once been, searching for MacGregor. Surely he had to be there, unless, for some reason he had never returned at all. She steered the horse through the carnage of blackened wood, through the smoke wisps drifting like ghouls in the night, searching for a familiar face.

"Hugh!" Maggie finally spotted him through the haze. "Thank goodness, you're here. Are you all right?" She hastened to him.

Leaning up against a corral fence, one of the very few enclosures still standing, the bent figure stirred slightly and turned toward the sound. MacGregor responded to Maggie as one who is awakened out of a deep sleep, slowly and confused. Behind him, a small campfire lit up the dark with its eerie glow, highlighting his profile. And before him, on the other side of the split rails, a cluster of Herefords milled uneasily, their breath forming clouds in the cold air, their smell all the more pungent because of their fear.

A lantern hung on a rail, its flickering light illuminating his eyes, swollen and reddened from the smoke.

"Maggie! Maggie McKennon! Where've ye been?" He

rushed to her, grasping Bonnniedoon's foamy muzzle in his hand to steady her.

"No need to hold her," Maggie smiled, sliding to the ground. "She'll stand."

"Why, she has nae bridle up'n her! No saddle, either! An' look at ye, frozen stiff. The mare's a steamin' sheet o' ice. But ye're safe!" MacGregor exclaimed. "Ye must tell me what happened? Wilcox thought ye'd perished when th' barn went down. Said he saw ye go in, but n'er come out."

Maggie slid off Bonniedoon's back and collapsed against MacGregor. "I went for an unexpected ride, that's all. But it's nothing compared to this!"

"How did ye get out? An' before ye did, did ye see anythin', anyone, anythin' a'tall that seemed suspicious?"

"Yes, perhaps I did. I heard the sound of a horse galloping away not long after you left. I told Wilcox but we couldn't figure out who it was or where it had gone. I thought that one of the men who came to the meeting might have stayed behind, but I couldn't be sure. What are you thinking? That someone intentionally started the blaze?"

"I don't seem tae know anymore just what I think, exactly, except that I dinna' believe there was anythin' left in this world tae live fer until this minute, Maggie. I dinna' think I could even face th' risin' sun wi'out ye here. I didn't care what th' reason behind this fire might be. Now perhaps, I do. Don't ye see, there's nae measurin' th' loss o' Rockrimmon, compared ta th' thought o' losin' you."

"Please, don't . . ." Maggie interrupted. "Don't go on. You're exhausted and so am I. We'll sort all this out tomorrow, see what's left. It had to be an accident, I'm sure . . ."

MacGregor shook his head. "There's nothin' we can be sure o' anymore . . ."

Maggie had never seen him so lost, bereft of hope. She

wondered which had taken its greatest toll—whatever had happened at the hearing or the burning of the ranch. Maggie began shivering visibly. "Where can we go? I'm freezing. And you must be too. Just look at you." Tears filled her eyes as she took his arm and drew closer to him. She felt overwhelmed by his pain, a blow inflicted upon one who surely didn't deserve it and who, seemingly, could no longer bear the weight of another loss.

Reggie Wilcox appeared from out of the dark behind her, and slipped a leather rein around Bonniedoon's neck.

"Gotcha!" he said, tightening the lead before the mare could duck out of his grasp. "Would ye look at that! The lady an' th' wild mare! Unless I'm dreamin', ye both got out after all." He smiled through his icicle-crusted beard and patted the horse upon the neck. "Never thought we'd see th' likes o' ye again. Returned from th' dead, did ye?"

"I think we both did." Maggie managed a weak smile. "Please Reggie, can you put her where she'll be safe?"

"Do me best, ma'am. Here, take this, ye'll be needin' it." He draped a blanket around Maggie's shoulders.

MacGregor drew Maggie to him, tightening the blanket around her. "I've lost th' battle, Maggie. Beaten by such heinous guile, had nae chance a'tall. As complete a takeover as ye'd ever imagine. From th' top tae th' bottom, e'ery man involved had his facts in place, his claims proven."

"Oh, Hugh . . ."

"They've pushed me out, lass, an' that's all there is tae it. But their time will come. I'll na' go tae war against a band o' hooligans. I may be finished here, but I still ha'e security in Scotlan'. All these years I made sure o' that. These vultures can take what they see here, what's left o' it—th' wind, blizzards, cattle an' all th' rest. Truth is, I've buried a good part o' me, maybe th' best years. But I'm na' dead yet. I'll be headin' back tae th' Highlands as I should ha'e long ago."

MacGregor guided Maggie toward the bunkhouse which had miraculously been spared, the lantern throwing spots of light across the snow. An emergency shelter with cots and blankets had been set up inside. They stopped outside the door.

"Is everyone else all right? Did anyone get hurt?" Maggie asked.

"Everyone's accounted fer," MacGregor answered, " 'cept the old collie. Queen wouldna' leave Elizabeth's room. Th' stubborn thin' burned t'ashes. I guess that's th' way she wanted it.

"Would ye look at that?" Hugh nodded in the direction of what had been the master wing. "From th' center down, where th' stone wall forms th' fireplace between th' two wings, na' a piece o' wood left. An' yet t'other side still stands . . ."

Though it was dark, Maggie could see that the west end of the house remained upright, smoke and water damaged to be sure, but the flames had moved through the east end only. It seemed as though fate had intended to cut the house in two.

MacGregor continued. "Though she's still upright, I doubt if we can lea'e her fer long. My guess is th' damage is far too great. Might as well burn th' rest too. Burn th' whole thin' tae th' ground."

"Shhh. You musn't speak of it. You can make no judgment now." Maggie stared at the grim spectre before them. The shock had started to hit her. She felt as if she needed to sit down, anywhere, even in the cold snow.

"MacGregor." Maggie could not acknowledge another word. "I need to rest. Please, let's get inside." They opened the bunkhouse door, the one building that remained intact, and stepped in. There, cowboys from the crew sat at makeshift tables and Mrs. Heiser and Sarah and the girls, bundled up in heavy coats, lay half-asleep on cots. All looked up in surprise. At the sight of Maggie, they jumped to their feet and gathered round.

"We'll be spendin' th' night here, what's left of it, considerin' it's th' only protection we've got," MacGregor said. "There's coffee. Find yerself a place tae lay your head, Maggie; ye need some sleep. I still ha'e work tae do. If ye're up t'it, I'd be grateful if ye'd help me assess th' damage in th' mornin'." Maggie nodded and headed for the first empty cot.

Morning dawned muddy and gray, the sun obscured by thick ground fog made worse by the lingering smoke. For once, the constant Wyoming wind had died down to a faint whisper, unfortunately, just when they needed it most.

"Where do we start?" Maggie asked, rubbing her cold hands together.

"If there's anythin' left tae salvage we'd better do it while we can," MacGregor answered. "I've checked th' house an' what's left seems sound enou' tae enter. But 'tis a disaster, I'll warn ye."

As they walked, their boots crunched on the glazed ice that had formed during the night. Maggie could see that the drovers had been at work since first light. Burned wood lay in piles like skeletons. By a miracle, few animals had perished and makeshift rope corrals contained those that might have strayed.

"I say, you don't mind if I interrupt here? Came just as soon as I heard the news." Benjamin Farrell stepped forward, imposing in his fur-trimmed black coat and derby. "Tragic! A fire of this magnitude! I am shocked. Saddened. MacGregor, sir, my sincerest regrets."

Remarkable, Maggie observed, *always ready to be of service. Benjamin Jackson Farrell certainly had a knack for well-timed appearances.* Maggie was glad to see him nonetheless, eager for whatever news he had to share.

"Any idea what caused all this, or who?" the attorney asked, getting right to the point. He didn't wait for an answer. "Let me be direct, Mr. MacGregor. I see you are quite compromised. I'd like to do what I can to assist you at this difficult time."

At least he's consistent, Maggie thought.

"Well then, please join us," MacGregor responded, "if ye care tae. But I'm na' hirin' at th' moment. If ye care tae help, ye may get yer hands dirty like th' rest. We'll start in my office an' pack up my records, if there's anythin' left. I have a suspicion that if nothin's there, it may not ha'e been th' fire that's cleaned me out."

"You really think someone's done this on purpose, don't you?" Maggie looked at the Scot gravely. "It makes me furious to think that you might be right."

Not answering, MacGregor helped Maggie around what had once been the front door, and on through the water-soaked foyer toward the library. The acrid smell of smoke made it hard to breathe and a fine layer of ash covered everything they touched. Together the three worked their way down the hall toward MacGregor's study, the door still shut since he'd left the day before.

"I don't ken what tae think," Hugh responded finally, pushing open the door. "Right now, I don't want tae think a'tall."

The rich, damp brown earth of South Park appeared through the snow like dark patches on a paint horse. Out in the greening fields the new Highland calves dropped as scheduled, leggy and lean and covered with a fine silky down. One by one, sturdy and strong, they were on their pink split hooves within minutes of their first breath. Maria christened each one with a name, keeping an accurate count.

April pulsed with a vengeance on the Cameron Ranch, new grass pushing up shoots, creeks full to overflowing. The sound of the meadowlark could be heard, returning as it did each year to the lush woodlands. Billy Munro headed out in the early hours to watch the deer wander down to feed, and savored the sight of the long-legged fawns, following their mothers like princes prancing through the sage.

Billy felt the urge to move, at least to walk or ride the land, to take his fill of the unfolding spring upon it. He wanted to head up into the hills and canter the gray gelding over the crests, but he stayed close. Sven assured him that he must, for he had to be there when the word came, telling them what was to happen next. Billy awaited each day with anticipation, hoping it would be the one which would finally set him free.

"Hold my arm, now. Steady, ye're doin' fine." Billy coaxed Silva out the door into the sunshine. The injuries from the cougar attack had healed on the surface, but a stiffness persisted. The old Spaniard refused to let this stop him from undertaking his chores. A long time lying on his stomach while being treated for his wounds left him irritable and anxious to return to a normal life.

"I can walk on my own," he insisted. "Let me go." Silva tottered forward, painfully trying to stand with the aid of a walking stick that Billy had carved out of a branch.

"Stay right where y'are!" Sven called out from the back of his horse, appearing in the clearing in front of the house. No one had expected him to return so soon from his trip into town. "Or sit down, the both of yu," he smirked. "Yu'd better be sittin' for what I've got ta say!" Billy grinned, and helped Silva to a rocky outcrop a few feet from the door, but remained standing himself.

"Had me a chat, bright and early, with the South Park sheriff down in Fairplay, Billy!" Sven dismounted and pulled a bottle of whiskey out from his pack. "I think it's time ta celebrate so I brought the celebrations with me." He pulled the cork and held the bottle in his right hand, as though checking the contents.

"According ta the sheriff, now, a posse was secretly advised of what's left of McKennon and have now taken charge of the corpse! I reckon I had a little to do with that. Had ta get the ball rollin', didn't I?" Sven downed a stiff swallow and exhaled audibly. " 'The man had been murdered,' he said. Seemed obvious enough. For the time bein', an investigation of the case is pendin'. Meanwhile, the list o' suspects names includes just about everybody on that cattle drive last fall who was holdin' a gun, not one of 'em still located in Colorado, 'cept yu Billy, but technically yu ain't here, putting the case on hold for the time bein'. Are yu with me?" Sven took a second swig, smaller than the first.

Silva and Billy didn't bat an eye.

"Go on," Billy said, cocking his head.

"Meanwhile, yu might be interested ta know that up at t'other end, somebody tried ta pin the murder of Kerr McKennon on Stewart Merrill who's been conveniently doin' time on the range north of Rockrimmon. He swears he had nothin' ta do with it. But he did say that gol-durned Pinkerton man showed up tailing the cattle drive, that much he remembers."

Billy listened intently, his eyes fixed on Sven's grizzled face, his arms folded across his chest.

"If yu ask me, that puts the so-called Pinkerton man behind the bullet. If so, he deserved what he gave. Seems yu saved the sheriff here in South Park from wasting serious time on a hangin', the likes of which ain't too good for the health of most folks anyhow." Sven stood before Billy, putting both hands on his shoulders.

"The way I see it, yu're guilty of nailing a bastard who had it coming ta him, but yu'd have ta return to the Territory of Wyoming ta get tried, if anybody knew it was yur gun that took him. And that ain't gonna happen."

"Why not?" Billy shook his head incredulously.

"Because. Here's the best part: Doc Holland, outta Cheyenne, the man who cleaned out Merrill's leg, likes to hunt with the coroner down in Fairplay." Sven's eyes twinkled merrily. "And what's that got ta do with the price a' beans? Well, accordin' ta the coroner, who likes ta talk, he says Doc told him that he recorded the killing of Kurt Skoll just the way Merrill explained it ta him before he passed out on MacGregor's kitchen table. I had him write down what he said real careful like so's I wouldn't make a mistake:

According to witnesses, the deceased was killed by a member of the droving party who shot in self-defense. At least three hired hands swore they drew their guns together and fired, therefore, the owner of the bullet remains unidentified.

Sven nudged Billy in the ribs with his elbow. "There yu go, Billy boy. Case closed. Yur outta' the picture. Have a swig and pass the bottle. In case yu didn't get all that, it's simple—as of this minute, yur a free man!" Sven shoved the spirits in Billy's face. "Did yu hear what I said, boy? Yu can do as yu damn well please!"

"Look at this," Maggie said. "Do you think it's important?"

MacGregor stopped the survey of his files to look at Maggie's odd find. Water-soaked but still intact, she retrieved the leather saddlebags that had once belonged to Kurt Skoll, stored next to a bookcase behind MacGregor's desk. He had gone through them a few days after the arrival of the Colorado crew back in November and found little of value that he didn't already know. Aside from a cache of gold coins, which he'd locked up for safekeeping, he'd forgotten they existed.

"Oh that. It's th' property o' that character who said he worked fer th' Cattle Commission. Funny, we reported his death an' they said they'd never heard o' him. I figured McKennon had hired him on fer some reason, but now I'll never know."

"Do you mind if I look through it?" Maggie asked.

"Before you do," interrupted Farrell, "might I have a word with you, in private, before you get distracted any further?" The portly attorney motioned to Maggie to follow him outside. Up till then, he'd been helping MacGregor load books and ledgers into a small wagon outside. Farrell had apparently been waiting for an opportune time to talk with his client in private.

"Certainly." Maggie followed him outside, wiping her sooty hands on her apron.

"Aside from the obvious," Farrell began, "I have rather bad news for you from home, I'm afraid."

"My father?" Maggie asked.

"Well, in a way, yes and no. He's not any worse. But he's not any better either. News arrived that he's panicked over the state of affairs and decided to sell off the Cameron Ranch to the Midland Pacific Railway who's been eyeing the property for another spur to Denver. Sounds like he plans to take their offer and convert the ranch to a depot and gaming saloon, with Charles Leeds as proprietor and owner. The liquor connections are obvious. Your brothers-in-law are clamoring to come West as well, ready to turn the business into the finest money maker in South Park, pub and all. And they don't plan to include you."

"You must be joking!" Maggie exclaimed.

"Strange as it sounds, I'm afraid your family has pushed you entirely out of the picture."

"That's what they think." Maggie's cheeks flushed with fury.

"Excuse me, but I'd like tae finish in here an' get out if we can." MacGregor appeared in the open doorway, prompting their assistance. "Th' buildin's doomed. Th' roof's so damaged it's bound tae collapse wi'in a day. I need ye now, if ye don't mind."

"Certainly, my good man. We'll be right there." Farrell turned to Maggie. "I have more to tell you. But it will keep." Their eyes met with the promise to continue the discussion later, and Maggie walked back inside seething with anger at the thought of her family destroying the Cameron to benefit the bank.

She cast aside the saddlebags, satisfied that MacGregor

had gone through them, and then, thought again, what was in those buckled compartments after all? Could anything be of use to her? She undid the buckles and pulled out the sheaves of folded papers, covered with meaningless notes. Having removed these, she peered into the leather interiors searching for whatever else might be hidden there. She wasn't disappointed. Peeking out of a slit in the wall of one of the pouches was the tell-tale corner of an envelope, soiled and bent. She pulled it out and opened it, revealing a dog-eared white calling card clipped to a letter. She stared in amazement at the name on the card: Charles Leeds, her own brother-in law.

Maggie turned to Farrell who was sorting out the salvageable. "Look at this," she urged, as she unfolded the paper to read its contents. "And this . . . !" as she spotted a familiar letterhead, the embossed stationery of the First Bank of Philadelphia. Hesitantly, Maggie began to read aloud.

"Allow me," said Farrell, noticing her hands beginning to tremble. He scanned the communiqué quickly and looked up at Maggie, pursing his lips and running his tongue across his teeth. "Well now, I do think we've got something here. And I think you've got what you want as well."

"What do you mean?" Maggie asked.

"Only this. In so many words, what I am reading is a formal contract describing murder for hire. At least, suggesting it. Kurt Skoll received instructions to open the path for First Bank's progress in Colorado, 'at any cost.' In all probability, with an autopsy, we can safely assume that the bullets in Kerr's body will match those from the gun owned by Kurt Skoll. That explains the obvious.

"Still, it would be comforting to know why Kerr McKennon had to lose his life to that worthless drifter," Farrell said, scanning the document. "The situation still doesn't add up." He took another look at the papers in Maggie's hand and reviewed the second page. "Then again," he murmured, "maybe it does. Based on this letter, it appears that the person with all the answers is your own father, Maggie."

"What?" she exclaimed. "What do you mean?"

"I'm really not surprised," Farrell continued. "When circumstances faulted in the cattle world, I recall hearing him discuss how much he regretted your marriage and the loan to the ranch. Kerr stood in the way of recouping his loss, and socially, the family alignment proved awkward for Magnes's financial reputation. I believe he intended to undermine your husband entirely. And with these instructions, he indirectly gave Skoll more leeway than anyone ever dreamed he'd take."

"What shall we do?" Maggie asked, shaken by the revelation. Feelings of rage burned within her. It was clear that Magnes was partially responsible for Kerr McKennon's death.

"What would you like to do, Maggie? The law is on your side."

Maggie could say nothing. She read the letter again. A sick feeling crept over her as she absorbed the brief instructions. *"To identify assets and debts, as well as assist in the obstruction of all further operations of the Cameron Ranch."* That was the part she would never understand. How could the vicious Irishman take that to mean murder? Or had her father or brothers-in-law intimated as much? If so, what a dissolute and viciously greedy group they had become.

MacGregor joined them and knelt by Maggie's chair as Farrell read the letter aloud. MacGregor put his arm around her shoulders and said softly, "I'm so verra' sorry, lass."

"Not as sorry as I," Maggie said solemnly, her face white with disappointment.

"Exposure is a terrifying thing if we make this public," Farrell cut in. "It will bring the Dowling house down completely. Destroy the bank, your family. Everyone. I hate to see guilty men go unpunished, but since there is a ready culprit, blamable for the crime, I suppose I myself could live with the ugly truth. Your family probably cannot as easily. But their peace of mind is none of my affair. I think they can well afford to keep this nasty piece of business a secret. It would never do for this to reach the board of directors. Indeed not. But with this truth, we can now be assured of your father's cooperation while I continue to protect you. And, in return, I believe your father might want to take care of my recent acquisition in Virginia where I've decided to retire, eventually."

"And what about the Cameron?" Maggie asked.

"Oh, I assume he'll reconsider giving the ranch to you, Maggie, loan payments deferred or overlooked until such time you've reached the kind of profits that will enable you to assume them comfortably. Oh, yes, and the railroad I made mention of earlier, will probably re-route through Jefferson, south of the ranch, if it is to run at all. That would be my guess."

"How ironic," Maggie said. "If my father had only understood the role I played, what I wanted, none of this would have happened."

"Possibly not. Then again . . . you may not know him, as a businessman, that is. May I continue to move forward on your behalf?"

"You do whatever seems necessary," Maggie confirmed, "as you have so far." Her father's unfathomable role in her husband's untimely death kindled a sense of rage she'd never felt before. Her voice broke as she attempted to make her feelings clear. "If I never speak to any of the Dowlings again, it really won't matter. Do what you must, sir. You will con-

tinue to represent me, I assume, until the entire matter is resolved?"

"By all means. Why not? This case has grown more interesting and more lucrative than I ever imagined."

"My thanks seem insufficient at this time, Benjamin, but I
owe you much. How can I ever repay you?" Maggie put her
arms around the attorney's wide frame, giving him a kiss on
the cheek and a heartfelt hug.

"I think you just did, my dear. Always wished you would
do that. Delightful, really."

45

The fire brought together anyone who had been connected to Rockrimmon Ranch, especially suppliers with accounts owed or those in MacGregor's employ, even from as far away as Chugwater. Stewart Merrill rode in later that afternoon, long after the meeting between Maggie and Farrell. He'd been running cattle on the northern roundup and headed down just as soon as he heard the news which had arrived with a summons for his return to the ranch. Upon his arrival, he dismounted in stunned disbelief and picked his way through the debris, seeking out Sarah, Jenny and Pat at the bunkhouse, rejoicing in their safety. Like many other cowhands, he then waited his turn to speak to MacGregor, hoping to find answers to what would be his next move.

Talk of the ranch fire consumed the town and locals were astir with assumptions. Blame was targeted at no one in particular, but gossip implicating the Stockgrowers seemed inevitable. Not a soul dared utter their name, but it managed to surface nonetheless.

Trying to stay out of the turmoil, Maggie, Sarah and the girls took rooms in the same hotel as Farrell and set about making plans to return to Colorado. They desperately needed something concrete to turn to. Maggie proceeded determinedly with her travel arrangements, but Sarah wasn't sure what to do since Stewart hadn't shared with her his decisions or MacGregor's advice. The women sat together in the hotel lobby awaiting Stewart who had promised to join them.

To their surprise, Stewart didn't arrive alone. Sheriff Thompson and Benjamin Farrell flanked him on either side. When they reached the foyer, Sarah rose and approached her husband. He greeted her with a brief hug, but then released her, saying, "Not now. I need to speak to Mrs. McKennon. In private."

Sarah retreated, her face red, and looked at Maggie reproachfully.

Maggie stepped forward and followed Benjamin and Merrill to a circle of chairs on the other side of the lobby. Sarah reseated herself, puzzled by the events. The sheriff placated her, taking Maggie's seat with a wan smile. This move intentionally put Sarah's back toward her husband. "They'll be awhile. Let 'em talk."

"Nothing you say here will jeopardize you any further, Stewart," Farrell stated in a low voice. "I believe your earlier report to the authorities now stands on record. Whatever else you choose to tell Mrs. McKennon is up to you. She will appreciate your sincerity."

For the first time, Maggie saw Farrell display tenderness as he patted Stewart paternally on the shoulder. "Go ahead," he encouraged. "I would also like to hear the details."

Maggie sat quietly. She'd been unprepared for the encounter and awaited whatever Stewart had to offer with apprehension.

"I hope you can forgive me, Mrs. McKennon," Merrill began. He looked at her, then stopped. "I hope Kerr can too. There hasn't been a day I haven't thought about him, haven't stopped blaming myself. I told Mr. Farrell here that I was determined to go to the authorities once I got to Wyoming. Only I never got the chance. Looks like I didn't have to. The fire brought them to me. Believe me, I didn't mean to hide this from you all this time. I never meant to keep it to myself."

Maggie now realized that whatever he had to say was what she'd been waiting for: undoubtedly, the rest of the story behind Kerr's death. It could be no other. "Please," she encouraged him. "Tell me what you must."

"Kerr McKennon deserved a better burial than the one I arranged for him," he said, a note of self-pity in his voice. "But I was that Irishman's hostage, ma'am. He had me in his sights the whole damn time. Me, Sarah, little Pat and Jenny. He wouldn't have stopped short of hurting others, taking another . . ."

Farrell intervened. "From the beginning, Stewart, may I suggest? I think that would be helpful."

Stewart Merrill took a deep breath and removed his hat, laying it carefully on the floor next to his feet.

"God help me, Mrs. McKennon. I hope I never have to tell this story again. Ever.

"On the second day of the drive, the stock detective, that man named Skoll, showed up while we stopped to water the herd. Kerr and him rode off a ways to talk, and it weren't but a few minutes before Kerr came back. He looked mad. I didn't pay the other fellow no mind, but I didn't appreciate seeing the boss upset. Kerr didn't want to talk about it so I just let it ride. That was the last I seen of Skoll during the drive.

"As the herd got strung out, Kerr and I got separated by late afternoon; I took the droving-end like I usually do and rode slow, looking for strays. By the time we bunched together again and made camp, I couldn't find Kerr anywhere. None of the other drovers had seen him, either. It was like he just disappeared, no word to anyone.''

Maggie sat quietly, her eyes fixed on Merrill's face. He looked away, staring out the window to the street.

"I headed toward the ranch and must have gone three or four miles before I found two sets of tracks, Bonniedoon's in front. Just as I lost sight of the hoofprints in the dusk, I heard a noise in a gully and I found them. That is, Kurt Skoll standing over a body, attempting to dig a grave. Bonniedoon was gone. Just Skoll's horse stood tied to a tree.

" 'What're you doing?' I demanded, startling him.

" 'Why, I found this poor man on the trail!' he said defensively.

"I didn't believe it for a second. 'Then we'd better get the sheriff,' I replied. 'Let me help you.' Then I saw who it was. 'My God! It's Kerr McKennon! Help me get his body on my horse and we'll take him into Fairplay.' I dismounted to pick him up.

"I don't know which was worse, Mrs. McKennon—my pain at seeing Kerr laying at his feet or my rage at this worthless killer that I knew was lying to my face. I attempted to pick up the body, then I saw the extent of damage. I was so shocked I laid him right back down. He'd been shot. Real bad. Looked so awful, I don't dare tell you what an ungodly sight, what was left . . .''

Merrill's eyes moistened with the memory and his hands began to tremble. He picked up his hat and held onto it, fingering the brim as he spoke.

" 'Nobody's callin' no sheriff,' Skoll insisted. 'It was just an accident, that's all. The man has been thrown by his horse.'

" 'I don't think so,' I answered. 'He's been shot and more than once! I think you've got some questions to answer, whoever you are,' I said. 'You're comin' with me.'

"Before I could finish my sentence, I found myself looking straight into the barrel of Skoll's gun. I stepped back, reaching for the rifle on my saddle. I was sorry I didn't have my sidearm on me. I'll never stop regretting that.

"For a minute, I was sure he meant to kill me too. Then he must have thought better of it because he said, 'Merrill, I think yer timing's perfect. Ye and me have got a secret. One ye're gonna keep the rest of yer life. No one needs to know about this, especially those drovers out there. Ye're right, this man's been shot. I killed him in self-defense. He drew a gun on me and wouldn't listen; kept pushing me out o' his way. Nobody pushes me. Well, no matter. He's dead and ye're gonna help me hide his body.

"And then ye're gonna head back to that cattle drive with whatever story ye can come up with. And stick to it because I'm headin' back to the Cameron and intend to make sure that ye do. I'll be watching yer family real close. If I hear a peep that the authorities are on my tail, I'm hittin' the trail and takin' your daughters and wife with me, one way or an-other. Do ye understand?' "

Merrill, now shaking visibly, bowed his head. His shoulders heaved as he sighed, and he laid down his hat once again. He covered his eyes with his right hand, his left clenched tightly upon his knee.

Maggie sat in disbelief as the story unfolded. But she needed to hear it all. Farrell sat grim and stern-mouthed, aghast at the brutality of the deed, the callousness of the killer, and the apparent helplessness of the man who told the tale.

Stewart Merrill sat limp, as if telling the story had stolen his very spine. Reluctantly, he continued.

"We dragged the corpse into a cave and filled the opening with rocks. I made note of where it was so I could find it again. Skoll released me with a gun in my back and I returned to the drive with the story about Bonniedoon. Told them I took the body on in myself. Later, the mare coming back to you helped make it more believable. I was able to construct the rest and pull off the dummy funeral too, although the Spaniard, Silva, saw me make the fake body. He never said a word, I don't know why.

"I have lied to so many people who trusted me, it got so I was afraid to open my mouth or to look anyone in the eyes. I forfeited everything Kerr ever gave me, ever entrusted me with. That sonofabitch Skoll should have killed me too. He might as well have. He took everything that mattered: my integrity, my self-respect.

"But how could I know he didn't mean what he said? I couldn't risk my family and I didn't know what to do. So I played along, his victim, hoping for a way out. Every day the lie got bigger; every day my guilt and fear tore me to shreds. And I had to pretend that everything was the way I said it was. Finally, just so I could do my job, I tried believing my own tale. Tried to see it the way I said it happened. By day it worked. At night, I couldn't sleep from the truth. And all along, I hated myself for submitting to my fear. Intimidated by a criminal who had me as good as bound and gagged. I hoped he'd leave so I could feel safe, but he never did.

"My only hope was MacGregor. If I told him the tale, maybe he would know what to do. Know how to protect my family. Once the Cameron was shut down, I couldn't believe it when Skoll latched onto the ride up to Cheyenne. I was ready to blow his head off every step of the way. We got as far as Rockrimmon when he tried to make a move, and I fired a warning to scare him off. He shot back at me and then, in the panic, the Scottish hand, Billy, fired a bullet at him. It hit. The rest you know. And that's about all. Oh,

God, I wish that was all."

Merrill broke down and covered his face with his hands, a sob shattering his composure. He rested his elbows on both knees and remained, head bowed in agony, humiliated before Maggie and Benjamin, tears moistening both his weathered hands.

When he straightened up and looked at them with red-rimmed eyes, he added, "I had a dozen chances to tell this story. Only I couldn't. I didn't know if anyone would believe me. How could I prove I wasn't an accomplice? After all, I knew where the corpse was hidden. How would anyone know I didn't do it myself? The real culprit was dead. No one could get his confession. So I decided to bury the truth, as much as I could. And as long as I could hide up there with a thousand Herefords, I could pretend the killing never happened. God knows I tried. It didn't work. Some days I thought I couldn't stand it. Like I said, Mrs. McKennon, Kerr deserved better. I know I've failed him. And you."

"No, you haven't failed us," Maggie answered softly. "And you've suffered enough." Though she regretted Merrill's inability to take a stand or reveal the truth, she had to find room to forgive. "I'm sure that no one would have reacted differently. You did what you had to do. Please don't think you owe me anything—please." She put her arms around the trembling man and embraced him, then wiped away her own tears. "Kerr would have forgiven you, I think, as I do. And I don't believe that anyone will accuse you."

With this remark, she looked pleadingly at Farrell, hoping she was right, then smiled at Stewart and took his hand. "You see, the body's been found and you're not to be blamed. The bullets matched Skoll's gun. Thank goodness no one else was hurt."

"Maggie's correct," Farrell added for Stewart's benefit. "And just so you know, Mrs. McKennon," he added, turning to Maggie with a forced formality. "The authorities cleared Stewart earlier this afternoon of any blame in the murder. He still may have to account for what he reported to the coroner. Other than that I believe this matter is closed."

The Denver Pacific ran two trains a day from Cheyenne to Denver and back, composed of stock cars, dining, sleeping and passenger cars, and freight. Like the great ocean ferries, the trains made distant cities into neighbors and bore animals and people alike across the grassy sea of the plains.

A stock handler led Bonniedoon into the angled opening of the freight car and lined her up next to a dozen other horses traveling to Denver that day. Even a silver-maned Welsh pony, brushed and beribboned, stood tied for the journey, on its way to a lucky young lady's birthday in town.

Maggie rode alone in the comfort of a first-class car, not caring that she was dressed for riding in a split skirt, high boots, and a hip-length gored jacket. She traveled light, carrying nothing except a shoulder bag with her ticket and necessities. She'd come aboard with a saddle and bridle which she stored in the luggage compartment in lieu of a valise. The rest of her clothing had been packed in freight boxes and sent to their final destination via the local forwarders.

Stock cars headed farther west would be re-assigned at Denver's Union Station to be picked up by smaller lines, traveling on to South Park and beyond. Once over the pass, the animals still on board, including Bonniedoon, would be unloaded at the depots in Como or beyond.

As the wheels clacked along the rails, Maggie watched small pronghorns race beside the train, the only flash of life in the empty prairies as far as she could see. She was not sorry to be leaving the flat horizons, the vast openness. To her, despite its austere beauty, Wyoming would always feel threatening and bare. Her thoughts filtered back to her departure that morning from the station in Cheyenne.

"Don't go," MacGregor had begged her as they said goodbye at the platform.

"I must. Please don't make it hard for me."

"Dammit, Maggie. I'll nae' plead wi' ye." MacGregor's voice sounded hoarse. "It's beneath me tae do so. But I'm askin' ye tae reconsider. Look at me . . ."

She couldn't. She couldn't bear the look in his eyes, and hadn't been able to for the entire week. She didn't want him to see the flicker of doubt in her own, the hint of commitment that had crept into her heart while she was unaware. How hard it was to deny those feelings, how difficult not to bend. Had it not been for Billy Munro . . .

"Listen tae me," MacGregor said. "There's a life ahead fer th' two o' us, th' likes o' which ye canna' imagine. A sweetness, an ease, that ye ha'e a right tae know. It can all be yers."

"Please, don't make this harder than it is," Maggie protested. "I don't doubt your offer. But if it's meant to be, we'll both know in the future. I won't deny the possibility. For now, there's much at stake I need to determine on my own. My dearest Hugh, you've given me the best of yourself, taught me everything you can. Cared for me, protected me. Don't think I'll ever forget that."

"None o' what I've done fer ye compares tae what ye've done fer me, lass. Ye ga'e me back a part o' my life an' a reason tae live it. When th' world was dark, ye were my light. Belie'e it or na', there's an old sayin' back home abou' th' moon . . ."

"I know," Maggie cut in. "Kerr told me once about

MacGregor's Lantern, about the reivers. A full moon, he once said, is all a man would need in order to . . ."

"That's right," MacGregor stopped her short. "That's th' one. Only ye can forget that tale. I ken at last, for myself, what a man—what this man, really needs tae find his way. A woman like yerself. Y'are my lantern, Maggie, an' always will be. Y'are th' light in my life."

MacGregor's eyes moistened as he struggled to finish. "Lea'e me then. Go if ye must. But know that my door is always open. Nae matter when, nae matter where. Ye may write tae me care o' th' Royal Scots Bank, Edinburgh. They'll know where I've settled, how tae find me. An' if ye reach out in any way, trust I'll be sure t'answer."

For the last time, MacGregor took Maggie in his arms. He held her in an embrace so fierce she could feel his impassioned heart beating through her jacket. This time he did not hesitate to seal their farewell with a kiss, his lips crushing hers in a desire to express what he felt, and had felt, for a long time. Finally, Maggie gently eased him away.

"I have to go. I'll remember you always," she said. She loved him, but dared not tell him, lest he take her ticket and tear it up on the spot. She struggled with the truth of it, the searing pain that said this was a man she could perhaps spend a life with. If only there hadn't been another.

"Good luck wi' th' Cameron," MacGregor said softly. "For yer own sake, I hope ye'll succeed. Perhaps we'll meet again . . . Whate'er happens, I will always remember ye, lass. Fer as long as I live."

Bonniedoon picked the trail across the Park from the station as though she'd followed it a hundred times before. She carried Maggie up the wagon road toward the ranch, exactly the same way she'd carried Kerr nearly a year before.

The sun shone upon the damp ground and the first May buds of lavender pasque peeked through the pale green grass. Maggie stood up in the stirrups to better see the trail ahead. With a quick brush of her heels, she coaxed the horse into a trot and headed across the broad plateau. Riding with easy confidence, she kept her eye on the ground and the woods a few miles ahead. With luck she would arrive by late afternoon. As she rode, she felt as if she were guided toward her future by predestined forces, benevolent and strong. Her choices now were her own and she would assume responsibility for them. The events of the previous few months had transformed her former view of life into something entirely new. The old Maggie lived only in memory.

She regretted coming unannounced but hadn't written to Sven, for there had been no time. She'd made up her mind to leave for the Cameron as soon as Benjamin Farrell told her she could. Once he'd contacted Philadelphia, Maggie had only a few days after the fire to gather her things. Wherever she chose to be, Farrell had promised he would keep her informed of his new leverage with her father and the bank and the progress on her circumstances. At this point, Maggie felt as distant from the Dowlings as if they'd been strangers. She wondered if her sisters had any inkling of the truth.

As she rode on, and the mare shifted into her lilting, ground-covering canter, Maggie was filled with a sense of her own potential and a surging sense of hope. No one could ever tell her again what was or wasn't possible, and she wouldn't rest until she had determined where and how her boundaries would be drawn. For now, the resurrection of the Cameron meant everything. Tomorrow perhaps, would hold the promise of even more.

Letting go of the end of Rockrimmon, the fire, and the feeling that she might have broken MacGregor's heart,

Maggie knew she had witnessed the fall of innocence in the wake of the times. She knew she couldn't share the blame for any of it. Both MacGregor and McKennon had failed before the onslaught of change, propelled by powers too great for any one man to stand up to alone. She could grieve for them and knew that she would, but she needed time. Eventually, she would become all the stronger for having known them both.

The earth gave way with a spongy softness under Bonniedoon's agile hooves. She cantered easily down the last half mile of the trail near the Cameron's edge and from the last rise, Maggie could finally see what it was she'd been longing for those many months on the plains. Before her, exactly as she remembered them, were the rambling stone house with its tile roof nestled near the trees, the clean waters of the river rushing to the south, and the endless swells of the park rising in every direction. The layered ranges of the Rocky Mountains, still snow-capped, jutted skywards, and framed the clear horizon.

Before her in the meadow grazed the small, multi-colored herd of Highland cattle, quietly chewing upon the timothy and tender willow. A thicket of curving horns rose and clicked against each other as massive heads turned to assess the rider, approaching across the field.

Maggie urged Bonniedoon into a slow gallop, her chest pounding as they neared the house. Riding into the clearing, she picked up the scent of wood smoke from Maria's kitchen and noticed an old Highland brood cow standing next to a white-coated heifer in a pen. A mule and a small red roan lounged in the shadows of the barn. With joy flooding her heart, Maggie slowed to a halt. Taking a deep breath, she inhaled the smell of home. As she prepared to dismount, she heard a familiar sound, the high-pitched whinny of a horse she knew all too well.

Bonniedoon pricked her ears and nickered softly in response. Turning, Maggie then saw the most welcome sight of all; a slate-colored pony with a dark mane and legs, his head over the corral fence. It neighed again, this time, more loudly. Smiling, Maggie slipped to the ground and led Bonniedoon toward the barn, thrilled by the sight of Billy Munro's stalwart gray.